AN EARL LIKE NO OTHER

She was, of course, not wearing that infernal mobcap at this hour. "Your hair—" He reached to touch it, then thought better of doing so and dropped his hand.

She gave a nervous laugh and swiped a hand over her head and along her neck. His gaze followed her hand.

"Luckily it will grow back," she said. "At least I needn't plait it every night now."

"A silver lining behind every cloud, eh?"

She shrugged, but made no move to end the encounter. Wanting to prolong it, he asked, "And your hands? Are they healed now?"

"Nearly." She held them out and turned them this way and that. "Some redness. I wear gloves for most tasks."

"Allow me." He took her hands gently in his own and steered her across the threshold toward the better light on her nightstand. "They seem to have healed nicely. With luck, there will be little scarring."

He raised his gaze to hers and seeing a corresponding degree of sheer need in her eyes, he gave up control, put his arms around her, and lowered his mouth to hers . . .

An Earl Like No Other

WILMA COUNTS

KENSINGTON BOOKS
KENSINGTON PUBLISHING CORP.
www.kensingtonbooks.com

TO

LONE MOUNTAIN WRITERS

Thank you! Thank you! Thank you!

for always helping me

make it better.

CHAPTER 1

May, 1815

Mr. Thomas Logan wore a battered top hat and other remnants of the conservative, plain dress of his position as a London solicitor. His clothing, appropriate for a very junior associate in a large law firm in that great European city, was decidedly out of place in the frontier town of St. Joseph in the Louisiana Territory of the New World. Logan's wardrobe had taken a beating during a journey of several months' duration to this center of the fur trade. In the latter stages of his trip, he had been acutely aware of the sniggers of white men and open curiosity of Indians he encountered.

St. Joseph, a port on the Missouri River, was crowded now with mountain men gathered to sell the pelts they had accumulated over the winter. He recognized accents from Europe—French, German, and Spanish. Who would have thought so many men from civilized parts of the world would have chosen this life? Admittedly, he used the term *civilized* rather loosely, for he possessed the true Londoner's sense of superiority. He could not distinguish either languages or dress of the natives, whom he thought of with a shudder as mere savages. He quelled these thoughts as he had done for some weeks now. Thomas Logan was a man on a mission. Mentally bracing himself, he went about his task of locating a fur trapper named Jeremy Michael Chilton.

Logan's ordeal had included a two-month ocean voyage, then another two months trekking across nearly half of the North American continent by stagecoach, horseback, riverboat, canoe, and now horseback again. Having finally arrived in St. Joseph, he found locating his quarry easier than he had anticipated. The town was a frontier outpost, but saloons, brothels, and mercantile stores abounded to serve fur traders.

"Chilton? Yeah, I know him," a grizzled, unkempt man said in the fourth or fifth establishment Logan visited. "He's with a tribe of Arapahos 'bout a mile and a half north of here."

"Arap . . . uh—*what*?"

"Arapahos. Plains Injuns."

"I see . . ." Logan did not see at all.

"We'll find 'im fer ya, Mr. Logan."

This assurance came from Bill Hansen, one of the five experienced mountain men Logan had hired in Kentucky to guide him into the deeper wilderness. At first, his new comrades had been wary and faintly contemptuous of the fastidious Londoner. Gradually, though, his perseverance in the face of the hardships of the trail had won them over. He supposed the turning point had come as he took a dunking when a canoe capsized. He had also endured hours and hours on horseback. No London cabs in the wilderness, he reminded himself.

"Lead on then, Mr. Hansen."

Half an hour later, they entered an Indian camp full of tepees, women bending over cook fires, and men idling in the late afternoon. The smell of wood smoke blended with that of roasting meat; adults called out to each other or to reprimand noisy children. Logan could see little to distinguish this from any of the other heathen encampments he'd seen. His group's horses and pack animals were immediately surrounded by a gaggle of scantily clad brown-skinned children who giggled and pointed. "Impolite, uncouth little monsters," Logan muttered to himself. Hansen asked directions in a guttural native language and they were pointed toward the edge of the camp. Logan's anticipation rose. Was it possible that he at long last could discharge the duty that had brought him so far?

Among the tepees Logan spotted a proper English tent such as a soldier might have used on the Iberian Peninsula—indeed, it was not unlike Logan's own traveling accommodation. *Well, perhaps the man has not gone entirely native,* he thought.

As they neared the tent, a tall man, probably roused by the mayhem in the wake of Logan's arrival, emerged and pinned up the opening flap. Logan noted dark brown hair and blue eyes. Hansen and Logan dismounted and pushed forward as others of their party held back with the animals and packs.

"Are you Chilton?" Hansen asked.

"I am."

"This here's Mr. Logan. He's done come all the way from England lookin' fer you." Pride and amusement showed in Hansen's voice as he gestured toward his smaller companion, who maintained the aura—if not the semblance—of a proper English gentleman. Logan stepped aside, clutching a leather attaché packet, and sought to ignore several mongrel dogs sniffing and growling at his feet.

"Thank you, Mr. Hansen," Logan said. "Perhaps you and the others could set up our camp while I convey the message I came to deliver."

"Sure thing, Mr. Logan."

Logan lifted his battered hat and tried to maintain his dignity as he shook a foot at a particularly impolite dog. He bowed. "I am happy to find you at last, my lord."

The tall man smiled, apparently amused at this incongruous scene. "I'm afraid you miscall me, sir. It's just 'Chilton' here."

"Ah, but in England, my lord, you are now the Earl of Kenrick."

Chilton drew in a long breath. Color drained from his face. He looked as though someone had landed a solid punch to his midsection. "I'm *what*? You can't be serious. My father? My brothers—Charles, Edgar?"

"Deceased, I am sad to say." Logan's tone was somber. "Your brothers drowned in a boating accident in the Irish Sea. Your father succumbed to complications from illness—his liver, you know."

"When?"

"Your brothers a year ago and your father some three months later."

Chilton shook his head, clearly overwhelmed. His expression was grim, but color was returning to his face.

"I'm sorry, my lord. I'm sure this news comes as a shock."

"Indeed it does." Chilton's voice caught. "All this time I've thought of them as alive and well and . . ."

"Your older brothers were lost at sea, but your father was laid to rest in Kenrick chapel," Logan said gently.

"Others of my family? I've been away for nearly ten years and have had only a few letters."

"They are well. Your stepmother remained in London after your father's death. His sister, Lady Elinor, chooses to remain at Kenrick. You surely know your sister Margaret married the Honorable William Talbot six years ago."

Chilton nodded and Logan went on. "She has twin sons and a daughter, so you're an uncle, my lord."

Chilton grinned. "A girl as well, eh? I knew of the boys. And Bobby?"

"Your younger brother, Robert, was still in Belgium when I left London."

"He is still in harm's way, then," Chilton said. "Even here we heard of Napoleon's escape in March." He looked off into the blue sky, his gaze focused on something within. "Hard to think of Bobby as a seasoned soldier. He was only sixteen when I left. My father— Charles—Edgar . . ." He shook his head again.

Logan shifted from one foot to another. "Is there some place we can talk, my lord?"

"Of course."

With a gesture, Chilton invited him into the tent and let the flap down. Soon they were seated on what Logan thought of as very civilized camp stools. Logan, holding his attaché case primly on his lap, started to speak again in a formal tone. "I represent the Phillips law firm handling Kenrick business affairs. When your brothers drowned, your father was most anxious to have you return to England. When we received no response to our letters, Mr. Phillips prevailed upon me to make this journey. That would be the younger Mr. Phillips— Mr. Walter Phillips, that is. His father passed on in 1812."

"I know Wally very well. So he's in charge now, eh?"

"Yes, my lord. Mr. Walter instructed me to find you—no matter how long it took. It has been a most interesting adventure, I must say."

Chilton gave him what seemed to be a sympathetic smile.

"I am pleased to have found you, my lord," the lawyer said, drawing some papers from his packet.

Before he could continue, however, the tent flap whooshed open and a child of perhaps four years bounced in, uttering something in the heathen language and sounding highly excited. The child, who appeared to be female, ran to Chilton and clutched at his knee.

Chilton put a hand on her shoulder and turned her toward Logan. "Cassie, you are being rude to a guest." He looked at Logan. "My daughter, Cassie—that is, Cassandra Margaret."

The child stamped her foot. "Little Willow, Papa."

"Ah, yes. Also known as Little Willow."

"Your daughter?" Logan murmured. The London man was shocked as he examined the child more closely. No gentleman of his acquaintance would parade his by-blow quite so blatantly. The little girl was a comely creature, her hair in two long shiny black plaits; she wore a buckskin dress and a beaded headband. She glanced up shyly and Logan looked into very clear, very intelligent, very blue eyes.

"Greet the gentleman properly, Poppet—and in English," Chilton said with a light push at her back.

"How . . . do?" She bent her knees in a shy curtsy, then hugged herself closer to her father, but never took her eyes from the stranger.

"I—I am pleased to meet you, my—uh—lady," Logan managed, pleased with himself at having controlled his shock—even to the point of according the child a title he was not at all sure was rightfully hers.

Chilton gave the little girl a gentle shove. "You run out and play now, Cassie. And tell Running Fox I said to behave himself."

She skipped away and Chilton met the lawyer's gaze directly, but with a hint of defiance.

"H—her mother?" Logan asked, unable to contain his curiosity.

"Dead," the new Lord Kenrick said flatly. "My wife, Leah—or Willow—died giving birth to our daughter."

"Y—your wife? But she was . . . she was—"

"Half Arapaho. My wife's mother is white—lives in St. Louis. And Willow *was* my wife. First by tribal ceremony and then by a Christian ceremony in St. Louis where the marriage was registered. So, yes, it appears that my daughter is, as you say, *Lady* Cassandra Margaret."

"Y—yes, my lord." Logan digested this information, then asked, "Are there— uh . . . any others?"

Chilton chuckled, apparently amused at Logan's discomfort. "No. Only Cassie. Believe me, she's enough."

"Yes, my lord." Logan sat even straighter and began to shuffle through his papers. "As your brothers left no legal heirs, you, my lord, became heir to the earldom when they died. As I said, we tried to contact you then."

"Communication is no easy matter in the wilderness, Mr. Logan."

"You have the right of it there, my lord," Logan said ruefully, then he continued. "In any event, when your father too left us, it became crucial that we locate you, for you, my lord, are now the Earl of Kenrick, and there are certain matters of a rather urgent nature."

"I shouldn't think there's much left of the Kenrick earldom," Chilton observed. "Is there even enough to merit the name?"

"Well, yes. A good deal of movable property has been sold off—paintings and some other art pieces, many of the horses, a carriage or two. The real estate, no longer entailed, as you know, has been heavily mortgaged."

"I surmised as much. The process started long before I left England."

"The elder Mr. Phillips had more or less given up on the matter," Logan explained, "but Mr. Walter thinks that, with proper management, the earldom might thrive again. To that end, he secured extensions on the loans."

"Wally always was an optimist."

Logan smiled politely. "He seems confident that you will agree to take on the task of saving Kenrick."

Jeremy Chilton, new Earl of Kenrick, saw Mr. Logan settled into the camp Hansen set up, and he agreed to Cassie's urgent pleas that she be allowed to spend the night with her cousins, Running Fox and his sister Butterfly. Their mother had been a half-sister to Cassie's mother. Finally, he had time to consider the full impact of the lawyer's message.

As a third son, Jeremy had never entertained any notion of inheriting the title. Nor had he harbored any envy or regret that there were two brothers in front of him. Early on he had faced several important facts: his father's profligate habits were depleting an already floundering earldom; his older brothers were likely to finish it off; and there was nothing—absolutely nothing—a third son could do about it. Not only would there be no inheritance for him from Kenrick, but there was no rich relative, no fairy godmother lurking in the wings. He would be on his own, a fate that was often the lot of younger sons.

As a boy he had dreamed of running away to sea to make his fortune as a pirate. As an adolescent, his ambitions were nobler: He would join the army and fight the Corsican monster trying to subdue all of Europe. In the end, he had been persuaded by a fellow Trinity College student—another impoverished younger son—to go adventuring in the New World. Jeremy had lost track of Walthorp, who had lasted in the wilderness only one year, then taken a desk job with Astor's American Fur Company in New York. Jeremy, however, had taken to the rough frontier life, though initially he thought of it as a temporary sojourn. He would one day take up a more settled way of life, but probably in America rather than England. Before settling down, though, he must add to his savings in the St. Louis bank with another year or two out here in the fur trade.

Now—suddenly—he was no longer "just Chilton" but Earl of Kenrick! He could stay where he was—let those creditors collect on the debts his father had amassed. Let an empty title eventually fall where it would—perhaps to his younger brother Robert. Let the tenant farmers, mill workers, and others fend for themselves. They would probably have had to do so anyway if either Charles or Edgar had inherited.

Memory conjured up faces from the past: A stable hand who taught him how to ride. Farmers who taught him the value and rewards of hard work. A gamekeeper who shared secrets of nature with a lonely boy. The vicar who instilled a love of Homer and Marcus Aurelius. Not just faces. People—families—all dependent on the fate of the Kenrick earldom.

One of his reasons for leaving England was not wanting to see such people reduced to penury or sent to workhouses. While his father and brothers lived, he could have done nothing. But now? Wally Phillips had always been a sensible sort and he seemed to think one Jeremy Chilton could turn things around.

But what about Cassie? How would she react to being uprooted? Well, children often adapted to change more easily than adults did. His daughter was resilient; she blended easily with her cousins in the Indian village—and with her white relatives in St. Louis. Since her birth and her mother's death, he had been determined to see that she had the best he could offer, including a decent education that would allow her entrance to any society of her choice. To that end, he had a good deal of money saved—not a fortune, but a start. But—did he dare require that Little Willow become Lady Cassandra?

Could he live with himself if he failed even to try to save the earldom—to preserve a heritage that his daughter had a right to? And what about all those others? Did his very name not carry a responsibility to them?

He wrestled with the dilemma for three days, but in the end he saw little real choice in the matter. He would have to take on the task of trying to save Kenrick.

CHAPTER 2

London
Spring, 1816

Katherine Emma Newton Gardiner arrived one evening in late March on the doorstep of her husband's solicitor, gripping her son's hand in one of her own and clutching a large traveling bag in the other. The boy carried a smaller bag and the mother had a guitar slung across her back.

"Oh, please, do be at home," Kate prayed as she set the bag down and lifted the door knocker.

After some time, the door opened a crack and an imperious male voice said, "*Ye-s-s*?"

"I am Lady Arthur Gardiner and I wish to see Mr. Phillips. It is a matter of some urgency," Kate announced.

The butler seemed unsurprised by the anxiety she could not quell. He gave her a penetrating look that also took in the boy standing quietly at her side. The servant weighed her words, then opened the door wider and motioned them in. He took their bags and the instrument, set them inside the door, and motioned mother and son to a nearby bench.

"Wait here. I shall see if Mr. Phillips is in."

Presently, Phillips himself appeared along with the butler. Phillips was a sandy-haired man in his thirties.

"Lady Arthur. What a pleasant surprise. Come in. And Lord Spenland. How nice to see you." Phillips greeted the child in an adult manner, giving him a slight bow, which the little boy returned politely and expertly.

"I am not at all sure you will deem it such a pleasure once you know why I am here," Kate said.

"A crisis, I take it?" Phillips responded. "Well, let us deal with it over tea. Martin, another pot of tea, please—and some of those ginger cakes for young Lord Spenland."

"Right away, sir."

Kate removed her cloak and her son's outer coat and handed them to the butler, who then promptly went to do his master's bidding.

Phillips ushered mother and son into a drawing room containing furniture that appeared to be valued for comfort as much as style. A fire burned in the fireplace and a lamp on a side table between two winged chairs splashed warm light into the room. One of the chairs was occupied by a plump, pretty blond woman.

"You remember my wife, do you not, Lady Arthur?" Phillips said.

"Yes, indeed." Kate smiled at the other woman, who immediately stood and curtsied politely.

Mrs. Phillips held a book she had been reading, her finger marking the place. "I shall ring for more tea."

"Already taken care of, my dear," Phillips assured her.

"Oh. Then, as I presume this call involves some legal business, I shall excuse myself," Mrs. Phillips offered.

"I would not drive you from your own drawing room!" Kate said. "I came because Mr. Phillips was a particular friend of my husband—as well as his solicitor."

"Never mind, my dear. It happens all the time. But if you prefer that I stay . . ."

"By all means," Kate said politely.

"Perhaps you would rather your son had his tea in the kitchen?" Mrs. Phillips had apparently noted a degree of anxiety about their guest. "We have a new family of kittens next to the cooker," she said warmly to the little boy and laid aside her book.

"Thank you, Mrs. Phillips. Ned would like that, wouldn't you, son?" Kate nudged the child to accompany the woman to the kitchen.

When the door closed behind them, Phillips pointed to a place for

Kate on the sofa, sat himself on a chair nearby, and said, "Now. What is it that has you so upset?"

"Does it show that much? I thought I had calmed myself during our long coach journey." The sympathy and concern in his voice nearly undid her careful control. "Oh, Mr. Phillips, I made such a terrible mistake in taking Ned to Wynstan Castle."

"I feared as much," Phillips said, "but we all hoped it would work for the boy's sake, his being the heir and all."

"That's precisely why I agreed to go, despite Arthur's careful plans. His grace offered such a plausible argument. Since Ned will eventually become the duke, his grandfather insisted that it would be best if he grew up on the land he would one day inherit. I had misgivings, but I was persuaded to that viewpoint."

Phillips nodded. "At the time, I must admit I was inclined to agree with you. I mean to say, Arthur could not have foreseen that his older brother would die within months of his own demise. With young Ned now heir to the Wynstan dukedom, it made perfect sense to all of us."

"Still—I should have remembered Arthur's stories of his childhood. I should never have given in to my father-in-law's arguments," Kate said. "Nor should I have pestered you and Captain Lawrence to agree."

"I do not recall such a deal of pestering, Lady Arthur," Phillips replied with a smile. "Captain Lawrence—it's Major Lawrence now—and I readily accepted our joint guardianship of young Ned, but we both knew that your husband would have made you *sole* guardian—were one allowed to name a woman to such a position."

Mrs. Phillips returned, followed by the butler bearing a tea tray. "I left your son happily consuming ginger cakes and playing with the kittens."

"Thank you," Kate said, accepting the cup of tea Mrs. Phillips offered her.

"We were discussing the boy's guardianship," Mr. Phillips explained. "You recall the case, I am sure." He turned to Kate. "My wife has a fine hand—*and* a fine mind— and she often copied documents for me until recently."

"I see," Kate said.

Mrs. Phillips settled herself on the sofa next to Kate. "I *do* recall the case. I distinctly remember questioning why a duke's son would take such extraordinary measures to eliminate members of his own family as possible guardians."

"My husband spent an unhappy childhood under his father's iron hand," Kate explained. "The duke was not just strict with Arthur. He was decidedly cruel at times."

"Good heavens!" Mrs. Phillips said. "His own son?"

"Arthur was under the impression that his father thought not," Kate said quietly.

"What are you saying?" Mrs. Phillips wore a frown of consternation and her husband too focused a curious gaze on Kate.

"Arthur thought perhaps he was *not* Wynstan's son, though the duke never publicly questioned his paternity and certainly his brother Frederick and his sister—both some years older than Arthur—were the duke's children."

"But the duke *told* Lord Arthur this?" Mrs. Phillips asked in an appalled tone.

"I do not think he said it very precisely, but that was the impression Arthur had from some things the duke did say and, of course, from his rather bizarre behavior toward Arthur. The duke favored the others inordinately, especially his heir, Frederick," Kate said. "That much was clear in the time Ned and I were at Wynstan Castle. The duke's treatment of Ned and me was, I think, an extension of his treatment of Arthur."

"Oh, you poor thing," Mrs. Phillips murmured sympathetically.

Phillips broke in matter-of-factly. "So what happened? What brought you here?"

"I—I knew of nowhere else to turn." Kate took a swallow of the hot tea, savoring its warmth, then set the dish down. "And I wished to discuss the funds Arthur left."

"Give us the whole story," Phillips said. "After all, I have neither seen nor heard from you since you left my office nearly a year ago."

"It is not pretty," Kate warned. "Once Ned and I removed to Wynstan Castle, we became virtual prisoners. I did not mind so much for me." Her hands in her lap, she twisted the wedding ring she had never removed and cleared her throat. "I am somewhat embarrassed to tell you this—but without Arthur, it really made little difference *where* I was."

"But you had your son," Mrs. Phillips said gently.

"Yes. And a blessing he is. I honestly thought he might thrive in the country."

"Did he?" Phillips asked.

"He *would* have done so. He *did*—at first. But the duke kept demanding more and more of him. And Ned tried so hard! The duke required that he learn fencing and boxing. When Ned did not immediately take to swords and fisticuffs, Wynstan accused him of being a silly female and a mama's boy. Ned has only eight years!"

"Good heavens!" Mrs. Phillips said again. "What did you do?"

"I tried to reason with the duke, but he said I had 'coddled the boy long enough. The future Duke of Wynstan should be made of sterner stuff.' " Kate tried to affect the duke's cold tone.

Phillips shifted in his chair. "Somehow, I doubt this is the whole story of why you are here."

Kate sighed. "No. It is not. He . . . he insisted that Ned learn to shoot and hunt. Ned is terrified of guns. Even now he occasionally wakes up with nightmares in which he relives hearing guns in battle—especially that last battle at Toulouse."

"Go on," Phillips urged.

"The duke forced Ned go on a rabbit hunt. There were several men and boys and a pack of dogs." She closed her eyes against the memory.

Mrs. Phillips, perched on the edge of the sofa, turned toward Kate. "You were there too?"

"Oh, no. This was a men-only affair. I just heard about it afterwards. It was terrible, though. This was not a hunt to rid farmers of pests. It was only for sport. There were loud shots. And blood. A great deal of blood. Ned was sick and vomited. The duke insisted Ned try shooting, but he couldn't—in part because the duke's gun was far too large for a small boy. But Ned was also terrified, you see?"

Again Mrs. Phillips gave a sympathetic murmur and reached to place her hand on Kate's.

Kate went on. "The duke was embarrassed in front of his friends." Even now, in the retelling, she felt herself trembling at what was coming next. "He—he was so angry he picked up the bloody carcasses of two of the rabbits and draped them around Ned's neck and made him carry them home that way." She stifled a sob.

"Good grief!" Phillips said.

Kate nodded. "Ned was nearly hysterical. He kept saying to me later, 'That was how Papa died, Mama. I know it. In a field with blood everywhere.' " Now, weeks later, remembering the utter despair in her son's voice, Kate felt tears on her cheeks.

"No wonder you wanted to leave," Mrs. Phillips said, motioning to her husband, who eventually understood that he should hand over his handkerchief to their visitor. "I cannot imagine how Mr. Phillips and I might react if such a thing happened to one of *our* sons!"

"Oh, there's more," Kate went on bitterly after wiping her eyes. "Later, the duke called Ned down to the library. I went with him, but Wynstan would not allow me in. However, I stood outside the door—and I heard it all."

"Heard what?" Mrs. Phillips asked in an appalled whisper.

"The duke shouted that he would teach Ned a lesson he would not forget. Ned was, he said, just like his father and needed the same treatment. Then . . . there was a horrible slapping sound. He was using a leather strap on my little boy! Ned screamed. I screamed too, and pounded on the door. Finally, it stopped. The duke jerked open the door and cursed at me, but I shoved past him to Ned, who was cowering over a chair, sobbing his heart out."

"As well he might be!" the other mother said.

"You indicated that you were virtually held prisoner at Wynstan Castle," Mr. Phillips reminded her in a lawyerly tone meant, she supposed, to defuse the emotions aroused by her story.

"Yes. He refused to allow us to leave. *I* could leave, but 'the boy will stay here,' he insisted. He even set the servants to watching us."

Mrs. Phillips gasped. "My heavens! How utterly dreadful for you."

"So how did you make your escape?" the husband asked.

"I waited. Eventually, they would let their guard down. And they did. It happened when Wynstan came here to London—something to do with Parliament. One of the grooms whom Arthur had rescued years ago from a beating helped us. I had a little money hidden away. We took the mail coach three days ago and arrived here this afternoon." She paused, exhausted by her emotions—anger and fear had assailed her anew as she told the tale. "Will you help us?"

"I will do what I can," Phillips said. "Arthur deserves that and more from me. Do you have something in mind?"

"I—I am not sure. At first all I could think was to get away—as far from Wynstan Castle and the duke as possible."

Phillips gave a rueful chuckle. "So you came to London—right where the duke is."

She smiled feebly. "I thought he would not expect that. He will probably think I have gone to my parents in Surrey, though he cannot know how unlikely that would be."

"You may be right about his not expecting that course of action. But eventually he will trace you here. He knows of my connection to Arthur."

"I know," she said glumly, "but I cannot allow that evil old man to hurt my son again. There must be some way—some place—we can hide. Arthur left us some funds. I intended to save them for Ned— that is, until . . ."

"Until he was no longer the penniless son of a second son, but the heir to a very rich, very important dukedom," the lawyer supplied. He stood and began pacing the room.

"I . . . I *could* go to the United States—the war has long been over there too—or to Canada, perhaps," Kate said. "I think there is enough money for passage."

He paused in his pacing. "Yes. There is. And you could manage for two or three—perhaps four—years, but then what?"

"Something will turn up. It always does," she said brightly—too brightly.

"No. No. That will not do," he muttered and continued his pacing. "You must also consider the fact that the present duke will not live forever. Your little Ned will one day be a very important man in *England*."

All three were silent for several moments. Then Mrs. Phillips spoke again.

"Husband, you *can* help her, can you not?"

"I shall do my utmost," he said.

He rested one elbow in the palm of the other hand and stroked his chin thoughtfully, frowning in concentration. "Hmm." He paced some more, lost in thought. "Perhaps—" He turned to Kate. "Can you manage a large household?"

"Well . . . I—I don't know. I managed—or helped to manage—my father's household when I was growing up. There were only ten or twelve servants, but I had six brothers and sisters—I mean six who survived."

"That should do. Kenrick is a desperate man."

"Kenrick? Desperate?" Kate felt she was floundering in a great bowl of jelly.

"Do stop pacing and explain yourself, my dear," his wife demanded, but her tone was indulgent.

He resumed his seat. "The Earl of Kenrick. He too is one of my clients. He needs someone to bring order to his household. In Yorkshire. Which is quite some distance from Wynstan Castle in Devon."

"Has he no wife to do so?" Mrs. Phillips asked.

"She died," he said abruptly. "Five years ago or more. There's a young child—a girl, I believe."

"He has no housekeeper, either?" Kate asked.

"Not any more. She was elderly and went off to live with her sister or cousin or some such. The dowager countess lives in Bath. There is an elderly aunt at Kenrick, but she is crippled with arthritis and somewhat blind. Of course, it would not be a *permanent* solution, but it could buy you some time in which to come up with a better plan."

"Possibly . . ." Kate said slowly.

"An earl? He surely would not entertain the idea of the mother of a future duke as his *housekeeper!*" Mrs. Phillips was clearly scandalized.

"*No-o-o,*" Kate said, turning the idea over in her mind. "But he might welcome plain Mrs. Gardiner and her son Ned."

"Well, he should know what—or whom—he is getting involved with," Phillips said.

"No!" Kate said sharply. "Please. No one but you—and Major Lawrence—should know where we have gone. This Lord Kenrick might not want us if he thinks we are not just ordinary people."

Phillips agreed reluctantly. "Perhaps you are right. The fewer who know, the better. However, first you must get past the hurdle of an interview with Kenrick. Then—if he hires you—you can decide yourself how much to tell him and when."

They were all silent for a moment, then Kate had a thought. "No. Not *Mrs. Gardiner.* That is Wynstan's family name. I shall be Mrs. *Arthur.* Just plain Mrs. Arthur. And her son Ned. Wynstan and his servants never referred to Ned as anything but 'Master Edward.' The duke hated calling Arthur's son 'Marquis of Spenland.' Spenland had been his precious Frederick's title."

Phillips took a deep breath. "As you wish, my lady. 'Mrs. Arthur' it shall be. I will send word around to Kenrick tomorrow morning—I think he is still in town."

"Meanwhile, you and your Ned can stay here until all is decided," his wife said, patting Kate's hand again.

"That is very generous of you, Mrs. Phillips. Frankly, I don't know what I would have done had you not offered such hospitality." Kate hated being in such a vulnerable position, but lately she had had to swallow much of her customary pride.

Later that night, tucked into a spare room with a now sleeping Ned, Kate had thought with no small degree of apprehension about the coming interview. She found herself in a familiar, if one-sided, discussion with her dead husband.

"Oh, Arthur, this just has to work for us!"

She hoped the Earl of Kenrick would not prove crotchety and difficult to please. She gave an inward shrug. What did it matter? Yorkshire was far enough from Devon and Wynstan Castle to ensure safety for Ned. For that, *she* could endure almost anything. This was a temporary solution.

She supposed she *could* have sent Ned away to school— there were children as young as he in boarding schools—but she was sure that Wynstan would have found some way to foil that plan. And besides, she could not face the idea of giving up her son so soon. Eventually, she would have to make a decision about Ned's education—about a proper education for a future duke. For now, though, she could continue to teach him, but bright, eager Ned would—all too soon—grow beyond what his mother could give him.

She sighed. That bridge would be crossed in due time.

CHAPTER 3

Wishing himself on the road back to Yorkshire, Jeremy Michael Chilton, Earl of Kenrick—seventh of that line—paced about his suite in Grillon's Hotel, awaiting the arrival of his solicitor. He fervently hoped this delay would prove to be worth the wait. The note from Phillips said he had found a housekeeper for Kenrick Hall. Would that it could be so!

In recent months Jeremy had become acutely conscious of the fact that he himself was most inept at managing his own household—nor was his frail Aunt Elinor up to the task, even though his financial affairs had forced him to close off one whole wing of the house. The consequent reduction in staff meant fewer people to direct, but managing menus and housekeeping schedules was simply too much on top of acting as his own steward and supervising farmworkers. After all, the farms and mills had to be productive—or there would soon enough be no house to keep. Saving Kenrick was proving every bit as difficult as he had anticipated. And tiring, for Jeremy worked long hours, side-by-side with his workers.

A visit from his sister Margaret had served as the catalyst to rouse him to action regarding the household. One evening, long after Aunt Elinor had retired, Margaret had upbraided him.

"Jeremy!" She sounded exactly like their old nurse. "This will not do!" She ran a handkerchief across a table in the library. "Look at this!" She held up the dust-besmeared bit of linen and lace as she took a seat next to her husband William on a sofa. "Poor Aunt Elinor cannot see it, but surely you can see the filth you are living in!"

Jeremy gave her a quizzical glance and set aside a pamphlet on farm management he and William had been discussing. He was vaguely aware that housekeeping matters were not quite what they should be. Now that he had guests, he noticed the shortcomings—and he was aware of the inadequacies of his kitchen.

Margaret seemed to read his mind. "And your table! Are you aware that we have had the exact same lunch and the exact same dinner three days running?"

"Three days?" He did not explain that a man who fell into bed exhausted every night hardly tasted his food.

"Three days. I will not eat another bite of roast lamb!"

Jeremy was saved from responding to this mild outburst when his brother-in-law chided her. "Now, now, my love. I am sure you were taught better manners in the schoolroom. Remember—we are guests."

"In the house in which I was reared!" she retorted. "If I cannot speak my mind here, where might I do so?"

Jeremy, feeling rather mischievous and appreciating a diversion from talk of crop rotations and breeding sheep, said lightly, "Mags has always been one to speak her mind."

She glared at him. "You know I *hate* being called Mags!"

"Why?" her husband asked.

"*He* knows why," she said.

Jeremy explained. "Nurse used to refer to her as 'Lady Maggie.' Robert twisted that to 'maggot' from which came Mags."

"And I never did achieve a proper revenge upon our dear little brother," she said. "I do hope his fellow soldiers have come up with some equally offensive sobriquet for *him*."

Her husband patted her hand and affected a tone of exaggerated sympathy, which his grin belied. "I understand why you hate it, my dear. I promise never to use such a demeaning term. What was it again? Ah, yes. Mags."

She slapped at him playfully. "You both stray from the subject at hand." Margaret turned to her brother. "Jeremy, since you don't have a wife, and Aunt Elinor is unable to help, you must have someone to supervise your staff, plan menus, and so on. What happened to Mrs. Preston? One of the maids told me she left. So you've no housekeeper at all? I found Sally Jenkins in the kitchen. Sally Jenkins! A dairy maid for a cook? Mrs. Jenkins is able enough, but lacks imagination."

Jeremy sighed. "I'm lucky she took on the task. Mrs. Preston gave up housekeeping duties here three months ago after she took a nasty fall. She went to live with her daughter in Nottingham."

"And Cook?"

"She received a better offer."

"A better offer?"

"Mortimer offered her twice what I was paying her."

"Who is Mortimer?" she asked.

"The man who bought the Barkley estate—and rebuilt it virtually from scratch. You must know of him. He and Father were apparently very close. Mortimer owned a mill in Lancashire and made a fortune during the wars with Napoleon."

"Oh, yes. I vaguely recall meeting him once. Mortimer stole your cook?"

"He did," Jeremy admitted. "He has also hired away one of my grooms and offered better terms to two Kenrick tenant farmers."

"Who?" she demanded.

"Thompson and Banks."

"Alfred Thompson? He left Kenrick lands? I cannot believe that! Why, his grandfather worked this land for our grandfather!"

Jeremy shrugged. "I know. But there have been few improvements to the land or the cottages and barns on Kenrick since Grandfather's day. Thirty years of neglect takes its toll—on people and places."

"We were just discussing land improvements, my dear," her husband put in.

"I know Father spent a great deal of his time in London," she said, "but what about the steward—Stevens?"

"I couldn't afford to keep him on," Jeremy admitted. "In truth, he didn't perform well. Father liked him because the two often played cards and drank together—along with Mortimer. So—I am handling everything myself."

"Except the household," Margaret said.

"I try." He thought he sounded defensive. "The truth is—as long as Cassie is properly cared for—the household is the least of my worries. And Cranstan seems to handle matters in the nursery well enough."

"Perhaps. . . ." Margaret appeared to have reservations. "Nurse Cranstan does see to your daughter's physical needs adequately."

"As she is supposed to do," Jeremy said. "Of course, in another year or so I expect I shall have to hire a governess to provide lessons for Cassie. Meanwhile, Cranstan keeps her fed and dressed properly."

"Like a little doll," Margaret said.

Jeremy frowned at the hint of disapproval he detected in her tone. "Yes. Cassandra Margaret is a very pretty child and, since coming to England, she exhibits none of the tomboy proclivities of her namesake aunt." His grin softened this taunt.

She sniffed. "Hmph. *I* had fun as a child. And it would appear that carefree fun is decidedly missing in Cassie's life."

"You may have a point," he conceded, "but bear in mind that Cassie is surrounded by adults now. You always had Robert."

"Yes, I did. I am sorry William and I have not visited more often since your return—though I am sure Cranstan thinks the nursery has been contaminated by our three wild ones."

The conversation then drifted to other matters, but Jeremy had absorbed Margaret's points. As he bade his guests good-bye a week later, he gave his sister two promises: he would spend more time with his daughter and he would find a housekeeper.

Both tasks were harder to fulfill than he had anticipated.

Lately, the Earl of Kenrick found his daughter somewhat bewildering. She had changed profoundly since leaving North America. He had foreseen a period of adjustment, but she seemed to have lost her spirit. The giggling, prattling child of the frontier had turned into a withdrawn, but very proper young member of the *ton*, always respectful and subdued—almost wooden—in her behavior.

Jeremy had tried to break through the wall that had arisen, but to no avail. As Margaret had pointed out, Cassie was like a doll. A porcelain doll that might break if handled too roughly. He doubted either her Indian family or her white grandmother would see anything of the vivacious, fun-loving Little Willow in this very prim English child. Yes, he wanted her properly prepared for a role in English life, but he had not considered that her personality might be so altered with a change in geography. He had purchased a pony for her, thinking that might help. And it did, but still he worried.

"Give her time, my lord," Nurse Cranstan had assured him. "She is learning our ways rather well, I think. She will be a proper English child. You'll see."

Nor had he been able to find a suitable housekeeper in his own village or other parts of Yorkshire. Since arriving in London a week before, he had interviewed several women sent by an agency, but hired none. One had thought the pay inadequate, but that was a matter on which he could not budge. Two refused to remove to the "wilds of Yorkshire." Another seemed altogether too slovenly—he suspected an affinity for the gin bottle with her. Yet another seemed too eager to work in the house of a virile man who conveniently had no wife. Jeremy quickly shied away from that one. Unlike his predecessor, the new—seventh—Earl of Kenrick was not one to trifle with women in his employ.

He had mentioned the problem in passing when he consulted Walter Phillips on other matters. Though Phillips was the Kenrick solicitor and Chilton now the earl, the two men had quickly dispensed with formalities and regained their schoolboy friendship. They were Wally and Jeremy again. Beyond the friendship, the two had become partners in a business venture involving cargo ships from the Orient. Both knew it was a risky proposition. Jeremy had put nearly all his savings into it, but the returns would be—could be—sufficient to take the pressure off the Kenrick holdings. Do or die, he had told himself.

But now there was this matter of a housekeeper, and Phillips had promised help there too.

A knock on the door heralded the arrival of a hotel attendant presenting a plate with a calling card. "You have visitors in the lobby, my lord."

"Thank you."

Jeremy followed the man down to the main reception area where he found Phillips sitting with a woman much younger than Jeremy had expected. Mid-twenties, he guessed. As Phillips introduced Mrs. Katherine Arthur, Jeremy noted dark blond hair under a modest straw bonnet. She wore a none-too-fashionable forest green cloak that emphasized hazel eyes framed with dark brows and lashes. He decided immediately that she would not do. Altogether too young to be a housekeeper. And too pretty. Still, he *had* to have someone. . . .

Suddenly, he became aware that she was subjecting him to as keen a scrutiny as his was of her. He glanced into her eyes and grimaced ruefully, sharing the discomfort of being "caught out," as it were.

Phillips indicated a table with chairs set near a window that looked out onto the street. "Perhaps the two of you would like to hold your discussion over there. I shall just wait here for you, La— uh—Mrs. Arthur." He picked up a newspaper lying on a sofa.

When she had been seated, Jeremy took the opposite chair. He stared at her, and was disconcerted to find her holding his gaze rather than lowering her lashes demurely. Her demeanor was honest and open, rather than bold.

"You seem rather young for a housekeeper," he said bluntly. Privately, he also thought she was far too attractive to be hired by most ladies of society who would not want their men distracted by a charming servant. Housekeepers were regularly middle-aged frumps—not women who would spur a man's mind toward the bedroom.

"I am nine and twenty," she said.

"*Mrs.* Arthur. You're a widow?"

"Yes. My husband died on the Peninsula. I have a son who must accompany me."

He liked the fact that she was so forthright. "A son? Phillips said nothing of a child. How old is he?"

"He is just short of his eighth year."

"I see." He drummed his fingers absentmindedly against the arm of his chair. "Hmm. Well, that should not prove to be an insurmountable problem. In fact, perhaps not a problem at all. Might be better if he were a girl, though."

"I beg your pardon?" Her voice held a hint of umbrage.

"Oh. Sorry," he said. "I was thinking aloud. My daughter is nearly six and my sister is convinced she needs more association with other children."

"Oh."

"I assume you are experienced at managing a rather large household?"

"Uh . . . how large?" she asked nervously.

"Thirty or thereabouts. Could you manage such a staff?"

"I *think* I can, but I feel I must be quite honest with you. I have not supervised so many on a regular basis."

"I appreciate your candor. Honesty is a quality I value rather highly." He thought he sounded insufferably pompous.

She glanced up at him, then quickly away. "I more or less managed my family's household of over a dozen people when I was just a girl. My father has a small holding in the south of England."

"More or less?" He raised a brow in skepticism.

She went on as though she had not noted the implied question. "And I often helped to set up portable hospitals and helped direct disposition of wounded when my husband served in the Peninsula."

"Good heavens. You followed the drum?"

"Yes," she said simply.

"A hard life for an English woman."

"A hard life for anyone," she replied.

He nodded and then surprised himself. "Well, Mrs. Arthur, as Phillips probably told you, I desperately need someone to take over my house so that I can devote my time to other matters. And frankly, I have been unable to find a suitable party. But if you are willing to remove to Yorkshire, I am willing to hire you on a trial basis."

"Yorkshire?" She sounded a bit breathless.

"Yorkshire. I don't see why so many Londoners consider Yorkshire the end of the earth."

"I'm not a Londoner. Yorkshire would be perfect, my lord." She smiled fleetingly. "The end of the earth is a campaign trail in the Pyrenees."

He noted how even the wisp of a smile animated her features, but there was also a haunted look in her eyes. He sensed vulnerability and was startled by his own regret at seeing such. Only much later did it occur to him that she had not said where she was from. Nor had he thought to ask.

"I shall take your word for that. My younger brother served with the Forty-sixth Rifle Regiment. Captain Robert Chilton. Might you have known him in the Peninsula? He's with the army of occupation in France now."

She raised her brows in surprise. "Yes, I did know then-Lieutenant Chilton—slightly. He was one of my husband's fellow officers."

He thought her response seemed evasive, but he could not waste time worrying about it. "Shall we agree to a trial period of three months?"

"That will be acceptable, my lord."

They discussed the details of a modest salary, time off each week, and arrangements for her and her son to travel by mail coach to Kenrick, a small town in Yorkshire. Jeremy explained that he had not brought a carriage to the city and would begin his ride back the next day. He thanked Phillips, saw the two of them to the door, and gazed thoughtfully after them.

This trip to London might, in the end, prove very satisfying. Investing in cargo ships was a gamble, though. Was he turning into his father? Still, he felt some relief at having hired a housekeeper.

As Phillips escorted her to the carriage and then back to his own house in Bloomsbury, Kate allowed herself the luxury of looking to the immediate future with something resembling optimism for the first time in months. She realized the stay at Wynstan Castle had been far more oppressive than she had thought at the time.

She had been nervous about meeting the earl, for so much had depended on this interview! What if he had dismissed her out of hand? He was younger than she had expected, though Mr. Phillips had said they were once schoolfellows. She thought he was probably near her own age. He was rather a large man, but it was not physical presence alone that made him seem a downright imposing figure. It was that direct way of looking at one. His blue eyes were flecked with a darker color, like unpolished lapis lazuli. Heavy dark brows over a once straight, now slightly crooked nose gave him a forbidding demeanor. Carelessly styled dark brown hair showed a touch of gray at the temples. He certainly did not *look* impoverished. His attire, while not of the first stare of fashion, was refined and altogether fitting. He might have been a most attractive specimen if he had smiled, but the man had not smiled even once.

Not since those earliest days with Arthur had she been so intensely aware of the mere physical presence of a man. When he took her thinly gloved hand in his work-roughened clasp, she had raised her eyes to his and felt something electric pass between them. But now she put that bit of utter foolishness down to her own apprehension about the outcome of the interview.

"Have you been to Kenrick Hall?" she asked Phillips.

"Not in recent years," he replied. "Kenrick comes to town when he needs to see me. He was one of the clients I inherited when I took over my father's practice, though I also knew him in school. Father always said the earldom had gone downhill—he was distressed by what had happened. However, I think that it still has great potential."

"By which you mean?"

"That with good management—something that was significantly absent when the current earl's father was in charge—the estates might reap a very nice income. In fact, my father always thought Kenrick *could* be a very rich man indeed."

"But the current earl is not?"

"No, he is not. His grandfather was rather indifferent to what he referred to as 'newfangled ideas' of agriculture. Kenrick's father, of course, was a wastrel and brought the place to near ruin."

Kate must have looked mildly shocked at this revelation, for Phillips continued, "No, Lady Arthur, I am not telling tales out of school. The whole *ton* knows the sixth earl was sinfully profligate and that Jeremy Chilton inherited a title laden with debt and mortgages."

"Were the lands not entailed?" Kate's curiosity was crowding out good manners.

"The entail died with Kenrick's grandfather—the fifth earl. And his son—the current Lord Kenrick's father—managed to squander or mortgage nearly everything."

In for a penny, in for a pound, she thought, and said, "You seem on closer terms with the earl than is usual for a mere business relationship—rather like that between you and my husband."

He chuckled. "You are a most observant woman, Lady Arthur. Remind me not to underestimate you."

"Please—you must call me *Mrs*. Arthur."

"You're right. I almost slipped with Kenrick. To answer your question, Kenrick is a year or so older than I, but we knew each other as schoolboys at Winchester, then we went off to Oxford, but were in different colleges. We drifted apart when I left to study law at Lincoln's Inn. After that, he was in North America for a number of years. Never expected to return. They say the test of a friendship is how two people react after a prolonged absence. In that regard, Kenrick and I pass the test. As with Arthur, Jeremy is not just a client—he's a friend."

"I do not recall Arthur's ever mentioning him."

"That's not surprising. Arthur never knew him. That is, I don't *think* the two ever met. If so, it would have been very fleetingly. As I said, Jeremy was a year older—and a far more serious student in those days than either Arthur or I." He chuckled at some distant memory.

"So," she said lightly, "you have obtained a position for me with an impoverished earl."

"I hope not. I doubt he will become truly impoverished. He is not without prospects or potential." But the sensible solicitor offered nothing more on that topic.

"In any event, this temporary position suits my needs perfectly and I do thank you!"

CHAPTER 4

A week later, Kate and Ned stood in the open yard of the only inn in the town of Kenrick. The coach in which they had arrived had left only moments before. Mother and son were both tired, having been cooped up in a coach for four days, though Phillips had seen to it that they had sufficient funds for accommodations along the way. He had also arranged for his own middle-aged housekeeper to accompany the young widow and her child. Mrs. Sealy was overdue for a visit with her brother in York, the Phillipses insisted over Kate's protests. Ned had fidgeted and fussed during this last morning, asking repeatedly, "Are we there yet?" Now, here they were in the courtyard of an inn and no one to meet them.

"Mrs. Arthur?" The man's voice startled her. He tipped his hat to her as she turned. "I'm Cuthbertson, Lord Kenrick's coachman. His lordship sent me to collect you and the boy." The man's accent was so heavy Kate had to strain to define the individual words. "He would've come hisself, but they needed 'im in the birthin' barn."

"Birthing barn?" she asked.

"Sheep. A couple of prize ewes are having a tough time."

"Sheep," she echoed, feeling decidedly stupid.

"This here's sheep country," he said. "Finest wool in England. Kenrick's got some o' the best. An' this bein' lambin' season an' all..." He took the bag Kate had been holding and glanced at the bag and the guitar at her feet. "Where's your trunk?"

"We have no trunk. This is all we have."

He seemed surprised at this, but said nothing as he stored the luggage and the instrument in the rear of the carriage. He opened the door and pulled down the steps. Kate motioned for Ned to scramble to his seat.

"How far is it to the Hall?" she asked.

Cuthbertson handed her in as he answered. " 'Bout half an hour."

Once under way, Kate pulled aside the heavy curtains on the carriage windows and fastened them so that she and Ned could see the area that was to be their new home, however temporarily.

"Look, Mama!" Ned giggled at the antics of new lambs in a field.

The white sheep, some with black faces, stood out in stark contrast to the green of fields and rolling hills. Here and there sharper projections of gray stone or clumps of trees provided variety to the landscape. Stone fences separated fields, some with sheep, others with crops. Above, a blue sky dotted with wispy clouds added another dimension of color to the scene.

Kate gradually relaxed. She had expected to be on edge until she settled into the routine of this new stage in her life. But already the contrasts of comforting colors and intriguing landscape were creating a sense of calm and well-being. Perhaps this had been a good move after all.

She felt the carriage slow and sensed the horses straining to ascend a hill. At the crest, she looked across the way to see a mansion of gray stone with a slate roof. Imperiously, it dominated an elevated crop of land on the far side of a green valley. Yet it seemed to blend in perfectly with its surroundings. Very picturesque, she thought.

"That must be Kenrick Hall," she said to Ned.

" 'Tis big, Mama. But not so big as Wynstan Castle."

"It is large," she agreed, "larger than I expected. But you must remember, my darling, not to mention Wynstan to anyone."

"I *know*, Mama," he replied impatiently.

Kate glanced out the window again. Silently, she questioned Lord Kenrick's informing her of a staff of thirty or so. Surely it would take at least twice that many for a house this size! Though she had seen only the front of the building, she conjectured it would have at least two, possibly three wings—each with three stories and an attic and cellar as well.

From the crest of the hill they had climbed, she could see the road winding down and through a lane of trees showing the green-gold of early springtime leaves. It crossed an ancient stone bridge, then took a wide sweep in front of the mansion. The carriage rounded the building and came to a stop in the rear.

A servant hurried forward to open the carriage door. Ned jumped out and stood shyly waiting for his mother. The servant helped her alight and she held Ned's small hand in her own as an anchor to familiarity, for she was suddenly aware that she had not dispelled *all* her nervousness about this adventure she was embarking upon. A heavy oaken door opened to reveal a man who looked about sixty and walked in a stiff, upright manner. He had rather thin hair, a gray mustache, and a very precise air about him.

"Welcome to Kenrick Hall, madam. His lordship told me to expect you. I'm Wilkins, the butler."

Kate nodded her acknowledgment. "Thank you, Mr. Wilkins. I am, of course, Mrs. Arthur and this is my son, Ned."

"Lord Kenrick warned me about the boy," Wilkins said.

"*Warned*?" She raised a brow. "His lordship assured me that my son would pose no problem for the household."

Kate knew it was important to establish herself immediately. The Good Lord knew she had seen enough new officers take over existing regiments to know what her role would be in this household.

Wilkins swallowed visibly and replied in a slightly mollified tone, "He told me. But 'tis unusual, you know. I assume you will ensure that the child is no hindrance to the staff."

"You may depend upon it," she said. "Now, if you will show me to my room, I will attend to my son and then someone may show me around."

"Yes, madam. His lordship would like to see you in the library when you are ready."

"Please tell him I will be there very shortly."

They had moved into the kitchen. It was large with a slate floor and two long worktables in the center of the room. Kate noted two large ranges, but only one seemed to be in use. The whitewashed walls were streaked with soot from the coal-burning stoves. Wilkins introduced her to the cook, an older woman named Sally Jenkins, and three younger women, obviously kitchen maids.

Kate nodded at each in turn and noted that they cast inquisitive looks her way. Sally Jenkins was a robust, gray-haired woman of mid- to late-forties, Kate guessed. She had a round face reddened by an open fire over which she had been tending a roast on a spit.

"Smells good," Kate said appreciatively, but she noticed the girl who'd been introduced as Rosie roll her eyes behind the cook's back.

Mrs. Jenkins acknowledged the introduction hastily and muttered something about having to get the midday meal on the table.

Rosie was a slight girl of perhaps fifteen years. She had reddish brown hair and a ready smile. Wilkins instructed her to show Mrs. Arthur to the housekeeper's rooms and wait to show her to the library.

"Yes, Mr. Wilkins," Rosie said with just a touch of sauciness in her tone.

He frowned at her, but turned on his heel and left the kitchen.

Rosie kept up a patter of chitchat as she led Kate and Ned down a narrow hall to two plainly furnished rooms. "Old Mrs. Preston had these rooms. The bedchamber is rather crowded since we put in a cot for your boy, but the sitting room is proper comfortable enough."

Kate looked around. "Yes, I can see that it is."

The furniture—a couch, a wing chair, and a small table with two straight chairs—was worn, but, aside from needing a thorough dusting, it was clean. "Lord knows you have lived happily in surroundings far less elegant," she told herself, recalling accommodations she and Arthur had endured on the Peninsula. She quickly removed her hat and cloak, glad that she had not entirely put off her sober half-mourning clothing; it would do very well for a housekeeper. She forced stray wisps of hair back into the severe bun, wishing she had time to redo it entirely. She wet a cloth in the basin and wiped her face, then dug around in one of the bags to find the mobcap she had secured as a badge of her new station in life.

She sat Ned down at the table in the sitting room where she gave him not only the last of the biscuits they had occasionally munched on during their journey, but also a piece of paper and a graphite pencil with which to amuse himself.

She kissed the top of his head. "You be a good boy, son. I'll be back soon."

"Yes, Mama." He was already engrossed in his drawing.

"I'll keep a watch on 'im for you," Rosie volunteered as she showed Kate the way to the library.

"Thank you, Miss Davis."

"Nobody calls me Miss Davis—just Rosie."

"*I* shall call you Miss Davis," Kate said firmly.

Rosie grinned. "Well, ma'am, that could get confusing as my sister Nell, she works here too, and she be a Miss Davis too."

"Hmm. That does present a problem," Kate said and then admitted defeat with a smile. "Very well, then, Rosie it is."

Rosie was quiet for a moment, then she said shyly, "You seem rather young for a housekeeper."

"I suppose I am," Kate admitted, "but there is no age requirement for doing a good job, now, is there?"

"No, ma'am." Rosie paused again then said, "We downstairs folks are that glad you've come, ma'am."

"Oh?"

"Yes, ma'am. Mrs. Jenkins, she's a good soul—an' she does know how to cook all right, but she don't have much imagination. We're hopin' our meals might change some now you're here."

"I . . . see."

"Mind you, his lordship don't stint on food for the help," Rosie hastened to explain. "An' he ain't one to try to trap a girl beneath the stairs none, neither."

"I should hope not," Kate said.

"They's lot o' them what do," Rosie said knowingly.

"You have worked in other houses, then?" Kate asked.

"Oh, no. Only here. Me da's one o' Kenrick's tenant farmers, but I got friends in other houses around. There ain't no place so good as here," she said proudly, " 'spite o' his lordship's troubles."

Kate was spared an improper or quelling response to this, for they had arrived at the library door. The moment they passed through the door separating the service areas from the family's quarters, she was intrigued by what she saw. Not surprisingly, the halls here were wider, the furnishings more lavish. But everywhere there were signs of neglect. Yes, the earl certainly needed someone to take charge of his household. She waved Rosie a farewell and rapped lightly on the library door.

"Yes. Come in," a deep voice answered. "Ah, Mrs. Arthur." He rose behind the desk to greet her. A small, white-haired woman seemed to have been dozing, but sat upright on hearing his voice.

Today, the Earl of Kenrick did not resemble any peer of the realm she had ever seen. He was dressed much as a common laborer might have been in a well-worn pair of buckskin breeches and an open shirt, the sleeves rolled up to his forearms. Open at the neck, the shirt revealed a bit of dark hair. He gestured for her to be seated in a chair in front of the desk. She noted the hard muscles of his arms and that his shoulders made an ordinary worker's shirt a most interesting garment, despite its stains.

She quickly gave herself a mental shake and tried to concentrate on what he was saying. Which was hard to do—distracted as she was by watching his hands idly playing with a small paperweight as he talked. He looked comfortable enough behind the desk, but she suspected he was a man who was more at ease out of doors than in. She tore her gaze away from his hands and looked into his eyes. Oh, dear. That was an error. One could get lost there! Unable to look away, she held his gaze for what seemed an eternity. Then he cleared his throat and said, "Mrs. Arthur, allow me to introduce my aunt, Lady Elinor Chilton Baxter."

"My lady," Kate murmured politely and bobbed her head in acknowledgement.

"I trust your journey was a pleasant one." The older woman's voice was strong and firm in contrast to the slightly vacant look in her eyes and a cane near her elbow.

"Yes, thank you."

"Wilkins will have someone show you around after the midday meal and you may begin your duties as soon as you are settled in," her employer said.

"Yes, my lord."

"I trust you know far more about housekeeping than I do," he said. "I have made it clear that you are in charge. Mind you, Wilkins has his nose slightly out of joint, but he will get over it."

"I—I don't understand." Lord. Was she going to start off on the wrong foot with the butler? Had she already done so?

The man behind the desk ran his hand nervously through previously disheveled hair. "The truth is, the manor needs more than a mere housekeeper. It needs an overseer—someone to take charge. A chatelaine, if you will."

A wife, she thought, but of course she could not say that.

"In most houses, a wife performs the role I am outlining for you," he said, just as though he had read her mind. "But mine is a bachelor establishment—and likely to remain such."

"My nephew wants a housewife, but not a wife," his aunt interjected.

"Yes. Something like that." He looked slightly embarrassed, but grinned briefly, flashing even white teeth against a tanned complexion.

Oh, Lord, Kate thought. *You smile at the ladies like that and you will have a wife—a real wife—forthwith.*

"One of the maids and a footman must be available regularly to attend Lady Elinor, but if you need to hire additional help, we could—perhaps—do with one or two more—but no more than that." He ended on a note of caution.

"Let me consider the matter," Kate said. "I cannot make such a request until I know the house and the staff better."

"Of course."

The interview over, she saw that her son was fed, then she joined the staff in the servants' hall for the midday meal. Wilkins stood at the head of one long table and motioned her to that place at the other one.

"This is Mrs. Arthur, the new housekeeper," Wilkins announced, still standing along with Kate.

She felt all eyes focused on her. "How do you do?" she said. "It will take me a while to become acquainted with all of you, so do bear with me."

They nodded politely, some smiling their welcomes.

Then Mr. Wilkins said grace and there was much scraping of chairs and benches as the servants—well over thirty of them—took their seats and set about busily digging into the meal. It consisted of roast lamb, potatoes, boiled cabbage, and bread and butter. A hearty, but not especially attractive meal, she thought as she took her seat.

Rosie happened to sit near Kate and said softly, "See? This is our midday meal most days. Always the same."

"Oh?" Kate tried to keep a neutral tone.

"Breakfast is always porridge, except for Saturdays and supper's always bread and cheese—always the same cheese too."

"I . . . see," Kate said as a couple of brave souls near Rosie nodded agreement. "I make no promises, but perhaps something can be done."

She was mindful of Arthur's telling her that Napoleon had once said an army travels on its stomach. She supposed the same might be true of an army of servants and laborers.

The meal finished, Rosie and the other kitchen maids set to clearing the table and washing dishes. Wilkins handed Kate a large brass ring with a number of keys on it and assigned a chambermaid—Nell, Rosie's sister—to show the new housekeeper around.

"I expect you will find your way around quickly enough," he said, dismissing her.

"Yes, I suppose I shall," she replied. *With or without your cooperation*, she added mentally.

Nell proved to be nearly as much of a chatterbox as her younger sister. Must run in the family, Kate thought.

"The oldest part of the house was built in the sixteenth century," Nell said as they walked a long corridor, "during the time of Queen Elizabeth. Seems the first earl found favor with her majesty."

"Yes. I read as much in a guidebook."

"His lordship closed off the east wing when he took up residence about a year ago."

"Oh?" Kate encouraged.

"Had to. Couldn't afford it no more. Had to let a lot of the staff go too."

"How sad."

"But he were fair about it," Nell assured her. "He kept 'em on till they got new places—an' he helped 'em get new jobs too."

Kate was not sure why this information pleased her so, but perhaps the earl would be equally kind when it came time for her to leave.

"I should like to see the whole house, including the east wing," Kate said.

"You'll want a wrap, then," Nell said. "It's pretty cold in that part of the house."

They took time out to obtain shawls, then continued the orientation tour. Kate saw ample evidence of the decline in grandeur the house had suffered. There were spots on some walls where paintings had once hung, though a long gallery still included a number of family portraits that looked to be quite valuable. She thought she recognized one as a Holbein. Mr. Phillips had told her much of the moveable property had been sold to defray debts, but apparently even the profligate sixth earl had demurred at disposing of family portraits.

She found draperies—both for windows and for beds—in need of thorough cleaning and repair. The linen closets were full of items needing mending and carpets cried out for serious beatings. A coating of dust lay over most of the house—even to some extent in the most used rooms: the library, a drawing room, the dining room, Lady Elinor's chamber, his lordship's chamber, and the nursery. Well, that was one chore that could be handled immediately.

Nell was obviously embarrassed at seeing matters through the new housekeeper's eyes. "It—uh—needs some doing," she offered.

"It needs a great deal of doing," Kate said. "But never mind—soap and water, some beeswax—and a healthy dose of elbow grease—will bring things about." Kate deliberately made her voice more confident than she felt.

The truth was, she found the task daunting, but not impossible. It was, she thought, a wonderful house. Her first impression had been right. The house was large—far larger than any she had known intimately before the move to Wynstan Castle. Unlike the cold showplace that was the castle, though, this house fit comfortably into its surroundings.

"The house appears to have been constructed from local stones," Kate commented as she and Nell crossed the slate floor of the entrance hall.

Nell chuckled. "Well, you might say so. The stone was originally quarried for the abbey up the Kenrill River. The first earl used stones from the abbey for this house—least, that's what me da says."

"A not uncommon practice when the monasteries were destroyed in Tudor times," Kate observed. She liked that bit of history about the house. And she loved the use of natural stone and heavy, natural timbers throughout the building. A wonderful home, but sadly neglected. She shook her head in mild dismay.

Nell seemed to read her expression and offered apologies. "Lady Kenrick—his lordship's stepmother—she never liked it here. Used to live in London mostly. She's in Bath now. Lady Elinor is near blind. An' Mrs. Preston—well, she was gettin' on, you see."

Kate murmured sympathetically as they climbed the stairs to the nursery rooms, only three of which were in use. One was a large general purpose room that doubled as a schoolroom and playroom, one the nursery maid's chamber, and the other belonged to the earl's young daughter. The other five chambers in the nursery suite were kept closed, Nell explained. One was a larger bed-sitting room for a governess. They were all cold and smelled faintly musty.

Kate and Nell found the nurse and her charge in the larger room, which had clearly been designed to accommodate a good many more people than the two it now engulfed.

Nell made the introductions. "This here's Nurse Cranstan and Lady Cassandra," she said, sounding very formal. Kate thought the young maid's voice had taken on a reserved, even apprehensive note.

"Mrs. Cranstan," Kate said with a nod. "I am Mrs. Arthur, the housekeeper."

"Yes, I know." The other woman's tone was almost curt. "And it's Miss Cranstan—or just plain Cranstan."

Kate judged the Cranstan woman to be in her fifties. Her dark auburn hair was liberally streaked with gray and worn in a severely drawn back bun. She was a tall, spare woman with plain features. She had a brusque, no-nonsense demeanor.

The child seated quietly at a small table, however, was far from plain. She was small with straight, coal-black hair that hung nearly to her waist. She looked up when Nell said her name, turning on Kate a pair of blue eyes that were especially startling, given her very dark hair and golden complexion.

"What a beautiful little girl," Kate said softly. "How do you do, Lady Cassandra?"

Before the child could react, the nurse spoke in an admonishing tone. "How do you greet someone properly, Lady Cassandra?"

The little girl scooted down from the chair and executed an awkward curtsy. She turned solemn, intelligent eyes on Kate, but said nothing. Nor did she smile.

"She doesn't talk much," the nurse said. "And she still has a lot of heathen ways about her. I doubt we will ever make a proper lady of her, but his lordship insists we try. And heaven knows I *do* try." The woman heaved a much-put-upon sigh. " 'Tis hopeless, though. Her hair won't take a proper curl, no matter how hot the iron or how tight the rags, and she is as stubborn and contrary as any wild animal."

Kate was appalled at the woman's crass speech in front of her charge. The little girl gave Miss Cranstan a dull, enigmatic stare. There was none of the liveliness or interest one would expect in a child of five or six years. Nevertheless, Kate had the distinct impression that Lady Cassandra, despite her extreme youth, possessed a very accurate view of her nurse.

"Children do have minds of their own." Kate tried to sound noncommittal and bit her tongue against adding that wise adults treasured and nurtured those independent minds.

"Well, this one certainly does," Nurse Cranstan confided. "Why, just getting her dressed of a morning is a chore."

Kate looked more closely at Lady Cassandra's dress. It was an elaborate pink affair with a high ruffled neck and a profusion of ruffles and ribbons. She wore fancy slippers. The little girl looked uncomfortable in garb that could hardly be considered standard schoolroom or play attire.

"Is something special planned for her ladyship's day?" Kate asked.

"Oh, no," Cranstan said with a note of superiority. "I always try to dress her properly, though." The nurse snatched up a porcelain doll with yellow hair and a dress similar to the one worn by the child. Cranstan thrust it toward the girl. "Here, darling. Go and play now." The endearment seemed forced.

The girl took the toy and retreated to a window seat, where she sat looking disconsolate. Kate, feeling sorry for her, followed her gaze to a high shelf on which sat a rag doll dressed in an outfit Kate thought must be some sort of American Indian clothing.

Cranstan noted the direction of their attention and gave a mild snort. "Can you fathom that? She'd rather play with that filthy rag than the beautiful doll his lordship brought back from London for her. Had a devil of a time getting that—that *thing* away from her."

Kate surmised that it was not a new housekeeper's place to correct the child's well-established nurse, but her instant fury at the woman's obtuseness would not allow her to remain silent. "Perhaps it is merely a matter of wanting to cling to something familiar," she said.

The nurse sniffed. "She needs to get rid of her heathen ways and learn to be a proper English girl, though how she will ever be accepted in polite society with those Indian features is beyond me."

Kate bit her tongue and exited the nursery along with Nell.

Immediately the maid seemed more at ease. "Nurse Cranstan, she's pretty strict."

"It would appear so," Kate said.

"Miss Mortimer recommended her to Lord Kenrick's attention," the girl said.

Kate did not want to encourage gossip among the servants by asking who Miss Mortimer was and why his lordship had given such credence to her recommendation, but she left the nursery with a much lower opinion of her employer than she had heretofore entertained. How *could* the man subject that beautiful child to such a rigid, restrictive atmosphere?

CHAPTER 5

Jeremy watched his new housekeeper leave the library. What on earth had possessed him to hire a woman whose appearance and demeanor recommended her more for a ballroom than a stillroom? An apron about her waist emphasized delectable feminine curves, and that ridiculous mobcap did little to hide the soft, wispy curls about her face. He shook his head in self-disgust. He supposed he had been thinking with some part of his anatomy other than his brain. And *that* line of thought would not bear pursuing at all. She was, he reminded himself, an employee—and *this* Lord Kenrick, unlike his predecessor, would not be dallying with the help! Three months. In three months, perhaps Margaret could find him a proper housekeeper.

"Well, Aunt," he challenged. "What do you think?"

"Your new housekeeper *sounds* efficient. Young, though. Is she pretty?"

"Pretty?" He feigned disinterest. "Yes, I suppose she is—for whatever that matters."

"Oh, it could matter," his aunt said sagely. "Time will tell."

Jeremy snorted. "The vicar's wife is reading novels to you again, isn't she? The two of you—filling your heads with romantic nonsense."

His aunt laughed merrily. "You, my boy, could use a bit of romance in your life!"

He heaved an exaggerated sigh. "Finish your nap, Aunt Elinor. I have work to do."

In the next two days, he became aware of subtle—and some not so subtle—changes in the Hall. He noticed the smell first. Fresh air and beeswax chased away the pervasive mustiness. He had come into the library one afternoon to find the windows wide open and papers on his desk exactly where he had left them, but firmly anchored by a paperweight, an inkwell, and an intricately carved, fist-sized image of a buffalo, given to him after his first hunt with the Arapaho. A young maid was on her knees industriously polishing the legs of the furniture.

"Should I leave, my lord?"

"No. Finish your task," he said.

"I'm near done. Mrs. Arthur, she wants it done proper-like. She wouldn't let me touch the top o' the desk none, though."

"Good," he said firmly. His desk was messy—but it was sacred territory. He was glad the housekeeper realized that.

He also began to notice what appeared on his plate at mealtimes. Suddenly, his meals presented not only an eye-pleasing variety of color and texture, but subtle blends of herbs and spices added to meats and vegetables enticed the palate. The second evening, he sent a footman for the housekeeper. She appeared in the dining room as he and his aunt were finishing the evening meal.

"You wished to see me, my lord?"

He wiped his mouth with the napkin and leaned back in his chair. "Yes, Mrs. Arthur. We'd like to compliment you on the meal." Well, that was true, he told himself, as he carefully ignored that he had also just wanted to see her. "It was quite fine."

"Thank you. I shall pass your praise on to Mrs. Jenkins."

"*Mrs. Jenkins* was responsible for this?" He gestured at his empty plate.

"This meal bespoke a hand other than that of Mrs. Jenkins," Lady Elinor said.

"Well, I do make an occasional dish. I love to cook and Mrs. Jenkins is kind enough to share her domain. I happened to notice the herb garden—it was quite overgrown. Also, I found an assortment of spices in a chest in the housekeeper's rooms. I imagine Mrs. Jenkins simply did not know they were there."

"Hmm," the earl grunted noncommittally. His aunt merely nodded.

"Will that be all, my lord?"

"Yes—uh, no." He felt an inexplicable urge to keep her near. Later he attributed it to the fact that, other than Aunt Elinor—whose conversation centered on local gossip—there was no one else in his household he could engage in real, non–duty-related conversation. Only recently had he become fully aware of this lack in his life. In America, he had enjoyed the camaraderie of fellow fur traders in the wilderness, and during the months he and Willow spent in St. Louis, he had developed a companionable friendship with a local minister and a lawyer. All of those people had been his equals. Here, he was in charge—responsible—and it was hard to discuss philosophical or political issues with people whose very existence depended on getting along with him. Here was a woman who struck him as knowledgeable and conversant with affairs of the world—and she was decidedly easy to look at too. "How are you getting on?" he now asked the housekeeper.

"Quite well, my lord. The staff have been most helpful."

"Even Wilkins?" he asked, not bothering to mask a shade of amusement and concern.

"Yes. Even Mr. Wilkins," she replied with a smile.

"Very good." He felt they both knew they would not openly discuss the butler's offended sensibilities unless it proved necessary to do so. "And have you had time to consider your duties overall?"

"I have, my lord. And I have examined the household books. I believe we can manage as is—for a while, at least."

He raised a brow in surprise. "Indeed?"

"Yes, my lord."

Reluctantly, he let her go then.

Leaving the dining room, he saw his aunt to her chamber, then visited the nursery. It was his habit to spend time each evening with Cassie, regardless of how much—or, lately, how little—time he had spent with her earlier in the day. His visit gave Miss Cranstan a break each evening during which she could sip cider and socialize with other staff members. And it gave him precious time alone with his daughter.

She was, as usual, prepared for bed when he arrived. He hugged her close, savoring the fresh, clean smell of her. With her long black hair braided into two plaits, she reminded him strongly of her mother, though Cassie's eyes were a brilliant blue where her mother's had been what he thought of as deep Indian brown.

He was not sure why, but his dead wife had occupied his thoughts even more than usual lately—always with a tinge of regret. And guilt. He had long since let go of his grief, though he supposed the regret for what might have been would always haunt him.

What might have been—had either of them been of a different temperament. There was a wildness about the beautiful Willow that had had nothing to do with her being half Indian. On their very first meeting she had captivated him—as, indeed, she captivated all men. He could hardly believe his luck when she chose him among all the men pursuing her. Rich fur traders and brave Indian warriors seemed to have more to offer her than a greenhorn Englishman. Perhaps it was his being "different" that attracted her. He had not cared. All he wanted was her. And the feeling was mutual—for a while.

Familiarity breeds contempt, he thought. Well, it had seemed so at any rate for the capricious, volatile woman he had married. In retrospect, he realized that she had already shown signs of restless dissatisfaction when she—unhappily—found herself pregnant.

"Papa is sad?" Cassie's plaintive question roused him from these less-than-happy memories.

"No, Poppet. You always make me happy."

He nuzzled her smooth cheek and tickled her lightly, making her giggle. She was his carefree Cassie again, but only for a moment. Then she seemed to remember herself and she straightened.

"How was your day?" he asked. "Did you and Ned play outside today?" The two children had become acquainted the day before—when it had rained all afternoon.

"No, Papa. English girls don't play wild boy games." There was a note of regret in her voice.

"They don't? Who says so?"

"Miss Cranstan. She says proper English girls must not run around like wild heathens." She reported this in total innocence.

Jeremy thought the nurse's remark decidedly crude, but he could not bring himself to believe it had been truly malicious. "Perhaps Nurse Cranstan is right—at least partly," he said. "But it is all right for you to have fun."

"Yes, Papa," she replied in a serious tone.

"Shall I tell you a story of a beautiful girl who could run faster than any of the boys in her village?"

"Oh, yes, please!"

Her eagerness showed a spark of the old Cassie. So, transplanting the characters from Greek myth to an Arapaho tribe, he related the story of the fleet-footed Atalanta.

"That was a good story, Papa," Cassie said with grave approval.

He grinned and hugged her tighter. Miss Cranstan returned and he kissed Cassie good night. He waited as the nurse put the child to bed.

"A word, Miss Cranstan," he said when she came out.

"Yes, my lord?" Her tone was coolly superior.

"I should not think it necessary to speak of 'wild heathens' to my daughter," he said.

"If, indeed, I used such a term, I meant nothing untoward by it," she said defensively. " 'Tis but the sort of thing one says in passing. I often did so with Miss Mortimer."

"Among themselves English people often use such terms indiscriminately, not realizing how advanced many other cultures truly are. I want my daughter to accept and take pride in her heritage—English *and* Arapaho," he explained, then added in a firmer tone, "I prefer that you not use terms like *wild heathens* with Lady Cassandra."

"Of course, my lord. I had not realized she was quite so delicate in terms of language." Her tone made it clear that she thought he was overreacting, and Jeremy did not want to exacerbate the issue, so he let it drop.

The next day Nurse Cranstan's former charge, along with her parents, came to call. Jeremy and Lady Elinor received the visitors in the formal drawing room, which was larger and more elegant than the comfortable room the family usually chose.

In the interest of keeping the proprieties, Sir Eldridge Mortimer announced, he had accompanied mother and daughter when they had seen fit to pay a neighborly call on a fellow landowner, an unmarried man at that. One could not be too careful with a young lady's reputation. The man had greeted Aunt Elinor politely, but these comments seemed to overlook her presence. In any event, there the three were: in the Kenrick drawing room, sipping tea and making small talk.

Mortimer was a robust man in his fifties with a shock of black hair that refused to show more than the barest hints of gray. Jeremy's acquaintance with him had occurred only in recent months, for Mortimer had moved to the area while Jeremy was in America. Mortimer was one of those ambitious self-made men one often saw on the fringes of society: men whose financial ambitions had been realized and who now turned their aspirations—or those of their wives—to the social sphere.

Well, why not? Jeremy reasoned in a live-and-let-live manner of thinking. Mortimer's knighthood was a recent one, conferred, according to Phillips, after a hefty "loan" to the always financially pinched Prince of Wales.

Jeremy turned his attention to his female guests. In contrast to her more flamboyant husband and assertive daughter, the mother was a gray little pigeon of a woman. She seemed content to allow her husband and daughter to carry most of the weight of the social amenities, though she had graciously inquired after Lady Elinor's health.

Miss Mortimer was a comely young woman in her early twenties—no longer fresh from the schoolroom, but one who was not yet clearly upon the shelf. Her thick, dark hair was a sharp contrast to a clear, pale complexion and pale gray eyes. Her features were unexceptional, her smile practiced. Jeremy had met her at a dinner given by another neighbor on his return, and he had danced with her at local assemblies. He had dined with the Mortimers on two occasions as well. Now, in the earl's drawing room, Charlotte Mortimer kept up a steady flow of light conversation designed, apparently, to show her merry, amiable nature. It was accompanied with secret little smiles and much fluttering of eyelashes.

Jeremy was both amused and nonplussed by her so openly flirting with him. He dared not look at his aunt, knowing she must find what she discerned of the scene to be marvelously ridiculous.

During a pause in his daughter's chitchat, Mortimer spoke. "Local gossip informs us you hired a new housekeeper during your recent trip to London, Lord Kenrick."

"Yes. Mrs. Arthur has joined my staff." He was silently grateful that, thanks to that same Mrs. Arthur, much of the house was now presentable for guests.

"My wife and daughter have not visited here as often as I have,"

Mortimer said. "Came for a ball once, I think." He cast a glance at his wife, who nodded meekly. "It was one of those rare occasions when Lady Kenrick was here."

"My stepmother is skilled at entertaining." For a fleeting moment, Jeremy wondered to what degree she practiced her skills now that she resided in Bath, her circumstances much reduced from the lavish lifestyle she had enjoyed in London. He shrugged inwardly. Amelia would find a way.

"I have not seen much of your home, my lord," Miss Mortimer hinted broadly.

Before Jeremy could respond to this, the young woman's father spoke again to address Lady Elinor. "Perhaps her ladyship would be so kind as to show you around."

Lady Elinor's raised eyebrows as she glanced in Jeremy's direction clearly showed her reaction to the knight's imperative tone. "I beg your pardon," she said.

"Oh, my dear, we mustn't impose," Lady Mortimer said, her tone at once embarrassed and placating.

"I have some business to discuss with Lord Kenrick," her husband said brusquely.

Aunt Elinor planted her cane firmly next to her chair and rose somewhat unsteadily. "Jeremy, my dear, perhaps you could have Mrs. Arthur give them the tour and I shall excuse myself."

"Of course." Jeremy tugged at the bellpull harder than necessary.

When Wilkins appeared, Jeremy instructed him to accompany his aunt to the morning room and locate Mrs. Arthur to show the ladies as much of the house as could be shown.

Shortly, Mrs. Arthur arrived, her cheeks slightly flushed, a touch of flour on her nose, but wearing a freshly starched apron. Jeremy had to stop himself from grinning at the sight. He introduced her to his guests and explained the request. She nodded agreement and soon he was left with his remaining guest.

Jeremy assumed Mortimer wished to discuss the mortgage and other vouchers of debt the neighbor held against Kenrick properties. Although Jeremy had managed to whittle it down some by leasing the London townhouse and other economies—like a severely reduced stable—the debt was still of overwhelming proportion.

And it was all held by this man.

"Sir?" Jeremy prompted politely.

"You must be thinking me rather high-handed in suggesting a tour of another man's house," Mortimer said.

"Tours are not an uncommon phenomenon in houses of historical significance—though I am not sure Kenrick Hall qualifies as such."

"In this district, it is the only house that does," Mortimer scoffed. "However, that was not why I had you send the ladies away."

"You want to discuss financial matters," Jeremy said flatly.

"Well, yes—and no."

"My solicitor assures me that the debt is not finally due until mid-October." Having come this far in the last year, Jeremy refused to give in easily or quickly.

"True. Nor did I have in mind to press for early payment."

"Then . . ." Jeremy let his voice trail off. This was Mortimer's scene. Let him play it out as he would.

The older man shifted uncomfortably in his chair. " 'Tis a rather delicate matter," he began slowly, "but I'm a patient man and I've given you some months now to get your footing." He paused. "Were you aware that there was an understanding of sorts between your brother Charles and my daughter?"

"No. . . . That is, I *have* heard some gossip, but there seems to have been no announcement."

"No. No. Things had not progressed to that point. Charlotte wasn't sure of her feelings, despite the possibility of becoming a countess. Your father encouraged the match, of course." Mortimer did not meet Jeremy's gaze.

"I see . . ." Jeremy wondered where this was going. He had seen nothing of the pining lover in Miss Mortimer's demeanor.

"Well, now. The truth is, my little girl wants to be a countess. And she seems somewhat taken with you, my lord." Now the man gave Jeremy a direct, assessing look.

"I—uh . . . was not aware. That is—Look! I hardly know your daughter, sir."

"In the higher circles of society, that is not a major consideration," Mortimer responded.

"Perhaps not, but it is important to *me*."

"All her life I've tried to give my Charlotte whatever it is she wants."

"A commendable position, I'm sure," Jeremy said, trying to absorb the shock of what the man was suggesting.

"She thought she would like to be Lady Kenrick, so I did my best to ensure her heart's desire."

Jeremy sat quietly for a moment. "I confess I did wonder how—or why—*all* my father's debts—and my brother's too—ended up in the hands of one person."

"I bought them all," Mortimer said. "Seemed a prudent step to take."

"In case Charles proved a reluctant bridegroom?" Jeremy asked coldly.

Mortimer ignored the tone and chuckled. "Oh, he wasn't reluctant—not in the least. He liked the idea of having a generous allowance and leaving the work of managing things to someone else."

"Did he now?" Jeremy knew it was true. Neither Charles nor their father had been overly interested in the most basic matters of estate management. As long as the money poured in—

"Of course, he was also not averse to my daughter's person. She is, as you have no doubt observed, a lovely woman. They would have made a match—I'm sure of it—but for his untimely death."

"I think death is rarely timely."

"Right."

They sat in silence, Mortimer apparently allowing his host to absorb what had been said. Offended by the audacity of the conversation, Jeremy was furious at the man's blatant attempt, even now, to manipulate matters at Kenrick. But it was impotent fury because, so far at least, the other's machinations had put his quarry right where Mortimer wanted him. The fact that the quarry had changed identities seemed to matter not at all.

Mortimer now added, "After your brothers died, your father thought that, once you understood matters, you would be agreeable to our plan."

"So what—exactly—is it that you two had in mind?" Jeremy challenged, determined to force this arrogant bully to expose the full extent of his vulgarity.

"I think you probably understand." The man sounded smug. "I offer you exactly what I offered your brother."

"And that was . . . ?"

"I would ensure a generous settlement on my daughter, including an allowance for her husband—in addition to expunging all debt of the earldom."

Jeremy frowned. "And *you* would get . . . ?"

"A father's assurance that his child was happy." He said this piously and with a straight face. Then he added in a coldly matter-of-fact tone, "There are conditions. First, I assume title and control of all Kenrick properties—the lands and farms, the mill, the mines, and the brewery. And, secondly—although you keep the peerage and a seat in Parliament—you will take the name of Mortimer. You may add it to your own family name with one of those fancy hyphens, if you wish."

Jeremy snorted. "You would strip the entire earldom of its very meaning."

"Not precisely. I should expect that all would be restored to my grandson one day."

"Lucky for you that my child is a female," Jeremy said bitterly.

"No. I would say it was lucky for *you*," Mortimer said. "If the brat had been a boy, I would have foreclosed immediately instead of granting that extension Phillips was so keen on negotiating."

"And if Miss Mortimer does not care for such a match now?" Jeremy asked.

The lady's father waved his hand in a dismissive gesture. "Oh, she wants it. I think she likes you better than she did your brother Charles. She and her mother both like the idea of moving in the best circles."

"And I suppose *you* like the idea well enough too."

"Yes. I admit it. I do." Mortimer seemed now to become more affable. "So—you can see it would be in all our interests if you two were to come to an understanding."

"I cannot like the crassness of this discussion," Jeremy said.

A flush of anger suffused the older man's face. "You, my lord, cannot afford such refined sensibilities," he sneered.

"You're probably right." Jeremy tried not to allow his despair and disgust to show in his expression or tone, but inwardly he faced the bleak truth. He could walk away from Kenrick—the Hall, the estate, and all the other properties and concerns—not to mention the people dependent on the earldom. He had already proved, in the New World, he could make it on his own. And, in truth, what difference would it make? If he were to give in to this bully's demands, would the results not be the same as if he *had* walked away? Somehow Kenrick pride would not allow him to surrender helplessly—not now. Not ever. He might still lose, but—by God!—he would not allow himself to be manipulated like a puppet. He still had time. There was still a chance to save Kenrick.

Mortimer must have sensed some of this inner turmoil. "Well, you think on it some, my lord. I am sure you will come to the right decision. Meanwhile, I grant you my permission to pay court to my daughter."

The knight's smile was a cold, mechanical grimace.

CHAPTER 6

Kate knew that, in an owner's absence, it often fell to the house-keeper to show visitors around a grand house. Nevertheless, she wondered briefly at this task she had been given. First of all, the owner was in no way absent. And, secondly, the parts of the house that could be shown were no longer so very grand.

"His lordship has closed off much of the house," she explained apologetically.

"Never mind. We shall see what we may," the younger woman said airily.

They had already seen the entranceway with its elegantly carved staircase winding upward, the stairwell towering fully three stories. She showed them the library, still well-stocked with books. Kate knew it to be a varied collection—everything from ancient classics to Shakespeare and contemporary novels such as Miss Austen's works—along with collections of poetry, sermons, and treatises on modern farming and animal husbandry.

"This room has a lived-in look about it," Miss Mortimer commented.

Thinking the young woman sounded slightly disapproving, Kate said, "I believe it is his lordship's favorite."

"He is a reader, then?" Miss Mortimer asked as she idly ran a hand over the spines of several volumes, but taking no note of the titles.

"I—uh—suppose so," Kate said. She knew he often read late into the night.

She had first discovered this habit of her employer on her second night in the Hall. It had been nearly midnight; unable to sleep, she thought a book would help by either making her sleepy or at least providing a diversion. She threw on her rather nondescript robe and her bedroom slippers. Her hair hung loose in two long braids. Grabbing a candle in a holder and lighting it, she had been surprised on stepping into the hallway of the family area of the house that the footman charged with extinguishing lights at night had failed to do so, for light shone under the library door.

She discovered why as she stepped into the library. Lord Kenrick was ensconced in a comfortable leather chair, reading. On a table at his elbow a gaslight shone brightly; a half-empty glass of dark amber liquid sat near the lamp. She uttered a small gasp of surprise on seeing him. He looked up and started to rise on seeing her.

"No, please, do not get up," she said, pleased, nevertheless, that with this man simple courtesies were extended to servants as well as elegant ladies. "I—I did not think to find anyone here so late. I thought to find a book—I shall leave you in peace."

He sank back down. "No. No. By all means—" He gestured to the laden shelves. "I'm afraid the books are not well organized. What might you be interested in? Aunt Elinor has some novels over there by the window."

"But I thought she—"

"She has a friend who reads to her. I do sometimes as well."

"Oh. A novel would defeat my purpose," she said with a laugh. "I'd be awake all night to find out what happens next. I thought maybe some poetry—"

"To the left of the fireplace."

They were both silent as she surveyed the shelves he indicated. She felt his eyes on her as she did so and was acutely aware of the impropriety of her being here with him at this hour, dressed as she was. Strangely enough, she did not feel uncomfortable, though.

She took two books from the shelves.

"Ah, you found something."

"Blake and Wordsworth. Both favorites of mine."

He raised his eyebrows. "Really? I should not think there are many housekeepers whose tastes run to those two poets."

"I suppose there is no accounting for taste," she said, but mentally kicked herself for stepping out of the conventional housekeeper mold.

"No, I don't suppose there is."

"Good night, my lord. And—thank you."

He had waved a hand as she made her escape.

Now she added to the Mortimer women, "You must know that I came here only a few days ago."

"Yes, I had heard that," Miss Mortimer said. "I also heard that he found you in London after rejecting local women for the post—older women, that is. You have a son, have you not?"

Kate did not like the other woman's tone, but she answered quietly. "I do."

Miss Mortimer raised one brow. "But . . . no husband?"

"My husband died at Toulouse," Kate said shortly.

"How sad," the older woman murmured with a glance at her daughter, whose brow was still raised in skepticism.

Kate changed the subject. "Much of the house is closed, as I told you, but I will show you the ballroom and the gallery, if you like."

As she opened the gold velvet drapes, she apologized for the chill air in the ballroom and said a silent *thank you* for its having been dusted and aired out the day before, though Holland covers still shrouded the furniture along the walls. Mirrors along one wall reflected light from French doors opposite, which led to a large balcony. Two elaborate chandeliers would provide ample lighting at night. A painted ceiling depicted classical scenes of pastoral happiness.

Miss Mortimer skipped to the center of the room and whirled herself in an elaborate spin. "Oh! This is marvelous!" she gushed. "We *must* have a ball here, Mama."

Her mother frowned slightly and chided, "Yes, dear. You might suggest as much to his lordship."

"Can you not just see this room full of distinguished guests—all waiting anxiously for an important announcement?" Miss Mortimer swished her skirt in another spin about the room.

"I believe the green and gold decor is original," Kate offered. "The room is patterned after the ballroom at the Palace of Versailles, though this one is square, whereas the one at Versailles is a long gallery."

Something in Kate's tone seemed to have arrested the other young woman's attention. "You've been to Versailles?"

Kate could have kicked herself, but she answered honestly. "Yes. With my husband. During a temporary peace, which, unfortunately, did not last long."

"Oh." Miss Mortimer gestured dismissively. "I do not keep up with politics. I am perfectly content to leave that subject to the gentlemen."

Who usually make a royal mess of things, Kate thought, but she bit her tongue against saying this aloud.

In the gallery, Miss Mortimer had much to say of the costumes of the women in the portraits. She seemed quite knowledgeable about styles and fabrics. She showed little interest in the people in the portraits, which for Kate was just as well, since the housekeeper had not yet been given a thorough tour of the gallery herself. Then they came to a huge canvas depicting the late earl, his second wife, and his five children.

Kate looked closely at the young men in the picture. It had been made when the current earl was a very young adolescent, but already he had shown the high cheekbones and fine physique that would characterize the grown man. His older brothers, on the other hand, seven and nine years older than he, had—even then, in their twenties—shown signs of dissipation. She studied closely the two younger children in the portrait, a little girl about five, and a little boy of perhaps eight years. This child was of special interest to Kate, for he had grown up to become Lieutenant Robert Chilton, a particular friend to Arthur and to her. She smiled at seeing the man's friendly grin on the face of a child Ned's age.

"Hmm. I must say, Lord Kenrick—the current one, I mean—does not resemble his eldest brother," Miss Mortimer commented. "Which is probably a blessing," she added with a giggle.

Kate did not respond, but showed the ladies to another section of the house. She opened the drapes in the music room and in another, smaller, drawing room, which was sparsely furnished.

"This room will be perfect for entertaining lady friends," Miss Mortimer said.

"Charlotte!" her mother admonished.

Kate pretended not to notice the older woman's speaking look at her daughter.

Miss Mortimer laughed. "Never mind, Mama. We both know I am not one to count my chickens before they are hatched." She laughed again—triumphantly, it seemed. "And I believe mine are being hatched even as we speak."

Again, Kate politely ignored the exchange between mother and daughter, but she could not ignore her own inward reaction. Miss Mortimer's crassness and her possessive attitude were grating, but as Lord Kenrick's housekeeper, Kate could evince little interest in her employer's personal life.

They continued the tour with the housekeeper dutifully showing such of the guest rooms as were presentable. Chambers occupied by Lady Elinor and Lord Kenrick were, of course, out of bounds, but the adjoining chambers of the master suite—those of the long absent countess—were not.

"A charming suite," Miss Mortimer pronounced them, "though, please, not lavender and purple." She put a finger to her cheek. "Hmm. Bright yellow, perhaps. I am one of those rare women who can wear yellows."

Kate was fast developing a disgust of the other woman's seeing everything in terms of herself. But the behavior of a guest was none of the housekeeper's business, now, was it?

Finally, Miss Mortimer asked, "Have we seen it all, then? That is, all that is showable now?"

"All but the nursery," Kate said. "That section of the house is the domain of Lady Cassandra, who is cared for there."

"Oh, but we *must* see that too," Miss Mortimer insisted.

"If you insist . . ." Kate was reluctant to thrust strangers upon the child.

"But of course. We could not possibly visit Kenrick Hall without paying our respects to dear Crannie," Miss Mortimer gushed. "She was once *my* nurse, you know and lately Mama's companion. She is like a member of our family. It was I who recommended her to his lordship."

In the nursery's main room, she gushed even more. She made a point of greeting Nurse Cranstan effusively and Kate noted that the nurse basked in such attention.

"How *are* you, really, Crannie? I would not have you unhappy."

"I am quite well, miss. I do what I can. I must say, though, I haven't such fertile ground here as I once had." This was said with a coy tone and a sidelong glance at the child whose quiet play had been interrupted.

Miss Mortimer sympathized. "One can only expect so much. I am sure you do your best, but blood *will* tell, will it not?"

Cranstan nodded vigorously. "Ah, yes." She lowered her voice to a conspiratorial tone. "And when it is mongrel blood, it fairly shouts." She seemed unduly pleased with her little play on words.

Miss Mortimer smiled her appreciation of the simple joke and patted Nurse Cranstan's shoulder. "Well, you just do what you can, dear Crannie. You will be amply rewarded for your efforts."

"Thank you, miss."

Miss Mortimer then turned her attention directly to the child. "And how are you, Lady Cassandra? Have you been learning your letters and numbers?"

The child nodded solemnly and Nurse Cranstan barked, "Answer the lady properly."

"Yes, ma'am."

It was not clear to Kate whether the little girl responded to Miss Mortimer or to Nurse Cranstan.

Miss Mortimer spied the golden-haired doll on a chair and picked it up. "What a beautiful doll. You must love this toy very much."

Lady Cassandra looked as though she wanted to please, but did not know which woman to please at the moment. Kate caught her gaze and gave her an encouraging smile, which the little girl returned fleetingly.

"Where did you get such a lovely doll?" Miss Mortimer went on in the same false, condescending manner many adults used with children.

"My papa . . ." the child said softly.

"Your papa gave you this? How very nice." Then she added, sotto voce to the adults, "Not exactly a match, would you say?" She fingered the blond tresses of the doll.

The little girl gazed from one woman to another in some bewilderment. Kate wanted pick her up and hug her and tell her everything was all right. Already Nurse Cranstan put a hand on her charge's shoulder to direct her back to her play.

Miss Mortimer absently put the doll on a nearby table and said, "I believe we have seen everything now. You may escort us back to the drawing room, Mrs. . . . . Arthur, was it?"

"Yes, miss."

Kate happily took her leave of the Mortimer ladies at the drawing room door. However, she was deeply disturbed—not only by the young woman's proprietary attitude toward the Hall, but, more profoundly, by what she had observed in the nursery. Cranstan's attitude toward young Lady Cassandra angered Kate. And her anger quickly shifted to the child's father.

Why on earth would a loving, caring parent entrust his child to a woman who felt as Cranstan obviously did? Or was he loving and caring? She had seen him only twice in the company of his daughter. They had walked through the kitchen on Kate's and Ned's first morning at the Hall. Father and daughter had both breakfasted already and were on their way to the stables. Ned had been sitting at a side table in the kitchen, finishing his own breakfast.

The two children were introduced and eyed each other warily—embarrassed as children are wont to be with adults hovering about.

A short while later, from a window in the kitchen, Kate had seen the earl and his daughter ride out, he on a fine-looking gray and she on a chestnut pony. He had seemed loving enough then. The next day he had brought her to the kitchen in the afternoon to suggest that the two children might enjoy playing in the garden—there was a maze there and the earl had asked a young footman to keep an eye out for them—and lead them out of the maze, if need be. He explained that this was Nurse Cranstan's half day off.

Later, Kate had asked Ned how the playtime had gone. He shrugged and said it was all right, he supposed. And had he enjoyed getting to know Lady Cassandra? Kate pursued.

"She's all right—for a girl," Ned said.

"Oh, high praise, indeed," Kate teased, ruffling her son's hair.

Kate thought her employer's child was mostly quite lonely. But despite Kate's deliberately discouraging servant's gossip, she knew that the earl made a ritual of spending time with his daughter every evening.

She shook her head. This business with Cranstan just did not make sense. And was he seriously considering Miss Mortimer as a possible stepmother? "Blood will tell," indeed!

* * *

When the Mortimer women returned to the drawing room, both men rose and Sir Eldridge asked that his carriage be summoned. Jeremy managed—barely—to uphold his share of civilized conversation. He was grateful that it was of short duration.

"Oh, what a fine house you have, Lord Kenrick," the daughter said with bright enthusiasm.

"Very nice, indeed," the mother offered more calmly.

"Thank you, Miss Mortimer, Lady Mortimer." Jeremy gestured for them to be seated and, when all were sitting, added, "Unfortunately, some of the house has suffered neglect for quite a long while."

"But it could be put right in no time," Miss Mortimer said. "Isn't that right, Papa?"

Her father nodded. "As you say, my pet."

"The ballroom is magnificent," Charlotte Mortimer went on. "Oh, my lord, you really must give a ball! Mama and I would be very pleased to help you do so—send invitations and plan decorations. Wouldn't we, Mama?"

"Of course, dear."

Jeremy thought the knight's wife looked slightly embarrassed, though she maintained a placid expression.

"I fear a ball must wait on other matters," Jeremy said. "Perhaps in late autumn, or next spring. . . ."

He was deliberately vague, but Miss Mortimer clapped her hands together and said, "Autumn would be perfect. A harvest ball! Absolutely perfect!"

Jeremy put up a hand in the universal *halt* sign. "Please. I said *perhaps*. Much could happen between now and then."

Miss Mortimer affected a pretty little pout for a moment. Then her voice and manner became distinctly coy as she held Jeremy's gaze. "Yes, it could, could it not?"

Her father interjected at this point by clearing his throat. "Hold on, daughter. Don't rush your fences. Patience, my dear. Patience."

The pout returned. "But, Papa, I've not been to a real ball in such a long time . . ." Her voice trailed and Jeremy thought perhaps a subtle sign from her father had warned her off.

"We missed the London season this year because of her grandfather's passing." Lady Mortimer's quiet explanation filled an awkward gap.

"I'm sorry," Jeremy murmured.

"It was months ago," Sir Eldrige said, "but it would not have looked good for us to be frolicking about in society then."

Jeremy had no reply for this conversational gambit other than a nod. Wilkins announced the carriage to be ready and Jeremy saw his not-quite-welcome guests to the door. He then returned to his desk and sat in growing darkness, for outside the windows a storm threatened. Good! He hoped the Mortimers were thoroughly drenched. He shook his head at the pettiness of this thought. Again, he went over that bizarre conversation with his chief—his only—creditor. He wondered just how much of the scheme the daughter was party to. Clearly, she was aware of much of it.

Trying to view the matter in a cool, detached way, he thought Miss Mortimer pretty enough. Such arrangements as the knight suggested were not uncommon among the ton, especially between financially strapped peers and the so-called "made men" of the merchant class. Some men would leap at the father's proposition. All that money and a handsome woman on one's arm to boot. Enticing offer, that.

Enticing—*if* one were primarily interested in appearances; the appearance of wealth and independence, the appearance of an enviable marriage. His father had opted for that—twice. Both his father's marriages had been contracted with pretty girls who came to the title of countess well dowered. Jeremy had not known his mother well; she had died when he was four. He remembered laughing blue eyes and an exotic scent. Cassie had those eyes.

For some years, there had been no strong female presence at Kenrick Hall, though his grandmother had wielded a wicked tongue on occasion. Then his father had brought home a new bride, the laughing, bubbly Amelia, scarcely ten years older than her youngest stepson. The boy Jeremy had immediately developed a hopeless infatuation for this splendid creature. She seemed the epitome of his adolescent view of ideal womanhood—beautiful and pure. His love for the younger sister and brother she later provided had, at first, been an extension of his naive adoration of the charming Amelia. In time, though, he learned to love Margaret and Robert for themselves alone.

The death of his obsession with Amelia had long been a painful memory. During his last year at Oxford, Jeremy had been sent down for some minor infraction. Bored and restless, he had gone to the music room one day to work off some of his ennui at the pianoforte—only to discover his beautiful stepmother there locked into something more than a mere embrace with a man definitely *not* Jeremy's father.

Jeremy's surprised gasp had wrenched their attention away from what they were doing. The man, one of his father's younger friends, seemed only slightly embarrassed as he nonchalantly straightened his clothing.

Amelia had rolled her eyes and said in a bored tone, "Oh, dear, Reginald, I do believe we have shocked the poor boy."

Wanting to cling to his view of Amelia—that boyish dream of female perfection—Jeremy had turned his fury on the man. "You, sir, are a—a—scoundrel!"

"Yes, I probably am," the man agreed calmly. "But there's no need to make a Cheltenham tragedy of this."

"Indeed not," Amelia chimed in, hooking her arm gaily into her lover's. "You *must* know by now that such is the way of society."

Her tone made Jeremy feel like the greenest of schoolboys. He even felt himself blushing!

She went on brightly, "We shall keep this our little secret, shall we?"

Jeremy had mumbled incoherently and fled the scene, Amelia's laughter echoing behind him.

He had told no one of what he had seen. He had considered telling his father, but this would hardly have been an ordinary father-son conversation, even if he and his father were given to such—which they were not. One could not stroll up to one's father and casually offer, "Oh, I say Father, are you aware that your wife is cuckolding you?"

And, to be honest, was her behavior so very different from her husband's? After all, his father kept a mistress in one of the lesser sections of London.

Nevertheless, the secret had gnawed at him—and it had certainly altered his view of half the human race. Now, he thought with disgust, he had learned nothing—nothing—from that experience. He had been as wrong about his wife's character as he had been about Amelia's. These two events had undermined his confidence in his judgment regarding women.

Was he now to walk blindly into another such misconception? Not bloody likely! "Twice burned, forever cautious," he told himself, not at all sure he quoted the adage correctly.

On the other hand, he remembered his comment to Miss Mortimer's father. It was true that he hardly knew her. He should at least be fair to *her*. After all, she should not be held accountable for her father's boorishness.

No. It went beyond mere boorishness. The man had an agenda, and he did not care how he achieved it. Jeremy could not shake the deep, offended anger that he felt at Mortimer's outrageous plan. The man had bought himself a knighthood. Was that not enough?

Jeremy answered his own question: No, it was not enough. Not for a man like Mortimer. His knighthood was valid only in the knight's lifetime. Mortimer's plans were more far-reaching. That business with the name change proved that much. Sir Eldridge Mortimer not only intended to appropriate the earldom, he would steal the earl's very identity.

"Think again, sir!" Jeremy vowed silently. "I still have several months."

His mind drifted to a far more pleasant subject: Cassie. It occurred to him that now that the weather was generally nicer—this threatening storm notwithstanding—his daughter needed to get out more. Being cooped up all winter had been an alien way of life for his little Indian maiden.

With this, another thought occurred to him. He rose and reached for the bellpull. When Wilkins responded, he again sent for the housekeeper and stood staring out the window as he waited for her.

She arrived momentarily. How was it that this woman's very presence had a calming, comforting effect on him?

"Ah, Mrs. Arthur. I apologize if I have interrupted an important task."

She smiled. "No, my lord. An onerous one, but necessary." He raised a brow. "The chambermaids were helping me inventory linens."

He nodded absently. "I wanted particularly to thank you for the improvements I have noted—and for your showing the Mortimer ladies around."

"It was merely my duty."

"Even so, I am grateful. But that is not the only reason I sent for you."

"My lord?"

"Would you object to your son's taking riding lessons?"

"My lord?" Surprise in her voice told him he had caught her off guard.

He explained. "My daughter is being introduced to English riding, and it occurred to me that she would find the lessons more enjoyable if she shared them with another child."

"Oh, I . . . see." She spoke rather slowly, almost as though she were weighing her words carefully.

"It will not be dangerous, you know," he assured her. "Has he ever ridden before?"

"Yes, though not lately."

"Well, it would not take him long to regain his skill."

"No, I don't suppose it would."

Again, he detected some reluctance in her tone and he wondered at it. "Being able to ride might be advantageous to him one day—should he want to be a stable hand or a coachman. Most boys like the idea of learning to handle horses," he said persuasively.

"Oh, I know Ned would enjoy any time spent around the stables."

"Then it is settled," he said firmly. "Tomorrow morning—unless this storm is still upon us—he shall join Cassie for her lesson."

"Yes, my lord. And—thank you. Ned will love the idea."

Yes indeed, he would, a troubled Kate thought, as she returned to the servants' area of the house. This was a problem she had not foreseen—and she should have done so!

An ordinary housekeeper's son would probably not be conversant with fine riding cattle. Ned, however, had been riding ever since he could sit on a horse. As an army officer, Arthur had been a capable rider and had loved seeing his young son master each new technique. She recalled with a twinge of nostalgia Arthur's proudly showing off the little boy's skill.

Kate had deliberately not explained to her son anything more than he absolutely needed to know about their current living situation. He knew, for instance—and was glad—that his mother was keeping him away from the grandfather whom Ned disliked and feared. She did not think he understood their decline in status, though. For him, this was another wonderful adventure—his whole life had so far been mostly about change.

Would he now inadvertently reveal his mother and himself as impostors?

CHAPTER 7

When the next day dawned dry and sunny, Kate found herself of two minds about it. On the one hand, she and a gardener could begin to take hold of the kitchen herb garden, and on the other, Ned would join Lady Cassandra's riding lesson. Unfortunately, Ned's mother would find it hard to be in two places at once.

His eyes glowing with excitement, Ned eagerly welcomed the prospect of being on a horse again. He chattered happily through his breakfast. Lord Kenrick and his daughter met the housekeeper and her son in the kitchen.

"Ah, I see young Ned has proper attire for this outing," Lord Kenrick observed. Kate suspected that surprised him.

"Yes," she said. "His father wanted him to have correct riding clothing." She did not add that Ned had long since outgrown the clothing Captain Lord Arthur Gardiner had provided.

She noted that Lady Cassandra seemed a bit fidgety in a child's riding outfit of a short skirt over matching pantaloons. The outfit was blue, bringing out the color of the child's eyes.

"You look very pretty, my lady," Kate said as she held out a small basket of apples from the cellar. "Here is a treat for your equine friends."

"*Ek-ine*?" The little girl wrinkled her brow.

"Horses!" Ned said with true male superiority.

"Come along," Lord Kenrick said, taking the proffered basket. He looked at Kate. "It will go fine. I promise. If you can get away, you are welcome to come down to the stables to observe."

"A little later, perhaps," she replied and bit her lip nervously as she watched Ned leave with the other two. Not since their arrival had Ned been truly out from under his mother's watchful eye. As the trio made their way to the stables, she noted that Lord Kenrick had a hand on Ned's shoulder while he and his daughter gripped the handle of the basket of apples on his other side. Both children chattered happily and both kept looking up at the big man between them. It crossed Kate's mind that Ned was starved for male attention. Now, what in the world was she to do about *that* problem?

She busied herself for the next half hour in the herb garden. Then she tossed down her trowel and removed her gardening gloves. She instructed the gardener on finishing the task and strolled toward the stables, trying to look unconcerned as she did so. Nearing the stables, she could hear adult cries of encouragement and childish squeals of delight.

She observed Lord Kenrick leaning casually against the arena fence along with two stable hands. As she approached, one of the other men spied her and moved aside to make room for her next to Lord Kenrick. Their arms not quite touching, she could nevertheless feel the warmth of his body. He gave her a rueful smile, his eyes crinkling at the corners.

"You gammoned me, Mrs. Arthur," he said.

"I beg your pardon?"

"You said young Ned hadn't much experience. Look at him! Perfect form."

Ned sat erect in the saddle as an older man put the horse through its paces.

"Let him go! Please," Ned begged. "Faster!"

The man in the arena looked to Lord Kenrick, who looked questioningly at Kate. She nodded slowly. There were three training jumps set up in the arena and Ned, freed from the restraining hand of the groom, urged his mount to take the jumps. Kate heard Lord Kenrick suck in his breath. She ignored his glance at her. She tried to seem oblivious to any sense of danger. He returned his gaze to the boy and watched with apparent astonishment as the child assumed the position of a champion rider and took each of the jumps smoothly. His lordship let out the breath he had been holding.

"Yes, indeed, Mrs. Arthur, you gammoned me."

"I did not intend such, my lord," she said quietly.

Ned rode his mount close to the fence where Kate and Lord Kenrick stood.

"Did you see me, Mama?" he asked excitedly. "Wouldn't the duke's grooms be proud of me?"

Kenrick looked at Kate. " 'Duke's grooms'?"

"I—uh—we were in a duke's household for a while."

"You worked for a duke?" he asked. "Phillips omitted that bit of information in your references."

"It—it did not work out—with Ned—you see."

Kenrick gave her an oblique look. Then he shrugged. "The duke's loss is my gain, it seems."

She glanced away, then returned her gaze to his and smiled. "You might say that."

She thought he would have responded, perhaps to press her for more information, but just then Lady Cassandra called to him.

"Papa! You promised . . ."

"All right, Poppet. Yes, I know." He motioned to the man in the ring. "Do as she wants."

To Kate's surprise, the man lifted the little girl from the child-sized sidesaddle. Lady Cassandra stood impatiently as the groom removed the saddle and handed it to a young man along the fence. Some sort of silent communication must have gone through the stable, for suddenly there were two more stable hands and other outdoor workers hanging over the fence around the arena. The man in the center lifted the child onto the horse's bare back and gave her the reins.

Kate was astonished as Lady Cassandra gave a loud whoop and began to race her horse around the arena, kicking her heels into the horse's side. Kate noted with no small degree of pride that Ned easily controlled his startled mount near the fence.

"Good heavens!" Kate exclaimed softly.

The child had magically leapt to a standing position on the back of the galloping horse.

"See, Papa?" she called to her father, who seemed totally unconcerned for her safety.

"I see," he called back. "Now, do stop showing off, Cassie."

Kate became aware of another presence. Nurse Cranstan stood on the other side of Lord Kenrick.

"Really, my lord!" the nurse admonished. "Such behavior is most unseemly, most unladylike. How *will* she learn to ride as ladies do if you encourage these Indian ways?"

Lord Kenrick looked chagrined. "You're right, of course. But Cassie needs to be free—just free—at times."

"You hired me to teach her ladylike behavior and I do my best," the woman complained. "This—" She gestured to the child still in the arena. "This surely undermines much of my work."

"It's all right, Miss Cranstan," Lord Kenrick said firmly. "My daughter will certainly learn the lessons needed by a proper young Englishwoman. But she needs freedom to be herself too."

The nurse said nothing in response, though she seemed to give a small sniff of disapproval. Kate was mildly surprised at the depth of understanding shown by the father. Well. Perhaps he understood more than Kate had thought he did.

"Lady Cassandra is already quite a skilled horsewoman," Kate observed quietly.

"Arapaho children learn to ride almost before they walk," Lord Kenrick said. "But Miss Cranstan is right—my daughter needs to learn to ride as an English lady. That is, of course, what we are about with these lessons."

"Of course," Kate murmured.

"I hope you are reassured about allowing young Ned to join the lessons." He waved toward the groom still in the arena. "Jack here is an excellent rider and teacher. He will oversee the children at all times."

Kate agreed to continuing the lessons, in part because she had seen the sparkle return to Ned's eyes as he rode. He'd not been so carefree and happy in months! His mentioning "the duke's grooms" alarmed her, though. What else might he let slip? She did not want to quash his joy or frighten him, but she had to make him aware of the need for secrecy.

He was excited and bubbly that evening over his supper. Full of details about the ride and the horses, he even accorded Lady Cassandra a measure of admiration. "She's just a girl, o'course, but she knows lots of tricks."

"Is that so?" Kate sat down in the chair next to him.

"Oh, yes," said, very serious. "She's going to show me some."

"Well, you be careful, Ned. You must mind what Jack or his lordship tells you."

"Yes, Mama." He concentrated on his plate for a moment, then asked in a wistful tone, "Mama, do you think I'll ever have a horse of my very own?"

"Of course, my dear. When you grow up, you'll have a whole stable of horses!"

"When I'm a duke, you mean?"

Instinctively, Kate glanced at the door to be sure it was closed. It was. She spoke quietly, "Yes, some day. But you must remember not to talk about that to anyone. Not to anyone."

He nodded. "It's a secret, huh?"

"Yes. A very, very important secret. We don't want to go back to Wynstan, do we?"

"No!"

"So you must be careful and not mention your grandfather, or the castle, or the stables. Can you do that?"

He turned a searching gaze on her. "Is it all right to talk about Papa?"

"Yes, love." She quelled threatening tears and hugged him hard.

Just when he thought life could not be more hectic, Jeremy found himself busier than ever. Several herds of sheep, augmented since the new lord's return with prize rams and ewes, roamed Kenrick fields. Tenant farmers and shepherds and their dogs watched over the flocks closely. As he rode from farm to farm, field to field, Jeremy's heart swelled with pride and humility. Large sections of green separated by stone fences gave witness to organization on Kenrick lands. Some fields had sheep grazing; some showed new growth of hay that would be harvested later; others were fallow—given over to a profusion of yellow, white, and purple—wild crocus in bloom. The landscape was dotted with stone barns here and there for storing hay and sheltering animals from the extremes of Yorkshire winters.

The farmers and herdsmen themselves, along with other workers, lived in two small villages, Upper Kendale and Lower Kendale, as well as the larger town of Kenrick. This was Kenrick land. These were Kenrick people. And he was *damned* if he would turn them over to the likes of one Eldridge Mortimer without a fight.

It was only mid-afternoon, but Jeremy and Thomas Porter, who managed the home farm, had already put in several tiring hours, struggling with a ewe attempting to birth twin lambs the wrong way. As sometimes happened, the new mother simply rejected one of her offspring.

"I'll take 'im in, my lord," Porter said. "Me wife and daughter are already hand-feeding one from last week. Another'n won't make much difference."

"Thank you, Porter. These two little fellows are important to improving our flocks. Though why they all have to arrive at the same time is beyond me!"

Porter chuckled. "That's sheep tendin' fer ye. First the lambin' and then the shearin' makes springtime real busy. Hard work, it is."

"That's next, isn't it—shearing," Jeremy said. "Looks like we'll have a good return, though, on the animals we added last year."

"Aye, my lord."

Jeremy enjoyed working with men like Porter. They were honest, hardworking, and proud. But, not unlike men he had known on the American frontier, one had to earn their respect. The new earl was not at all sure he had achieved that goal yet. However, he knew Porter and others appreciated his asking—and often taking—their advice on matters.

As he rode home, his mind drifted again to that silent vow to thwart the plans of his chief creditor. Now that Kenrick was his, he wanted to keep it. For himself, yes, but also for Porter and others like him. And for Cassie. A legacy for Cassie.

Cassie. Had he made a serious mistake in uprooting her from America? He had anticipated a period of adjustment. That was to be expected. He had tried to ease her transition by hiring an English-woman to school her in the ways of her new life. But now, a year later, she was still too quiet, too withdrawn. The other day in the arena, he'd seen a spark of the old Cassie—of his Little Willow. Maybe she was coming around. . . .

Coming in from the stables, he entered the main house through an outer room that had two doors, one leading to the kitchen, the other to a hallway that allowed access to living quarters of upper servants: the cook, the butler, and the housekeeper. Beyond those rooms the hall led to a stairway, giving servants access to chambers for the family and, above those, the attic rooms for maids and footmen. Beyond the stairway was a wider door, padded against noise, leading to the family living areas.

Hearing laughter and childish giggles coming from the kitchen, he opened that door and beheld his daughter kneeling on a stool at one of the worktables. She and Ned were cutting out figures from rolled dough. Both children wore outsized aprons and judging by the amount of flour on their hands and faces and on the floor, they had been at this task for some time. The kitchen staff were enjoying the show even as they tended their own chores. Jeremy paused, feeling like an intruder as he watched and listened.

"See?" Ned was saying. "My man is a soldier. I'm putting a sword in his hand."

"He's a fine soldier," Mrs. Arthur said. "What are those raisins on his chest?"

"Mama! Those are medals."

"Oh. How many medals did Ned give his soldier, Lady Cassandra?" the housekeeper asked.

The child counted slowly, pointing to each one, then said tentatively, "Five?"

"Yes. Five. A brave soldier, indeed."

"I want to make a gingerbread lady." Cassie looked at the housekeeper with an expression that was at once imploring and adoring. "Can I make a lady?"

"Of course you may," Mrs. Arthur said. "See? We'll just cut her a skirt—like this—then you can decorate it."

One of the kitchen maids glanced up and saw Jeremy. "Oh, my lord." Everyone paused as in a tableau.

Then Cassie called, "Papa!" She scrambled down from her stool and flung her flour-dusted arms around his legs. "We're making gingerbread!"

He laughed. "I see that. Looks like you are wearing half your flour."

"Oh, dear. I fear you are now wearing some of it too, my lord," Mrs. Arthur said with a smile. "Rosie, do hand his lordship a towel to brush that off."

" 'Tis nothing." He set his daughter back on her stool, then dutifully brushed the flour off his breeches. He murmured admiring words over the efforts of both children and was about to leave when Nurse Cranstan burst into the kitchen.

"Ah, *there* you are, Lady Cassandra. I've been looking all over for you!" Her voice was stern and accusing, and had an immediate effect on her charge, who went very still and seemed to shrink within herself. Then Miss Cranstan noticed her employer and modified her tone. "My lord."

"I'm sorry," Mrs. Arthur said. "I sent Nell to tell you that her ladyship was being looked after. Did she not tell you?"

"She told me. But that was over an hour ago. You are disrupting the child's schedule."

"I apologize," the housekeeper said. "The children were having such fun—"

The nurse wore the same forbidding expression she'd had the other day at the arena. "Yes. Well. I hardly think a female of Lady Cassandra's station needs to concern herself with cookery." She glanced at Kenrick, apparently seeking his confirmation.

"No harm was done," he said. "Sometimes flexibility is a welcome thing in a schedule. Let her finish here and she will rejoin you in—say—an hour?" He looked at the housekeeper, who nodded.

"Children need the discipline of a firm schedule," the nurse declared even as Jeremy held the door for her, then followed her out with a parting word of, "Carry on, then." He smiled and winked at Cassie and saw some of her sparkle return.

"A word, Miss Cranstan," Jeremy said as the kitchen door closed behind them.

"Yes, my lord?"

"Perhaps you should relax your schedule somewhat."

"As you wish, my lord. But, frankly, I believe that would be a mistake. As I said, children need discipline. Lady Cassandra scarcely knows her letters and numbers. Her needlework is a disgrace."

"In my view, children also need to feel carefree and happy— which my daughter is at the moment. Having a playmate has been good for her."

"If I may say so, my lord, this association with the lower orders is not quite the thing for the child of a peer."

"Nevertheless, you will build some flexibility into your schedule to allow her more time with her new friend."

"Yes, my lord." Her disapproval plain, she nodded curtly. "Will that be all, my lord?"

"For now."

He watched her stride down the hall, her posture stiff. He sighed. That had not gone well. Thinking to get some paperwork done before supper, he went to the library. Among the items of mail on his desk were two missives of special interest.

He eyed ruefully an invitation from the Mortimers to a dinner party next week. He wondered if there were any excuse short of an attack of the plague that he could offer as a polite refusal.

A letter from his younger brother brought forth a far more joyous response. Robert would arrive in June for a prolonged visit!

CHAPTER 8

Lambing season was scarcely over when Jeremy found himself thrust into the organized chaos of shearing adult sheep. Clipping the fleece from a squirming, bleating full-grown animal was no easy task. After trying it himself, he readily left that job to men who knew what they were doing. He marveled at the friendly competition among those shearing: who could shear an animal fastest; who produced the most complete fleeces in one piece.

"That's some mighty fine wool we be gettin'," the farmer Porter commented.

"Yep. It's real fine all right," one of the shearers said, "but the market ain't so good right now."

"Maybe wait a month or two to sell it," Porter suggested.

"Good idea," Jeremy said. "We have storage available—at least until the haying season is upon us. We'll put the bulk of our wool in the north barn on the home farm."

"Be easier to ship from there," Porter agreed. "An' who knows? Might get a better price later on."

"I hope so," Jeremy said. "I do hope so." What he did not say was that the future of the entire earldom might well depend on the sale of a barn full of stored wool.

This grim thought stayed with him as he rode home and then dressed for the Mortimers' dinner party. He tied and retied his cravat for the formal evening attire, annoyed that he had not come up with a viable excuse for avoiding this engagement. But he was sure *any* refusal would be taken as an affront, and he saw no reason to deliberately antagonize a neighbor. Or a creditor.

Arriving at the Mortimer estate, Jeremy was glad to see that a number of guests had been invited. At least tonight there should be no repeat of that uncomfortable conversation in his own drawing room. A very correct butler announced his entrance.

"Ah, Kenrick. So glad you could make it," Sir Eldridge said.

Jeremy bowed politely to the knight and his wife. "Thank you for inviting me."

"Well, we could hardly exclude our highest ranking neighbor, now could we?"

Glancing around the room, Jeremy noted a number of very eligible young men in the group, as well as young women arrayed in colorful gowns. Of these, Charlotte Mortimer stood out in a red silk gown embroidered with silver roses. Her dark hair was swept up and pinned with silver clips. She was, he silently conceded, a very good-looking woman. His gaze moved on until he spotted the Dennisons talking with the vicar and his wife, but before he could move in that direction, Mortimer grabbed his elbow and steered him to the group that included Miss Mortimer.

"My daughter has looked forward all day to your arrival," Mortimer said.

"Really, Papa!" she protested with a laugh. "You must know that we women like to keep men guessing."

"Been a long time since I did any courting," Mortimer replied.

Jeremy saw raised eyebrows and speculative looks directed his way at this comment.

"Courting? Who's courting?" old Mrs. Spencer, one of the neighborhood's few octogenarians, called from a nearby chair where she was holding court.

"Never mind, Mama." Her middle-aged son patted her shoulder.

"Young people get so much freedom these days," Mrs. Spencer went on in the high-pitched voice of the hard-of-hearing. "In my day, a girl had a chaperone at all times."

"Ah, but my grandmother told me how you and she used to outwit them," a woman bystander said.

"That we did!" The old woman giggled like a schoolgirl. "Why, I remember one time—"

Charlotte had moved to stand near Jeremy. She spoke in a low voice so he was forced to bend close to hear her. She wore a heavy, musky perfume. "I am glad you could come, my lord. When Mama and I planned this little soiree, it never occurred to us that the whole of Yorkshire would be preoccupied with shearing sheep!"

"I know only of my part of 'the whole of Yorkshire,' Miss Mortimer, but it is true that at Kenrick we have had a few busy days."

She put a hand on his forearm and gave him an intimate smile. "Please, do call me *Charlotte*."

Aware that others watched them, though they could not hear, he glanced pointedly at her hand, then into her eyes in which he perceived a strange mixture of hope, triumph—and maybe—desire? "For the time being, I am more comfortable with *Miss Mortimer*," he said quietly.

Her expression tightened and she removed her hand. "As you wish, my lord."

Jeremy surmised that Miss Charlotte Mortimer was unaccustomed to having even the most trivial of her wishes thwarted.

Dinner was announced and, as the guest ranking highest in the neighborhood's social hierarchy, Jeremy was seated to the right of his hostess. He had not been at all surprised to find that his dinner partner, seated now on his right, was his hosts' daughter. Still determined to judge her on her own merits and not blame her for her father's heavy-handed behavior, he was nevertheless mildly surprised at the number of times her arm or hand "accidentally" encountered his own. He listened halfheartedly as she engaged him and the gentleman on her other side in what Jeremy thought of as typically vacuous dinner-table conversation. To entertain himself, he tried imagining the other guests at an Arapaho feast after a buffalo hunt. He grinned involuntarily at a vision of his host leading a dance around an open fire to reenact a kill.

"Do you find the behavior of the Princess of Wales amusing, my lord?" Miss Mortimer sounded mildly shocked.

Jeremy suddenly felt himself the focus of attention in their part of the table. "Well, I—"

Lady Mortimer sniffed. "Caroline of Brunswick shows little regard for English customs or, indeed, for her own position as our future queen."

"But really, Lady Mortimer, what can one expect? She *is* German, you know," said Mrs. Hartwick from farther down the table.

"The royal family have many strong German ties, do they not?" Jeremy asked. "The current king's father spoke English only with a marked accent."

"Oh, but our current royals have been polished by three generations of English influence," Mrs. Hartwick asserted.

"In any event," the young man on the other side of Miss Mortimer put in, "the princess's behavior is not so very different from that of her husband, now is it? Sauce for the goose is sauce for the gander."

This speaker was young Baron Whittley, who had only lately come into his father's title. Jeremy had noted earlier that the baron flirted outrageously with Miss Mortimer. Now he wondered cynically if Sir Eldridge would settle for a mere baron for his daughter.

Mrs. Hartwick, apparently feeling the conversation was entering improper territory, changed the subject to comment on the Chinese decor of the dining room. Jeremy went back to assigning Arapaho character and dress to other guests.

Dinner finished, Lady Mortimer led the ladies in returning to the drawing room. Servants efficiently cleared the table and the male diners settled into rounds of port, politics, and other subjects thought unsuitable for feminine ears. Jeremy had always thought this custom silly; several women of his acquaintance—including his Aunt Elinor and his American mother-in-law—were quite capable of contributing to any subject gentlemen might wish to discuss.

When the conversation turned to local matters, there was much grumbling about the price of wool.

"You'd think with Napoleon safely tucked away, the market on the continent would open up," Squire Dennison said.

"Put it in storage. Wait a while. That's what some are doing—eh, Kenrick?" Hartwick, one of the area's largest landowners, said.

"Ah, but how long can one store such a huge number of bales of wool?" Sir Eldridge named a figure that was uncannily accurate to the bales Jeremy had only this week stacked in a barn on the home farm.

Jeremy, who gave his host a hard look and thought the other man looked decidedly smug, merely shrugged. "A temporary measure."

"Well," Hartwick said, "you know what they say: 'Hope springs eternal.' I wish you well."

"Thank you," Jeremy said evenly, but he was profoundly irked that Mortimer kept such close watch on Kenrick affairs.

Finally, their host drained his glass and rose, saying, "Gentlemen, I'm sure some of you young bucks are anxious to rejoin the ladies— and I did have rather strict orders from my daughter not to dawdle over the port."

In the drawing room, they found the ladies idly listening to Miss Mortimer and two other young women around the pianoforte, singing country ballads as a fourth one played the instrument. When the gentlemen joined them, an older woman took over the playing for a round of dancing.

Seeing his offer as a social duty, Jeremy asked Miss Mortimer to dance. She eagerly accepted and rested her hand on his arm rather longer and more often than strictly necessary by the movements of the dance. Jeremy was again aware of raised eyebrows and curious glances cast their way. He later danced with two other ladies; then, feeling he had satisfied the social amenities, was on the verge of taking his leave when Sir Eldridge, his daughter on his arm, approached the group with whom Jeremy was talking. It included Squire Dennison and Baron Whittley, as well as the squire's wife and daughter— the latter a comely young woman with silvery blond hair and blue eyes.

"I say, Kenrick," Sir Eldridge said during a lull in the conversation, "I don't believe you've seen our orangery, have you?"

"No, I haven't," Jeremy replied. "I think you mentioned adding one some months ago."

"It's finished now and I doubt there's a finer one in all of Yorkshire," the knight said. "Charlotte, my dear, why don't you show his lordship the orangery? It is quite well lit. I had special lanterns installed."

"Oh, I'd love to," she said. "My lord?"

Heeding the warning bells clanging in his mind, Jeremy said, "Such a delight should be shared. Perhaps the others would care to join us?"

The squire and his wife demurred, saying they had already seen this new feature of the Mortimer estate. The other two young people, pleased to join the earl and Miss Mortimer, were unaware of a certain tightness about Sir Eldridge's expression or resignation in the set of Miss Mortimer's shoulders as she led them to the orangery. She pointed out not only exotic fruits being grown there, but also some nonnative flowers.

"I'm especially fond of the orchids," she said.

"So delicate. So beautiful," Baron Whittley murmured with a meaningful look at Miss Mortimer.

"Yes, aren't they?" she responded. "Do have a look at this one, Lord Kenrick. Father and I are very proud of this addition to our collection."

With this comment, she led him into a small alcove housing some tall pillars with plants spiraling up them. They effectively screened Jeremy and Miss Mortimer from Whittley and Miss Dennison. Miss Mortimer pointed to two large delicate purple-pink blossoms.

"These will be especially beautiful in a wedding bouquet," she murmured for his ears alone.

Embarrassed at both their seclusion and her intimate tone, he deliberately stepped aside. "Do have a look, Miss Dennison, Whittley."

They cast him curious glances, but dutifully examined the exotic blooms. Charlotte Mortimer compressed her lips in what might have passed for a smile.

"The plants themselves look rather sturdy," Miss Dennison said.

Jeremy voiced appropriate and general admiration of what was undoubtedly—as Sir Eldridge had said—the finest, most elaborate hothouse in the county.

They returned to the drawing room to find the party breaking up with carriages and cloaks already called for. Jeremy noticed a brief communication pass between Charlotte Mortimer and her father: The knight's inquiring glance at the young woman was answered with a slight shrug and grimace of defeat.

Jeremy rode home with a vague feeling of foreboding, no longer harboring any doubt as to Miss Mortimer's full compliance in her father's machinations.

Kate had kept busy the last several days. Along with her usual duties she and the staff prepared bedchambers for anticipated guests to the manor. Wilkins had informed her that Lord Kenrick expected at least one male guest, perhaps more. Kate wondered fleetingly who such guests might be, but quickly decided any friends of her employer could scarcely be of any significance to the housekeeper. After all, she had never been a part of that strata of society when she was young, and certainly not as a widow later.

They dusted, scrubbed, and aired three rooms, but no guests arrived. There had been a delay, Wilkins said. After a while, the process was repeated and curiosity rose among the staff, for, aside from a short visit from his sister, the earl had had no overnight guests since his arrival at Kenrick.

May gave way to June with days growing ever warmer. Lady Elinor began to spend an hour or two each afternoon in what the household referred to as the rose garden, but which actually sported a profusion of blooms at this time of the year.

"I dearly love the smell of the lilacs," Lady Elinor announced to Kate when the housekeeper approached the padded wicker couch on which the earl's aunt sat. "That's your scent, is it not, Mrs. Arthur?"

Kate had long since ceased being surprised at the partially blind Lady Elinor's uncanny ability to identify each and every person around her. "Yes, it is. Well, mostly lilac."

"Mm-hmm. There's a fresh, woodsy touch as well. Clara fancies lilac too, but I can always tell the two of you apart because she always smells of rosewater as well." Clara Packwood, the vicar's wife, was Lady Elinor's friend.

"Actually, I've come with a message from Mrs. Packwood," Kate said. "She sent round a note that she will not be able to visit today. Her daughter has gone into her confinement."

"Oh, how exciting! This is Clara's first grandchild. Still, I am disappointed to hear she's not coming. We were going to start this new book today. Selfish of me, isn't it?" The older woman touched a book within reach on the table nearby.

"No, not selfish at all." Kate knew how much Mrs. Packwood's twice-weekly visits meant to Lady Elinor. The two women shared a love of popular novels. Regularly, Mrs. Packwood read for a while, then the two women had tea or lemonade and speculated on where the story was going.

"Not selfish," Kate repeated. "Human, I'd say. However, I have some free time at the moment. My son is at the stable for Lady Cassandra's riding lesson and the staff are about their duties. I would be happy to fill in for Mrs. Packwood—that is, if you think Mrs. Packwood would not mind."

"Oh, would you?" Lady Elinor eagerly pushed the book toward Kate. "Clara has already read it—she was merely accommodating me."

Kate opened it and read the title. "*Pride and Prejudice*—by a lady. I've heard of this book!"

"It came out a couple of years ago, and Clara read it then with great enjoyment. We both liked *Sense and Sensibility*."

"Well." Kate smoothed the page and began, "*It is a truth universally acknowledged that a single man in possession of a good fortune must be in want of a wife*."

Lady Elinor chuckled. "A single man in possession of a fortune— or of a title!"

Kate went on with the story, thinking not much got past Lady Elinor. Both women had heard, but neither talked about, the rumors that dominated local gossip after the Mortimers' dinner party. Kate was dismayed by the speculations she heard, but reminded herself repeatedly that it was none of her business. Besides, she was concerned only on behalf of Lady Cassandra. Wasn't she? She gave herself a mental shake and soon she and Lady Elinor were engrossed in the story of Elizabeth Bennett and the enigmatic Mr. Darcy.

Thus it was that Kate's duties evolved naturally to include her reading to Lady Elinor whenever Mrs. Packwood, now much occupied with a new grandson, was not available. In truth, Kate enjoyed her time with the older woman. She and Lady Elinor had similar tastes in reading materials and they shared an ironic sense of humor. Except for a few wives of fellow officers, Kate had had no female friends since leaving her childhood home, where she had always had her sister Beatrice, only a year younger, to confide in.

Beatrice. Always, any thought of her four sisters and three brothers brought nostalgia and regret. And burning anger at a father who could so coldly cause an enduring separation of siblings who loved each other. She wondered if Beatrice had married? Goodness! Mary would be of a marriageable age now too. So would Suzanne. And her brothers? Surely they had gone away to school and then university. They would have escaped that iron hand to some extent.

It was mid-morning a few days later when Lord Kenrick sent for his housekeeper. He rose from behind his desk, gestured for her to take a comfortable barrel chair, and reseated himself in its mate. As he crossed his legs, she sat on the edge of her chair and tried not to stare at the way his breeches molded to muscular thighs.

"I understand you have taken on an additional duty," he began.

"My lord?" She found his tone and expression difficult to read.

"Lady Elinor informs me you are regularly spending time reading to her."

"Oh, yes. But only when Mrs. Packwood is unable to do so. And I do assure you, my lord, I am not neglecting my regular duties. Have you a complaint? Has Mr. Wilkins—"

He held up a hand. "Slow down, Mrs. Arthur. I've no complaint. Nor has Wilkins, to my knowledge."

"Then—"

He uncrossed his legs and leaned forward in his chair, clasping his hands in front of him. "My aunt brought this new turn of events to my attention."

"And you disapprove?" She held her own hands tightly in her lap, trying to quell her nervousness.

"Do stop jumping to conclusions." His voice was stern, but not angry.

"Yes, my lord."

"Lady Elinor is concerned that she might be imposing on your good graces. After all, she said, you were hired to be a housekeeper, not an old lady's companion."

"She does not take up so very much of my free time. And I truly do enjoy her company. We have much in common, despite our differences in age and station."

"So she tells me."

There was a touch of irony in this comment and Kate wondered just how much of their conversations his aunt had repeated. Both women had lost husbands whom they had loved very much. Lady Elinor had also lost a son at a young age to an epidemic of scarlet fever. "He would have been Kenrick's age," she had confided. "Perhaps that is partly why I am so fond of Jeremy." Lady Elinor had grown up an earl's daughter and Kate as the eldest child of a wealthy country squire, but they had much in common in terms of education and interests, though Lady Elinor's infirmities limited her activities at this stage of her life. "I seem to be living vicariously," she'd said with a chuckle. Still, Kate worried, how much might she have revealed that she should have kept hidden?

Lord Kenrick smiled. "Don't look so worried. My aunt has not been telling tales."

Kate emitted a nervous little laugh. "Well, that's a relief."

"However, she did want to establish that you are truly satisfied with things as they are."

"Yes, I am. Her ladyship is not unduly demanding."

"And you still find the staff adequate?"

"For the nonce."

"So be it, then. Both my aunt and I thank you."

When he could contrive no other reason to detain her, Jeremy reluctantly allowed his housekeeper to return to whatever he had interrupted. He sat at his desk considering the effect of a trim figure, dark blond hair, and a set of hazel eyes that seemed to flit from almost brown to almost green, depending on light and emotions. Plus a faint scent of lilac, he reminded himself. *And you'd probably do well to expend those kinds of thoughts on the Mortimer chit.*

Several days in the field with farmers and sheep had seen the pile of paperwork and mail on his desk grow astronomically. He had ignored long enough problems of labor, supplies, and equipment for the cotton mill. A flooded shaft in the coal mine demanded attention as well. Perhaps if he cut the hours of shifts in the mill, he could avoid letting workers go. The mine manager assured him the pump could be repaired—this time.

This time. He ran a hand distractedly through his hair, wishing he had someone to talk all this out with, someone to help him see the issue more clearly. What could he do if those cargo ships failed to make port? What if the price of wool fell even lower? What if . . . ?

He spied a missive from Phillips. It was an unusually weighty letter. Speaking of cargo ships . . . Opening it, Jeremy was amazed to see another letter from Phillips—this one addressed not to him, but to his housekeeper! Phillips was writing the housekeeper? Jeremy had left London in such a hurry, it had not occurred to him to wonder how Phillips had happened to find the available Mrs. Arthur—who had previously worked in a duke's household, at that. Jeremy reached for the bellpull to send a footman in search of the housekeeper again.

Meanwhile, he read the message Phillips had sent him:

I do apologize for being the bearer of bad news, my friend, but it appears that at least two vessels of the fleet of five in which we invested went down during a storm in the Indian

Ocean. The five were traveling together to ward off pirates, you know. This information comes from survivors whose lifeboats had drifted far off course. They suffered egregiously, but were eventually picked up by a clipper that only this week arrived in England. There is no word yet on the other ships, but surviving crew members fear the worst.
P.S.
    Would you be so kind as to deliver the enclosed letter to Mrs. Arthur? I am relying on you to handle this message with the utmost discretion.

J

Jeremy sat stunned for several minutes, thinking of the lost lives, lost ships, and lost cargo. Having himself battled the furious storms of a capricious Mother Nature for years in North America, he thought he could appreciate fully the sacrifices—and the drive—of men who went to sea. Still—such a terrible waste of life. . . .

There was also, of course, the matter of ships and cargo. He wondered if other investors had put as much of themselves into this venture as he had. It went far beyond money. He had, in effect, wagered his and his daughter's future—as well as that of the entire earldom. The profit would not in itself have paid the debts Mortimer held, but along with the mill, the mine, and the sale of the wool, he just might have managed to squeeze out from under the knight's weighty boot. Now, perhaps he and Phillips and the others could realize *something.* He recalled Hartwick's comment the other night: "Hope springs eternal."

He shook his head in resignation and drummed his fingers on the desk. Time will tell, he thought, and meanwhile, it simply was not in his nature to give in without trying to salvage what he could.

He reread the letter, dwelling this time on the postscript and the letter for Mrs. Arthur.

Utmost discretion? Bloody hell! What was going on here? Was there some sort of liaison between Phillips and Mrs. Arthur? Had she been his mistress whom Phillips just happened to help to a job out of town? He shook his head. No. Impossible. That would be totally out of character for Phillips; Wally was besotted with his pretty blond wife. And Jeremy would have staked a bundle—if he had one—that such behavior would be totally out of character for Mrs. Arthur too.

Mrs. *Katherine* Arthur. Why was there no man's name in front of that *Arthur*? And why had he not questioned that before? Was Mrs. Phillips involved in some sort of charity helping fallen women? No, that scenario did not fit his Mrs. Arthur, either. *His* Mrs. Arthur? Perhaps she would open up after reading the message from Phillips.

Answering a second summons from her employer in less than an hour, Kate knocked tentatively on the library door and entered at his bidding.

"Yes, my lord?"

"I have here a letter from Walter Phillips for you," he said, giving her a keen look.

She felt her whole being go very still. She imagined the color draining from her face. "A l—letter? F—for me?" Oh, dear Lord. It could only be bad news.

"A letter." He held it out to her.

"Thank you." Her hand trembled as she took it. He might have been extending a hot poker to her for all her eagerness to take it.

"I hope that yours, at least, is not bad news," he said. "However, if you need anything—"

She took a deep breath and regained some of her composure. "I'm sure it isn't. Mr. Phillips handled a minor legal matter for my husband. This is probably the final confirmation. But, if you will excuse me—"

He nodded, his expression unreadable.

She scurried from the room, berating herself. If she had to lie, surely she could have come up with something more believable than that! She went to her rooms, glad Ned was engaged in solving the riddle of the garden maze. She ripped open the letter, scanned it quickly, then reread the brief message more slowly, fear clutching at her painfully.

My dear Mrs. Arthur. (At least he had remembered not to address her as *Lady Arthur*!) *I do not want to alarm you unduly, but Wynstan has hired a Bow Street Runner to trace your whereabouts. My wife and I put him off by informing him of your family ties—in Cornwall, we thought—but I fear he will come back to question us and our staff again and eventually, he may put you and your son on that mail coach north. (In retrospect, perhaps having Mrs. Sealy accompany you was not*

such a good idea, matters of propriety notwithstanding.)
Lawrence is keeping me apprised of the duke's actions. We
should be able to give you ample warning if the situation be-
comes critical.

    P.S. You may want to divulge your circumstances to Kenrick.
He is a good man.

She sat down heavily and clenched her fists. No. She would not
panic. Not yet. As a diversionary tactic, their coach ticket had been to
Durham, a hundred miles farther north. The runner would have to go
north and fan out from there into dozens of towns and villages.
Surely she and Ned were safe for some time yet. And if worse came
to worst, she could return to London and book passage to Canada.
Thank God that Arthur had engaged men like Mr. Phillips and Major
Lawrence to look out for her interests.

    As for informing Lord Kenrick of who and what she was—no.
The fewer people who knew, the safer Ned would be. And—how
could she reveal herself as such a fraud?

CHAPTER 9

The next day, as Jeremy set about solving the most immediate problems of the huge concern that was the earldom as a whole, he received welcome news: The mine was once again in full operation. The labor problems at the cotton mill, however, required his presence, so he informed his aunt and Cassie that he would be gone for a day or two. He also made such members of the staff who needed to know aware of his plans: Wilkins, Miss Cranstan, and Mrs. Arthur.

His aunt, of course, wished him well and assured him she would be fine. He needn't worry about *her*. Cassie was another story. In a comfortable chair in the nursery, he held her on his lap as he told her he was going away. Her chin trembled and tears trickled down her cheeks.

"Can't I go with you? Please, Papa. I'll be good. I promise."

He held her tighter and pressed his head to hers. "I know you would, Poppet. But the mill is no place for a little girl." Even as the words left his mouth, he had a mental image of children scarcely older than his daughter working long hours in both the mill and the mine. Child labor was a fact of life, but that did not mean one had to like it or approve of it. Faint rumblings of protest were heard now and then in political circles, but it would take an act of Parliament to effect any change—and the Seventh Earl of Kenrick had yet to take his seat in that august body.

Cassie patted his cheek. "I could stay in the carriage," she begged.

"No, sweetling. You couldn't. Now stop crying, please." He wiped tears from her cheek with his thumb. "I'll be back soon and then we can do something really fun. All right?"

She brightened. "A picnic?"

"If you'd like."

"Can Ned and his mama come too?"

"If you'd like."

This promise mollified her and she kissed him good-bye with an eager smack.

Although he could have left it up to Wilkins to inform the rest of the staff of his impending absence, Jeremy chose to inform Mrs. Arthur himself. He felt an inexplicable urge to see her. Well, maybe not so *very* inexplicable—but he was also still intensely curious about that message from Phillips. Instead of summoning her to the library, he tracked her down in the stillroom. She was sorting a basket of fresh flowers and herbs and hanging them to dry. She was not immediately aware of his presence and seemed lost in thought—or worry—her brows knit.

"Mrs. Arthur."

She turned abruptly, knocking the basket to the floor, spilling fragrant greenery. "Oh, my lord! You startled me."

"I'm sorry. Shall I go out and come back in?"

She smiled. "No, of course not. Did you need me for something?" She stooped to gather the spilled herbs.

Oh, yes, he thought, admitting to this realization as he bent to help her. Their hands touched briefly and their heads were close as they retrieved the basket's contents. He was aware of the fresh, earthy smell of the herbs and of the light lilac scent he had come to associate with her. They both stood and he handed her a sprig of something pungent. His gaze holding hers, he was acutely aware of her person and he thought there was answering awareness in her eyes.

He cleared his throat. "I came to tell you I am leaving for a day or two, depending on what I find at the mill."

"I see. We shall try to ensure all is safe while you are away."

He thought she was trying to convey a pleasant optimism she might not feel, for a strained look about her eyes belied her tone. "Well," he said lamely, "I just wanted to be sure you were all right, that your news from Phillips yesterday was not upsetting."

"I'm fine," she said cheerfully.

He was sure he detected a certain false note to her tone, but he could not force her to confide in him, now, could he?

"You seem to have restored order to this room." He looked around just as though he knew what a stillroom should look like. However, he had seen this one on his initial tour after arriving back in England. Messy and neglected and dirty, it was then of little concern to the new lord. Now he observed a number of jars on dust-free shelves, all neatly labeled, and several branches of herbs in various stages of dryness hanging overhead. Two covered crocks stood in a corner.

Mrs. Arthur turned quickly, picked up a sprig from the worktable, and held it out to him. "Doesn't this smell wonderful?"

He sniffed it. "Mint."

She held out another. "Try this."

He bent nearer to smell it. "Mint as well?"

"But different. Spearmint and peppermint." Her voice seemed to catch as she held his gaze again.

Slowly, almost without being conscious of the action, he pulled her to him and pressed his mouth to hers. For a moment she was very still, then her arms encircled his neck and she responded feverishly, hungrily, pressing herself closer. He uttered a low groan and deepened the kiss. She still held a sprig of mint in her hand and he later supposed it was that smell that brought him to his senses. He released her abruptly and stepped back.

"I—I *am* sorry, Mrs. Arthur. I—I should not have done that."

"There's no need to apologize, my lord." She did not look away, but she did look embarrassed.

"I would not take advantage," he stumbled on.

"Please. Forget it." She looked down at the sprig of mint still in her hand. "It must have been obvious that I—that it—it was—well, mutual." She lifted her eyes to his again, her own earnest and honest—and showing a degree of fear he wanted immediately to erase. "But I agree: it should *not* have happened. No offense offered; no offense taken."

He broke the eye contact. "Well, then—"

"Did you have some special task for me to fulfill in your absence, my lord?" Her tone now was very businesslike.

He assumed the same demeanor. "No. However, I've promised Cassie a picnic when I get back, and she specifically ask if Ned and his mama could come too."

"I'm sure Ned would enjoy that."

"And his mama?" He smiled.

"Hmm. She might too. We'll see."

Inexplicable need, indeed, he chastised himself repeatedly on the long ride to the mill. "Just could not control yourself, could you, Kenrick?" He relived the warm earthiness of the stillroom coupled with the light scent of lilac and mint and recalled the absolute rightness of their bodies molding together. Was he turning into his father after all? Even as he berated himself, he recalled with infinite pleasure the way she had responded.

Kate too was subjecting herself to a good deal of self-censure. She should never have allowed that to happen. And to have responded as she had was totally improper. Why, she was no better than those wanton widows soldiers used to joke about so! Worse, she had been oblivious to the very real danger the incident could pose. What if the earl thought her so lacking in morals he would dismiss her? Never mind his own role. Romantic dalliance between masters and servants invariably ended with servants paying the price of such. Oh, dear God. If she lost this position, what would happen to Ned?

Well, she would just have to see that it never happened again, she decided, as she went about her usual duties. She was annoyed, though, that she had to come to that decision over and over again.

The housemaids at Kenrick took turns overseeing the nursery so that Miss Cranstan could have her dinner with the rest of the staff in the servants' dining hall. Kate knew that, in the hierarchy of servants, Miss Cranstan valued herself at the top and felt everyone else should do so as well. The woman dearly loved to gossip, though her conversation lent itself more to pronouncing her opinions than exchanging information and ideas with others. Among the staff, Miss Cranstan made no secret of her opinion that the Kenrick earldom would have a countess in charge of the Hall before the year was out—and that the front-runner for that role was her former charge, Miss Charlotte Mortimer.

No one contradicted Miss Cranstan at dinner, but Rosie Davis later expressed the fervent hope that the woman was wrong.

"My cousin is a housemaid for the Mortimers," Rosie said to Kate as the two of them arranged a tray for Rosie to take up to Lady Elinor.

"An' that Miss Mortimer—she's spoiled an' hateful! Had a girl fired because she overheard a footman say the girl was pretty."

"That surely can't be true," Kate said.

"That's what Cousin Jane said. An' she also said Miss Mortimer don't like it none that Lord Kenrick dotes on his daughter so. Said stepchildren belong in boarding schools."

"Good heavens!" Kate said, feeling guilty that she allowed Rosie to divulge this much. "Jane should probably guard her tongue more. Most employers do not like having private business broadcast so."

"That's what me 'n Nell told her." Rosie looked contrite and left with the tray.

Kate returned to the servants' dining room as the others were finishing. Miss Cranstan was saying in a put-upon tone: "He said he'd be gone a day or two. But my half-day off is day after tomorrow and he made no plan for what I'm to do with the child. Usually *he* does something with her then."

"I'll be glad to watch over Lady Cassandra for you if his lordship has not returned," Kate offered.

Miss Cranstan pondered for a moment. "Well—I would not want to put you to any trouble—"

"It's no trouble. She can join Ned's lesson, then the two of them can play outdoors if the weather is nice."

"Well . . ." The nurse sounded only slightly reluctant. "I really did have special plans. Miss Mortimer and her mother are sending a carriage for me to visit them."

"It's settled then. I'm sure his lordship won't mind."

Kate saw Lord Kenrick's absence as an opportunity to give carpets in the most heavily trafficked portions of the house a thorough cleaning. To this end, she set footmen and maids about the tasks of removing the carpets, hanging them over ropes strung between two posts, and beating them vigorously with paddles. The servants involved treated the job, a deviation from routine duties, as an adventure; there was a good deal of laughter and horseplay.

Mr. Wilkins and Miss Cranstan complained about the commotion and the dust and retreated to their respective rooms—sans carpets. When the floors had been scrubbed and the carpets replaced, Kate gave the staff free time and treated them to ale and cakes Mrs. Jenkins had prepared. Wilkins and Cranstan sniffed at this too, muttering things like, "When the cat's away . . ." and "They'll just take advantage . . ."

The following day was as dry and sunny as the previous one. Extending effusive, if not wholly sincere, words of appreciation to Kate, Miss Cranstan left to keep her appointment with the Mortimer women. Lady Cassandra happily joined Ned's lessons and Ned happily showed off the very superior knowledge a two-year advantage gave one. The lesson over, Kate considered the little girl's attire.

"Ribbons and ruffles for outdoor play? I don't think so." Telling Ned to finish a line of sums, she took Lady Cassandra up to the nursery rooms.

"So," Kate said. "Where are your play clothes kept?"

The girl opened a closet door and Kate examined several garments. "No, darling. Your *play* clothes."

Lady Cassandra looked puzzled. "I wear these. 'Cept for riding."

"Well, there must be *something* here," Kate muttered and began opening doors and pawing through drawers. "Ah-hah!" She found a plain cotton dress and a matching cotton pinafore. "This will do nicely—easily washed and ironed."

Once they were outside, Ned eagerly proved to the two females that he had mastered the maze. Leaving the children to run through it again—and again—Kate joined Lady Elinor at the wicker lawn furniture to read a day-old newspaper.

"Labor unrest. The price of bread. Nothing changes much, does it?" Lady Elinor sighed.

Before Kate could reply, Ned appeared before her with Lady Cassandra right behind him. "We're tired of the maze," he complained.

"Hmm. All right. Would you like to do something really useful?"

"What?" He sounded skeptical.

"Grass is crowding out the good plants in the herb garden. Could the two of you pull the grass? Then use the bucket and dipper to water the good plants?"

"I guess so." Ned sounded reluctant, but the two children dashed off to this new venture.

"Just the blades of grass, now," Kate called after them.

"That was tricky of you," Lady Elinor said with a chuckle.

"One uses what one has," Kate said airily as she picked up the paper again. She had chosen the herb garden because it was directly on the other side of the hedge behind which she and Lady Elinor sat.

She could easily keep track of the two youngsters even as she and Lady Elinor read and talked—sometimes over mild squabbles and giggles on the other side.

From the crest of the hill, Jeremy paused to drink in the scene of his home. He loved this view across a small dale. It had been this picture, especially, that had come to him on the rare occasions when he'd felt truly homesick during those years in North America. When his older brothers were alive, it would never have occurred to him to feel such a rush of possessive pride and fierce longing to keep hold of all this. His struggles of the last year had only intensified his will to hang on. The crisis with the mill and the mine were not wholly resolved by any means. Thirty years of neglect could not be corrected in a matter of months. What they really required was a huge infusion of money to modernize equipment. And always there was what Jeremy invariably thought of as "the Mortimer debt." He sighed. So much uncertainty . . .

His attention was diverted by a carriage in front of the entrance to Kenrick Hall. Even at this distance, he recognized the Mortimer vehicle and saw the figure of Miss Cranstan emerge and climb the steps. He'd forgot this was her half-day off! The carriage moved on, and Jeremy breathed a silent thank-you that he would avoid any of its other passengers.

Thirty minutes later, his horse having gone lame, Jeremy was walking down his own driveway, leading his mount. His mind was preoccupied with tending to his horse and finding a nice, cool drink for himself. As he approached the back gardens on the way to the stable, he heard loud voices and urgent cries. He started to run.

"You vile, vile little animal!" Nurse Cranstan was screaming. "Just look at you! Covered in mud! You'll never be anything but a little savage!" She jerked at Cassie's arm, causing the child to stumble and fall.

Before Jeremy could reach them and intervene, Ned jumped to help the fallen Cassie. "You leave her alone!" he shouted.

"Vermin." Cranstan slapped the boy; he howled in surprise and pain.

At this point, the boy's mother rounded the end of the hedge and grabbed at a very startled Nurse Cranstan. "How dare you strike my child!"

Cranstan tried to push the infuriated mother away from her. Mrs. Arthur pushed back and Nurse Cranstan slipped, landing on her bottom in a large puddle of mud with a loud yelp and dragging Mrs. Arthur down with her.

"Why, you—" The nurse struggled to rise, but kept slipping.

Mrs. Arthur found better purchase and scrambled to her feet, looking as ready for battle as a mama bear protecting her cub.

"Here! What's going on here?" Jeremy shouted.

All eyes turned on him, horror in the nurse's eyes, chagrin in the housekeeper's, and mere surprise in the children's. A babble of voices erupted as they all responded at once.

"Papa!"

"We were just—"

"The children have been—"

"Help me up, please."

He extended a hand to Nurse Cranstan and was rewarded with a handful of mud. Now that he knew no one was injured, he wanted to laugh at the whole farcical situation, but thought better of any mirth. "One at a time," he ordered. He pointed at the nurse. "You first."

Miss Cranstan's attempt to look dignified was belied by mud on her gown and face. She had also lost some hairpins; she pushed hair off her face, thus leaving another streak of mud. Belligerence and apprehension vied in her tone. "This, my lord, is what comes of allowing your daughter to associate with the lower orders. The child, as you can clearly see, regressed to her heathen ways the moment my back was turned. And it is all this woman's fault. She encourages children to be out of control."

Jeremy felt his lips tighten, but before he could formulate a response, the nurse rushed on.

"Mrs. Arthur was to look after Lady Cassandra. My half-day off, you know. She assured me you wouldn't mind—"

"No, I—"

"But, *look* at her ladyship. Just look! She isn't even wearing the garments I personally dressed her in this morning!"

"She needed play clothes—not ribbons and lace!" Mrs. Arthur said.

"And what would *you* know about rearing a child of the ton?" the nurse barked.

A deep flush suffused the housekeeper's face, but Jeremy did not allow her the explosion he saw coming. "Ladies, enough! I'll send for each of you separately when we've all cleaned ourselves."

Seeing that the altercation had attracted the attention of several other staff members, he ordered his horse taken to the stable, picked up his daughter, and carried her into the house. When he set her down in the kitchen, he chuckled at the sight she presented.

"You have streaks of mud on both cheeks," he said.

"It's war paint, Papa. I was showing Ned—"

"You were going to war with Miss Cranstan?"

She giggled. "No, Papa!" Her expression became serious, apprehensive. "Are you angry, Papa?"

"Not with you, Cassie. Not with you."

"Papa?"

"Hmm?"

"Papa, what's a *sabbage*? Miss Cranstan said—"

"Never mind what she said." He managed to control his anger. "She was upset. She didn't mean to say that."

"Oh. It's a naughty word?"

He seized on this. "Sort of." He motioned to the maid Rosie, who hovered nearby. "Take her up to the nursery and clean her up, then take her to the drawing room where I'll ask Lady Elinor to sit with her. But do not trouble Cranstan with her."

"Yes, my lord. Come along, my lady." Rosie took a grubby little hand in her own.

A half hour later, Kate dutifully reported to the library. Apprehensive, she scarcely dared to breathe freely. This altercation with Nurse Cranstan after her own lapse in behavior in the stillroom might well be cause for dismissal. Lord Kenrick stood in front of French doors that opened onto a slate patio. The light behind him, she could not read his expression. He motioned to the set of barrel chairs and they both sat.

"What *was* that all about?" he demanded without preamble.

"What she said, for the most part." Kate explained her volunteering to look after Lady Cassandra so Nurse Cranstan could keep her engagement with the Mortimer women. "I—uh—perhaps overstepped with the change in clothing. And I should have foreseen that children would find playing in mud hard to resist." She spread her hands in a helpless gesture, "But they were having fun and children *are* washable—"

"As are adults," he said with a rueful smile.

"Are you—are you going to dismiss me, my lord?" She voiced her immediate concern. After all, Miss Cranstan had been in the earl's employ much longer than one Mrs. Arthur!

"Dismiss you? Whatever for?"

"Well, we did agree on a trial period and it's almost up and I don't think Miss Cranstan likes me and she *is* an important member of the staff and—"

"Hold on," he interrupted. "You're jumping to conclusions—again." He held her gaze and grinned. "Are you always so impetuous?"

She felt herself blushing, for she knew he was remembering—as she was—her response to his kiss. "I—I—sometimes. I guess."

He stood and extended his hand as he said, "For the record: no, I am not dismissing you." His grin broadened. "At least not today."

"Oh, that's a relief," she said in the same light vein he had used. She smiled, grasped the hand he extended, and rose from the chair. There was an arrested moment between them, then he released her hand and she moved toward the door. But, she thought, it truly was a relief. She had been sorely afraid—worried for two days. And now this. Few employers could tolerate friction among upper staff members. Perhaps his lordship would be able to smooth things over and she could school herself to a more tolerant attitude toward Cranstan—or at least avoid her as much as possible.

Miss Cranstan stood in the hall as Kate emerged. In the interest of toleration, Kate gave her a tight little nod of recognition—and received a frigid stare in response.

Jeremy stood behind his desk as Nurse Cranstan entered the room. He gestured to a straight-backed chair in front of the desk for her and, when she had taken it, he sat himself and folded his hands over a letter lying on the blotter.

"I see you've already spoken with the housekeeper," she said nervously. "I do hope that woman has not twisted the truth out of all semblance of proportion."

"Mrs. Arthur essentially corroborated what you said outside earlier."

"She did?"

"She did."

Miss Cranstan seemed to relax. "Well, then. You know, my lord, I simply do the best I can."

"I am sure you believe that," he said, "but I am letting you go."

"Letting me—" Anger flashed in her eyes and two red blotches appeared on her cheeks. "So! She *did* fill your head full of lies about me. Women like that. Flit themselves in front of a man and he loses all sense of what is right and proper."

"Miss Cranstan. You forget yourself. This has nothing to do with Mrs. Arthur or anything you may imagine she said. It is entirely about your own behavior."

"My behavior?" Her voice rose and Jeremy feared she might become apoplectic. "*My* behavior?"

"Yours. I specifically asked that you create a freer atmosphere for my daughter and that you respect her as a person by not using abusive language with her. Yet that is precisely what I happened upon this afternoon."

"I admit I lost my temper, my lord," she said more contritely, "and I do apologize, but that woman simply should not be allowed to gainsay her betters. You must see that." She ended on a plaintive note.

He raised a hand. "Again. It is not about Mrs. Arthur." He lifted the letter from his desk. "I have written you a letter of recommendation. I have not laid out any objections. It simply says you worked here and gave satisfactory service in the physical care of your charge."

"If it was so satisfactory—"

He interrupted her, his voice hard. "I cannot—I will not risk having my child—or any child for which I have any degree of responsibility—treated as you treated those two today. I've included a bank draft for your wages to the end of the quarter. Cuthbertson will drive you to the coaching inn tomorrow—or anywhere else you want to go within a day's drive." He rose and walked around the desk to hand her the letter. "I expect you to be gone from this house by this time tomorrow."

"As you wish, my lord." Her voice, stiff and icy, seemed threatening. "I am quite sure you will live to regret this decision."

"I sincerely doubt it, but I wish you well."

The next day he was not surprised to learn that Miss Cranstan had had Cuthbertson drive her to the Mortimer estate.

CHAPTER 10

"Are you sure that is a good idea?" Lady Elinor asked when Jeremy told her at breakfast the next morning of his plan to take the housekeeper and her son along on a picnic with him and Cassie.

He shrugged. "Why would it not be?"

"Oh, come Jeremy! You know such a thing cannot be kept a secret."

"Why should it be a secret? There's nothing immoral or improper about a simple picnic!"

"Are you being deliberately obtuse, my boy? You know very well you'll set tongues wagging throughout three or four neighborhoods if just the four of you go off in the woods alone. That—on top of your dismissing the Cranstan woman—why, the gossip mongers will be fairly salivating!"

"Well, let them." He was annoyed, but he knew his aunt had a point. "I promised Cassie—"

"I know. And one should keep promises made to a child."

"One should keep promises, period."

"Of course, but—"

"I have it!" he interrupted. A teasing grin showed in his voice. "You must accompany us."

"I must—Jeremy, have you lost your wits?"

"Why not? You'd enjoy it. I know you would. We can take a maid and a footman, too, to help you. Three extra adults should quell any undue gossip."

"Oh, Jeremy—" she protested, but he could tell she welcomed the idea. "I would not want to be a burden—"

"Impossible—and it's settled. Tomorrow—weather permitting."

The weather cooperated, so five adults and two eager children set off for a picnic the next day in an open carriage. Lord Kenrick and the footman, Thomas, occupied the driver's seat, the others rode in the back with food and other essentials, including a somewhat battered guitar that Jeremy assumed belonged to the footman. The maid who accompanied them was Rosie, who was being rewarded for temporarily taking over the duties of the nursery maid.

Jeremy drove to a spot on the Kenrill River he remembered from his childhood. It was as he had seen it in memory a thousand times: idyllic. Under an oak tree a large patch of grass sloped gently down to the water's edge, from which a gravel bar jutted into shallow water. He drank in the blend of fungal odors of woods, grass, and solid earth.

"What a beautiful spot," Mrs. Arthur said as the carriage came to a stop. "A huge oak tree, warm sun sparkling on the water, just enough shade. It's perfect!"

Jeremy cast an appreciative glance her way, sure her inventory of the site was primarily for his aunt's benefit. While he and Thomas took care of the horses, Mrs. Arthur and Rosie spread blankets and pillows, and made Lady Elinor comfortable. Leaving Thomas to finish with the team, Jeremy, carrying the picnic basket, strolled toward the women. Ned and Cassie had their heads together in earnest discussion.

"Ask them," Ned said.

"No. You ask."

"No, you do it."

"Ask what?" Jeremy demanded as he set the basket down.

They both spoke at once. "Can we go in the water?"

"*May* we," Jeremy corrected automatically.

"May we—*pleeease*?" Both children bounced up and down in anticipation.

Jeremy looked at Mrs. Arthur, an eyebrow raised in question.

"Is it dangerous?" she asked.

"No. It's only ankle deep for about twenty feet out. Probably a bit cold at first."

"I could go with them," Rosie offered eagerly.

Mrs. Arthur nodded. "All right, then."

Quickly, before capricious adults could change their minds, the two children plopped down on the edge of the blanket to remove their shoes and stockings. Ned, wearing the short pants customary for a boy his age, was ready in a flash and jumped up.

"Wait for Cassie—Lady Cassandra—and Rosie," his mother said, helping the little girl remove her footwear, roll her pantaloons up to her knees, and tuck the hem of her dress into her belt, as Rosie, in a show of proper modesty, performed these same tasks for herself behind the meager screen of a low bush.

When the chaos of Rosie and two children racing into the chilly water had subsided, Mrs. Arthur said, "I'm sorry, my lord. I am so used to hearing Ned chatter about *Cassie*, you see."

"Never mind. She can be *Cassie* for the day, at least. Honorifics seem a bit silly for children." He sat on the edge of the blanket, his knees drawn up.

"Ah, but they *do* serve a purpose," his aunt put in.

"And that is—" he said.

"They maintain decorum," Mrs. Arthur said, pausing momentarily in the process of laying out food. "Rather like the use of ranks in the military."

Lady Elinor nodded. "Precisely."

"But people with military ranks are adults," he argued. "The natives in America have a more sensible solution."

"What?" Both women spoke at once.

"One can have one name as a child and quite another as an adult. The adult name is often earned—for a skill or an act of bravery."

"Such as?" Lady Elinor said.

"Basket Woman was skilled at weaving baskets from river weeds and willows. Buffalo Killer is obvious. And Thomas here," he added with a gesture as the footman approached, "might be called He Who Laughs."

"And did you have an Indian name?" his aunt asked.

"Uh, yes . . ." He gave a sheepish grin; how had he allowed this conversation to take such a turn?

"Well. What was it?" Lady Elinor demanded.

"I—it's not important," he said.

"Nonetheless, I should like to know what it was," his aunt pursued. "And I am sure Mrs. Arthur is interested also."

"Oh, yes." His housekeeper's grin at his obvious embarrassment was as wide as that of the nodding footman.

"You're ganging up on me," he protested. "Even Thomas has joined you, betraying his sex."

Thomas's grin widened and Lady Elinor said, "Come, my boy. Out with it."

He sighed. "All right." He lowered himself to a reclining position and rattled off the name in the Arapaho language.

"What?" they all said.

He repeated it.

"Too many syllables," Lady Elinor protested with a laugh. "I could never master all those vowels! What does it mean?"

"It boils down to something like 'Willow's Choice.'"

"A tree chose you? There must be a story there," Mrs. Arthur said with a smile as she finished laying out food and utensils and sat back.

"Oh, yes. A very long story." He allowed himself a rueful note. "*Willow* was my wife's Arapaho name. Actually, her name translated more accurately to something like the Singing Willow of the Evening."

"How interesting," Lady Elinor said.

"I'm sorry, my lord, if we intruded," Mrs. Arthur said.

He glanced at her and smiled, touched by her empathy. Then he shrugged. "Not at all." He was surprised at the ease with which he had shared even this most trivial information, and at the absence of the pain and regret memories of life with Willow usually conjured. "It was an interesting life," he added.

"One not many Englishmen can lay claim to," Mrs. Arthur said.

"No, but few English*women* have endured the hardships you must have encountered on the Peninsula campaign," he said to change the subject.

"Well, it was not so *very* bad." She seemed to have picked up on his desire to shift the topic. "The marches between battles were not wholly unlike prolonged picnics. Much more serious, of course, but—still—a very casual way of life."

A loud scream erupted from the river. Instantly, Jeremy was on his feet and he and Mrs. Arthur ran onto the gravel bar, the footman Thomas right behind them.

Jeremy could not stifle a laugh at the scene that greeted them. Rosie sat in the stream, her legs straight out before her, her skirt billowing up around her. Ned and Cassie stood looking on in awe.

"Are you hurt?" Mrs. Arthur called.

"No," Rosie said. "Just me dignity, I guess. I slipped. Felt somethin' on me leg. Scared me and I fell."

"Probably a minnow," Jeremy said. "I'll help you up."

"I'll do it, my lord," Thomas offered, rushing to the rescue.

"You children come out too," Mrs. Arthur said. "Our lunch is ready."

Thomas set Rosie on her feet and she and the two children stepped gingerly over the uneven pebbles of the gravel bar and up to the edge of the picnic blanket.

They described the incident to Lady Elinor, who said, "Rosie, you'll need to remove your wet dress. You'll catch cold."

"Oh, my lady! I couldn't do *that*."

"Thomas, there's another blanket in the carriage. Will you get it, please?" Mrs. Arthur asked.

"Certainly, Mrs. A." He ran to do so.

Jeremy was struck anew by the easy relationship between Mrs. Arthur and the other servants. Of course, they owed her respect. As housekeeper, she wielded tremendous influence over who was fired and who was hired. But he thought this went far beyond that simple fact of life. They genuinely liked her. Even Wilkins had come around to the point of seeming pleased when Jeremy informed the butler she would be staying beyond the trial period.

Now he was aware of her cajoling Rosie into removing her dress behind the bush—though he and Thomas and Lady Elinor kept up a low conversation and pretended not to listen. Rosie's part of the discussion was an occasional whimper. Mrs. Arthur alleviated the girl's offended sensibilities by assuming a practical, no-nonsense tone.

"Put your stockings back on—they will keep your legs warm. Yes, you can keep your drawers on—they'll dry soon enough. Now here— wrap this blanket around you—just hold it like so. I'll put your skirt and petticoat in the sun to dry."

This was followed by a tremulous "thank you" and the two women emerged from behind the bush.

"Papa!" Cassie giggled and pointed at Rosie. She launched into a vowel-ridden commentary in Arapaho.

"Cassie! English, remember? You are being rude," Jeremy said.

"I'm sorry."

"What did she say?" Ned asked.

"She said Rosie looks like Chief White Eagle's favorite wife—who is a very pretty woman, by the way."

At first Rosie looked uncertain about this comparison, but then she preened a bit. "Why, thank you, Lady Cassandra."

The afternoon mishap had little effect on anyone's appetite. Roast chicken, savory cheese scones, fresh baby carrots, and strawberry tarts disappeared in a flash. Afterwards, the children happily went about finding and picking wildflowers, promising not to stray out of sight. Relishing a feeling of lazy contentment, free of worldly concerns, Jeremy stretched out on the blanket near his aunt. Buzzing insects and an occasional birdcall lulled his senses. Rosie and Thomas sat off to the side talking softly; Mrs. Arthur was finishing the last of her tart.

"Well, done, Mrs. Arthur," Jeremy said.

"My compliments as well," Lady Elinor said.

"Mrs. Jenkins did the food," Mrs. Arthur said.

Lady Elinor heaved a comfortable sigh. "Such a very pleasant day—Rosie's little contretemps notwithstanding. Thank you, nephew, for letting me be part of it."

"And how could I not?" he responded. "You, dear aunt, are part of the Kenrick package."

"Mrs. A," Thomas said shyly as the housekeeper brushed crumbs from her skirt, "would you play for us?"

"Of course—that is, if it is everyone's wish." She held Jeremy's gaze.

"The guitar is yours?" he asked, feeling foolish.

"Yes. I learned to play on the Peninsula."

"You are a woman full of surprises, are you not?" Rising to a more erect position, he scarcely noticed a momentary look of apprehension in her expression. "And did you play for the great Wellington himself?" he teased.

"Only once," she said.

"Oh. Well, then . . ." He gestured to Thomas, who ran to the carriage to retrieve the instrument.

Mrs. Arthur took it, strummed a few times, adjusted the tuning, and paused. "What shall it be?" she asked.

" 'Barbara Allen,' " Rosie suggested.

Jeremy prepared himself for a rather ordinary amateur rendition of one of England's oldest and best-loved ballads. What he heard astounded him. Her voice was basically a sweet contralto, but she demonstrated—effortlessly—both range and control. She handled the instrument with ease and expertise. Jeremy was himself an accomplished musician; he had played the pianoforte since he was ten and had furthered his musical education during his years at Oxford. He knew a masterful performance when he heard one. And this certainly was such.

He listened raptly, as did the others. They all applauded vigorously when the last note faded. She launched into a happier comic ballad that had them all smiling and clapping their hands in tune. The children, who had rejoined them, took special glee in this one, as she directed specific lines to them.

"Do Papa's song," her son begged.

"Oh, but it is so sad," she protested.

"*Pleeease*?" He stretched the word out to three syllables.

She shrugged and said to the others, "This is a Portuguese ballad of tragic love—rather like Romeo and Juliet. A haunting song of loss, personal and devastating. My husband liked this one very much." She smiled sadly at her son.

She sang in Portuguese, so the words were meaningless to her immediate audience, but her voice and the music crept into their very souls. Jeremy was profoundly moved by the music, recalling losses he had experienced in his own life. He observed that the two servants and his aunt were equally moved: the women had tears in their eyes. Even the children were sobered.

She allowed the last note to hang in the air before saying, "I told you it was sad."

"But very beautiful." Lady Elinor said. "Very beautiful."

"Yes, indeed, Mrs. Arthur. You are a woman full of surprises. Where did you learn to sing like that?" He held her gaze for a long moment and this time he saw it. Was that anxiety, perhaps fear, in her eyes?

She shrugged. "Here and there. The family circle, you know. All girls learn to sing."

Not like that, he told himself. Not like that. That voice had a very good coach at some point, but he kept this thought to himself.

Feeling faintly apprehensive, Kate busied herself with the task of gathering up the picnic paraphernalia. After a moment, Lord Kenrick rose and said, "The sun is getting quite low. Come, Thomas, let's see to the team."

"Rosie," Kate said, "your skirt may be dry enough to wear now."

Rosie checked the skirt and pronounced it damp but wearable. She put the dress back on and returned to help Kate finish gathering things together. By the time the men brought the team and carriage around, all was readied.

"This has been a most delightful day," Lady Elinor said as Lord Kenrick helped her into the carriage. "I do thank each and every one of you."

"See? I told you you'd love it," her nephew said.

She caressed his chin and said quietly, but with a laugh, "Jeremy, dear, no one likes an *I-told-you-so*."

Kate smiled at this and on the return journey tried to keep up her end of casual conversation with Lady Elinor, but found her mind repeating his lordship's question: "Where did you learn to sing like that?"

Could he tell she had had superior training? Her father had been an unforgiving tyrant, showing little affection to any of his children, but he recognized talent when he saw it and insisted that it be nurtured. No, a few folk songs could not reveal so much. It was not as though she had been warbling operatic arias. She dismissed the worry and fell to agreeing with Lady Elinor about what a wonderful day it had been.

As they approached Kenrick Hall, a traveling coach was pulling up to the door. Lord Kenrick stopped behind it, turned his own reins over to Thomas, and jumped down to help his passengers alight. A tall man emerged from the other vehicle and called out, "Jeremy! Oh, I say! Perfect timing, eh?"

Kate felt herself freeze inside.

No! This couldn't be happening.

But it was.

She kept her head down, foolishly hoping her mobcap afforded some cover, and instructed Rosie to take the children up to the nursery.

"Both of them?" Rosie asked.

"For the moment. I shall come for Ned as soon as I can." She could not just desert Lady Elinor.

"Bobby!" Lord Kenrick grasped his brother's outstretched hand, then enclosed him in a bear hug. "I did not expect you until next week!"

"You know how government works—its clocks have different timing mechanisms than those of ordinary folk." Robert Chilton looked over his brother's shoulder and spied their aunt. "Aunt Elinor! You are still the most beautiful girl in Yorkshire!"

"Oh, go on with you, you honey-tongued devil, you." She hugged him and Kate saw tears on her cheeks.

Kate tried desperately to make herself least seen, but Robert Chilton spied her and took a step toward her.

"What the—? Kate? Kate, is that you? By Jove! Lady Arthur! I never thought to see you here!"

CHAPTER 11

Kate's mind was in a whirl. Robert faced her; Lord Kenrick was slightly in front of her, his eyes focused on his brother.

Lord Kenrick's brows shot upwards. "*Lady* Arthur?"

Kate tried to convey her sense of urgency with a warning look to Robert even as she answered Lord Kenrick in a light tone. "Oh, pay that no mind, my lord. It was a silly game we played on the Peninsula. You must know how utterly bored soldiers can get—even officers." She shook her finger at Robert. "And *you* must know these games do not play well at home where imaginary titles are frowned upon."

Robert's eyes widened in astonishment. "Imagi—. Oh. Right. I was just so surprised to see you."

"And I, you, Captain Chilton," she said. "It is a real pleasure and I do hope we will have an opportunity later to catch each other up. Right now you must be anxious to renew your acquaintance with your family."

Another gentleman emerged from the traveling coach and Robert quickly introduced him as Captain Ralph Clemson. "He joined the regiment just in time for that little dustup at Waterloo," Robert explained and made the man known to his brother and his aunt. He then turned to Kate, who was holding her breath against another faux pas that could bring down her house of cards. "Unfortunately, Clemson, you missed knowing our 'Angel of the Forty-sixth.'"

"Mrs. Arthur. I am the housekeeper here at Kenrick Hall," Kate offered, with a brief curtsy and a glance at Robert to be sure he had absorbed her name and position.

"Pleasure." Clemson nodded in her direction.

Wilkins and a footman appeared to help with the luggage.

"We should move indoors," Lord Kenrick said, offering his arm to his aunt. "I am sure Mrs. Arthur will see to some refreshments for us."

"Yes, my lord." Kate was glad to make her escape, but also worried that Robert might let something slip before she could talk with him. And what might Captain Clemson know of the Angel of the 46th?

She saw to it that refreshments were taken to the drawing room and that a suitable supper would appear in due time. It was a point of pride with her that Lord Kenrick's household not be found deficient on any score. Trying not to allow herself to become obsessed with worry, she kept very busy for the entire evening.

It was late before Jeremy had any time alone with his brother. Lady Elinor had excused herself immediately after the evening meal, saying she had had a long day. The gentlemen then sat for a long while at the dining table over port and brandy, sharing stories of their separate adventures of several years and on two continents. At first, Jeremy had privately wondered about the sort of person an adult Robert might have become. After all, his younger brother had been a mere schoolboy when Jeremy had seen him last. He was pleased to find his doubts were groundless. The three men established an easy rapport and talked for a long while before Captain Clemson politely left the two Chilton brothers to cap the evening.

Jeremy and Robert moved into the family drawing room and were ensconced in comfortable chairs, their last drinks in hand when Jeremy turned to the topic that had niggled at the fringes of his consciousness since that scene at his brother's arrival.

"So—Bobby. You knew my housekeeper in the Peninsula."

"Jeremy, I haven't been *Bobby* in over a decade," his brother protested. "And I think our sister has been Margaret lo! these many years, though I did enjoy twitting her about 'Mags' when I visited." He had mentioned earlier his visiting the Talbots.

"All right. *Robert.* I shall try to remember." Jeremy suspected the younger man deliberately avoided the question, and he was not inclined to allow that. "Mrs. Arthur? The Peninsula?"

"Ah, yes. Kate. We called her the Angel of the Forty-sixth. That little woman showed more courage and fortitude during the entire campaign than any six fighting men!"

"Is that so?"

"Saved lives too. Some women—especially officers' wives—complained and carried on. But Kate—she helped the medical people. I know of at least three fellows who would not be treading the earth today but for her."

"Is that so?" Jeremy said again, trying to be encouraging.

"That *is* so," Robert said firmly and sipped his drink. "She saved my arm! Blasted surgeon wanted to lop it off here." He pointed to a spot above his right elbow. "Kate persuaded him to wait. She cleaned the wound herself, applied poultices and such for over a week. So . . . I'm here, and I'm still right-handed. Thanks to her."

"Impressive. But what do you know of her background?"

"What do *you* know?" Robert parried.

"Well, I admit to knowing precious little. I was desperate, you see." He explained the circumstances of hiring Mrs. Arthur. "I trusted Phillips. I trusted her, in fact, but as I look back on it, I had little real information. She is a soldier's widow; she was forthright about her son; she did not mind removing to Yorkshire; she came from the South of England; and she's done an exemplary job since she came here. Oh, and she worked for a duke. So—what can you tell me about her?"

"She worked for—"

"For a duke."

Jeremy watched an unreadable flurry of thoughts and emotions flit across his brother's expression before Robert looked away.

After a long pause, Robert said, "She comes from Cornwall—or Surrey. I forget which. Father was a country squire and a high stickler. Disowned her when she married against his wishes. Husband's family disowned him too, but he was able to buy a commission." There was another pause. "That's about all I can tell you."

"*Can* or *will*?" Jeremy suspected there was more—much more—that Robert could tell him.

Robert shifted uncomfortably in his chair. "At the moment, *can*. I owe her too much not to respect her privacy."

Jeremy smiled, torn between admiring his brother's loyalty to a friend and his own intense curiosity. "I can accept that. Mind you, I am not satisfied—far from it, in fact—but I respect your position."

He decided to let the matter drop for now. "So, you've seen the inimitable Maggie—uh, Margaret—and her lot. Have you seen your mother?"

"Oh, yes. Clemson and I stopped in Bath a few days before coming up here." Robert drained his glass and waved away Jeremy's offer of a refill. "Mother is, as you can imagine, not best pleased with you."

"I know. I have a note from her every few weeks or so telling me that Bath is just not London. I offered her the dower house here, but she said, 'Society in Bath is decidedly inferior, but society in Yorkshire is nonexistent!' "

"That's my mama." Robert sported an understanding grin.

"To be perfectly honest, Robert, I *had* to let the London house. If certain other ventures don't go well, I am likely to lose it anyway. Hell and damnation! I'm in real danger of losing everything. Amelia will still have her fortune, though, and she can live comfortably forever in Bath. Your grandfather knew what he was about in negotiating her marriage settlements with our father."

"He was a sharp one, all right. But I'm sorry to hear matters are so lean with you."

"It will work out—or it won't." Jeremy stifled a yawn. "Before we call it a day, what about you: What are your plans?"

"Clemson and I are on a sort of reconnoitering tour."

"Oh?"

"We are both keen on selling out. His grandmother left him a holding in Scotland. He'll be going on alone in a few days to check it out."

"And after you sell your commission?"

"I could live for a while on the proceeds. Also, both Margaret and I had modest legacies from our maternal grandmother." He shrugged.

"I see."

"Made the settlements easier for Margaret's marriage. But I think Talbot would have had her in sackcloth." Robert chuckled, "Still would too."

"They are quite taken with each other," Jeremy agreed, feeling a twinge of envy as he thought fleetingly of his own marriage to the captivating and capricious Willow. "So," he said, again shifting the topic, "you're set to become a true Corinthian, eh?"

Robert snorted. "Hardly. I won't be *that* plump in the pocket. Or such a fribble. God knows this family has had enough of those."

* * *

The next day the three gentlemen went out shooting early in the morning. Privately, Kate thought it a deal of foolishness when one thought of the paltry number of fowl they were likely to produce for the table. Chicken was more available, was a more versatile dish, and tastier besides. Still, the men would have their sport. Throughout the morning she fretted silently and, though she tried not to let her anxiety spill into her dealings with others, it was inevitable that it do so.

When Rosie made some trivial comment about yesterday's embarrassment, Kate snapped at her, "Do try to be less absorbed with yourself."

The maid looked hurt, mumbled, "Yes, ma'am," and scurried away. Kate immediately felt contrite. *Self-absorbed? Look who's talking*, she told herself and resolved to make it up to Rosie later.

She also snapped at Ned, who pestered to be able to play with a bow and arrow. "No. I haven't time this morning and there's no one else to set up a target and supervise."

"I don't need a target set up. I'll be careful."

"I said *no!* Go do the page of sums I gave you."

"I already did," he said resentfully.

"Cassie will be down soon for the riding lesson. Go and change your clothes so you can join her."

This met with less resentment and Kate was glad to know that Ned and Cassie would be looked after very well by the stable crew for a while.

Since Cranstan's leaving, Kate had assumed some of the responsibilities for Lady Cassandra's care. Rosie had been appointed temporary nursery maid, seeing to the little girl's routine physical care and sleeping in an adjoining room in the nursery suite to be on call. Still, Kate had to supervise Rosie. His lordship had mentioned the need for a "real" nursemaid, but then his brother had arrived and God alone knew when—or if—the vacancy would be filled.

Kate knew that to a certain extent she was dwelling on the issue of Lady Cassandra's care to distract herself from her own problems: a Bow Street Runner trying to find her, and what Robert Chilton might reveal to his brother.

By mid-morning, the gentlemen had returned from their shooting expedition with a few ducks and a goose for the Kenrick table. After a late breakfast, Captain Clemson was writing letters, and Lord Kenrick was engaged in some paperwork of his own. With the children now occupied, Kate seized the chance to talk with Robert.

She found him sitting in a wicker chair in the back garden, smoking a cheroot. "I hope I'm not intruding."

"Not at all," he replied. "I was hoping for a chance to speak with you. Have you time for a little stroll?"

"Of course."

When they were out of earshot of any chance listener, he said, "All right, Kate. Out with it. Tell me what is going on with you. Last I heard, you and Ned were at Wynstan Castle—and here I find a member of a duke's family as my brother's *housekeeper*? Incredible!"

"I suppose it does seem that way." As they walked slowly along the garden paths, she explained briefly the circumstances of her being where she was and what she was.

"And you had no alternative?"

"None that I could see. The law favors men over women, you know, and a powerful duke, well . . ." Her voice trailed off in despair.

"What about your family? Surely after all this time—"

"My father's response would be 'You made your bed—now you must lie in it.' *If* he deigned to respond at all. Nor would he ever even *think* of defying a duke. He was very emphatic in washing his hands of me when Arthur and I returned from eloping to Gretna Green."

"Why? Most fathers would rant a bit, but then they'd come around."

"Not mine," she said bitterly. "He sets great store by orders of precedence in society. He refused permission for the marriage merely because he knew Wynstan disapproved."

"And Wynstan disapproved because—?"

"Because he *always* disapproved whatever Arthur wanted to do. And because the daughter of a mere country squire could never measure up to his expectations for his family connections. He is quite pretentious about his position in society, you see. Also, he had chosen a wife for Arthur: the daughter of an earl who was to inherit a property adjoining Wynstan's main holding. Wynstan hates—positively hates—having his wishes thwarted. He simply will not tolerate opposition."

"So he refused permission."

"Right. But both Arthur and I were of age. Our parents' permission was irrelevant. We went to Gretna Green."

"And both fathers disowned you."

"Yes."

"That must have been very hard for you."

"It was very painful at the time," she said. "It still is. Even now I shed tears over losing my brothers and sisters. Papa threatened to disown them too, if they acknowledged me. And he would. He would. I tried to visit my family when I first returned to England. Papa had a manservant turn me away at the door."

There was a catch in her voice as she stopped walking and faced him. She had a fleeting thought that Robert's gray eyes reflected layers of emotion much as his brother's blue eyes did, but she continued her tale. "Arthur and I had a difficult time financially at first, for we had only what was left of Arthur's quarter allowance. Wynstan cut that too, though he offered to restore it if Arthur would agree to have the marriage annulled. It was Arthur's maternal grandmother who came to our rescue. She gave Arthur the money to buy his commission." She spread her hand in an open gesture. "There you have it. Rather a sordid story, is it not?"

"My dear lady." He pulled her into a spontaneous and warm embrace. "The only sordidness is in the behavior of two autocratic old men." He released her and they walked on. "I knew the basics of all this, of course, but not the details," he said.

"W—what have you told Lord Kenrick?"

"Only that you were from Surrey—I thought—and there had been trouble over your marriage. I did *not* tell him that the Angel of the Forty-sixth is, in fact, Lady Arthur Gardiner and that her son is heir to the Duke of Wynstan."

"Oh, thank goodness."

They walked in silence for a few moments, then Robert said, "But you should."

"Should?"

"Tell him. Tell him who you are."

She shook her head. "I cannot. I would lose my position. Lord Kenrick would have to let me go. I must protect my son. No. Lord Kenrick must not know. Please, Robert. Please."

"Jeremy is a good man."

She stopped and faced him again. "I think he is that, but what could he do? Nothing. And I would have to leave here—and there's no place to go. Please, Robert." She tried, but knew she failed, to keep the panic out of her voice.

He gripped both her hands in his own and held her gaze. "All right. I will keep your secret, but I think you are making a very serious mistake."

Kate felt her worries had been alleviated a bit at least. The Bow Street investigation still loomed, but she could put it out of her mind for a while yet.

Jeremy had been standing at the library window and observed his brother embrace Mrs. Arthur.

Bloody hell! What was that all about?

Should be obvious even to someone as obtuse as you, Kenrick.

Robert had not kissed her, though, had he?

It was just a friendly hug.

Uh-huh. A friendly hug. Between a virile young man and a very attractive woman.

You have no right to these feelings, he told himself. *No right at all. You need to quell that green-eyed monster about which Shakespeare wrote so profoundly.*

Pretend you never saw it. Pretend it never happened.

Oh, yes. Pretend.

His curiosity about the background of Katherine Arthur went unsatisfied, but he was forced to push it to the back of his mind as he dealt with routine crises: a farmer's cottage that needed a new roof; a dispute between tenant farmers over assigned landholdings; a mysterious illness in a certain flock of sheep. Also, the Mortimers—father and daughter—continued to remind him not only of their existence, but that they felt certain proprietary rights regarding his own existence. Jeremy found their attitude annoying and intrusive, but to make an issue of his feelings would have him behaving as boorishly as they, though he had to admit that the daughter was a bit more subtle than her father.

Sir Eldridge Mortimer arrived one morning alone and unexpected just as Jeremy, his brother, and Captain Clemson were finishing breakfast. Determined to keep his dealings with Mortimer on a rather formal level, Jeremy had the man shown into the library and excused himself from the breakfast table.

"Sir Eldridge? Please have a seat." Jeremy gestured to a wing-backed chair on one side of the fireplace and took the matching chair on the other side. "May I offer you something to drink? Coffee, perhaps, at this hour of the morning?"

"No, nothing. Thank you." The knight sat and tapped his fingers on his knees.

"Sir?" Jeremy prompted.

"I'm here about Miss Cranstan," the knight blurted.

Jeremy made no effort to disguise his surprise and answered coolly. "I beg your pardon?"

"Miss Cranstan. Your nursery maid."

"I know who she is: my *former* nursery maid."

"Miss Cranstan has served my family for many years—first as nursemaid to my daughter, then as companion to both my wife and daughter. She is virtually a member of the Mortimer family. Your turning her off without cause has greatly upset the Mortimer women, especially my daughter."

Jeremy maintained the same chilly tone. "And you have come here to . . . ?"

"To see that you hire her back."

"Why would I do that?" Jeremy was torn between anger at the man's sheer nerve and amused curiosity about just how far he might go.

"Primarily to maintain felicity and harmony in your household in future. Take it from me, my boy, an English wife likes to handle these matters herself."

Jeremy, in an effort to maintain a semblance of civility, paused before responding, then said, "First of all, sir, I am not your 'boy.' Secondly, your advice would be relevant, though hardly welcomed, if I had—or when I have—an English wife. Until such time, while I appreciate that you feel you have a concerted interest in my affairs, I assure you that I can manage to deal with what goes on under my own roof without outside assistance." He paused, then added, "For the record, I do not make such decisions about staff members without cause."

Mortimer grimaced and seemed uncertain how to react. Then his jaws tightened visibly and he said, "I thought that might be your view of the matter, my lord, but, under the circumstances, such an intransigent position is truly not in your best interests, is it?"

Feeling his own jaws tighten, Jeremy refused to respond. He stood. "Was there anything else, sir?"

"Not today."

The knight took the not-so-subtle hint and departed, leaving Jeremy shaking his head in wonder at the sheer nerve of this particular neighbor.

CHAPTER 12

Midsummer had been much celebrated in the town of Kenrick long before a Tudor monarch had made a grateful follower the first Earl of Kenrick.

Nobody knew the exact origins of the holiday, but legend had it that faeries danced in circles this night and the town's oldest and most superstitious folk swore to marvelous miracles and strange acts of supernatural vengeance on or near this date in the distant past. Most people dismissed these tales and devoted themselves to the serious business of having fun—and watching their neighbors do so as well. The celebration was a daylong affair, starting with an early-morning church service, proceeding to footraces and a treasure hunt for the youngsters. It also included picnicking on the green and culminated in the Midsummer Ball sponsored by the town fathers.

Jeremy explained all this to Mrs. Arthur one morning when she conferred with him after being plagued with questions by the staff, particularly the younger employees. The earl and his housekeeper were strolling back from the stables where they had watched fondly as Ned and Cassie showed off their riding skills. Captain Clemson and Robert had joined them for a time and been suitably impressed with the children's skills before going out riding themselves.

A light rain had fallen in the night, but the day promised to be a fine one. Jeremy drank in the clean freshness. And with it, he caught a whiff of the lilac-woodsy scent he associated with the woman walking beside him. If he buried his face in that enticing spot between her ear and her shoulder, would he get more than a whiff? A well-deserved rebuff would be more like it, he thought ruefully. Her voice brought him back.

"Midsummer in this part of Yorkshire sounds like a joyous occasion."

"It is," he replied. "And you may put staff doubts to rest—if, indeed, any doubts remain. Kenrick always participates."

"The young people will be pleased."

"And you? Will you dance at the Midsummer Ball, Mrs. Arthur?"

"I, my lord? A ball?"

"Londoners would view it as more of a country assembly than a ball. The Midsummer celebrations here are very democratic—all of them. For one day of the year, we manage to put aside distinctions of social rank."

"Really?" She stopped and stared at him.

"You find it strange?" he asked with a grin. "Perhaps it offends the sensibilities of rank and decorum you and Aunt Elinor value so highly?"

"Now you are deliberately making fun of me, my lord." Her eyes twinkled merrily. "Tsk, tsk. Using your rank to browbeat a lowly servant."

"Is that not one of the privileges of rank?"

She laughed and conceded. "Perhaps it is."

Delighted that she had responded in kind to his teasing tone, he wanted to hug her, to kiss her, but decorously maintained his distance. Damn decorum anyway!

As they walked on, he said, "You did not answer my question. Will you dance at the Midsummer Ball?"

"I think not. Surely someone must stay here at the Hall."

"Wilkins will handle that. He tells me he is too old for such frivolity."

"I cannot leave my son unattended for such a long time."

"It will be only a few hours," he assured her. "Children join the festivities during the day. In fact, many activities are precisely for the younger folk. One of the maids will be paid extra to see to their care during the ball."

"I—I'm not sure—"

"You deserve a break, Mrs. Arthur, and I intend to see that you get it."

"Thank you, my lord, but—"

"No *buts*. It's settled."

Jeremy could not help wondering at a trace of anxiety in her expression. Most servants would be eager for a break in routine. But then she was not "most servants," was she?

When he had taken time to think about her—and lately that had occurred far more often than it should—he found anomalies that simply baffled him. There was her well-trained voice, for instance. Her speech—both diction and accent—were definitely upper class. He recalled her interest in Blake and Wordsworth. Chance comments of Aunt Elinor's and bits of conversation he had overheard showed a level of understanding and education beyond that of the average housekeeper, even one who had served a duke. And that was another thing: Which duke? When?

And what was the nature of her relationship with his own brother? Robert had clearly been surprised to find her here; just as clearly they had a special friendship of mutual, equal respect. He was sure it did not go any deeper than friendship—yet. But perhaps in time . . . He frowned at that idea.

She did not fit any conventional idea of a housekeeper, yet she performed her duties in an exemplary fashion; she got on well with the entire staff; and—and too many things did not add up. Should he challenge her? Or would she eventually trust him as she seemed to trust his brother?

Kate avoided making a decision about attending the Midsummer celebration. In fact, she wondered if she even had a choice. Lord Kenrick had made his wishes known and he obviously felt he was granting her some sort of boon in urging her to take part. To refuse outright would raise questions she did not want to answer. Instinctively, she felt safer at Kenrick Hall. She sought Robert's advice on the matter one afternoon when she knew he was alone in the library. He invited her to join him on a long couch where he sat on one end facing her, his arm resting along the back. Fully aware of the impropriety of the housekeeper doing so, she occupied the other corner, twisting her hands in worry.

"I can't see that you have much choice if you continue to refuse to take Jeremy into your confidence," was Robert's blunt response when she laid out her concerns.

"But what if I am recognized?"

"There is not much likelihood of that happening. Did you not tell me you'd never been north of Coventry before?"

"True."

"Our town of Kenrick is not exactly on a main thoroughfare—nor is it much of a metropolis," Robert said.

"But with thousands of demobilized soldiers unleashed on England now that Napoleon is no longer a threat . . ." Her voice trailed off.

"There were very few men from Yorkshire in our regiment. I am not saying it is impossible you would be exposed—just highly unlikely."

She nodded.

"Besides," he added, with a gesture at her attire, "people see what they expect to see. You are the housekeeper at Kenrick Hall—mobcap and all. Though, you might draw attention in a fashionable ball gown."

Just then the library door opened and Lord Kenrick walked in. Kate quickly got to her feet.

"Am I interrupting?"

"No, my lord. I was just leaving," she said.

"A fashionable ball gown? What was that all about?" Jeremy asked his brother when the door closed behind her.

"Kate was just concerned about the Midsummer festivities."

"I thought I explained them to her rather thoroughly," he said, as he rifled through a drawer in his desk.

"You know how women are—afraid she won't fit in."

Jeremy grinned. "I was not aware, little brother, that you were such an expert on the fair sex."

"Me—and Don Juan."

"Don't tell me you've become a follower of that exhibitionist, Byron."

"Not him, but his poetry. He has some really fine work—and it's very popular with the ladies!"

Jeremy laughed, but he was certain that he had interrupted something of more significance than feminine nerves.

The day after her discussion with Robert, Kate still had reservations about the Midsummer festivities, but these were quickly pushed aside by a weightier matter: her son's education. Lord Kenrick asked to meet with her after the midday meal. Once again, the two of them occupied the comfortable barrel chairs in the library. And once again, he leaned back casually, far more at ease than she who had fretted inwardly since receiving his summons.

"I hope you have not thought me remiss in the matter of a nursery maid," he began.

"No, my lord."

"As a matter of fact, I have given the matter a great deal of thought and discussed it with my aunt, but I should like your view of the matter as well."

"I am flattered, my lord."

"You needn't be. My motives are somewhat self-serving."

She raised her brows. "I don't understand."

"First of all, I am aware that Cranstan's departure has necessitated some additional duties for several people and that you have been saddled with the logistics of juggling their assignments."

"It has not been so *very* bad, but—"

He put up a hand. "Hear me out."

"Yes, my lord." She settled back in the chair and with a gesture made a light show of giving him the floor.

"I also wish you to be satisfied with your situation at Kenrick."

"Oh, but I am, my lord."

"More satisfied, then."

She was quiet as he went on.

"I am told that you are yourself seeing to lessons for your son."

"Yes, I am. But I assure you, my lord, Ned's lessons do not interfere with my duties."

"I did not mean to imply that they did." He sounded impatient and he frowned, but his grin and laughing tone belied his stern words. "Suppose you stop jumping to conclusions and allow me to finish."

"Yes, my lord." Wanting to laugh at his tone, she tried to sound contrite.

"Instead of a new nursery maid, I intend to hire a governess to provide lessons for my daughter and it occurred to me that not only would Cassie enjoy her lessons more if they were shared, but that she might learn more too."

"Shared with whom?"

"Your son, of course. He's the only other child in this house that I know of." He paused, then continued, "I told you my motives were self-serving. This arrangement would also free you to devote more attention to the ongoing needs of the Hall and the staff."

She sat in stunned silence for a moment, then said slowly, "What you are proposing is most unusual. A housekeeper's son taking lessons with an earl's child? It—it is simply unheard of!"

"I will admit to its being out of the ordinary—"

She laughed. "Extraordinary in the extreme: a housekeeper's son—"

"Ah, but an extraordinary housekeeper and an extraordinary son." His tone turned serious. "Your Ned truly is extraordinarily bright. He should have every chance to realize his potential."

"I do not mean to be impertinent, my lord, but are you quite sure your years in America have not rendered you unfit for English society?"

He chuckled. "Well, you *are* being impertinent—but you may have a point. Still, what do you think of the idea?"

"I think it a very generous offer and that I would be a fool to refuse it."

"Good. I have already set the wheels in motion. In a few weeks I shall interview possible candidates for governess and I should like you to be present when I do so."

"As you wish, my lord."

"There is one other related matter," he said.

She waited.

He cleared his throat. "Uh—I confess to breaching certain matters of protocol. I—uh—I had Wilkins show me your quarters the other day."

"You . . . ?"

He rushed on. "They were designed for a single woman. In a house this size, we have— what? Twenty? Twenty-five bed chambers?—not counting servant's quarters. There is no reason you and Ned should share one."

"I like having him close by," she said weakly.

"Yes. But it would be better if he were near the schoolroom, too. There are at least seven chambers in the nursery wing. You may have adjoining chambers there. And you may retain use of the house-keeper quarters on the first floor as you see fit."

"That too is very generous of you, my lord. I—I hardly know what to say." She felt tears of gratitude gathering.

He stood abruptly. "Never mind. As I said: mostly quite self-serving. Effective immediately, by the way."

Kate also rose and held his gaze for a long moment, wanting to kiss him, and not just as a show of gratitude, she realized. She merely murmured sincere thanks and excused herself.

Overwhelmed, she hurried to her room to sort out this turn of events. Good heavens! The man had no idea what a gift he had just given her. Just as she was thinking Ned's education would suffer ter-ribly so long as she was a housekeeper, Kenrick had offered a perfect solution. Well, perhaps not *perfect*, but certainly workable for a year or two. Then—who knew? One thing was certain: Lord Kenrick in-tended her and Ned to remain here on a long-term basis. Eventually Phillips and Lawrence would find a proper school for Ned. When it came to that. Meanwhile, there was still the potential threat of that Bow Street Runner.

Three days later, Kate found the Midsummer festivities more or less exactly as Lord Kenrick had described them. All available car-riages and wagons from the Hall itself and the nearby home farm were called into service to transport the earl, his guests, and most of his household. Kate and Ned joined the other staff members on one of the farm wagons, but once they arrived in town, people scattered to find friends they might not have seen in weeks or months.

Initially somewhat shy in the crowds, Ned and Lady Cassandra gravitated toward each other, pulling their indulgent parents along with them. Captain Clemson and Robert trailed behind them.

"It's like a medieval fair!" Kate exclaimed on seeing the array of colorful tents and booths set up to sell cider, ale, sausages on buns, and sweetmeats.

"It isn't all fun and games, though," Robert pointed out. "See those folks over there? They are seeking new positions—carrying emblems of their trade."

Clemson said, "Ah, yes. There's a shepherd's crook. The fellow next to him is wearing a carpenter's belt."

"That young woman must be a dairymaid; she carries a milk pail," Kate said. She was torn between admiring their ingenuity and being grateful she had been spared such scrutiny in her own quest for employment.

Cassie and Ned were fascinated by a man with a monkey on a leash that danced as its owner played a concertina. They moved on to a larger gathering of people around a small, curtained stage. It was a Punch-and-Judy puppet show that brought forth laughter and giggles from all ages.

After a while, Robert said, "Clemson and I are going to check out the horse races. Maybe place a bet."

"All right," Kenrick responded. "Squire Dennison's black is said to be the odds-on favorite. And Mortimer has a chestnut he is proud of."

"No Kenrick cattle in the running, though," Robert said with regret. "Too bad."

"Not for several years, I'm told," his brother said. "But one day . . ."

When Clemson and Robert had taken their leave, Kate felt a twinge of nostalgia as she and her employer and their children wandered along. Almost like a family, she mused, but quickly quelled that thought.

They paused to watch a juggler perform before a sizable group.

"We can't see," Ned said. "Come on, Cass." He grabbed Cassie's hand and pushed through the group to stand in the front with a number of other children, leaving Kate and Lord Kenrick on the fringes.

Kate glanced up at him. "It appears we have been deserted, my lord."

"So we have been. Left quite alone in a sea of people." He gazed into her eyes and smiled. Something almost tangible passed between them, as intimate as a kiss.

The moment was abruptly shattered by a female voice.

"Oh, Lord Kenrick, how wonderful to see you!"

Kate turned to see Charlotte Mortimer accompanied by her parents and Miss Cranstan. Kate dipped a brief curtsy to the group and was promptly ignored as Miss Mortimer and her father greeted Lord Kenrick effusively with a barrage of small talk about what a fine day it was. The other two women gazed about them, refusing to make eye contact with Kate.

Having exhausted the profound topic of the weather, Charlotte

Mortimer looked from Lord Kenrick to Kate and smiled, her expression displaying nothing of warmth or cheer. "La, my lord. I see you do take seriously the unspoken rule that this holiday be 'classless.' Such gracious condescension, my lord—but what a blessing it comes only once a year, could you not agree?"

Kate would have liked to give the woman a proper set down, but held her housekeeper tongue.

"Oh, I don't know," Kenrick said. "It seems to me that respect and conviviality among people—not to mention good manners—can only be positive factors at any time."

"I quite agree," Miss Mortimer said, just as though she had not really registered his comment. She glanced pointedly at Kate. "But, in general, society functions best if we all stick to our own kind."

Sir Eldridge looked from his daughter to Lord Kenrick and back. He wore a slight frown. "Come, Charlotte, I do not want to miss the race."

"Yes, Father." She tapped Lord Kenrick playfully on the arm. "I shall save a dance for you tonight, my lord. Or two, perhaps." She leaned closer so her breast touched his arm briefly and lowered her still very audible voice. "But only two. After all, we do not want to rush things, do we?" Her glance at Kate held a trace of triumph—or challenge.

Lord Kenrick was prevented from responding as Ned and Cassie rejoined their parents. Kenrick bowed toward the Mortimers, who took their cue and left.

"Papa! Did you see the juggler? Wasn't he wonderful?" Cassie said.

"I want to learn to juggle things," Ned said.

"Me too!"

"You must start with only three items," Kate cautioned, welcoming the shift in atmosphere as Ned and Cassie replaced the Mortimer party.

"Soft ones—not plates and knives," Lord Kenrick added. Did he too welcome the change?

"I shall make you some small cloth balls," Kate said.

"For me too?" Cassie begged.

"Of course."

During the rest of the day, neither Kate nor Lord Kenrick brought up the topic of the chance meeting with the Mortimers—if, indeed, it was a chance meeting, Kate thought.

When they had all returned to the Hall and turned the children over to the maid who would see to their care, members of the Kenrick household changed into evening attire. Jeremy, his brother, and their guest, along with Aunt Elinor, waited in the drawing room for Mrs. Arthur.

"Now, remember," Lady Elinor said, "I am there for the music and a bit of gossip. You sit me down in a likely spot and my friends will find me."

"Absolutely not!" Robert scoffed. "I claim at least one dance with you."

Lady Elinor laughed. "I would not want to make all the young ladies jealous."

When his housekeeper entered the room, she quite took Jeremy's breath away. She wore the customary mobcap—Jeremy often thought of it as armor of a sort—but instead of a gray dress such as she usually wore, she had on a lavender gown—silk, Jeremy guessed—with lace of a darker shade at elbow-length sleeves and a low neckline that revealed a hint of cleavage. She wore white gloves.

"I say! Lady Arthur!" Robert blurted. "You look splendid!"

She turned abruptly and frowned at him. "Thank you, Captain Chilton, but please—we really mustn't continue that joke."

"Oh. Yes. I forgot. Old habits, you know."

"You do look very fine, Mrs. Arthur," Captain Clemson said with a bow.

"I concur. Fully," Jeremy said. "Except for that infernal mobcap. You certainly may dispense with it for the evening."

"I—I am not so sure. Would that not be going too far? Lady Elinor?"

"It's Midsummer," Lady Elinor said. "Our little world goes mad only one day of the year. And Kenrick is the lord of the manor. Best do as he wishes."

Mrs. Arthur reluctantly removed her badge of office and laid it on a nearby table. Jeremy drew in another breath. Her dark blond hair was arranged in a thick, shiny braid from the crown of her head to the nape of her neck. Streaks of lighter blond also caught the light and soft curls that shaped her face.

"Much better," Jeremy said, holding her gaze momentarily. He wondered what all that hair would look like strewn about on a pillow, then mentally kicked himself.

She turned to the other two men, who were dressed in their regimental uniforms. "I must say, Captain Chilton and Captain Clemson, you bring back memories for me."

"Like the prince's ball in Lisbon, eh?" Robert said. "You were surely the belle of that ball."

A look of fear flashed in her eyes. Jeremy might have missed it had he not been staring at her. She looked away and waved her hands dismissively. "Another time, another place."

Storing away this observation to examine later, Jeremy decided to rescue her. "Shall we go?"

As was to be expected, the arrival of Lord Kenrick's party at the ball caused quite a stir. Two soldiers in their resplendent uniforms caused flurries among many female hearts. Jeremy was aware that he himself cut a respectable figure in the stark black and white of formal evening wear, but it was Mrs. Arthur who raised several eyebrows, and he was determined that she not be subjected to undue notice or criticism. To this end, he made sure that he escorted his aunt into the assembly room and Mrs. Arthur appeared on Robert's arm. He admitted to himself a twinge of envy of his brother at this arrangement. She then sat on the sidelines near Lady Elinor.

The Chilton brothers and their guest commanded so much attention that they were scarcely allowed to sit out a single dance. Jeremy noted that Mrs. Arthur twirled about the floor nearly as much as he and the two captains. Telling himself he had no right to such feelings, he quelled what he readily recognized as sheer jealousy at seeing her on the arms of others.

He dutifully danced with Charlotte Mortimer, who was flirtatious and polite—and determined in her goal of snagging him for a second dance, which he knew would cause tongues to wag as nothing else could. They chatted of inconsequential matters until the movements of the dance caused them to intersect with Mrs. Arthur and Robert, her partner of the moment.

"Your housekeeper is making a spectacle of herself, my lord," Miss Mortimer said.

"I see nothing untoward in her behavior," he said.

"All those different partners. And that gown she is wearing is sadly out of date, but it was certainly not purchased on a house-keeper's wages!" Miss Mortimer said. "Unless, of course—"

Jeremy interrupted before she could go wherever she was headed with this thought. "Household staff are often given items of clothing by their employers, are they not? The garment Miss Cranstan is wearing is remarkably like one you wore last autumn." He stopped short of commenting on the number of partners she herself had had.

"I am flattered that you remembered a gown I wore. That is a very good sign, my lord." She gave him a coy smile.

Jeremy was glad when the dance ended and he could return her to the care of her parents, who stood talking with Squire Dennison and his wife and daughter. Robert and Clemson joined the group and Jeremy introduced them to the others. Miss Mortimer continued to stand close to Jeremy, her hand lightly—possessively—on his arm. He thought he saw a subtle communication pass between Mortimer and his daughter, then Mortimer excused himself and walked toward the musicians. The group continued ballroom chitchat, with a good deal of fluttering of eyelashes from the young women and smiling goodwill all around.

During a lull in the conversation, Robert bowed slightly to the squire's daughter. "Miss Dennison, I wonder if you would favor me with the next dance?"

She laughed and said, "Of course. But, good heavens, Robert, I'm still Delia—the same girl you rescued from that apple tree!"

"Um. Not exactly the same," he said appreciatively. "Dilly Delia managed quite a transformation while I was off fighting for king and country."

She blushed prettily, but said with another laugh, "Ran away to play soldier, you mean."

Jeremy turned to Clemson. "I say, Clemson, if you are free for the next dance, Miss Mortimer is a marvelous partner."

Clemson accepted the suggestion and bowed to her. "Miss Mortimer?"

She gave Jeremy an oblique glance and emitted a brittle tinkle of a laugh, but her eyes were a hard stare. "La! Can you fathom this? The man is trying to get rid of me," she said to the group in a forced teasing tone. "Well, so be it, Captain."

"Kenrick's loss is my gain," the captain said gallantly, extending his arm.

"Quite so," she said in a tight little voice and exchanged a look of chagrin with her father as he rejoined the group.

Having watched Mrs. Arthur take the floor with both Robert and Clemson as well as the footman, Thomas, and even his coachman, Jeremy approached her himself and bowed. Only when they stood on the dance floor and heard the music did he realize his error. It was a waltz.

While it was true that the waltz had made it even to the back-country of Yorkshire, it was also true that many country folk considered it quite scandalous. If she had drawn censure before, this dance might fan the tongues even more. "A waltz," he said. "Are you up for this?"

"Oh, yes. The German regiment brought it to the Peninsula early on."

"That isn't exactly what I meant," he said. "Too late now." He took her hand in his and put his other hand at her waist as she rested her other hand on his shoulder. He closed his eyes momentarily. My God! This was so right. So absolutely right.

"What did you mean?" she asked.

"The waltz has yet to gain universal approval," he said, regaining his inner composure, but still keenly aware of the woman in his arms.

"Yes. I know. Silly, is it not?"

He laughed and deliberately pulled her closer in a swirl of the dance. "Mrs. Arthur," he said, feigning surprise, "I do believe there is a bit of the rebel in you."

She smiled. "Perhaps. My father would certainly have agreed with that assessment."

"Really? There must be a story behind that comment. Would you care to share it?"

Although she did not falter in the least, he sensed a sudden stillness in her. She answered seriously. "Perhaps I will—someday."

"I shall hold you to that." He kept his tone light and changed the subject, but stored away yet another clue in the ongoing mystery of the elegant housekeeper.

For Jeremy that dance was the high point of the evening and he was sure Mrs. Arthur had enjoyed it too, but the evening was to present a spoiler of sorts—another encounter with a Mortimer. This time it was the father, whom Jeremy had come to view as his nemesis. Jeremy was at the refreshment table to fetch a glass of punch for his aunt when Sir Eldridge accosted him.

"A word, Lord Kenrick." It was more of an order than a polite request.

"Certainly, sir." The two stepped to the sidelines.

Mortimer cleared his throat. "That scene—you waltzing with your housekeeper—well, it was not in the best of taste, now was it? Neither my daughter nor I should like to see a repeat of such behavior."

"I beg your pardon." Jeremy riveted a steely glare on the man.

Mortimer averted his gaze. "What I meant to say, Kenrick, is this: Your fobbing her off on your friend and then waltzing—waltzing!—with that Arthur woman hurt Charlotte's feelings. I do not like to see my little girl unhappy." The last sentence ended on a note of threat.

For a moment, Jeremy was speechless.

Mortimer went on in a slightly more conciliatory tone. "Now, I'm sure you intended no harm, but, son, you just don't seem to realize that English women are not like those you knew in the colonies. Our ladies are more fragile, more delicate."

Jeremy did not want to make a scene, especially one that might end with Mrs. Arthur's name being bandied about. Finally, he found his voice. His jaw clenched, he spoke in a quiet, distinct tone that could not be heard even ten feet away, but that would be unmistakable to his immediate listener.

"You, sir, are too presumptuous by half! I am *not* your son, nor have I encouraged you in any way to address me as such. But this is not the first time you have had the unmitigated gall to advise me on matters in which my own father would never have presumed to meddle. I will thank you not to overreach so again."

Mortimer's face turned a fiery red, but Jeremy did not allow him to speak. "I would not intentionally hurt a woman in any way, but I am *not* responsible for your daughter's feelings—nor yours either. Now, if you will excuse me." Ignoring the sheer rage of the older man, Jeremy turned back to the punch bowl for Aunt Elinor's drink.

He struggled to hide his fury, but he should have known his aunt would sense any change in his demeanor.

"What is wrong, Jeremy?"

He sat in the empty chair next to her. "Nothing serious. I just had an unpleasant conversation with Sir Eldridge Mortimer."

"Oh." There was a wealth of understanding in that single syllable. "Then you are aware of the rumors he is fomenting."

"I have an idea of them." Jeremy did not elaborate.

He was glad when the Midsummer Ball was over for another year.

CHAPTER 13

When the Kenrick party returned to the Hall, the ladies immediately excused themselves, Lady Elinor to her chamber accompanied by her maid, and Mrs. Arthur to her new bedchamber in the nursery wing. Jeremy, Robert, and Captain Clemson settled in the smaller family drawing room for a nightcap. All three men had loosened their neck cloths as they sprawled on the most comfortable chairs. A low fire in the fireplace and soft light from a lamp lent a warm glow to the room.

"I enjoyed this day even more than I expected to," Robert announced, accepting the brandy Jeremy offered him, "even if I did lose that bet on the squire's black. I'd quite forgot what fun we had when we were growing up!"

"Country fairs are often as enjoyable as a grand state holiday in London," Clemson said. "Especially if the local females are both fair and friendly."

"Speaking of female pulchritude," Robert said with a raised eyebrow and a grin directed at his brother, "what is the story with you and the Mortimer chit, Jeremy?"

"There is no story," Jeremy said.

Robert elevated the inquisitive brow even higher. "Uh-huh. Well, she and her father seem to have a different view. She said something about one day welcoming me to Kenrick Hall. And her father hinted at the possibility of an 'interesting announcement.' So—have you made an offer or not?"

"I have not."

"I thought you would surely have mentioned it if you had," Robert said.

"She is a fine-looking woman—very fair indeed," Clemson observed.

"Yes, she is," Jeremy conceded, "but my acquaintance with her is somewhat limited. There was an arrangement between her and Charles."

"Really? I never heard of it," Robert said. "It never made it to the papers. Even in the Peninsula, we got the papers. Sometimes weeks late, but we got them. And read them to tatters."

"It hadn't reached that stage yet," Jeremy said.

"So she transfers her affections from Charles to you just like that?" Robert snapped his fingers and laughed.

"Sounds biblical—medieval, at least," Clemson commented.

Jeremy sipped his brandy, then said slowly, "I'm not sure that affections actually fit into the picture. Suffice it to say, there are other considerations."

"Are you thinking of offering for her?" Robert's tone showed only curiosity.

"I did not say that," Jeremy said. He ran his hand through his hair. "Let's just say the situation is . . . uh . . . complicated."

"Well," Clemson said, stifling a yawn, "I think I'll leave you two to sort out the matter of Cupid's arrows and all. I need to get an early start in the morning. Still a three-day journey to the Highlands."

Jeremy and Robert bade him good night, then settled back in their chairs. There was a long silence.

Finally, Robert said, "How complicated?"

Jeremy hesitated. How could he satisfy Robert's curiosity without burdening his younger brother with his own problems? "Sir Eldridge and Father were negotiating marriage settlements when Charles and Edgar drowned."

Robert frowned. "Charles was not involved in the negotiating?"

"I gather he was agreeable to whatever they decided."

"Probably didn't care. He had his London ladybird safely tucked away."

Jeremy looked at Robert questioningly.

"Ton gossip spreads far and wide. But I actually met her once. Pretty. An opera dancer."

"I see," Jeremy said slowly, still wondering how much to tell his brother.

Robert sat up straight. "I think I see, too." Jeremy glanced at him, but did not respond. "Back to you, big brother. Are you engaged in marriage settlements? Or do I overstep?"

"No. And no. After all, you *are* the heir."

Robert snorted. "Temporarily—until you produce a real one."

Jeremy waved a dismissive hand. "For however long, you are it. So . . . you have a right to know how things stand." With these words and a myriad of thoughts and emotions behind them, Jeremy made his decision. He explained the circumstances surrounding the Chilton family's precarious hold on the earldom.

"Good God, Jer. I knew the situation had deteriorated, but I had no idea it was so bad." Robert shook his head. "And Mortimer holds *all* the debt?"

"He does now. Bought it all up even before those unfortunate deaths in our family."

"Bought his knighthood as well, according to local gossip." When Jeremy cocked his head at this, Robert grinned and added, "You thought all those rides Clemson and I have taken were just for sport, eh? I have been reacquainting myself with my boyhood home. And the people."

"Have you now?"

"Yes. And I must say it does look better than it did the last time I saw it."

"Even without a steward, eh?"

"I heard about that too. You are well rid of that one. Stevens was lazy as sin. I never did understand why Father kept him on—except as a drinking crony."

"That was about it," Jeremy said.

"Kenrick is a lot to handle without a steward. How are you doing?"

"The truth?"

Robert nodded.

Jeremy swept his hand through his hair again; his tone was bleak. "I'm in over my head. I had to let Stevens go, but I'm finding it very difficult to manage on my own. It's a vast change from the fur trade in North America! The mill and the mine, not to mention thousands of acres of farm and grazing land. And did you know there was a brewery? *That* came as a surprise to me."

"A brewery? I never knew of it."

"A brewery. Apparently it came to Father as part of *my* mother's dowry."

"Is it profitable?"

"Not very. Like everything else, it has been sadly neglected. But I think it could be. Phillips thinks so too. I have him discreetly looking into the matter of a new steward—though I can hardly offer the sort of salary a truly competent man could command. So, for the time being, I muddle through." It sounded hopeless to his own ears now that the words were hanging in the air between them.

"Has Phillips come up with anyone?"

"Not yet. He did suggest that someone might be willing to accept a more modest salary for a share in possible annual profits."

"That's an interesting concept," Robert said.

"I thought so too, but so far, no takers. Not a one."

Robert looked thoughtful as he lifted his glass and drained the last of his brandy. Jeremy found the ensuing silence pleasantly comfortable. It had been a long time since he had shared simple companionship with a friend. That this friend was a favorite relative was an added boon.

Finally, Robert said, "Would you mind if I had a look at your books tomorrow?"

Jeremy was surprised. "To what end?"

"Well, you know I'm looking for gainful employment . . ." Robert's response trailed off.

"You think to become a steward?"

"The Kenrick steward, perhaps—if you are amenable."

"But—a steward?"

Robert emitted a rueful chuckle. "We younger sons have to make our way somehow. Army life has not the attraction it once had."

Jeremy sat in stunned silence. This was a turn that had simply never occurred to him. "Hmm. Steward? Are you sure?"

"Look, Jeremy. It is precisely what I've been doing for the last five years and more: logistics and procurement. I even have a letter of commendation from the Duke of Wellington himself."

Jeremy stood and set his glass on a nearby table. "If you are serious, it is certainly something we can discuss. God knows, I would welcome you with open arms, but I cannot urge you to board what may well be a sinking ship."

Robert too, rose and gave his brother a gentle punch on the shoulder. "Let's see how much water she's taking on before we abandon ship."

For a long while Jeremy lay in the huge four-poster bed of the master bedchamber, staring at the canopy above him. The brocade did not seem so faded in the faint light from the fireplace. He marveled at the changes life had thrown at him since Phillips's man, Logan, had caught up with him in an Arapaho camp. He had traded the casual freedom of the American frontier for the faded opulence of old England. Sometimes he wondered if he had made the right decision—but, then, there had never been much choice in the matter, had there? One did not abrogate responsibilities to people who had served Kenrick earls for three centuries! Still, his efforts might be for naught. Moreover, he was not convinced the transition had been good for Cassie. Her life too, had changed profoundly. To what extent had he sacrificed his daughter on the altar of familial duty?

He sighed and at last slept better than he had in months, though his last conscious thought was a vision of Mrs. Arthur laughing up at Robert as they danced at the Midsummer Ball. Was she the reason his brother thought of staying on at Kenrick?

Lord Kenrick's housekeeper was not enjoying the same peaceful slumber as her employer. Kate had looked in on her son before retiring to her own chamber. Ned had kicked off his bedcovers; she drew them back over him and kissed his sleep-warm cheek. Impulsively, she went down the hall to repeat the process with Lady Cassandra. She was well aware of what she was doing: postponing a clear view of this day and the evening.

Despite her earlier reservations about attending the midsummer festivities, she had thoroughly enjoyed them. She readily admitted that the highlight of the ball—indeed, of the day—had been her dance with Lord Kenrick. She savored every nuance of that waltz—from the spicy scent of his shaving soap to the warm humor in his blue eyes. Even through the fabric of their gloves, she had felt the warmth of his touch, relished the closeness. She could not ignore the sheer chemistry between them, even as she cautioned herself repeatedly against it. Had he been a good husband? What kind of wife had he chosen? All anyone seemed to know of her was that she was part Indian. But what kind of woman had she been? And just why should any of that matter to his housekeeper?

She shook her head yet again. "All right, Cinderella, you've had your ball. Now come back to earth and be sensible." Nothing—nothing—must jeopardize her position at Kenrick Hall.

She turned her thoughts to other aspects of the evening. She had, of course, enjoyed dancing with Robert and sharing a bit of refreshment with him. It was nice to be able to drop all pretense with at least one person who knew the real Kate. Nor had she minded sitting on the sidelines with Lady Elinor. She recalled snippets of conversation she had overheard there. The vicar's wife had been filling Lady Elinor in on neighbors attending the ball.

"As is usually the case," Mrs. Packwood had said, "there are three or four people here I simply do not know. Two gentlemen and a married couple who are staying at the inn. I believe the couple are seeking a property to rent. One of the other gentlemen, a Mr. Hoskins, spent an hour with my husband yesterday. Just wanted to familiarize himself with the community, he said. Nice man."

Mrs. Packwood prattled on, describing for Lady Elinor the ladies' dresses and commenting on the behavior of people they both knew. The vicar's wife was not inclined to be suspicious of anyone, but Kate had felt her entire being freeze at these words. A stranger asking questions? She could not quell a frisson of fear and tried surreptitiously to see who it was that Mrs. Packwood was talking about, but she was herself too much of a stranger to be able to tell. In any event, guests of the inn were customarily included, were they not? Perhaps she was just borrowing trouble.

All the next day, though Kate knew Lord Kenrick and Robert had seen Clemson on his way to the Highlands, she saw little of the Chilton brothers. They were sequestered in the library until late afternoon. A footman who delivered fortifying pots of tea reported they were "studyin' the books with lots o' notes and columns of figgers."

The next morning, Lord Kenrick called in his butler and the housekeeper to announce that he and his brother would be away for a few days inspecting various properties and enterprises. He gave them the particulars of his itinerary in case of an emergency, and then they were off. To Kate, Kenrick Hall suddenly seemed empty, despite a staff of dozens of people.

While she assiduously discouraged servants' gossip about their employer, Kate knew there was a good deal of speculation and apprehension among the staff about the financial state of the earldom. After all, what would happen to *them* were there to be a turnover at the top? She suspected the servants had a far better understanding of the matter than his lordship might wish them to have. They had no details, of course, but they "knew" that "that upstart cit, Mortimer" held something over his lordship's head, probably having to do with the previous earl's profligate ways.

Kate was human enough to worry privately about how these matters might affect her and her son. However, there was nothing she could do, was there? Wait and see. But uncertainty was unnerving. She understood all too well the feelings of other staff members. And she recognized an added dimension to her own uncertainty: this chemistry or undercurrent of attraction between her and her employer. She engaged privately in an ongoing argument with herself.

Your feelings are entirely improper!

One does not control feelings *easily.*

Where do you expect such feelings to take you?

Nowhere.

Oh, really?

They can go nowhere. Once he knows the truth—and he will eventually—his disgust will surely spell finis to what might have been.

So treasure what you have while you have it.

No. I need to put this foolishness out of mind and concentrate on Ned. The possibility of losing my son is very real.

One day at a time, my girl. One day at a time.

Meanwhile, she went about her duties of supervising housemaids in the everyday upkeep of a large house: sweeping, dusting, making beds, cleaning fireplaces, polishing furniture, planning meals. Wilkins and his band of footmen saw to polishing brass and silver, serving at meals, and sundry heavier duties, but Kate also oversaw the laundry, the dairy, and the kitchen. The gardeners and stable hands, who ordinarily answered to a steward, now took orders directly from his lordship.

In addition, Kate continued to make time for Lady Elinor and for both the children now. The two women moved on from Miss Austen to Sir Walter Scott. Determined to instill in her son her own love of literature, Kate had for years read or told stories to Ned at bedtime— fairy tales, Bible stories, myths. Now, Lady Cassandra happily joined this ritual. Kate sat on a couch in the schoolroom with a child, already dressed for bed, curled comfortably under either arm.

That was precisely where Lord Kenrick found them on the evening of his return from the inspection tour with his brother.

As usual when he'd been gone for awhile, Jeremy missed his daughter profoundly. He and Robert had pushed their horses hard to arrive home as darkness was laying claim to the land. Knowing it was already Cassie's bedtime, he rushed up to his daughter's bedchamber.

She wasn't there.

He heard voices from the schoolroom and stood outside and listened for a few minutes. Mrs. Arthur was reading a story apparently about animals, for it was punctuated here and there with appropriate animal sounds and accompanying childish giggles.

"No. No, Mama. Let Cassie do the owl," Ned said.

"Very well. She does an owl much better than I," Mrs. Arthur said with a laugh.

"Talks-with-Animals showed me," Cassie explained and produced a perfect owl hoot. "I can do a squirrel too." She immediately demonstrated.

Jeremy smiled to himself and just stood there, relishing the freedom and pure joy he heard in his daughter's voice.

Finally, there was a pause.

He heard Mrs. Arthur say, "All right. Off to bed, you two."

"Just one more, please?" Ned begged.

"Please?" Cassie added.

"No more stories tonight," Mrs. Arthur said firmly.

"A rime, then?" Ned suggested.

"The Psalm we've been learning," his mother countered and began, "The Lord is my shepherd . . ." and both children haltingly echoed her.

Jeremy waited until they were finished, then pushed into the room.

"Papa!" Cassie squealed in delight. She disengaged herself from the housekeeper's arm and ran to her father, who gathered her to him, sweeping her off her feet. He savored the feel of those little arms around his neck and the scent of the soap from her bath.

"I missed you, Papa."

"And I missed you, Poppet."

"I rode Toby every day," she babbled. "An' Ned learned me the maze an' Petunia had kittens and Mrs. Jenkins said I could have one for my very own if you said I could. Can I, please? *Pleeease*?"

"We'll talk about it tomorrow," he said as he saw Mrs. Arthur and her son move toward the door.

"Welcome home, my lord," the housekeeper said.

"It's good to be home," he replied, suddenly aware that the scene he had stumbled upon here gave his comment an undercurrent of meaning he would not have thought possible even an hour ago.

"Good night, Cassie. My lord," Mrs. Arthur said.

"G'night," Ned echoed.

Cassie stiffened in her father's arms and reached a hand toward the housekeeper. "Wait. Aren't you going to tuck me in?" There was a note of hurt and longing in Cassie's voice.

Mrs. Arthur's look at Jeremy clearly sought his response. Feeling himself a bit of an outsider, he merely nodded. The four of them moved down the hall to Cassie's room where Jeremy stood at the door with his hand on Ned's shoulder as Mrs. Arthur tucked the little girl into bed, along with her favorite doll, the Native American–clad figure. Cassie's arm clung around the woman's neck as Mrs. Arthur kissed her cheek and murmured, "Sweet dreams, my dear."

The look she gave her employer was almost apologetic as she stepped away from Cassie's bed to allow Jeremy to bid his daughter good night. Mother and son left the room and when Jeremy left Cassie's room, Mrs. Arthur was coming from her son's room where, Jeremy assumed, she had repeated the "tucking in" ceremony. They both spoke at once.

"Mrs. Arthur—"

"My lord—"

He stopped and gestured for her to continue.

"I—it—it just sort of happened," she explained, sounding nervous. "Rosie prepares her ladyship for bed as I supervise Ned's bedtime, then we read a story and the children retire. I—I hope you have no objection."

"*N-no*. Why would I? My daughter is well cared for."

"Yes. She is."

As they stood there in the hallway, he wanted to prolong this moment alone with her. "What is this about a kitten?"

"Three weeks ago, the kitchen cat had five kittens under the back door stoop. She is now sharing them with the world and Lady Cassandra desperately wants one of them."

"She does? Why?"

"To love. To have as her own."

"The pony Toby is her own."

"She cannot cuddle a pony as she could a kitten."

"I am in unfamiliar territory here," Jeremy admitted. "As a mother, what do you think of the idea?"

She answered slowly, thoughtfully. "I think this little girl has been very lonely for quite some time. Perhaps a pet would alleviate her sense of abandonment."

"My child has hardly been abandoned." He sounded stuffy even to his own ears.

"I did not mean to imply that she has been, but I think she has *felt* that way. After all, this past year of her life has been very different from what she experienced in earlier years."

"True, but perhaps you are reading too much into too little," he argued, conceding only to himself that his reaction might be prompted by a sense of guilt.

Her lips tightened and she gave a small shrug. "Perhaps I am." She did not sound as though she believed this. "In any event, both Mrs. Jenkins and I have repeatedly told Lady Cassandra that the decision would be yours and yours alone." With that, she moved toward the door leading to the back stairs to the kitchen. "I'll see to some refreshment for you and Captain Chilton," she added and slipped through the door.

"Bloody hell," he muttered to himself. She had as much as said he'd neglected his duties as a father!

"*You* asked the question," he reminded himself. "She answered it. Had you rather she had dissembled, lied to you?

"Well, perhaps. . . ."

The conversation had certainly changed the tone of his homecoming.

CHAPTER 14

Kate knew her position as housekeeper at Kenrick Hall was most unorthodox, for she had more authority—and more responsibility—than such a position usually entailed. But had the earl not made that clear from the beginning? Many of her duties—planning menus, deciding on household projects—would have been performed by a countess were one in residence, or by Lady Elinor were she less infirm. Occasionally, rumors, raised eyebrows, and snide questions dotted local gossip, especially in the days following Nurse Cranstan's departure. However, Lady Elinor's consequence and her friendship with the vicar's wife helped deflect negative comments. Also, according to gossipy Rosie, servants interacting with friends and relatives over tankards or teacups protested vehemently against scurrilous rumors. Kate herself maintained a professional demeanor with both her employer and her fellow employees.

But it was not easy.

Often of an evening, the staff would gather in the servants' dining room downstairs to play cards, dominoes, or draughts even as they were on call to serve the family upstairs. On rare occasions, Kate joined the group with her guitar for an informal song fest. At such times, Ned and Cassie frequently joined in as well. The gathering always broke up for an early bedtime, not so much for the sake of the children as for the fact that, in any well-run household, servants were expected to rise long before their masters. Kate treasured her camaraderie with the staff, but took care to preserve an invisible line of decorum.

Such a line was not so easily maintained on the other end of the spectrum. The history—and now the secret—she shared with Robert precluded treating him privately as anything but what he was: a valued friend. Robert continued to press her to tell Kenrick the truth, but Kate demurred, partly from fear of the unknown. What action would Lord Kenrick feel compelled to take? And what would he think of her? Had he not at their first meeting made a point of telling her how he valued honesty and integrity?

Lately, though, her concerns had extended to Kenrick himself. She had overheard him mention to Robert that he expected to take his seat in the House of Lords when Parliament met in the new year, for he had decided views on reform measures being bandied about in the highest circles. A scandal involving a connection of the powerful Duke of Wynstan and a not-so-well-known earl would render the earl's political views meaningless before he uttered them. Her very presence in his life offered a potential hazard.

Maintaining stiff formality with Lord Kenrick was proving very difficult indeed. Her mind would not let go of that kiss, the waltz, his occasional gentle teasing, the kindness he extended to Ned, and—most of all—the sheer magnetism of a fine masculine form and compelling blue eyes.

"Oh, good heavens," she admonished herself. "Robert has fine eyes and a fine physique as well. You are not daydreaming about him like some green girl!" The truth was that with each passing day, her feelings for Lord Kenrick grew stronger. She found herself even thinking of him as *Jeremy* instead of the title his position—and hers—required. She was sure that he was attracted to her to some degree. There had been that kiss, after all. . . .

But there was tension as well. She occasionally caught him looking at her with speculation and curiosity. Did he suspect that she was not the person she purported to be? She was tempted to tell him the truth. She wanted to share the problem—as she had often shared issues with Arthur. But no. Such a move would change—destroy—the status quo. Best leave things alone. The unknown was too frightening. Eventually she and Ned would have to leave. She could explain then—maybe write a letter.

* * *

The morning after his return from surveying Kenrick holdings with Robert, Jeremy went to the stables with a handful of carrots, thinking he would accompany Cassie and Ned on their morning ride. Perhaps Ned's mother would be there too, and he could smooth over any awkwardness of last night. Cassie and Jack, the stable hand who usually oversaw the riding lessons, were alone.

"Where is Ned?" Jeremy asked.

"He can't come today," Cassie said in a matter-of-fact tone.

"Can't come? Why? Is he ill? He seemed perfectly fine last night."

"He's not allowed for three days," Cassie explained.

"Who does not allow him?" Jeremy looked from Cassie to Jack.

"His mama," Cassie said with the same all-knowing frankness of children.

"You know anything about this?" Jeremy asked of Jack.

"Yes, my lord." But Jack seemed reluctant to elaborate and glanced at Cassie.

Jeremy handed Cassie the carrots. "See if Toby would like these."

"Oh, I know he will." She scampered out of hearing of the two men.

"So—why is Ned not allowed to ride?" Jeremy demanded of Jack.

Jack drew circles in the dust with the toe of his boot. "Well, my lord, you know how boys can be at times. The lad were just feelin' his oats. But he made the mistake of letting his ma hear him."

" 'Feeling his oats'? Explain that, Jack."

Jack sighed. "We come back from a sort of long ride couple days ago. He were tired an' it was rainin' an' he didn't wanta put the horse up proper-like. I told him as how you'd made that part of their ridin' lessons."

"And?" Jeremy prodded.

"Well, he got real uppity an' told me to do it myself since I was a stable hand an' it were my job an' all."

"*Ned* said that?"

"Yep. *You* know how young folks gotta try the fences now an' then. He added some other choice words you might hear around a stable. What he didn't know—me, neither—was his ma was just inside the stable door. Come down to wait for 'em."

"What happened then?"

"She come chargin' out that door like a whirlwind, grabbed that boy by his ear an' told 'im to apologize to me immediately and then laid into 'im somethin' fierce. Told 'im his behavior was totally unacceptable, how could he hope to take his proper place in society if he had no respect for the animals an' people who made his life easier—an' on an' on. Made 'im apologize to Lady Cassandra too, 'cause no gentleman would ever use such language in front of a lady."

Jeremy shook his head, pondering this.

Jack went on. "She ended by telling him—an' me—that he was not to come near the stables for three days. An' you know how that boy does love horses."

"Did he apologize?"

"Most definitely. He knew he done wrong. I think he was real sorry—not just for his careless words to me, but that his ma was shamed by what he done."

"What did she mean, 'take his place in society'?"

"I got no idea, my lord. But she were mad as hops!"

Jeremy was still mulling over this information and only half listening to his daughter chatter as the two of them set off on a leisurely ride, Jeremy holding his mount back to match the pace of Cassie's pony.

"Is that true, Papa?"

"Is what true?"

"What I just said. Weren't you listening, Papa?"

"I guess I wasn't, sweetheart. What was it?"

"Is a duke more higher than an earl?"

"Higher, not 'more higher,'" he corrected. "Yes. In the grand scheme of English society, a duke outranks an earl."

"Oh." She sounded deflated.

"Why do you ask?"

"Ned said when he grows up he will be a duke like Welgundon and then I'll have to curtsy to him. Is that true, Papa?"

Jeremy chuckled. "You mean Wellington, love. But yes, if he managed to become a duke, you might. Of course, you could marry a prince, and then Ned would have to bend *his* knee to *you*."

"Then that is what I shall do," she said, lifting her chin for emphasis. She abruptly changed the subject. "This is tomorrow, Papa. Can I please have one of Petunia's kittens? *Pleeease?*"

"When we get back, you may show them to me," he said, already knowing he would give in on this issue, not only to make his daughter happy, but also to prove to Mrs. Arthur that he was not as heartless as she might think.

As they continued the outing, his mind reverted again to his housekeeper. More pieces to the puzzle. A place in society? A housekeeper's son a member of the aristocracy? But how did these pieces fit the picture? Could be a mother's natural ambition for her child, on the one hand, and childish babble based on soldiers' gossip when Parliament elevated Wellington, on the other hand. Perhaps he would ask Robert—assuming Robert could answer without betraying a confidence.

Meanwhile, there was still the matter of the kitten. As he accompanied Cassie to the back entrance of the hall, they found the mama cat and her babies cavorting near the stoop. Jeremy could not help smiling at their antics, jumping over plants and each other, chasing shadows.

"They are having such fun!" Cassie said with a giggle.

"They are that," he agreed. "So which one has stolen the Lady Cassandra's heart?"

"This one!" She snagged a ball of fur sporting splashes of brown, white, amber, and black, and hugged it close.

"Why that one? Why not this little yellow one with white stripes?"

"I like this one." She hugged it closer. "She makes me think of Running Fox."

"She does?" Jeremy was mystified by the connection between this small feline and Cassie's erstwhile Arapaho playmate.

"His pony, Lobo. 'Member all the patches? I am going to call her Lady Lobo. Can I keep her? Please, Papa?"

"Yes, you *may*," said, sure his correcting her grammar went entirely unheeded.

She nuzzled the kitten. "Did you hear that, Lady Lobo? Papa said yes!"

Jeremy's idea of asking his brother about Mrs. Arthur was overshadowed by Robert's greeting when the two met in the library later.

"Jeremy! You must have a guardian angel looking out for you!"

"Oh?"

"The market for that wool you are sitting on is up this week. Up! And just when we need that space to store hay!"

Robert's excitement was contagious.

"Maybe luck is swinging our way," Jeremy said. "I stopped by the home farm to speak with Porter this morning. He said we should start cutting hay tomorrow. When we finish we can have the cutters load the wool on the wagons to haul it to market in York."

"Sounds like a good plan. Do we still make a holiday of the mowing the hay on the home farm?"

"We did last summer. But I had only just returned then."

Mowing hay on Kenrick holdings was a communal activity. Able-bodied men brought their scythes and pitchforks and went from one tenant farm to another cutting grass for the winter's fodder. The home farms were always the last of the Kenrick fields to be mowed, and the event culminated in a shared picnic at which farmers' wives tried to outdo each other with tasty dishes. The Earl of Kenrick supplied kegs of ale and cider; impromptu games of horseshoes, a tug-of-war over a freshly made mud puddle, and three-legged races supplied ample entertainment. As a child, Jeremy had always enjoyed this event and enthusiastically endorsed continuing the tradition.

When she heard the details of this Kenrick tradition, Kate felt none of the apprehension she had experienced at the Midsummer festivities. After all, this would be a much smaller gathering, involving only people directly connected to the Hall and Kenrick lands. She readily joined in preparations, overseeing the baking and packing food and utensils into baskets for the short journey to the home farm three miles away. The Hall's younger men, including Lord Kenrick and his brother, had been gone since dawn to get the most strenuous work done in the cooler morning hours.

Kate rode in the open carriage with Lady Elinor, Ned and Cassie, and Mrs. Jenkins. Ned, having served out his punishment, looked forward to the prospect of races and games with other boys; Cassie held her kitten close and chattered happily about what a wonderful pet Lady Lobo was. Others of the Hall's staff either walked or rode on the wagon, carrying food and equipment. When they arrived, Kate was pleased to see that much had already been done. Long tables and benches had been set up on a grassy area between the farmhouse and two barns some fifty yards or so away.

Their daughter being married to one of Kenrick's tenant farmers, the vicar and his wife were included in this affair. Kate was glad when Mrs. Packwood laid claim to her friend and whisked Lady Elinor off for a friendly coze on the sidelines. She was also grateful to Mrs. Jenkins and the Davis sisters, who saw to it that Kenrick's housekeeper was introduced to folks she had not yet met.

As the women spread large tablecloths and set out the food, Kate smiled at snippets of conversation she heard.

"Surely we could feed the whole of Yorkshire with this feast."

"Oh, Martha, you say that every year."

"We never have to carry too much of it home with us."

"Haying makes men real hungry."

"I'm that glad to see Mrs. Porter made her spice cake."

"And Mrs. Edmunds her gooseberry tarts."

Talk of the food was interspersed with news of weddings, births, deaths, which young man was sweet on which young woman, and so on. Kate reveled in the general atmosphere of gaiety and friendship, with children of all ages scampering about, adults exchanging greetings and news. It reminded her of similar gatherings in her youth— ordinary English life she had missed during those years on the Peninsula and later in a duke's castle. She experienced twinges of regret with these memories. Surely her brothers and sisters still did such things in Surrey.

The men arrived looking a bit tired and sweaty and definitely ready for the feast. As they washed up at a bench set off to the side with basins of water and towels, Kate noted that both Lord Kenrick and his brother fit right in with the other men, sharing the horseplay and general pleasure in finishing an annual job vital to everyone. All in all, the day was offering Kate an idyllic departure from the stress of worrying about her future.

There seemed no protocol for seating at the tables. When mothers had seen to feeding their youngest children, the women spaced themselves about the tables and the men then joined them. Kate winked at Robert when she saw him sit next to Squire Dennison's pretty daughter, Delia, who just happened, Kate had learned earlier, to have been visiting the eldest Porter daughter exactly when the mowing season reached a climax. Then she felt that now-familiar visceral reaction when the earl folded his long frame into a place on the bench next to her.

"Thank you for seeing to Cassie's care," he said softly, leaning close. He smelled of sunshine and fresh-cut grass.

"You are welcome, of course." She consciously steered her mind to something besides the very masculine form near her.

"I'm glad to see that Ned is back in your good graces."

She gave him an inquiring look.

"I saw him at the stables this morning."

"Oh. He was never *out* of my good graces, my lord, but like all children, he manages to challenge his elders at times."

"I see." She thought he wanted to say something else, but just then the vicar called for grace and gave a pleasingly short blessing. General conversation took over with some light competition about who had done best out in the field that day. Throughout the meal, despite her attempts to quell her feelings, Kate was keenly aware of the man seated next to her. When his knee happened to touch hers, she drew in a sharp breath at the intensity of her reaction.

"Sorry," he murmured.

She nodded but inwardly admitted to a small thrill of pleasure—then chastised herself for her unseemly reaction. She launched into another of those silent arguments with herself. Just why was it "unseemly"? After all, she was a normal, living, human being—with all the needs and desires of a mature woman. He was an attractive man. "And forbidden goods," as you well know, she told that other self. "And you know very well your feelings go beyond 'an attractive man' and 'a mature woman.' You can at least be honest with yourself, can you not?" She was thankful to be pulled out of this silent debate when she heard her name. Mrs. Jenkins, seated at the far end of the table on the opposite side, was telling the woman across from her that Mrs. Arthur, who had a way with seasonings, was responsible for a marvelous pudding.

Folks had eaten their fill and were lazily awaiting the start of the games. Some still sat at the tables; others had moved to sit or recline on the grass. Conversations were more subdued in tone, but just as lively in content. After all, such gatherings came infrequently; one had to store up information and relish the conviviality.

Lord Kenrick sat with his back to the table now, leaning back on his elbows, his long legs stretched out before him. Kate too sat facing the grassy area, idly watching the people around her as his lordship filled her in on who some of them were in relation to the earldom as a whole. He pointed out the blacksmith, named Carlson, a man whose brawny shoulders might well have announced his profession. "The fellow next to him is Taylor—a genius at grafting fruit trees. Mrs. Grimes there lives with her son—helps take care of the children. She makes wonderful cider."

"Perhaps she will share her secret," Kate said.

Kenrick laughed. "I'm told she guards it like the crown jewels."

Kate shrugged. "Nothing ventured, nothing gained."

Any response Lord Kenrick might have made to this was lost in someone's announcing, in an alarmed tone, "I smell smoke."

" 'Course ya do. We been eatin' roasted meat."

"No. This smells different."

"I smell it too."

"Look!" It was a shout and the speaker pointed to the larger of the home farm's two barns. A wisp of smoke spiraled up from the far side of that building. It was followed immediately by the first sighting of flames.

"Oh, my God! The wool!" Lord Kenrick yelled as he jumped up from the bench and ran toward the barn, his brother and several others on his heels.

Behind him pandemonium erupted.

People who had been lazily relaxing one moment jumped up in surprise, wanting to be of help, but clearly at a loss as to how.

Having taken in the details of the location of the fire, Kenrick yelled, "Buckets! Get them from the dairy! Form a line!"

Dairymaids and stable hands ran to do so. Mrs. Porter and her housemaids gathered buckets and small tubs from the farm kitchen and the laundry. A husky young man was already manning the pump over the well in the middle of the yard.

Immediately a line of men and women formed to pass buckets of water to those nearest the conflagration. Once she had ensured that Ned and Cassie would stay near Lady Elinor, Kate joined this line.

The men who had gone into the barn struggled to remove bales of wool through the rear door of the barn as those fighting the fire did so from the side of the building from which flames were now shooting. The stench of burning wool permeated the scene. Two fairly organized lines now struggled mightily against this force that had, from the beginning of time, been mankind's greatest blessing and most feared destroyer. One line manned the water buckets; the other passed the heavy bales to safety in the field behind the barn.

She heard Lord Kenrick shout, "Robert, check the other barn. Be sure it's all right." Robert and two others ran to do so.

It was a matter of minutes, but it felt like hours until people had formed themselves into a unified army to fight the monster. There was an occasional shout—an order or a warning—and yelps of pain now and then, but mostly they worked methodically. Kate concentrated on grabbing a bucket from Nell Davis on her left and passing it to Mrs. Weston on her right.

Suddenly, she saw a streak of movement headed toward the front door of the burning barn. Cassie's kitten! A yapping dog chased it. To Kate's horror, Cassie was right behind them; the dog veered away.

"No! Cassie! No!" Kate screamed as the little girl disappeared into the barn.

Kate jumped away from the line just as Ned ran to follow Cassie. She jerked him by his arm and in the sternest voice she had ever used with him said, "Stay here!" She shoved him in the direction of some onlookers who clutched him tightly, then she grabbed one of the tablecloths. She quickly dipped it into the nearest bucket and ran after Cassie.

Inside the barn smoke was overwhelming, stinging her eyes, blurring her vision. Her throat burned and she felt she was suffocating. She jerked off her mobcap to use as a mask; hairpins flew.

"Cassie!" she screamed. Where was she?

A wide space separated stalls on either side of the barn. Smoke was so heavy she could see only a few feet in front of her. Flaming debris fell from the loft above. She whipped the tablecloth over her head and felt more pins loosen in her hair as she did so.

"Cassie! Answer me!" she called again as she ran in a zigzag line to check the stalls. Oh, God, where was she?

The heat was oppressive; the smoke stole her breath; the stench of burning wool was almost palpable. She ignored the panic and despair and ran on. Then, in addition to the crackling fire and falling timbers, she heard a sob on her left. She whirled in that direction. Cassie was curled in the corner of a stall clutching her kitten, trembling in fear.

Kate extended her hand and tried to keep panic out of her voice. "Hurry, Cassie. We have to get out of here."

Cassie scrambled to her feet, still holding the kitten. Kate threw the tablecloth over the child and her pet, grasped Cassie's free hand, and ran for the door, stumbling awkwardly. A falling timber crashed to the floor, blocking their way. Kate picked up child and kitten and jumped over the flaming timber. There! The door was only ten feet away. Please, God. Please, God.

Another piece of flaming wood fell from above, striking Kate a glancing blow on her head, then her shoulder. She stumbled and lost her grip on Cassie.

"Run, Cassie! Run!"

Kate was relieved to see Cassie do just that—and to see the child swept up by a male figure and passed off to the arms of someone else.

Somehow—Kate never knew afterwards exactly how—they both had made it through the door. The fire emitted a terrible roar behind her with intermittent thuds of falling timbers. Kate was faintly aware that her hair was flying about her face and the hem of her skirt was ablaze. Her lungs bursting painfully, she sucked in fresh air. Someone threw a soaked cloth over her and beat at the flames on her clothing. She started to collapse, but strong arms prevented her doing so.

Darkness closed in on her.

CHAPTER 15

Jeremy had felt himself to be in several places at once since first sighting the fire; he was at the side of the building where the flames were fiercest when the fifteen-year-old Weston lad came running up to him.

"My lord! Your girl! She's in there!"

"Cassie?" he yelled, almost disbelieving. "*No-o-o!*" He dropped the shovel with which he had been throwing raw earth onto flames and raced to the front of the building and dashed toward the gaping door that framed the inferno within.

Robert and two other men stepped in front of him, grabbed his arms, and held him back.

"No, Jeremy!" Robert screamed. "Kate's gone after her. You'd never find them in that!"

"I have to try!" Shaking off the restraining hands, he lurched toward the open door again.

Suddenly, the hooded figure of his daughter was in front of him. He swept her into his arms and beat at flames on her skirt.

"Papa! Papa!" She sounded excited, even fearful, but she did not wince in pain when he grabbed her up.

Flames gone now, he whipped the cloth off her head and breathed a sigh—no, a prayer—of relief. Even as he assured himself of Cassie's safety, he peered over her shoulder into the holocaust, frantic for a glimpse of her rescuer.

Yes!

There she was.

He thrust Cassie into Robert's arms and ran toward the emerging Kate.

Tiny wisps of smoke rose from her hair and her skirt smoldered. A wet blanket was shoved into his hand. He threw it over her head and beat out flames threatening her skirt.

He felt her struggling for breath. Then she collapsed. He picked her up and clutched her to his chest, glad to see no more live flames about her person. The stench of burned hair assailed his nose. Oh, God, please let her be all right, he prayed silently.

He shouted at the nearest man, "Go for the doctor!"

"Yes, my lord." The man ran to a field where the horses had been turned out that morning.

Now things seemed to move ever so slowly.

"In here, my lord." Mrs. Porter directed him to the parlor of the farmhouse where he gently lowered his burden to a couch. She winced in pain as he placed her arm across her waist. Mrs. Porter hastily shoved a cushion under her head. Their patient's breathing was labored and she coughed intermittently, but she did not regain consciousness. Two other women, including Mrs. Packwood, hovered about, clucking sympathetically and seeking to be of help.

"I've sent for the doctor," he said, feeling foolish at stating the obvious.

"Yes, my lord," Mrs. Porter said, "but he won't be here for an hour or so. We need to know how bad she's hurt before he gets here."

"Well . . . uh . . ." Jeremy was at a loss for words. He did not want to leave. He wanted to stay near her, touch her, care for her—at least know the extent of her injuries. He could see burns on her hands and her hair—her beautiful hair—was frizzed. However, he needed to check on Cassie. Also, he knew how improper his staying would be and how it would reflect on Kate.

As though she had read his mind, Mrs. Porter said, "You go on, my lord. Me an' these other ladies will see to her. Me daughter's about her size. I'll find a clean gown of some sort."

"Thank you, Mrs. Porter."

As he exited the farmhouse, Cassie flew into his arms and Ned stood nearby, holding the kitten. Both children had been crying.

"Is my mama going to be all right?" Ned asked.

Hearing in the boy's voice the sheer terror of a child who had already lost one parent, Jeremy shifted Cassie so he could put an arm around Ned. "I think so, son. She's still unconscious, but she should come around soon." God! He hoped that was true!

"Oh, Papa, I was so scared," Cassie said. "Andy Phelps made his nasty dog chase Lady Lobo—an' she's just a baby!"

"Are you all right, my pet?" He kissed her cheek.

"My hand is burned. See?" She held up a bandaged hand. "Mrs. Jenkins put butter on it, but it still hurts."

"I'm sure it does," he said, trying to sound sympathetic through his overwhelming relief that he had not lost her. "Maybe if you put it in some cold water, the pain won't be so bad."

"Mrs. A found me an' Lady Lobo." He noted the use of the servants' affectionate name for the housekeeper.

"Mama wouldn't let me help," Ned said.

"She was worried about both of you." Jeremy briefly hugged the boy tighter. He then examined Cassie and was amazed not only that her sole injury was that burn on her hand, but that her pet had survived the ordeal unscathed.

"Can I—may I—see my mama?" Ned was obviously worried but just as obviously trying to be grown up.

"In a little while," Jeremy told him. "The ladies are taking care of her and you know how women are."

Ned nodded solemnly.

Jeremy continued to reassure both children for a few minutes, but then persuaded them that they—along with Rosie—should see to the care of Lady Elinor as he returned to check on Kate—Mrs. Arthur. He did not have time to consider just when she had become "Kate" in his private musings.

He looked toward the still-burning barn and saw with dismay that it was a lost cause. The fire fighters now worked to prevent its spreading to the roofs of the smaller barn and other buildings. Robert had taken charge, shouting orders and running to help protect the wool that had been saved. Matters out here seemed under control.

Back in the farmhouse, he found Kate still unconscious. Her eyes were closed; her chest heaved with each breath as she struggled for oxygen. She was now dressed in an outsized cotton nightdress and some of the ash and soot had been cleaned from her face. Mrs. Porter gave him a report as she set aside a basin and a wet cloth.

"We've cleaned her up as best we can what with them burns an' all. She has a lump on her head and burns on her hands and one arm. Havin' trouble breathin'—but that coughin' might be a good sign. I give 'er one o' my nightdresses, it bein' real loose on her, you see. There's some burns on 'er legs too, but they don't seem serious. Her skirt was wet from passin' them buckets; protected 'er legs, it did. Her hands are worst. An' 'er hair. Poor dear. She had real pretty hair."

"Yes, she did," Jeremy agreed. "Thank you, ladies. I'll sit with her until the doctor arrives." He saw the three women exchange questioning looks, but he simply had to be here. "She saved my daughter's life," he added—lamely, he thought.

"As you wish, my lord." Mrs. Porter placed a straight-backed chair near the couch.

The mad energy of his initial reaction having abated, Jeremy sat pondering the enormous debt he owed this woman. Yes, she had saved Cassie's life. But my God! He might have lost both of them! Suddenly, he realized the magnitude of that possibility.

"Good God! You're in love with her!

"You, who swore after Willow that you would never—never—fall into that trap again.

"Yet here you are.

"What about her feelings?"

Well, she did not seem totally averse to his person. He recalled her response to that kiss in the stillroom.

And Robert? One could not pursue a woman with whom his brother was in love! But . . . Robert did not seek Kate out especially. In fact, Robert had deliberately sought out Delia Dennison earlier today. Still, there was *something* between his brother and the Kenrick housekeeper.

What a coil this was turning into.

When Dr. Ferris, a slim, wiry little man of middle years, arrived nearly half an hour later, his report was anticlimactic, for his assessment paralleled the ladies' examination.

"Can she be moved?" Jeremy asked. "Can I take her back to the Hall?"

"Don't see why not," the doctor replied. "Just be careful of her head. That's quite a lump she's got there. She has a concussion, but she should come around in a few hours. Three or four, maybe. Maybe longer. The longer she's out, the more worrisome it is, though. Also, I think she strained her shoulder, but no broken bones. Luckily, her burns are relatively minor. Painful, though, I'm sure. I've put some salve and loose bandages on her hands. I'll come out tomorrow to check on her and I'll leave some laudanum now for the pain."

Jeremy thanked the doctor and asked him to check on Cassie as well. Jeremy was glad to learn that Cassie's wound was as minor as he had thought earlier.

Leaving Robert to supervise the cleanup, and holding the unconscious Kate on his lap, Jeremy accompanied his sad little party back to the Hall. Lady Elinor asserted her position as nominal lady of the house by organizing the logistics.

"When we arrive, Wilkins will show me to my rooms and you should put Mrs. Arthur in the countess's unused chamber," Lady Elinor told him. "It will accommodate caring for her better than having servants traipsing up to the nursery rooms. Rosie can handle the children."

"I hadn't thought that through," he said, "but of course you are right."

So, he did not hesitate at all before placing Kate in the countess's chamber, which connected to his own bedchamber through adjacent dressing rooms. Cassie and Ned, both of whom had been inordinately quiet on the return journey, followed him, along with the maid Rosie.

"Is my mama going to die?" Ned asked in almost a whisper on seeing his mother lying motionless on the canopied bed in the countess's bedchamber, a light cover over her body.

"No. You must not think that," Jeremy said. "She will be fine." He thought his own need for her to be "fine" was nearly as strong as Ned's.

"But why doesn't she wake up?" Ned persisted.

"She is sleeping. Sleep is sometimes the way God keeps us from feeling too much pain."

"Oh."

Jeremy was glad the boy accepted this explanation, but knew he himself would not be satisfied until she did wake up. "Now you and Cassie go on up to the nursery." He looked at Rosie, who nodded. "Rosie will see that you have some supper and I'll come to tuck you into bed later."

"And read us a story?" Cassie asked.

"And read you a story." He knew it was important to maintain routine for children in a crisis. It was, he was sure, what Kate would want for them.

Later, he turned over Kate's care to a maid long enough for him to get a hurried bath and change of clothes. In an open-necked shirt, his favorite buckskin breeches, and slippers, he reported to the nursery as he had promised. He gave Ned a reassuring report, hoping he was not being overly optimistic. The children were subdued, but readily accepted this new normality. Having read them a story and tucked them in, he returned to his post at Kate's bedside.

Some time later, there was a knock on the door to the main hallway. Jeremy looked up from a book he had been reading as the maid Nell opened the door and then left on an errand. Robert came in looking tired and begrimed.

"How is she?" Robert asked quietly, striding across the room to gaze down at the unmoving form on the bed.

"Still unconscious. Doctor said it could be a few hours. It's been over four. She's been a bit restless the last half hour or so."

"That's a good sign."

"Yes."

Robert drew up the chair the maid had vacated and sank wearily into it. "You want the good news or the bad news first?"

"The bad. Always save the best 'til last."

"The barn was destroyed—well, the roof, supporting timbers, and the stalls. Hard to destroy walls and floors of stone."

"I expected that," Jeremy said.

"It gets worse. That fire was deliberately set."

"What?"

"It was no accident. Arson. The evidence was pretty clear where it started. Rags and lamp oil."

"Who—?" But, instinctively, Jeremy was sure he knew the ultimate *who*. Who stood to gain the most from his inability to sell that wool? Proving his suspicion would be next to impossible. Mortimer was rich enough and clever enough not to involve himself directly.

Robert said, "Maybe someone with a grudge. Or paid. Or both."

Jeremy sighed. "Is there any good news?"

"Some. We saved the smaller barn—apparently the arsonist got scared before he could light his starter there."

"But no one saw or heard anything suspicious?"

"We think it was set after the men were in the field and the women had not yet arrived. Mrs. Porter said the dogs put up a fuss early in the morning, but when she sent one of her daughters to check on it, the girl did not see anything."

"Perhaps that child saved the small barn," Jeremy said.

"Could be. In any event, whoever set it might have had military experience."

"Why do you think that?"

"Timing. Someone who could time explosives could time the outbreak of a fire, but I think we should keep this whole arson business to ourselves for now. Ask around. See who knows what."

"I agree. Interesting that this should have occurred today."

"Happenstance, probably," Robert said. "Bad timing, maybe— and we were just lucky to be on hand to deal with it."

"Yes," Jeremy agreed absently, his mind still reeling not only with the idea that he had an enemy capable of such treachery, but, more importantly, what his personal losses *might* have been.

"And—" Robert's voice rose on a more optimistic note, "we saved about a third of the wool in the big barn. Not a total loss."

"But will it be enough?" Jeremy could not keep the bleakness from his tone.

"Don't give up yet, big brother. We'll have to reconnoiter again. This war is far from over." Robert stood and stretched. "I'm for a bath and some sleep." He gestured to the figure on the bed. "Keep an eye on our girl here."

As Robert left, Nell returned with a tray of food and a glass of ale. "Mrs. Jenkins sent this up for you, my lord."

"Thank you. Just set it on that table. Then you should get some rest, Nell."

"I don't know, my lord. Lady Elinor said—"

Jeremy chuckled, glad to find something to be amused about in the last few hours. "Mrs. Arthur's virtue is safe this night. You go on, now."

"Yes, my lord."

And Jeremy was thus left with his thoughts for company. *Our girl*? What did that signify?

He must have dozed off, for he was suddenly aware of Kate's thrashing about and muttering incoherently. He leaned forward to wrap his hand gently around her upper arm and murmur soothingly. His touch and voice seemed to quiet her. He released her and sat back. Almost immediately, she began flailing her arms about and hit her right hand on the bedpost, dislodging the loose bandages. Had she been awake, that blow would have been very painful, he thought. He replaced the bandage, retied the strings holding it, and restored the blanket she had kicked off. He was not immune to a glimpse of her shapely legs or the feel of her smooth, warm skin as he did so. Her muttering became more frantic. Occasionally, there was a coherent word or phrase— sometimes they even made sense.

"Run, Cassie! . . . Ned, be careful. . . . 'member: it's a secret . . . No, Robert, the duke . . . Can't tell Ken—. . . Runners . . . My son . . . Ned . . . Ned . . . No . . . No-o-o!" The last words came out in sheer terror.

When he had replaced the cover the fourth or fifth time, he gave up and lay on the top of it next to her, his arm cradling her head against his shoulder. Despite the smell of burnt hair, he savored her closeness. And she *was* calmer, her breathing less labored.

He lay there pondering her rambling cries. *Can't tell Ken*— Can't tell Kenrick what? A duke again. Which duke? Good God, there could not be that many dukes in the realm, could there? What was it that had her so frightened? Runners? Bow Street Runners? More pieces to the puzzle—and by God! Someone was going to answer these questions!

Finally, he slept himself.

In a bow to propriety, Jeremy had left the door to the hall slightly ajar. He awoke when there was a sharp knock on that door and Robert barged in. Light at the window showed it to be past dawn. Kate was quiet.

"Oh!" Robert said. "I—uh—"

"Come in, Robert. Don't be misled by what you see here." Jeremy untangled himself from the sleeping form beside him, slid his feet into his slippers, and stood. "She became quite restless and I could hardly grab her hands, now could I?"

"No. I suppose not. But you're damned lucky I—and not that chatterbox Rosie—caught you out. Even so, with Kate in this room, there's likely to be some talk."

"Ah, well—"

A groggy voice from the bed interrupted. "Lord Kenrick? Robert?

What am I doing here?" Then her voice became more alert—and alarmed. "Cassie? Ned?"

"They are both all right," Jeremy assured her, "and Dr. Ferris assured me yesterday that you will be too, as soon as these nasty burns heal."

She rolled her head to look at him and winced. "My head . . ."

"Yes. You suffered a blow there."

"The Angel of the Forty-sixth is up to her old tricks," Robert said with a grin. "But really, my dear, you could leave some of the heroics to us men!"

Jeremy immediately noticed the endearment, but he thought it might be just a casual turn of phrase.

"I—I don't understand," she said. "I remember the fire—the barn—stumbling—losing hold of Cassie. Cassie. Is she—?"

"She's fine," they assured her again as they filled her in on the basic details of yesterday's events.

"What caused it—the fire?" she asked.

Jeremy exchanged a look with Robert and said, "We are not sure yet." He cut off this line of discussion by reaching for the bellpull. "Nell will bring you some breakfast and see to your needs until your hands have healed." He looked at Robert to include him in his next statement. "When you are sufficiently healed, Mrs. Arthur, I think the three of us should have a chat."

"H—have a chat?" she repeated dumbly.

"Not now. When you are up to it. Ah, here's Nell now."

With that, he and Robert left the room.

The simple tasks of getting through the day prevented Kate's dwelling on Lord Kenrick's parting words that morning. In fact, they were swept to the nether regions of her mind as she dealt with the constant frustration of being almost totally dependent on others. With both hands bandaged and every movement painful, she struggled with even mundane things, such as lifting a spoon or a slice of toast. By the time the doctor had come to pronounce her on the mend, and she had had an audience with Ned and Cassie—and the ever-present Lady Lobo—her head hurt so abominably that she agreed to a small dose of laudanum, which allowed her to lose herself in sleep.

The next day, aware that her occupation of the countess's bed-chamber was likely to be viewed as most improper, she insisted on removing to her own room in the nursery wing. That day too some of the bandages were redone to give her more range of movement. Lady Elinor's maid managed to snip off Kate's damaged hair and create a most attractive, albeit short, hairstyle. From then on, she felt herself improving steadily and within the week was back to supervising staff members, if not always performing the hands-on chores she was wont to do.

In brief visits, Lord Kenrick checked on her frequently while she was still bedridden and, as she began resuming her duties as house-keeper, she encountered him far more often than had been usual before. He was always cordial and solicitous, but she could not shake the feeling that there was a good deal of speculation in his expressions of concern. Lady Elinor entertained her with *on dits* of local gossip—as did other members of the staff. Even Mr. Wilkins had climbed the stairs to the nursery wing. After the third day, Robert was conspicuously absent. Lady Elinor told her he was on a hasty trip to London to finish details of selling his commission.

Kate was grateful for Jeremy's concern. No. *Grateful* was far too mild a word. So was *concern*. She recalled now the utter contentment she had felt as she was entering a semiconscious state. Learning he had spent the entire night at her side had thrilled her, but also frightened her. Perhaps he did care for her as she cared for him. And if he did, how was she reciprocating that affection? With such deceit as might undo much of the good he was achieving with his earldom.

Was that to be the subject of his promised "chat"? Had he somehow learned the truth about her and Ned? She had pressed Robert, but he merely shrugged and said he had no idea what Jeremy had in mind. He told her not to worry about it. He did, however, once again urge her to confide in his brother.

Well, perhaps she would—when Robert returned. She knew it was cowardly, but with Robert there to support her, explaining herself should be easier. So long as Jeremy did not know her secret, she could postpone facing the issue of where she and Ned could run next. So long as Jeremy did not know, she could revel in being near him.

So, she avoided doing anything.

In the end, the matter was taken out of her hands.

CHAPTER 16

In the next two weeks, activities at Kenrick settled back to a semblance of routine as Mrs. Arthur recovered from her injuries and resumed more and more of her usual duties. The remaining wool had been shipped off to market and repairs begun on the burned barn, for the storage space was sorely needed for hay now. Jeremy rode out nearly every day to supervise the rebuilding and the harvesting, and to visit people on his own farms. Porter often accompanied him, and when Robert returned from London, he joined them. However, they gleaned little information about who might have set the fire.

Jeremy, Robert, and Lady Elinor were to attend a dinner party given by the Hartwicks. It was an invitation of long standing and Jeremy now dreaded it, for the Mortimers were sure to be among the guests.

As they were.

The Kenrick party had barely entered the drawing room when Sir Eldridge brought up the subject of the fire.

"The whole neighborhood is still abuzz with news of that unfortunate fire, Kenrick. But these things happen—"

"Some do not just 'happen.' " Jeremy held the other man's gaze until Mortimer looked away with a slight tightening of the lips.

Robert said, "The fire is still under investigation."

"Unfortunate, as I said," Mortimer replied. "But surely an accident."

Charlotte Mortimer stood near her father. She was dressed in a teal blue silk gown cut to show a tantalizing degree of cleavage. She murmured sympathetically. "At least no one was seriously injured. We must thank Providence for that."

"Not just Providence," Jeremy replied. "I might have lost my daughter but for the remarkable courage of a very brave woman."

"Oh, I did hear that one of your servants had ingratiated herself in the crisis. I assume you rewarded her quite adequately." Miss Mortimer waved her fan flirtatiously to dismiss the topic.

But Jeremy was not ready to let it go. "*Adequately*? I hardly think so. One cannot put a material value on a child's life. Or anyone else's, for that matter." He gave her father another direct look, but Mortimer merely averted his eyes again.

"Lady Elinor, you are looking very fine this evening," Miss Mortimer said.

"Thank you," Lady Elinor replied. "I do not attend many evening events, but my nephews insisted."

When dinner was announced, Jeremy was neither surprised nor pleased to find himself partnered with Charlotte Mortimer. He managed to keep up his end of conversations with her and with Mrs. Hartwick on his other side. Their talk involved such fascinating topics as the weather and travels on the continent now that Napoleon was firmly ensconced on the island of St. Helena.

"Hartwick's and my wedding journey was cut short by Bonaparte's adventuring," Mrs. Hartwick said. "I hope young people today will be luckier than we were."

"A wedding journey to the continent sounds heavenly," Charlotte cooed. "Do you not agree, Lord Kenrick?"

Robert, sitting on the other side of the table and two seats down, must have heard this bit of discussion, for he raised an eyebrow. Jeremy was glad etiquette prevented Robert's commenting, for his brother's gaze held a distinct glint of amusement. Jeremy was himself slightly uncomfortable, slightly amused, and slightly annoyed at this conversational gambit.

He cleared his throat, then shrugged and said, "In general, I feel sure ladies take far more interest in such matters than gentlemen do."

Robert grinned and nodded, the movement barely more than a tic.

"Oh, yes," Mrs. Hartwick said. "Mr. Hartwick would far rather talk of a hunting or fishing trip. I actually accompanied him one year to Scotland and found it a most enjoyable holiday."

Jeremy was grateful for the shift in topic.

Later, as the gentlemen were rejoining the ladies in the drawing room, Jeremy found himself and Mortimer momentarily separated from the others.

"A word, Kenrick."

"Sir?"

"I am mindful of the setback that fire dealt you, and I am not unsympathetic to your plight, but I feel I must tell you that I can allow no further extensions on the debt owed me." Mortimer's tone was firm, his expression hard.

"I believe the final date on the legal documents is still nearly three months away," Jeremy said evenly.

"Ten weeks," Mortimer said, "but in light of the sum you are likely to have had from selling your wool—"

Jeremy interrupted and struggled to maintain his even tone. "No doubt you know to the last farthing what we realized from the remaining wool."

"Yes, I do. I also know about those ships that went down in the Indian Ocean. I merely wanted to remind you that my offer some weeks ago still stands. I urge you to take it." Mortimer smiled, a baring of teeth with no warmth. "Otherwise, my lord, you will find yourself with an empty title and nothing else."

Jeremy was furious, but held his anger in check. Was there nothing of Kenrick affairs this man did not have a greedy eye fixed upon? Did he even have a spy in Lawyer Phillips's office? "This is hardly the time or place for this discussion, sir."

"Right. We should join the others."

As they entered the drawing room, Mortimer clapped a hand on Jeremy's shoulder and said in a loud, jovial voice, "I'm glad we understand each other, Lord Kenrick."

Jeremy clenched his teeth and moved away to join a group that included not only his brother, but also Charlotte Mortimer.

"What was that all about?" Robert asked quietly.

"Tell you later," Jeremy said.

Miss Mortimer laid a possessive hand on Jeremy's arm. "Oh, my lord, your brother was just telling us of the Richmond ball prior to that awful last battle with Napoleon."

"Was he now?" Jeremy stared at her hand, then lifted his gaze to hers. She quickly removed her hand, but her eyes held the same glint of control and triumph he had discerned in her father's. *You have not cornered this rat yet,* Jeremy thought. Aloud, he said to Robert, "I think we should say our good nights. We must not tire Aunt Elinor."

"Oh, right," Robert said.

In the carriage, Jeremy relaxed and chatted amiably with Robert and their aunt. He did not want to worry Aunt Elinor with the details of Mortimer's not-so-subtle hold on the earldom.

"I saw you talking with Hartwick and Brewster," Jeremy said to Robert. "Did they have anything to offer on the fire?"

"A great deal of sympathy, but no solid information," Robert said.

"Mrs. Dennison was telling me the Thompson boy has returned from soldiering on the continent," Lady Elinor said. "He used to be sweet on Delia Dennison." She laughed. "I think Mrs. Dennison wanted me to pass that tidbit along to you, Robert."

"Hmm," Robert responded noncommittally.

"Thompson used to work a Kenrick farm, but he is now on one of Mortimer's holdings," Jeremy explained to Robert.

"I remember them," Robert said. "Big family. Seven or eight children. Billy Thompson was—is—my age. He has a twin sister. Wilhelmina. Mina. Is she still in the neighborhood, Aunt?"

"Oh, no," Lady Elinor replied. "She left several months after her brother went off to the army. Just after we lost Charles and Edgar. They say she is in service in London."

"I always thought Mina and Frank Sutton were headed for parson's mousetrap," Robert mused.

"Frank Sutton married the Elmore girl two years ago. They have a baby boy," said Lady Elinor.

"You don't say." Robert stifled a yawn.

It occurred to Jeremy yet again that, despite her disability, his aunt missed very little of life around her.

When they arrived at the Hall, Robert saw Lady Elinor into the care of her maid, then sought his own bedchamber.

Having removed his boots and stripped down to his shirt and trousers, Jeremy decided to check on Cassie. Since the fire, he was very conscious of how close he had come to losing her and the need to just see her was often overwhelming. He put on slippers and climbed the stairs to the nursery wing. Through the open door of his daughter's room, a lamp in the hallway allowed sufficient light for him to see that Cassie slept soundly.

He was not surprised to see the kitten quite at home on his daughter's bed. He caressed Cassie's cheek and pulled the covers tighter around her.

"I see you have firmly established your place in this part of the realm," he said softly, holding the kitten in his cupped hands. It gazed at him solemnly and licked his hand with its small pink, surprisingly rough tongue. Jeremy settled the kitten back on the bed and left.

In the hall, movement two doors down caught his attention.

"Oh. 'Tis you, my lord," Mrs. Arthur said in a low voice as she tied the belt of her robe. "I thought I heard something—"

"I am sorry to have disturbed you." He drank in the sight of her and marveled that this woman, in a high-necked nightdress and a nondescript brown robe, elicited a far more profound response from his body than abundant cleavage in colorful silk had earlier in the evening.

"I—I was not asleep. Just reading," she said and he could see through the open door of her room a brightly-lit lamp at her bedside and an open book facedown on the nightstand. He also noticed a half-full glass of what looked like amber sherry.

She was, of course, not wearing that infernal mobcap at this hour. "Your hair—" He reached to touch it, then thought better of doing so and dropped his hand.

She gave a nervous laugh and swiped a hand over her head and along her neck. His gaze followed her hand.

"Luckily it will grow back," she said. "At least I needn't plait it every night now."

"A silver lining behind every cloud, eh?"

She shrugged, but made no move to end the encounter. Wanting to prolong it, he asked, "And your hands? Are they healed now?"

"Nearly." She held them out and turned them this way and that. "Some redness. I wear gloves for most tasks."

"Allow me." He took her hands gently in his own and steered her across the threshold toward the better light on her nightstand. "They seem to have healed nicely. With luck, there will be little scarring."

He raised his gaze to hers and seeing a corresponding degree of sheer need in her eyes, he gave up control, put his arms around her, and lowered his mouth to hers. With no pretense of reticence, she moved closer and wrapped her arms around his neck. The kiss was deep, searching—an urgent plea—no, *demand*—for more from both. His hands caressed her back and urged her closer to his own hard need. She tasted and smelled of the sweet sherry.

Finally, he lifted his lips from hers, but still held her close. His hands, it seemed, moved of their own volition over the curves of her back and sides, disarranging her robe. He heard a sharp intake of her breath as he reached inside the robe to caress a round breast; he moaned softly when he felt a rigid nipple through the thin fabric of her nightgown.

"Kate?" His voice a husky whisper, he realized fleetingly that this was the first time he had ever spoken her name aloud. It felt right. Natural.

Again, there was no pretense, only raw need in her response, "Yes. Oh, yes."

He was pleased that he had not lost all sense of the situation, for he did have enough presence of mind to close the door to her room before they lost themselves in feverishly disrobing each other.

He paused, put a bit of space between them, and drew in a sharp breath.

"What?" She sounded, alarmed, perhaps embarrassed.

"I knew there was real beauty beneath that infernal mobcap and housekeeper apron, but you—you—"

"Yes?" She sounded coy, teasing now.

"—are breathtakingly lovely, my dear—as I am sure you must know."

He drew her close again, his hands cradling her head as he kissed her eyes, her nose, the soft tenderness beneath her ears, then settled his lips on hers. He ran his hands through her hair, marveling at its silkiness and fresh lemony smell even as he recalled the smell of fire-damaged hair when he had lain beside her that night after the fire.

He nudged her onto the bed, where he was delighted to find no coyness at all. With a great deal of stroking, caressing, nonsensical words, and soft laughter, they brought each other to the brink of ecstatic pleasure. Then she lay beneath him, eagerly welcoming. In her eyes he beheld desire to match his own and he reveled in holding her gaze as he entered. She locked her legs around his and slowly, relishing every nuance of feeling, then with wild urgency, together they surged over the brink.

Afterwards, Jeremy lay at her side, idly caressing her naked body, kissing her neck and shoulder. She lay still, silent, but he could tell by contented sighs and small, accommodating movements that she was fully alert.

"Kate?" He nuzzled her neck.

"My lord?"

He chuckled. "In light of what we just did, I think you might use my name. Jeremy."

"Jeremy." She said it softly as though she were experimenting with the taste. Then she turned to look at him and spoke more firmly. "Jeremy. You—you know this was not a good idea."

"I enjoyed it immensely. I think you did too."

She giggled. "You say that like we just indulged in a—a strawberry pie."

"Strawberry pie is my favorite dessert." His voice was more seductive and his caresses more restive as he gently, subtly persuaded her into full cooperation with what he had in mind—well, what his body craved again. Pleased that his physical desire for her aroused a corresponding need in her, he also recognized a deeper, spiritual element—something to be treasured, to be cherished as he gave himself entirely in this ultimate act of sharing.

Again she lay quiet at his side. After a long moment of languorous contentment, he said, "Next time we do this in my room—where the bed is larger. Beds in the nursery wing were not designed for this."

She sat up and wrapped her arms around her knees. She gave him a direct look tinged with sadness. "Jeremy, there can be no 'next time.' "

"What are you saying? Of course there can."

She spoke slowly. "I . . . I think neither of us is the sort to indulge in—in reckless behavior."

"Look. We—you and I—have something wonderful here. Something to treasure. I care for you and I think you care for me. We can be married within the month—sooner, with a special license."

"M—married?" She sounded shocked. "We cannot marry."

"Why not?"

"An earl would not marry his housekeeper."

"This one would."

"There would be a horrible scandal. All your plans for the earldom . . . And—and—there are other considerations."

"Scandal be damned. It would blow over," he said with a dismissive wave of his hand. He paused. " 'Other considerations'? Like what? We are both free. Oh. Oh. You mean Robert. Oh, God! What have I done?"

"Robert?"

Ignoring what seemed like genuine surprise in her tone, he plunged on. "Robert and you. I knew there was something between you. And now we—I have—Ah, God forgive me!"

She jumped from the bed and stood with her hands on her hips, glaring at him. "You think—You actually think," she fairly sputtered, "that I would—that what just happened—Robert? Preposterous! Robert is my friend. A very dear friend. What a very high opinion you must have of me if you think I would—"

He wanted to laugh at the incongruity of her upbraiding him as she stood there stark naked, but then his sense of shame at having wronged his brother and his own temper rising in reaction to her scolding got the better of him.

"You must admit that it is a perfectly logical assumption."

"A logical—Oh! This is too much."

He too jumped from the bed and, mindful of her still tender hands, grabbed her by her upper arms. "A logical assumption," he said through gritted teeth. "But be that as it may—we should marry."

"Why?"

"Because, for one thing, I will not have a child of mine born on the wrong side of the blanket."

She jerked away from him. "Well, why don't we just wait to see if that is even a possibility?" Her tone was icily sweet as she wrapped the robe around her, then stood frowning at him, gripping the folds of the garment at her chin.

"Fine," he muttered. He pulled on his trousers and reached for his shirt. "We shall discuss this in the morning."

"That will not be necessary."

"Oh, yes it will." He knew he was being childish in this need to have the last word, but damn it . . .

Kate heard the door click shut behind him, then slumped to the bed and let the tears flow. Panic seized her. "Oh, my God. I've ruined everything. Ned. We will have to leave. But where will we go? Where?"

She fumed and fretted in this manner for some minutes, then allowed common sense to assert itself. After all, Jeremy had said nothing of her leaving. In fact, he had mentioned marriage. What he had not mentioned was love. She knew from personal experience that the time-honored institution of marriage was difficult enough when two people loved and cherished each other. Of course, many a marriage was contracted on other principles, but she had no interest in finding out what it would be like without those key ingredients.

Besides, he merely wanted to ensure that his child would not be born a bastard. Even as this idea popped into her musings, she knew she was being unfair. He had been gentle and caring in his lovemaking. On some level, he genuinely cared for her—he had said as much, had he not? And was a child not a valid consideration? Of course it was. She squared her shoulders and dried her tears. Good grief. A single sexual encounter needn't necessarily result in a pregnancy. Two, her conscience chided—and all it takes is one.

For a while she let herself relive those glorious moments: his hands, his lips exploring her body; her eager responses. She blushed at remembering her own passion, that urgent need to connect with this particular man, to be connected to him in the most primal way. In that respect, you are little better than those randy widows soldiers used to make such fun of, she chastised herself.

Why had she let this happen?

Part of the answer was that she had given in to her desire for him—for Jeremy. In doing so, had she now jeopardized Ned's welfare? The more complicated answer to the question of *why*, the more honest, more complete answer, was that she loved him. She cherished and respected his integrity, his loyalty, his gentle humor, his love for his daughter, his fondness for her son, his determination to do right by the people of Kenrick. Yes, she loved him. Hopelessly—for her very presence in his life was likely to bring disaster on him. Was she, in fact, about to invite calamity into the lives of the two people she loved most?

After a nearly sleepless night, Jeremy put aside not only his nervousness about meeting with Kate again, but his need to discuss the situation with Robert, and tried to immerse himself in estate business. He sat at his desk, not seeing the papers before him when Robert came in. Avoiding what was uppermost in his mind, he told Robert

An Earl Like No Other • 171

about his brief encounter with Mortimer, then turned to examining the books in light of the sale of the wool.

Jeremy ran a hand through his hair. "It cannot be done. I see no way to save us now."

"We've yet to hear about those remaining ships," Robert said. "They may still arrive to save our bacon."

"We cannot count on that happening. Mortimer is right: Those ships too are likely at the bottom of the Indian Ocean. Moreover, we have no idea what—if any—profit we may realize if they do make it to the London docks."

"There's still the money from my grandmother and from the sale of my commission."

"No!" Jeremy said sharply, then immediately softened his tone. "We've been over this before, Robert. If we go under, that is all you will have to start over with."

"And you will have nothing."

"I'll be able to return to America. Astor will take me on again. Maybe you will want to join us."

"Maybe. . . . Well, promise me this: If my money will make the difference—help us keep Kenrick—not just the name, but all of it— you will take it and never look back. After all, we agreed on a real partnership."

"Deal," Jeremy said. "If. It is a huge gamble, though" He ran his hand through his hair again. "God, how I hate this uncertainty."

Now the uncertainty extended to Kate. He knew little of her ties in England. Would he be able to persuade her to join him if he returned to America?

After surveying all Kenrick's enterprises some weeks ago, the Chilton brothers had agreed that Robert would be the new Kenrick steward. In addition to a modest salary, he would have a percentage of overall profits—if there were any. In effect, the brothers had drawn up a partnership. Jeremy had insisted on their drafting a legal document. And so they had. Robert had collected the papers from Phillips a few days ago—along with a still hopeful letter that in effect said "no news is good news" regarding their investment in cargo ships.

"There is another matter I want to discuss with you," Jeremy said. "It concerns Mrs. Arthur—"

But before he could continue, the sound of an arriving carriage with a large team and several outriders floated through the open French doors. Both brothers looked out to see what the commotion was.

"Do you recognize that crest—a rampant lion before crossed swords?" Jeremy asked and was surprised at seeing recognition and a profound sense of alarm on Robert's face.

"Oh, my God!" Robert said. "The Duke of Wynstan."

CHAPTER 17

As she oversaw the household routine the next morning, Kate pretended to herself that there had been little change in her status at Kenrick Hall. She met with gardeners who supplied the homegrown fruits and vegetables for the earl's table; she then conferred with Mrs. Jenkins about menus for the week, and set maids to turning mattresses, laundering bedding, and dusting furniture. None of the staff treated her differently; there were no sly glances, no sudden pauses in conversations when she approached. Her secret—hers and Jeremy's—seemed safe, and she hugged it to her.

She had not seen Jeremy yet and, after that quarrel, she was apprehensive about facing him. He was not a man to ignore an issue and pretend nothing was amiss. He would surely demand an explanation of her behavior. No matter how he might react to her deception, it was time—past time—to tell him the truth. She just had to find the right opportunity to do so.

It was mid-morning; Kate and Lady Elinor occupied padded straight-backed chairs as a small table in the morning room, so called because it faced east and caught the morning sun through tall windows. The family used it as an informal sitting room. Furnished for comfort rather than show and boasting light floral colors, it was Kate's favorite room in the Hall, even though it, like the rest of the house, showed signs of age and neglect: worn upholstery and sun-streaked draperies. Having dispensed with items from a day-old newspaper, Kate had just opened a new novel by Mrs. Edgeworth when Ned, closely followed by Cassie, burst into the room.

"Mama! Mama! He found us!"

Alerted by the alarm in her son's voice, Kate felt an answering frisson of fear—Ned's terror-filled reference to *he* could mean only one person. She sought to quell her own and Ned's emotions by speaking very calmly. "Good morning, Ned. Cassie."

Ned grasped her arm and shook it. "The duke, Mama. He's here!"

"Oh, dear God, no." The words exploded from her in a hoarse whisper before she could bring reason to control the fear.

"We saw the carriage. It's his crest. I saw the lion. Him too. He found us, Mama!"

Fear sought to grab and twist her innards; she fought nausea. Kate felt her life, her whole being crumbling as she put her arm around her son. "No. No." The words now came as a soft wail. She hugged Ned tightly and, despite the chaos churning within her, pressed her forehead to his and said softly, "We must not panic."

"What is it, my dear?" Lady Elinor asked.

"It's—it's Wynstan. He wants Ned," Kate said without thinking to dissemble in answering.

"Wynstan? The Duke of Wynstan? Cedric Gardiner?" Lady Elinor was clearly mystified.

"Please, Mama. We can hide, can't we? Cassie knows a place."

"Cassie knows a—? Cassie?" Lady Elinor shot a questioning look toward the little girl.

"In the dining room. There's a secret door." Cassie had caught Ned's sense of urgency.

"Ah, the priest hole." Lady Elinor calmly accepted and dealt with the excitement of the moment. "Cassie, my dear, why don't you show it to Ned while his mama and I sort this out? We shall call you when it is safe."

Cassie shifted the ever-present Lady Lobo to one arm and grabbed Ned's hand. "Come on, Ned."

"Mama?"

"I—it's all right, Ned." Taking deep breaths, Kate was regaining control of herself. She patted him on the back. "You go along with Cassie until we call you."

With a glance over his shoulder and reluctance in every step, Ned followed Cassie from the room.

Kate seized on the trivial to buy time to think. "There's a priest hole here in Kenrick Hall?"

Lady Elinor's matter-of-fact response barely registered as Kate frantically tried to think what to do. Her instinct was to grab Ned and just run. But where? How? She could achieve nothing alone.

"The first earl and his countess remained Catholic, though they publicly accepted the crown's new religion. Many people did, you know. But it was very dangerous in this area to receive church sacraments—hence a hiding place for a priest should they be interrupted." Lady Elinor paused. She had clearly resorted to this history-book explanation to allow Kate to collect herself, for her voice now became more firm. "Now, Mrs. Arthur, it is time you explained yourself. And I want the truth—as will Jeremy."

Kate sucked in a long, quavering breath. "It's a long story."

"Begin with your connection to Wynstan."

Kate took another deep breath. "My husband was Lord Arthur Gardiner, Wynstan's son."

Lady Elinor's eyebrows shot up. "Good heavens! Go on."

In a soft, resigned voice, wringing her hands nervously, Kate gave her a hurried summary of events that had brought her and Ned to Kenrick Hall. Occasionally, the older woman interrupted with a question or a comment, but mostly she just listened. When Kate finished, Lady Elinor sat quietly. Kate sat in misery and sheer terror at the thought of losing Ned. She had been so sure they would be safe for a while longer.

Finally, Lady Elinor asked, "Do Jeremy and Robert know all this?"

"Robert does. Jer—Lord Kenrick does not—or did not. I imagine he is being informed right now of what an imposter he has been harboring." Kate swallowed hard and clenched her hand on the table. "I did not know what else to do. I could not—cannot—allow the duke to mistreat my son." She fought tears of despair.

Lady Elinor reached across to pat Kate's hand. "Of course not. But, my goodness, what a predicament this is. Do you realize how it may affect Jeremy?"

"At first, I did not think of that at all. I just wanted Ned to be safe. I never counted the cost to others. But lately—Oh, Lady Elinor, what am I to do?"

Again the older woman patted Kate's hand. "Let's just see what happens. Jeremy and Robert are very capable men. Your son is safe for the time being."

Still apprehensive, but grateful for the older woman's sympathy, Kate gripped the hand of friendship. "Thank you," she whispered.

Further conversation was cut short by the appearance of Wilkins, who announced, "Mrs. Arthur, his lordship wishes to see you in the library."

"I am coming with you," Lady Elinor said.

Jeremy turned from the scene out the window to look intently at Robert. "Wynstan? You know him?"

"Know of him. He's here about Kate."

"Kate?"

"Kate. She needs our help, Jeremy. We both owe her. We must protect her. We must."

A sense of urgency swept from Robert to Jeremy, where it quickly blended with apprehension and anger.

"Kate? Kate needs protection? From a duke? What does that mean? Just what the hell is going on?"

"Just trust me, all right?" Robert begged over the furious knocking at the door. "Trust her."

Jeremy ran a hand through his hair. "Trust. There seems to have been an amazing lack of that commodity around here lately."

An open door from the library to the entrance hall allowed Jeremy and Robert to hear clearly an imperious male voice.

"Inform your master that the Duke of Wynstan wishes to see him immediately."

Jeremy stepped into the hall. "That will not be necessary, Wilkins." He then quietly instructed Wilkins to locate Mrs. Arthur.

Two men stood before him, but Jeremy had no difficulty distinguishing between them. The duke was a tall, thin man with a shock of thick white hair and heavy black eyebrows over granite-hard, almost black eyes. A square jaw and thin lips did little to soften one's impression. He was dressed in black and carried an ebony cane, though he held himself erect. The other man, heavier, and not as tall or as forbidding in demeanor, wore the signature red vest of a Bow Street Runner.

"I demand that you produce my grandson this instant," the duke said.

"How do you do, your grace? Welcome to Kenrick Hall," Jeremy said with exaggerated politeness and extended his hand. "I am Kenrick. This is my brother, the Honorable Robert Chilton."

Wynstan ignored the proffered hand. "I know who you are. And I know you are sheltering that slut who kidnapped my grandson. I have come to retrieve him and Hoskins here has a warrant from the London magistrate for her arrest."

Jeremy assumed a haughty attitude to match that of his boorish guest. "I am not accustomed, your grace, to allowing demeaning references to women in my home, nor to discussing important matters in my entrance hall. Please step into the library." He shot Robert a questioning glance and mouthed the question, *His grandson?*

Robert nodded glumly. Suddenly much that had puzzled Jeremy about his housekeeper and her son fell into place. But he still had a number of questions and he thought he might thoroughly throttle her once this was over. He had no doubt she was the boy's mother, but what was her relationship to the duke? Surely the man would not refer to his own daughter in such coarse terms. But just as surely Kate—his Kate—was a woman of quality; her education and speech proclaimed her such. She had deceived him profoundly, but he was damned if he would allow this man—duke or not—to mistreat her, nor to ride roughshod over someone under even the unknowing protection of the Earl of Kenrick.

Jeremy gestured to seats for their guests as Robert closed the library door. The duke looked around the room disparagingly and seemed to be withholding himself from the shabby elegance he saw. When Robert too was seated, Jeremy said, "Would you care to explain what, exactly, you are doing here, your grace?"

"I told you," Wynstan replied in the same superior tone. "Hoskins, you tell him in the simple terms he might understand."

The Runner looked uncomfortable, but explained as though he were reading a report. "After an exhaustive investigation, we have determined that the woman passing herself off as 'Mrs. Arthur' here at Kenrick Hall is, in fact, Lady Arthur Gardiner, widow of Lord Arthur Gardiner, youngest son of the Duke of Wynstan. The child Edward Arthur Gardiner is the Marquis of Spenland, heir to the Duke of Wynstan."

Jeremy looked at Robert for confirmation, but he knew, even before seeing Robert's nod, that it was true.

The Runner went on in the same rote tone: "As head of the family and in the absence of the child's father, the Duke of Wynstan is asserting his legal right to take charge of said child. He has sworn out a warrant for the woman's arrest."

"I am having her transported," Wynstan said. "Teach that baggage to cross swords with *me*."

"Careful of your language," Jeremy said softly. "Another slur, and, duke or not, I will have you thrown out of my home."

Red with outrage, the duke spit his words sliced through clenched jaws. "You would not dare such. Do you even know with whom you are dealing?"

"I am fully aware of who you are, but as a guest in my home—invited or not—you will behave accordingly."

"Just produce the woman and the child and let us get this over with," the duke ordered.

Robert addressed the Bow Street Runner. "Mr. Hoskins, I am sure you have a much better acquaintance with the law than I have, but have Lord Spenland's guardians been contacted in this matter?"

"Guardians?" The man looked in surprise at Wynstan. "Why—we assumed the duke had full legal standing. Male head of the family and all, you know."

Robert replied, "I happen to know that Lord Spenland's father appointed two respected and responsible gentlemen to serve as his surrogates should he be unable to manage his son's affairs."

"This certainly sheds a different light on the picture. You did not tell us this when you swore out that warrant, your grace," the Runner accused.

The duke issued a contemptuous snort. "Of course I did not do so. It was irrelevant. My position supersedes a scribbled paper." He turned to Jeremy. "Now will you produce the—uh—woman and the boy, or must I have this place ransacked looking for them?"

"You will do no such thing," Jeremy said. "You would need an army for such an endeavor, and I assure you those outriders who accompanied you would not be sufficient to the task. Nor will Mrs. Arthur—Lady Arthur—go anywhere against her will."

"I demand you require that woman's presence here and now." The duke rapped his cane against the floor. "And Hoskins, you are to arrest her forthwith."

"I cannot do that, your grace, until we know the legal status of guardianship," Hoskins said.

The duke turned to Jeremy. "Bah! Send for her! Now!"

"I am right here, your grace."

Kate, accompanied by Lady Elinor, stepped through the door.

The men, even the duke, stood as the women entered, though Kate noted that Wynstan studiously ignored her. She saw him frown in confusion at Lady Elinor and then turn away from her. When the women were seated, Kate ventured a look at Jeremy, but it was difficult to read his expression. However, she had heard enough of the conversation to know that he would not allow the duke free reign.

The duke, who remained standing, pointed an accusing finger at Kate and glared at her. "You! Who do you think you are, spiriting away my heir as you did?"

"I am his mother," she said simply. "And I shall continue to do all I can to protect him from being abused by you—or anyone else, for that matter. He has been happy here. Children should be allowed to be happy."

He responded with another derisive snort. "Happy! The boy needs discipline and training if he is to one day take my place. Discipline and training. And I intend to see he gets them."

"Over my dead body," Kate snapped.

"Oh, I shouldn't think it would come that," the duke said with a mirthless chuckle. His next words were stones flung directly at her heart. "But you *will* be out of the picture. The penal colony in New South Wales."

Kate felt an icy shiver course through her. She knew it was very possible for this cold specimen of humanity to achieve just such an end.

"Oh, for heaven's sake, Cedric. You always were an outrageous bully, but this is quite beyond enough." Lady Elinor's outburst focused surprised attention on her.

A deep flush suffused the duke's face as he peered more closely at the source of this affront to his person. "Eh? Who? Oh, I say—it—it cannot be. Lady Elinor Chilton?"

"Elinor Baxter, you old curmudgeon. As you well know. After all these years, you still think you can dictate to everyone. Browbeat people enough and they fall like dominoes, eh?"

"Well, I—I—"

"You could not dictate to Baxter and me years ago, and believe me, you cannot dictate here, either."

Kate watched, mesmerized, as Wynstan engaged in an internal struggle to regain the upper hand. Surprise, chagrin, and arrogance flashed across his features. Vindictiveness won.

"We shall see who has the final say on this matter," he threatened. "The law is likely to take a very dim view of a woman's grabbing a child from his ancestral home to take up residence in the establishment of an unmarried man. It's indecent, I tell you."

"Here, now—" Robert interjected.

Jeremy stood and held up a hand to halt any further outburst from the duke. "That's enough, Wynstan. You've gone too far. Too far by half."

Lady Elinor sat up straighter. Her voice dripped honey and vinegar. "And you forget, Cedric, that I am very much a part of this household. I do hope you are not attempting to question *my* character. I doubt our mutual friends in the ton would tolerate that."

"Oh, for—" The duke swallowed the rest of the utterance, then raised his cane and shook it at the lot of them. "Mark my words, one way or another that child will be returned to my management."

Kate felt a shiver of premonition. Instinctively, she looked at Jeremy, who gave her a slight nod as he took a stance at the fireplace, resting his arm along the mantel.

"Nothing will be resolved here and now," he said. "It will take a few days to get the legalities of this matter sorted out. Meanwhile Mrs.—Lady—Arthur and her son will stay where they are. And you, your grace, may find accommodation to your liking at the Kenrick Inn in town. I would offer you the hospitality of Kenrick Hall, but under the circumstances, I feel sure you would be more comfortable elsewhere."

Jeremy's tone left no room for quibbling and Kate felt a twinge of satisfaction at this slight to the duke's consequence.

Her satisfaction was short-lived, for as soon as the door closed on the departing duke and his companion, Jeremy's rather enigmatic gaze shifted from Kate to Robert and back to Kate. She squirmed inwardly, wishing this moment could have been avoided.

"*Lady* Arthur, Robert," he said, laying an ironic twist to her title, "I believe Aunt Elinor and I are entitled to some sort of explanation."

His voice was calm, detached, but Kate wished she knew what he thought, what he felt.

What Jeremy thought, what he felt as she told her story could be summed up in a single word: *betrayal.*

Amelia.

Willow.

Kate.

Three women he had cared for—and each of them had betrayed him. Even as he listened to Kate's story, he recalled his earlier misjudgments of women in his life.

So what if his feelings for Amelia amounted to adolescent infatuation—a boy naively equating physical beauty and an unassailable position in his father's household with perfection in character? His stepmother had found his puppy-like adoration amusing, his innocence laughable.

And then there had been Willow. She of the laughing brown eyes, she who clutched and clawed at life, demanding, taking whatever she wanted, whenever she wanted. He had been so utterly bewitched by her, so thrilled to have been what she wanted—that it had not occurred to him that she was capricious in her desires. In looking back, he did not doubt that she had loved him—in her fashion. But Willow was incapable of committing herself for long to anyone or anything. For her, the chase itself was the very stuff of life. He knew that much of the fault had lain with him, with his failure to understand her character. Willow's mother had tried to warn him.

"My daughter is very free-spirited, Mr. Chilton. She doesn't always choose wisely."

"And you view me as a bad choice?" he had asked.

"No. On the contrary. I think you the best choice she has ever made. I just hope—I pray—she will be satisfied—that you will both be happy."

They had been—for a while. He supposed, with the benefit of hindsight, that each of them had found the other exotic and fascinating. When the novelty wore off for her, Willow had been unable to settle for what had by then become familiar. What might have given comfort, she found tiresome. He sensed her restlessness, but felt powerless to deal with it. Then she became pregnant. Jeremy had longed for a child; Willow saw motherhood as a trap. It was all his fault, of course, for Willow was incapable of owning her share of blame for anything. He had often wondered if matters might have been different had Willow had a chance to know her daughter—or would she have come to resent her child as much as she had her husband?

And now Kate.

He had allowed it to happen again.

Would he never learn?

"So, there you have it," Kate said, interrupting his musings. "I hope, my lord, that you will not harbor any resentment toward Robert for agreeing to keep my secret."

"I think," Jeremy said slowly, feeling his way in this morass, "that it is not Robert's behavior that is in question."

Lady Elinor interjected, "But surely, Jeremy, you can see Mrs. Arthur's—Lady Arthur's position. Imagine if someone tried to take Cassie from us."

"Kate," said Lady Arthur. "Just Kate, please."

Jeremy gave her an oblique look and, seeing her blush, knew they were both remembering his use of her name just last night. He ran his hand through his hair and looked at both Robert and Kate.

"Are you sure about this business of guardianship?"

Kate nodded. "Yes. Since he could not give a mere woman legal authority, Arthur appointed his friends Mr. Phillips and Major Lawrence."

Robert rose to place a reassuring hand on Kate's shoulder. "I was there when Arthur received the papers in the regimental mail. Said he wanted me to see them as an extra precaution."

Noting the gesture, Jeremy said, "Nevertheless, Wynstan seems a very determined man. And you know what they say about possession being eleven parts of the law. We should curtail morning rides for the children—at least temporarily."

Fear flashed in Kate's eyes. "Yes! Wynstan can be very determined. He is used to getting what he wants."

"We shall do our best to protect your son, Mrs.—uh—Kate," Jeremy assured her.

"That we will," Robert affirmed.

"I fear all three of you are overlooking something," Lady Elinor said. They turned expectant gazes toward her. "Wynstan's slur about this being a bachelor household. My presence does lend a degree of propriety, but there is likely to be a great deal of gossip. Wynstan will see to it—out of sheer spite, if nothing else. He has done it before. He will do all in his power to sway public opinion. And he *is* very powerful."

Robert shrugged. "So? People always have to have something to talk about in Yorkshire. Especially in Yorkshire."

"So—this sort of talk could be very damaging to Kate, to her case, if it goes to court," Lady Elinor said. "What is more, the Kenrick name is likely to be muddied—yet again. Since the situation involves a person of Wynstan's rank, the talk most assuredly will not be confined to Yorkshire."

"But—but, as you told Wynstan, you have been here all along," Robert said.

"I was trying to divert him, but I doubt that a chaperone will account for much in ton circles," his aunt responded. "The vultures love gossip—the more salacious, the better."

"Oh, I am so sorry, my lord." Kate sounded devastated. "I never intended—I just wanted—"

"Well," Robert said, taking a practical tone and pacing about the room, "I suppose if one of us married her, that would solve the problem."

For a long moment no one said anything, then Kate spoke.

"Robert Chilton!" Her tone was a blend of anger and amusement. "If that is a marriage proposal, I do most heartily reject it!"

"Why? What do you find objectionable in me?" Robert asked.

Despite the underlying gravity of the situation, the other three laughed at Robert's little-boy-hurt expression and tone. Perhaps a bit of comic relief *was* in order, Jeremy thought.

Her amusement still very evident, Kate said, "Because, you lovable looby, you don't love me. Nor can I love you—at least not in the way a wife should love a husband."

Welcoming this information, yet still torn by his own conflicting emotions, Jeremy said, "Well, that leaves me."

Kate held his gaze for a long moment, her expression unreadable. She rose and smoothed her skirt. "Let us hope such a drastic step is unnecessary, though I do appreciate the willingness—of both of you—to make such a sacrifice. Now, if you will excuse me, I think I must go and rescue Ned and Cassie from the priest hole."

When she had gone, Robert escorted Lady Elinor for a stroll in the garden, and Jeremy stayed in the library, feeling the full weight of the morning's disclosures.

So his housekeeper was a member of one of the most eminent families in the realm. Her son—Cassie's playmate—was heir to a duke. So much for even a remote possibility of taking her and Ned with him to America.

They had stormed into his life under false pretenses.

She had been dishonest.

A sin of omission, he temporized.

A sin nevertheless, a streak of stubbornness insisted.

And he was damned if he was ready to forgive her.

Besides, there was still the matter of the duke.

Not to mention Mortimer, debt, threats, that mysterious fire—and the price of wool.

CHAPTER 18

A few hours later, Kate's earlier self-congratulations on seeing no change in her status in Kenrick Hall seemed a joke worthy of the gods themselves, for now the staff did, indeed, treat her differently. There were definite signs that the news had raced through the Hall: sudden pauses in conversations, speculative looks, confusion in greeting her with bows, curtsies, stumbling over her title. She was sad at losing all that she had achieved in the way of trust and rapport with other staff members.

She sought to put others at ease by carefully treating them with the same understanding and respect as always. She sought to quell her fear and uncertainty by taking refuge in mundane tasks. This ploy proved only partly successful in calming her inner turmoil. What should she do? What *could* she do? Grab Ned's hand and dash into the woods? A fairy-tale solution. To sneak away again would be impossible.

Besides, Lord Kenrick—Jeremy—had said, had he not, that he would protect her son? Regardless of what he might think of her now, she felt certain he would honor that promise—which made her love him all the more.

She was in the stillroom sorting and labeling herbs and spices when Wilkins notified her very formally that her presence had been requested for the midday meal with the family in the dining room.

"The family?" she asked, feeling stupid.

"That is what his lordship said." Wilkins looked beyond her.

She washed her hands, tucked an errant curl beneath the mobcap, and reported as instructed to find Jeremy, his aunt, and his brother already there. Four places had been set at one end of the table; a footman held a chair for her. When Wilkins and the footman had finished serving them, Lord Kenrick dismissed them and waited for the door to close before speaking.

"We have given the situation a good deal of thought, my lady," he said. "Henceforth, you will be an honored guest in this house. You will take your meals with us and you will remove to one of the guest bedchambers."

"Oh, I should not think that necessary," Kate protested. "I am quite satisfied in the nursery wing."

"As your hosts, we are not," Jeremy said, looking toward his aunt.

"You see, my dear," Lady Elinor said, "now that the servants know who you are, we can hardly relegate you to quarters that are less elegant than what any member of society would deserve as our guest."

"The sooner the servants view you as such, the sooner everyone else will," Jeremy explained.

"Better accept your new status, Kate," Robert said. "There is a good deal at stake here. Socially, politically, perhaps even legally."

Not to mention emotionally, she thought, and she again seized on the banal, the trivial, to avoid letting her mind drift to the painful. "But—but what about my duties as housekeeper? Someone needs to—"

Jeremy interrupted. "For the time being, you may continue to supervise as before. Wilkins will see that your instructions are carried out."

"I see . . ." His rather formal tone shredded her heart. She wanted to throw her arms around him and say, "I'm sorry, Jeremy. I'm sorry I was not more honest with you, more trusting. I'm sorry to bring such chaos to your world just when you were working so hard to right it." Instead, she sat quietly and listened as others managed her life—again.

Across the table, Lady Elinor offered a sympathetic smile. "For your sake as well as ours, we must try to deflect the gossip. Public opinion can be a powerful force in legal matters."

"And in political matters," Robert added.

"To that end," Jeremy said, "Aunt Elinor has invited the vicar and his wife, as well as Squire Dennison, along with his wife and daughter, to take supper with us tomorrow evening."

"Nothing elaborate," Lady Elinor assured her. "These are my special friends. We can rely on them to help us put a good face on this situation."

Robert chuckled. "And it does not hurt that Dennison is also the local magistrate."

Kate felt herself near tears at this show of support. "I do so appreciate your kindness, and I sincerely regret—"

"Now. Now. 'What's done is done and cannot now be undone' as a Scottish queen once put it," Lady Elinor said.

Kate gave her a rueful smile. "Lady Macbeth was a party to *murder.*"

Lady Elinor returned the smile. "Nevertheless, what we cannot undo, we must try to mitigate."

"How?" Kate asked.

"We—the three of us—have come up with something," Jeremy said. "If you are amenable, we have concocted a story that might suffice."

"And that is?"

Robert explained. "A mad relative of the Duke of Wynstan somehow got it into his head that he, instead of Ned, is Wynstan's heir and, fearing he would harm your child, you fled. Naturally, you sought the aid of your dead husband's friend—the intrepid Captain Robert Chilton—who persuaded his brother to allow you to pose as his housekeeper, but now the madman is safely ensconced in Bedlam and we are welcoming the glorious truth."

Kate laughed. "Preposterous. I was here long before you arrived."

Robert waved a hand dismissively. "That too was part of the plan." He paused. "The story is a little thin, but will serve to mitigate the gossip—or obfuscate."

Kate shrugged. "If you all think this will work . . . But what about Wynstan's version?"

"He was understandably worried about appearances and made foolish accusations in a fit of anger," Lady Elinor said.

"Which at least touches on the truth," Jeremy said.

Kate gave them a tentative smile, her gaze resting a moment on Jeremy's unreadable expression. "Then I had best see that Mrs. Jenkins serves up a truly remarkable supper tomorrow." Glad to have a project to occupy her, she rose.

Jeremy rose as well. "Mrs.—uh—Kate."

She turned at the door to see a distinct twinkle in his eyes.

"You may leave off those badges of office," he said.

"My lord?"

"Your helmet and armor. That infernal mobcap and apron."

"Oh. As you wish, my lord."

Well, she thought as she left the room, he did not seem unduly angry with her, but she was sure he still resented what he must see as—what was, indeed—her deceit. She regretted it, but what choice had she had? She could have told him sooner, as Robert had suggested, but somehow the timing was never right.

In bed last night?

Well, yes, she *might* have broached the topic then—had he not suggested she was so loose with her favors that she could wantonly bed one brother while having some sort of liaison with the other. The very idea!

Now—now she must put aside what might have been. She must concentrate on protecting Ned from a man whose idea of discipline and training meant torturing a child. And to do that, his mother needed help. In these enlightened, modern times women like the Princess of Wales and Lady Caroline Lamb might flout convention and assert a degree of independence, but woe betide a lesser woman who tried that—a country squire's daughter who openly opposed a duke. Ned's safety—his very being—depended on his mother's engaging help that could now come from only one source: the Earl of Kenrick.

Just when Jeremy thought this day could produce nothing more to complicate his life, it did.

Late in the afternoon, Nathan Porter arrived at the Hall and asked to see Lord Kenrick and Mr. Chilton. He was directed to the stables, where the two brothers leaned on a fence watching a trainer work a young horse Robert had purchased at Tattersall's before leaving London.

Greetings and praise of the new mount over, Jeremy asked, "What brings you our way, Porter?"

"I think I got a lead on that there fire, my lord."

"Are you sure?"

"Well, it could prove to be nothin' at all, but it seems worth lookin' into."

"Out with it, man," Robert demanded.

"Me 'n a couple of fellas was over at that tavern on Durham Road. Billy Thompson an' his pa was there—both of them drinkin' pretty heavy. Someone mentioned our fire, what a terrible accident it was an' how it was too bad it happened when the new earl was tryin' so hard to put things right an' all. Then Billy, he says real nasty-like, 'What makes ya think it was an accident?' Then the pa says, 'Watch yer tongue, boy.' He tried to get Billy to leave and he finally did, but as they left Billy says, 'Kenrick bastards didn't get near what they deserve.' "

"Interesting," Robert said, "especially when we've not spread it about that the fire was a case of arson."

"What did he mean about our not getting what we deserve?" Jeremy asked. "I know Thompson thought he would be better off as a tenant with Mortimer than with us, but I was not aware of bad blood or truly hard feelings about his move."

Porter stroked his chin. "I ain't real sure. After them two left, the barkeeper said they blamed one of your older brothers for some family problems, but he either didn't know what they was, or he wasn't gonna tell *me*."

Jeremy turned to his brother. "Have you any idea what that might have been, Robert? Something that might have happened after I left England?"

Robert's brow wrinkled in concentration. "No. . . . Not really. As I said before, Billy and his sister were my age, but once I went off to school, I saw them only during holidays. Billy and Mina were daredevils, though. Last time I saw them, I think we were all about seventeen. She was a pretty girl, but something of a flirt. Billy was quite protective of her, as I remember."

"I'd say that 'bout sums up them two," Porter agreed. "My wife used to caution our oldest girl not to behave like Mina."

"Hmm. Could be something there," Jeremy said. "Charles always fancied himself as quite a ladies' man."

"We can't confront the Thompsons with no more than that to go on," Robert said.

"You're right. We need to know more about our 'deserving' that fire. But don't forget, we do have some hard evidence: that oil-soaked rag meant to start a fire in the small barn."

"Pretty flimsy though," Robert replied. "Every household has old rags lying around."

"But they are not all white cotton with blue stripes," Jeremy said. "Let's bide our time another day or two, find out what we can before accusing anyone."

"My oldest daughter, Eve, might know something about Thompson family troubles," Porter said. "She knew Mina. Eve married the Edmonds boy over in Hollister Glen. I'll take a ride over there tomorrow."

"Aunt Elinor and her friends may be able to help too," Jeremy said, "but we have to be discreet—no sense stirring up any more needless, hurtful gossip."

Later that evening, with Robert off on what he had announced as a "reconnoitering mission," Jeremy and Kate has seen to the bedtime rituals for Cassie and Ned, the two parents tacitly agreeing to keep to the children's routine as much as possible. They had then joined Lady Elinor in the family drawing room, where the other two had prevailed upon Kate to give them a song and then another and another.

Jeremy thought the women as aware as he that they were avoiding discussing Wynstan's bombshell visit that morning. He was also conscious of how utterly comfortable he was in this very domestic scene, even though he refused to let go entirely of his sense of betrayal. He found himself fascinated by a wisp of a curl on Kate's forehead, and as she sang, he watched her mouth, remembering how those lips had responded to his the night before.

"So, tell us, Kate," he said to prolong the pleasant interlude, "how you came to be so musically adept."

"My father insisted all his children learn to play some instrument," she replied. "When my sister Beatrice and I showed a bit of talent on the pianoforte, he readily provided lessons."

"He made the right choice," Lady Elinor said. "You certainly are testimony to his wisdom in doing so."

"Thank you, my lady."

Jeremy noted a faint blush, but no false modesty in her demeanor. "That was a detail left out of our London interview a few months ago."

Her blush deepened. "I am truly sorry I deceived you so. I—it seemed a right solution at the time."

"And Phillips knew all along?"

"Yes, but to his credit, he did suggest I should tell you the truth."

"You should have."

She put aside her guitar and sat up straighter, a challenging glint in her eyes. "Now be honest, my lord. Would you have invited Lady Arthur Gardiner and her titled son—strangers—for an extended visit at Kenrick Hall?"

"Well, no, probably not," he admitted.

She gave him an arch look. "Given the issues you already faced, should that not be *definitely not*?"

"She has you there, Jeremy," his aunt said.

"Oh, all right," he said. "Back to the point I intended. Aside from your connection to Wynstan, just who are you?"

With occasional comments or questions from her two companions, she gave them a forthright, albeit brief, account of her earlier life.

No wonder they called her the Angel of the 46th, Jeremy thought. It took a very strong degree of courage and fortitude for a young, gently bred woman to defy an autocratic father and the conventions of society and then deal with the hardships of an army on the march.

On the heels of her last comment, Robert strolled into the room. "Confession time finally?" he asked with grin.

"You might say that," she said.

"I have some news that should interest all of you," Robert said and paused.

"Well?" Jeremy and Lady Elinor said simultaneously.

"Wynstan did not go to the inn." Again he paused.

"He left Yorkshire?" Jeremy asked.

"Oh, no. He is still in the area. He is a guest of Sir Eldridge Mortimer."

"He is a friend of Mortimer?" Jeremy asked with a glance at Kate.

She shrugged. "Not that I know of."

"I suppose he is now," Robert said. "Way I heard it, Mortimer was in town and dropped into the inn. He heard Wynstan come in and learned he had had some business here at Kenrick. He introduced himself and assured the duke he could offer accommodation more fitting Wynstan's rank than a mere country inn could."

Jeremy shook his head. "So the encroaching Sir Eldridge snagged himself a duke as a house guest."

"The innkeeper Finley was mad as hops about the loss of custom," Robert went on, "and Mrs. Finley was even madder."

"She is very proud of the bed and board she provides," Lady Elinor said. "Sir Eldridge likely offended her mightily. And Agnes Finley is not one to suffer in silence."

"Let us hope that knight and his new friend the duke don't come up with further mischief to plague our favorite earl," Robert said with a nod at Jeremy.

"Amen," Lady Elinor said.

Jeremy directed a look of understanding sympathy toward Kate, but one tinged with apprehension. What might those two powerful, tyrannical blackguards—his nemesis and hers combining forces—come up with to plague them further?

When Lady Elinor voiced her wish to retire, Robert, having as he put it, "had a sufficiently long day," offered to escort her above stairs to her chamber. Kate rose to do so as well.

Jeremy too was on his feet. "Kate, a word, if you please."

She turned from the door. *"Uh-oh. Here it comes,"* she thought. The dressing-down she deserved. "Yes, my lord?"

"Jeremy will do as well tonight as it did last night," he said, closing the distance between them, then the door as well. He gripped her elbow and steered her to a couch, where he sat beside her. She felt herself blush at his reference to the previous night, but, no, she would not allow him to disconcert her.

He ran his hand through his hair in a gesture she found endearing, for it showed a degree of vulnerability and uncertainty that she was sure he did not intend.

Finally, he took her hand in his and seemed to be floundering for his words. "Last night I . . . offered marriage to a woman I—uh—care for a great deal."

"Your housekeeper."

"My housekeeper." His tone became firmer. "Today, she is the same woman. My feelings have not changed."

"But? You are having second thoughts today?" Kate tried to hide her disappointment. "Never mind, Jeremy. I will not hold you to a bedroom declaration." She refused to look at him and tried to rise.

He slipped an arm around her shoulders and with his other hand gently turned her face to his. "No. I am not having second thoughts—not about the woman, nor about my wish to marry her."

"Even though you thought her capable of bedding one brother while carrying on with the other?"

He removed his hand from her chin, but held her gaze with his. "You distort what I meant then—and distract from the point I want to make now."

She moved away slightly, but his arm remained firmly around her shoulders. She said, "And the point is . . . ?"

He gave her a rueful smile. "There is more than one now. Yesterday, even hovering on the edge of genteel poverty as I may be, I had something to offer a housekeeper. Today, I haven't much to offer the mother of a son who will one day be a very rich, very powerful man."

"Today, she is in danger of being transported and—of—of losing her son." She was unable to quell sob.

"My dear Kate." He pulled her close and kissed her tenderly. "I shall do all in my power to prevent both those things from happening."

"H—how?"

"First of all, we announce our heretofore secret engagement." He put a finger to her lips when she started to speak. "Hear me out. We make the announcement—tomorrow night. If you want to cry off later—well, so be it. But no court would order that the intended wife of a peer be transported for anything short of murder or treason."

Feeling a twinge of hope for the first time since Ned had burst in with news of Wynstan's arrival, she gave him a faint smile that quickly faded. "What about Ned? Oh, Jeremy—I cannot lose him. I cannot have him harmed."

"Shh. Of course you cannot." He kissed her again.

Overcome by relief at being able at last to share this greatest fear, she returned the kiss fiercely. It deepened, and when he pulled away, they were both breathing heavily.

"Jeremy," she said softly, leaning toward him.

He stood and pulled her to her feet, giving her a lopsided grin. "I know I am going to regret this within minutes—but, no, I shall not take advantage of this moment. I want more than gratitude from you, Kate."

With that, he gave her a chaste kiss on the cheek and gently pushed her toward the door.

Surprised and taken aback, Kate climbed the stairs to yet another of Kenrick Hall's bedchambers.

Jeremy was right.
Within minutes he regretted sending her away.

CHAPTER 19

At breakfast the next morning Kate and Jeremy informed Robert and Lady Elinor of the plan to announce their engagement at supper that evening. When the other two offered hearty and sincere congratulations, Kate was uncomfortable.

"Please. I am willing to be party to a show for others, but I could not endure any more deceit with the two of you. This is a scheme—Jeremy's plan to forestall Wynstan's having me transported."

"That *is* the primary reason," Jeremy said. "But there is also the matter of the slurs he made about a woman of the peerage being so long in the home of an unmarried man."

"Wynstan and the Mortimers will make much of that, I am sure," Lady Elinor said.

"Be that as it may," Kate continued, "when the issue of Ned's guardianship is settled, I fully intend to release Lord Kenrick from such a commitment."

"But, my dear," Lady Elinor protested, "you will be called a jilt, thus justifying in some circles exactly what Wynstan suggested."

"Jeremy, you agreed to this?" Robert asked.

Jeremy shrugged. "It is Kate's life. Hers and Ned's. She must do as she deems best."

Kate thought she should be pleased with this response, but somehow she found it unsatisfying—then scolded herself for being so contrary. Aloud she said, "Any negative talk will have long since died down by the time Ned is of an age for it to matter to him."

Now that her true identity was known to all and sundry, Kate felt out of place in the servants' milieu and not wholly comfortable as a guest. Neither fish nor fowl again, she thought sourly. It had been that way ever since a squire's daughter had eloped with a duke's son. She had managed eventually to forge a place for herself on the Peninsula, and, until Wynstan's untimely visit, she had felt comfortable here too.

In between?

Well, at first she had simply not cared. Numb with grief as a new widow, she wandered through her days much like a sleepwalker. So long as Ned was cared for, nothing else mattered. Only when she found him suffering had she been jarred out of her lethargy.

Here at Kenrick Hall—her attraction to its master aside—she had truly begun to develop a sense of belonging, a sense of being in the right place. Her son was happy and the two of them were free, if only temporarily. Yes, it was temporary, but she had hoped it would last a few more months, perhaps a year or two.

Now . . . Now what? She felt so helpless. She *was* helpless. All her options were in the hands of others. Never before had Katherine Emma Newton Gardiner felt so powerless. The very worst of it was her inability to ensure her son's right to a normal childhood, his right to make his own choices and—yes—his own mistakes in life.

These thoughts haunted her even as she devised a menu with Mrs. Jenkins for the evening meal and conferred with Wilkins regarding wine and table settings. Then she sought escape from her worries in the herb garden. If only she could dispose of life's troubles so easily as attacking weeds or pinching off unwelcome buds.

That was where Wilkins found her: on her knees, cursing weeds.

"Ah, I thought this was where you might have disappeared to."

She stood. "Mr. Wilkins, you know me far too well." She immediately felt herself blushing at the irony in this statement.

"Yes. Well. Guests have arrived and your presence is required," Wilkins said.

"Not Wynstan, I hope."

"No. Not Wynstan. Two gentlemen from London."

Puzzled, she removed her gloves and a battered straw hat and wished she were wearing something more presentable than a dark cotton print dress.

"How do I look?" she asked nervously.

"You'll do," the normally austere butler said with a very slight twitch of his lips. Maybe that hard-won rapport had not been erased entirely.

In the drawing room, along with Jeremy, Robert, and Lady Elinor, Kate found two familiar, very welcome faces.

"Mr. Phillips! Major Lawrence! How very nice to see you!" She extended both her hands and a warm smile to each in turn. "You know that Wynstan—"

"Yes. That is why we are here, Lady Arthur. Kenrick and Chilton have been bringing us up to date," Major Lawrence said as the gentlemen resumed their seats in separate chairs and Kate sat on a couch next to Lady Elinor.

"As you know, I have a property near Wynstan's main holding," Lawrence went on. "Arthur was a particular friend of mine," he said for the benefit of the Chiltons. "Ned is my godson. When I heard that the duke was sure he had located them, I notified Phillips."

"And as I had some business to discuss with Kenrick anyway, we decided to come ourselves," Phillips added. "We have arrived rather dusty and travel-worn, but with the documentation required to put finish to Wynstan's claims."

"Oh, thank goodness," Kate said, feeling tears of relief threaten. She looked from the visitors to Jeremy and Robert. "Can we . . . can we notify Wynstan immediately?"

Robert laughed. "Phillips and Lawrence are quite ahead of us on that mission!"

"We encountered the Bow Street Runner, Hoskins, at the Kenrick Inn. He was satisfied that the two of us are Lord Spenland's guardians," Phillips said.

Lawrence added, "He was on his way to inform Wynstan when we left the inn. I do not envy the man that task."

"All's well that ends well?" Kate's voice was shaky.

"Perhaps," Jeremy cautioned. "I do not want to dash hopes here, but I think we must take Wynstan's parting threat seriously. Were he to have physical possession of the lad, we would have a serious problem, would we not, Wally?" He addressed Phillips. "You are the so-licitor here."

Phillips nodded. "We surely would. Probably take an act of Parliament to rectify. And Wynstan wields a deal of power in the House of Lords."

"Oh, dear God," Kate said softly, putting her hand to her mouth.

Jeremy rose to stand behind her and squeeze her shoulder. "You must not fear unduly, Kate. We will take precautions—like curtailing Ned's rides so long as Wynstan is in Yorkshire."

Kate saw Lawrence raise an eyebrow at Jeremy's gesture and his use of her given name, but she felt warmed and reassured by Jeremy's use of *we*.

"Thank you, my lord." She rose and smoothed her skirt nervously as she smiled at all of them. "And, now, since I am still the Kenrick housekeeper, I had best see to rooms for these gentlemen and additional places at the evening meal."

Supper that evening was not the first meal Jeremy had hosted for guests since his return to England, but was certainly one of the more enjoyable such occasions. Margaret should be here now, he thought. Mrs. Packwood and the Dennison ladies had oohed and aahed over the elegance of the table settings and flowers. The meal itself was outstanding, with subtle uses of herbs and spices to both fish and meat dishes.

But the Earl of Kenrick had an additional reason for feeling rather expansive this evening. Earlier in the day, as Major Lawrence and Robert, veterans of the Peninsula and Waterloo, refought a battle or two and caught each other up on their respective lives since, Phillips had been delivering some welcome news to Jeremy.

"I assume the business you mentioned to Kate had to do with certain cargo ships?" Jeremy asked as he and Phillips trailed behind the other two on the way out to the stables so Robert could show off his newest acquisition.

Phillips grinned. "It does. All three of the remaining ships docked four days ago."

"Cargo intact?"

"Cargo intact. We are not nabobs by any means, but we will realize a handsome profit." Phillips named a sum that had Jeremy's eyebrows shooting skyward.

"Great! More than we thought to realize, especially after that disaster with the other two."

"By itself not enough to get you out of the clutches of your chief creditor, but with other income, maybe—"

"We've had a setback on the wool production," Jeremy said as they neared the stable and heard Robert call to a groom to bring out his black. "I'll explain tonight, for I'd like your advice on how to proceed."

Thus had Jeremy approached this evening's gathering with a lighter heart than he might have otherwise done.

When dessert was served—a delicious peach tart—Jeremy leaned over to murmur to Kate, who sat at his right, "I might have preferred a strawberry pie."

She colored up just as he had expected, but managed to say calmly, " 'Tis not the season for strawberries, my lord."

He shook his head in an exaggerated grimace and said, "Just my luck."

She pressed her lips together and gave him a look of exasperation, but he was sure she was trying not to smile.

When the table had been cleared of dessert, Jeremy nodded to Wilkins, who produced the requisite glasses and filled them with chilled champagne. Jeremy looked at Kate, but refused to acknowledge a panicky question he saw in her eyes. He rose and, placing a hand under her elbow, brought her to her feet beside him.

"My friends, Lady Arthur and I want to take this opportunity to announce that she has made me a very happy man by agreeing to become my wife."

Shocked silence ensued as Jeremy lifted his glass in a salute to Kate, then the others quickly recovered and lifted glasses too.

"Oh, I say. Congratulations, Kenrick," Major Lawrence said to a chorus of "Hear! Hear!" around the table.

Kate was dumbfounded. Surely the news that Bow Street had no further interest in seeing her transported had made this announcement unnecessary. She had tried several times throughout the day to find an occasion to say as much to Jeremy, but always he was not alone, or nowhere to be found. Now she wondered if that had been deliberate.

But why would he go through with an announcement that now

seemed unnecessary? To protect her reputation? To do the right thing? She knew that the present Earl of Kenrick was a man motivated by a very strong sense of duty. Everyone knew that was in part why he was the present earl. After all, he could have stayed in America. She should be grateful for his protection. She *was* grateful. This thought brought an echo of memory: "I want more than gratitude from you, Kate."

She gave herself a mental shake. They would sort this out later. She managed to stumble through the rest of the evening without mishap, responding in conversations and performing those duties as hostess that Lady Elinor was unable to do, such as pouring tea when the party returned to the drawing room.

Later, as the local guests left, she received their good wishes for her future happiness with what she hoped was a satisfactory blend of enthusiasm and decorum. When the door closed on the last to leave, she hoped to corner and challenge Jeremy on that ridiculous announcement. However, he forestalled her.

"Kate, it is very late and I wonder if I might prevail upon you to see Aunt Elinor to her chamber? I have something of a particular nature I must discuss with the men."

He had made it sound rather urgent, and she could hardly protest in front of Mr. Phillips and Major Lawrence, so she said "Of course, my lord," but she was annoyed. Not that she minded accompanying Lady Elinor at all, though it was a task that could have been, and often was, performed by a servant. That infernal man had found a way to avoid a confrontation with her!

Half an hour later she lay in her own bed, replaying the events of this busy day. Perhaps Wynstan's spurious claim to Ned was a thing of the past. Maybe, in time, the duke might behave as a normal, caring grandfather. And pigs might sprout wings! She rolled over and pounded her fist into her pillow. She and Ned were back where they had started on that spring day of their arrival at Kenrick. She could not remain here as housekeeper. Not now.

Nor could she allow this sham betrothal to go on. Such a marriage would be disastrous to Jeremy's ultimate goals. She had been the instrument of Arthur's loss of status with his family and society. She would not be such to Jeremy. No. She would have to proceed alone—again.

She would consult Mr. Phillips and Major Lawrence in the morning as to how she could do that. As Ned's guardians, they were in a position to advise her.

In the drawing room "that infernal man" had ordered nightcaps of cognac, then settled himself into his own chair. The lamps and a low fire cast a warm glow about the room, making its daytime imperfections of age and neglect less noticeable.

Lawrence swished the amber liquid in his glass, sipped, and murmured, "Hmm. Quite nice, this."

"My predecessor had a long-standing arrangement with smugglers all during the troubles with Bonaparte," Jeremy said.

"Many an Englishman did," Phillips observed. "There are things the English find difficult to give up in even the worst of times—fine wine and good tea being among them."

Robert leaned back and said, "Did you have something on your mind in sending the ladies off as you did, Jeremy?"

"Yes, I did. The fire." With an occasional interjection from Robert, he described for the other two the barn fire and their suspicions about its origin. Phillips seemed somewhat shocked at Kate's role in rescuing Cassie, but Lawrence noted that the Angel of the 46th had acted totally in character.

Jeremy turned to his brother. "Robert, I saw you in a tête-à-tête with Dennison earlier. Did he offer anything of interest?"

"Just that he knew Thompson had expressed some rather vague ill-will toward our father and older brothers a couple of years ago, but he thought it had faded when you came into the title. Lately, since his son Billy's return, Thompson has been more vocal about feeling abused."

"No clue as to the nature of his complaint?" Jeremy asked.

"Not from him. But Delia—Miss Dennison—mentioned that Mina Thompson had had a tendre for Charles and Delia thought the two of them might have been meeting secretly."

"A tenant farmer's daughter and the heir to an earl? Not a very likely match under the best of circumstances," Phillips commented.

Robert snorted. "I doubt anything as honorable as a match even entered Charles's head."

"So far, this is just speculation," Jeremy said, "and it should not be bruited about outside this room."

The other three nodded agreement.

"You say you do have some hard evidence from the fire," Phillips said. "My suggestion would be to confront your suspect dead-on, without warning, and see what turns up. Mind you, you may never get enough to stand up in court, but at least you will know."

"My thoughts, exactly," Jeremy said, "but I am glad to have them confirmed by someone who knows the law far better than I do."

When the four of them retired, that was the general plan for the morrow.

But that plan had to be postponed.

The next morning Kate had just finished dressing and was about to make her way downstairs to see to the start of the Hall's usual morning routine, when there was a furious knocking at her door. She opened it to find the maid Nell Davis looking very distraught.

"Oh, my lady, please—you must come to the nursery. Rosie has been hurt and the children—" her voice rose in sheer panic—"the children—they're gone! Gone! Nowhere to be found."

Kate felt her breath stop. Fear clawed at her. She knew instinctively this was not a game the two children might have devised. She allowed herself only a single moment of panic. "Oh, dear God, no. No." Then she swallowed hard and said, "Go. Find Lord Kenrick and tell him. Quickly!"

"Yes, ma'am."

Kate raced up to the nursery where she found Rosie, still in a nightdress, seated at a table in the schoolroom while another maid wrapped a bandage around Rosie's head. There was a trickle of dried blood on her forehead.

"Rosie! What happened?" Kate asked

"Oh, Mrs. A.—that bounder hit me, he did. I tried to stop them. Really—I tried."

Kate spoke calmly, trying to soothe Rosie enough to get needed information. "Who, Rosie? Who hit you?"

"I don't know who he was," Rosie wailed. "I never seen 'im afore. But he were with Nurse Cranstan."

"Cranstan?"

Rosie nodded.

Just then Jeremy burst into the room. "What happened? What's going on?"

"We are about to find out," Kate said, her voice still deliberately controlled to calm both Rosie and him. She wanted to scream herself. "Start at the beginning, Rosie."

"I heard a noise, a voice, an' then someone yelled, but it were too early for the children to be awake. I come out o' my room and a strange man was there. He had ahold o' Master Ned. Ned was yellin' for him to let him go. Then I yelled too. I—I guess the commotion woke Lady Cassandra an' she come out o' her room. Nurse Cranstan grabbed her by the arm. I tried to stop them—an' that's when the man hit me. Near knocked me out when my head hit the table." She paused to take a long, shuddering breath. "Then, Cranstan, she grabbed Ned with her other hand an' nodded at me an' said, 'Tie her and gag her.' That's what he did. An' they left." She ended on a wail.

"Go on, Rosie. Did they say anything else?" Jeremy asked in a calmer tone than he had used before.

Rosie nodded and seemed to be trying to remember. "The man said somethin' like 'he didn't say nothing 'bout no girl, just the boy.' Cranstan, she says, 'We take her too. We haven't any time and she would yell to wake the dead. You can always sell a kid, especially a girl.' "

"Oh, good heavens!" Kate felt an icy chill at these words and reached for Jeremy's hand. He turned eyes of utter despair toward her, but as frightened and furious as he must have been, he remained outwardly calm.

"What time did all this happen?" he asked.

"J—just about daylight," Rosie said.

"A good two hours ago," Jeremy muttered. "Do you remember anything else, Rosie?"

"No, my lord. I'm so sorry. I should've—"

He patted her on the shoulder. "You did well, Rosie. Thank you." He turned to Kate. "Robert was with me, as were Phillips and Lawrence, when Nell brought me the news. Would you believe we were in the gun room? We are going after them."

"All four of you?"

"Yes. We'll take Jack and another hand from the stable. I'll send word for Porter and Weston to meet us too."

"Do be careful," she pleaded. "But, oh, do bring them back."

He stroked her cheek with the back of his hand. "We will be armed. Try not to worry." He added as he turned to leave, "I think they will try to go as far as possible as fast as they can to leave this area. That means toward York, then Manchester, probably. Send Thomas for the doctor to see to Rosie and have him also notify the magistrate, won't you?"

"Yes, of course."

Kate located Thomas and sent him on his way, then she informed Lady Elinor and the two of them spent the next several hours alternately sharing their worry and trying to bolster each other's spirits. Kate was devastated. The mere idea of losing her son was unimaginable. She could not believe that such pain would be any less endurable than what she had suffered in losing her husband. But she was glad of the companionship—the sympathy and optimism—of a woman who has suffered both those losses herself.

When Rosie had been seen by the doctor and given a sedative, and the doctor sent on his way, Kate and Lady Elinor, fortified by a pot of tea, met with Nell and Mr. Wilkins. The four of them sat around the table in the morning room, trying to piece together what must have happened.

"Miss Cranstan undoubtedly had a key to the back entrance," Wilkins conjectured. "One she either stole or forgot about having. And she would have been a familiar figure to the dogs—that's why they did not rouse the stable hands."

Nell added, "Mr. Cuthbertson said he sent a groom out to look around an' he found where a team and carriage and some other riders must have waited quite a while about a mile down the driveway."

"Nobody was up yet. They used the back stairs . . ." Lady Elinor heaved a heavy sigh. "One feels so—so violated! And those poor, dear children. They must be so frightened!"

Kate visualized Ned and Cassie being shoved into a carriage. Had they been beaten? Bound and gagged? "Oh, please, God, don't let them be hurt. Please." She was unaware she had spoken the prayer aloud.

Mr. Wilkins touched her arm. "Try not to dwell on negative images, Mrs.—uh—Lady Arthur. I feel sure Lord Kenrick will return them to us safe and sound."

"Oh, I hope so. He must. He simply must."

CHAPTER 20

Although his instinct was to ride as though the hounds of hell pursued him, Jeremy kept his small army to a steady pace in their own pursuit so as to get a degree of speed, but spare their horses for what might be a very long journey. They had been riding nearly three hours already but knew from inquiries along the way that they were on the right road. About an hour into the journey, Porter and Weston had joined them. Jeremy hoped he and his seven men would be up to dealing with the duke's entourage. Being able to count on the military prowess of Robert and Lawrence gave him an extra boost of optimism.

As they reached the top of a high hill, they had a panoramic view of a long green valley below them. "Hendley Dale," Porter said. "Looks real peaceful, don't it?" Spread out before them were vast green fields separated by the typical Yorkshire stone fences and occasional flocks of grazing sheep. The road followed the winding route of a rushing river. Also within their view, looking very small in the distance, was the duke's carriage. Two outriders in front and two behind the carriage provided the rich man protection from highway bandits—and pursuit. Through a telescope, Jeremy saw another man seated next to the driver.

"Six of them, counting the driver," he said. "There may be another inside with Wynstan and Miss Cranstan—along with Ned and Cassie."

He handed the telescope over to his brother. "We have to assume the driver and other men are all armed."

When Jeremy would have pushed ahead even faster now, Robert said, "Wait! Let's look at this terrain. See how the road follows the river?" He turned the telescope over to Major Lawrence.

"No bridges 'til you get to that village way off in the distance," Lawrence said.

"West Hinton." Porter named the village.

"Wynstan needs a bridge to get that carriage across the river," Robert observed.

"But we don't," Jeremy said.

Lawrence, having passed the telescope on to others, shaded his eyes with his hand. "Looks to me like we could cut across those fields off to the right, find a ford, and catch up to them at that long S curve. Plenty of trees along the river to provide cover."

"They might spot us crossing the field," someone said.

"They might do so," Robert agreed, "but remember: that carriage has to stay on the road and those outriders probably have orders to stay close to it. We spread out along the road—and hope the trees provide enough cover. We let the ones in front pass us by; then, Jack, you and Weston make sure they don't double back as we take on the rest. Phillips, you and Hank attack those riders in the rear. Shoot the horses if you have to—those fellows will be less trouble on foot. The rest of us take the carriage."

A hurried consultation followed as they tried to foresee possible snags, but in the end, they all agreed that this was a workable plan. The real danger, Jeremy thought, would come if—when—there was gunfire. He hoped Cassie and Ned would stay low, or that their un-feeling, misbegotten captors would keep them low. "Aim to injure, not to kill, but for God's sake, don't shoot into the carriage itself," he warned as they set their horses in motion again.

Events transpired more or less according to the plan devised at the top of that hill. Porter and Weston, who had often fished this stream, found a ford easily; then the whole lot of them waited silently, nerves on edge, in a copse of low-hanging willow, elm, and oak trees.

For Jeremy, this part of their venture was the worst: the waiting. Cassie must be out of her mind with fear. Did she think her father had truly abandoned her? Kate had suggested that, hadn't she? Kate. His heart wrenched at what she must be feeling now. At least he could do something to rescue their children. All she could do was wait. And Ned. He recalled how brave the little boy had been when his mother was injured. If there was a bright spot at all in this disaster, it was that Cassie and Ned might take some comfort from each other.

Robert broke into his musings. "Here they come!"

They allowed the front outriders to pass, then, as planned, Jack and Weston jumped them. As the carriage drew even with Jeremy and the main group of rescuers, shots rang out in front of it and the driver seemed instinctively to pull on the reins to stop the vehicle.

Then shots rang behind as well, and Jeremy, riding at the side of the swaying coach, heard a thump and an urgent cry from within.

"No! Don't stop! Go! Go! Faster! Faster!"

The driver cracked his whip and the carriage leaped forward. Jeremy and Robert, along with Lawrence and Porter, gave chase. The man sharing the driver's seat opened fire, but what with the violent swaying of the coach and having only a precarious hold on his seat, he had little control of his aim and his shots went wild.

There were shots from within the carriage too, but Jeremy thought they came from only one weapon. The Kenrick riders chased madly after the careening vehicle, trying to stay out of the range of fire, yet divert or slow the team. Then one of the lead carriage horses was hit with a stray bullet. It reared and upset the rhythm and balance of the rest of the team. Jeremy watched in horror as the carriage lurched off the road toward the river, carrying the hapless team with it. The driver and his companion were both thrown from their perch. The noise of grinding metal, breaking wood, neighing horses, and screams and curses from within the carriage added auditory as well as visual confusion.

The riverbank at this point was wide and sloped gently to the running stream. The carriage jounced heavily and might have turned completely over but for the fact that the team was still firmly harnessed to it. It came to a rest on its side, but was by no means steady, for the panicked horses kicked and fought to be free.

Jeremy jumped off his mount and screamed, "Cut the team loose!" He braced himself on a carriage wheel and reached to open the door. The interior presented a chaotic blend of arms and legs as three of the four people inside fought as hard to right themselves as the horses fought outside. Finally, he was able to grasp Cassie's arm and pull her free of the others.

Sobbing with fear, she threw her arms tightly around his neck. "Oh, Papa! I knew you'd come. I told Ned so."

He hugged her briefly, then loosened her arms from him, passed her on to Major Lawrence, and turned back toward the carriage. Inside, the duke lay strangely still, his body draped at an odd angle off the seat. Ned was sobbing hysterically. Nurse Cranstan seemed momentarily dazed, but she had picked up the duke's now useless gun. She quickly dropped it when she saw Jeremy's pistol trained on her.

She yelled, "We thought you were bandits! Now see what you've done! You've killed the duke! Get me out of here!"

"In due time," Jeremy said. "First, hand up the boy. Ned first, then you." "Though it would serve you right to leave you right where you are," he thought.

Ned was still crying and as Miss Cranstan grabbed at his arm, he let out a horrifying yowl of pain.

"Be careful!" Jeremy ordered.

Finally, the erstwhile nursery maid managed to lift Ned and, with a push on his rump, elevated him enough that Jeremy could get hold of his body. The boy's arm was twisted strangely and there was an ugly bruise on his face.

"Now get me out of here," the nurse immediately demanded.

Tempted for a moment to just walk away and leave those two villains in the wreckage, Jeremy said, "Calm down, Miss Cranstan. We shall see to you in a minute." He reasoned that her complaining was sufficient evidence that she, at least, was not seriously injured.

By now the rest of his group had joined those around the wreck and the team had been cut free. Jack and Hank sought to soothe the horses; they happily reported that the one shot had suffered only a flesh wound and would likely recover. Porter and Weston saw to the business of guarding the prisoners who had been relieved of their weapons.

"One of 'em in front got way," Weston said in disgust. "Just took off at the first shot. The driver's dead. Broke his neck in the fall."

Jeremy handed Ned to Robert. "Careful of his arm, Robert. I think it might be broken."

Robert grimaced. "Looks like it. Come on, my brave fellow, let's see if we can bind it up so it won't hurt so much."

"A—all right," Ned said with a sob. "It hurts real bad."

"I know it does, lad. Did that myself once—and I was much older than you. I remember I cried like a baby."

"You did?" Ned asked in wonder.

"Sure did." Robert walked over to one of the prisoners and ordered him to remove his jacket. The man looked puzzled, but did as he was told. "Now the shirt," Robert said, then exchanged the jacket for the shirt and ripped the shirt into strips from which he fashioned a sling for Ned's arm.

Jeremy was impressed with both the tenderness and expertise with which Robert handled the boy. Cassie appeared to be uninjured and immediately went to stand next to Ned and commiserate with him. "That old man hit Ned," she announced. "See his face?"

"Hit him? Why?" Jeremy asked.

" 'Cause Ned said we didn't want to go with them. The man hit him and said he'd do as he was told or else. We was really, really scared, Papa. Wasn't we, Ned?" She took Ned's good hand and held it gently. Ned nodded.

"Get me out of here!" Nurse Cranstan's abrasive whine came from the carriage.

Jeremy sighed. "Let's see if we can get this coach upright and get her out."

Soon enough the vehicle was somewhat upright—one wheel was broken and bent—and the irate female was allowed out of it. Her complaints reached a new pitch when—none too gently—they searched her for a weapon, then parked her with the other prisoners.

"The duke?" Robert asked.

Jeremy reached into the carriage and felt for the duke's pulse. "He's alive, but unconscious."

Not knowing the extent of his injuries and trying not injure him further, Jeremy and Robert struggled to get the still unconscious duke out of the carriage and lying on the ground.

"Careful," Jeremy warned. "It may be a back or a neck injury. We need something flat to put him on."

Using rope found in a storage compartment in the rear of the carriage, Kenrick's men bound their five prisoners. The four men seemed docile, resigned to whatever was coming. Miss Cranstan, though, continued to harangue and complain. It was indecent to tie her up with these men. The rope on her wrists was too tight. A woman deserved far better treatment, and so on and on.

Porter checked the rope on her wrists and, pronouncing it to be all right just as it was, added, "Woman, this treatment ain't nothin' to what you'll get on one o' them ships to New South Wales. Kidnappin' is a serious crime."

At this she went very pale and set to sobbing loudly. "They made me come—to—to help with the child. I'm just a nursemaid."

"Oh, shut up!" one of the other prisoners growled. " 'Twas your idea—partly, anyways. You it was told the duke you knew the layout o' the Hall. Quit yer caterwaulin'."

She subsided to an occasional snort or deep, pitiable sigh that everyone managed without much difficulty to ignore.

As Lawrence and Phillips continued to keep watch over the prisoners, the others managed to wrest the bottom of the driver's seat from the carriage to serve as a brace and they then tied the duke to it to prevent his moving around. He groaned a time or two, but remained insensible to his surroundings. His breathing was steady, but labored.

Jeremy dispatched Jack to race back to the Hall to inform Kate that they had successfully rescued the children. "Don't tell her the boy is injured, though. Spare her that worry 'til we get there."

"Yes, my lord."

"I'll ride into the village and get us some transportation," Robert offered. "Hank, you come with me."

Weston and Porter gathered up the horses and then they all settled down to wait for Robert and Hank to return. Jeremy sat on the grass with Cassie under one arm and Ned under the other. Ned cradled his injured arm and occasionally drew in a long, almost sobbing breath.

"I know it hurts, son," Jeremy said, checking the sling. "We'll try to keep it very still until we can get you to the doctor."

"What will he do to me?" Ned asked between shuddering breaths.

"He'll set the bone to make sure it heals properly."

"Will it hurt?"

"I'm afraid so, but afterwards, it shouldn't hurt so much anymore." Jeremy touched the boy's head, wishing he could absorb the child's pain himself. "You are being very brave, Ned. Your mama will be proud of you."

"Does mama know?"

"I sent Jack to tell her you are safe, but I'm sure she will worry until we get there."

Ned nodded sagely.

Very late in the afternoon, it was quite a procession of two vehicles and a small herd of horses that made its way back to the town of Kenrick. Besides a chaise and a farm wagon, Robert had procured bread and cheese for a hurried lunch. Jeremy thought perhaps Robert took seriously that adage about an army's traveling on its stomach. The duke's inert form was laid out on the wagon and his employees, Miss Cranstan among them, were arranged beside him.

"Not quite Wynstan's usual form of travel," Robert noted as he mounted his own horse, prepared with Lawrence and Weston to ride guard as Hank drove the wagonload of miscreants. Porter drove the chaise and Jeremy rode inside with the two children.

Miss Cranstan complained bitterly that she should ride in the chaise, but Jeremy thought Cassie and Ned had endured enough of her company.

In Kenrick, Wynstan's four remaining men were crowded into the only jail cell the town boasted; Nurse Cranstan was locked in one room at the inn, and the still unconscious duke was put into another. Dr. Ferris was called to treat Ned first, then the duke.

As soon as Ned's broken arm was set and the plaster cast dry enough, Jeremy set out with the children in the chaise for Kenrick Hall. Even though he had sent Jack ahead to give her the good news, Jeremy knew that Kate would continue to worry, that she would not be satisfied until she was able to fold her arms around her son.

Despite intermittent efforts to distract herself from worry with trivial tasks, Kate had spent most of this day fretting, and most of it in Lady Elinor's company. She was grateful for the older woman's companionship. By mid-afternoon, the two of them had moved into the family drawing room where Lady Elinor reclined on a couch and Kate sat in a nearby chair—when she sat. Jack's terse report that the rescue mission was a success had lifted a load of worry, but anxiety still clawed at her.

"You will surely wear that carpet right down to the boards beneath with all that pacing," Lady Elinor told her. "Come, dear. Let's have another chapter of Mrs. Edgeworth's novel now that we know the children are safe."

Kate gave a rueful laugh and glanced at the clock on the mantel yet again. "You're right. I just wish we could brush away minutes as we brush away dust. I hate this waiting."

"I know, dear, but 'they also serve who only stand and wait.' "

"I doubt this kind of waiting is what Milton had in mind. Ah, well—" Kate sat and opened the book. "Now, where were we? 'Chapter four . . .' "

In the early evening, the two women were having yet another cup of tea when they at last heard the carriage arrive. Dashing into the foyer, Kate was astonished to see Jeremy enter carrying a sleeping Ned in his arms, with Cassie walking beside them. Both children were still dressed in their nightclothes, though their captors had taken time to put shoes on them and find outer coats for them. Kate's eyes immediately riveted on the plaster cast on her son's arm.

"Oh!" she gasped, reaching to touch Ned's head. "He's hurt! Jack did not tell us—"

"His arm was broken when the carriage overturned, but he's fine now. He truly is," Jeremy assured her.

"Why is he unconscious?"

"Dr. Ferris gave him a very small dose of laudanum to ease the pain as he set the bone. Ned will sleep for quite some time, even though Ferris was careful about the amount for a child. Now, let us get our patient into his own room and I will tell you the entire story."

"Of course." Kate dutifully stepped aside and quickly enfolded Cassie in a tight hug. "Are you all right, my dear?"

"Yes, ma'am. Ned was very brave. He didn't cry much at all, did he, Papa?"

"You were both very brave," Jeremy said, starting up the stairs, "and we are very proud of you."

"We was real scared," Cassie said in a sober tone. "The carriage, it was going real fast. I think Miss Cranstan was scared, too, but she was real mean an' that old man, he was even meaner. He hit Ned! An' said he'd get more when we got where we was going. An' then the carriage went even faster an' there was shots an' then the carriage turned over an' we was all tangled together an' then Papa got us out. I was *so-o-o* glad to see Papa."

"I am sure you were." Although still concerned for Ned and anxious to see him cared for, Kate could not help being both alarmed and amused by Cassie's account and hugged her again.

They arrived at the nursery wing to find both Rosie and Nell waiting for them, though Rosie had been told Nell would take her place until Rosie herself was fully recovered from the blow she had suffered that morning. Kate was sure the proud Rosie was not about to give her place in the nursery even to her own sister.

Kate rushed ahead into Ned's room and turned down the covers on his bed. When Jeremy lowered his small form, she bent to kiss Ned's cheek and ran her hands over the rest of his body, careful not to jar his broken arm. Touching him was as important as seeing him in this miracle of his return.

"Is Ned going to bed in his shoes?" Cassie asked from the foot of the bed.

Jeremy chuckled. "No. We must not allow him to do that." He removed the boy's shoes and tucked Ned's legs under the covers.

"When is he going to wake up?" Cassie demanded. "We have things to talk about."

Kate exchanged a glance with Jeremy and they both smiled at Cassie's very adult proclamation. As Jeremy gently pushed his daughter toward the door, he said, "Ned will not wake up for a while—when he does, you will be in bed asleep yourself. You can talk to him in the morning. Now, let's have Nell get you a bath and some supper. And where do you suppose that infernal kitten has hidden all day?" He turned at the door and mouthed *I'll be back* to Kate.

Cassie giggled. "Oh, Papa! Lady Lobo isn't 'fernal. There she is!" She scooped the kitten into her arms and danced around with it, saying, "I missed you so much!"

"I'll be back later to read you a story," Jeremy said, turning his daughter over to Nell.

Kate had seen most of this father-daughter colloquy and heard all of it through the open door of Ned's room. She sat in a chair near the head of his bed so she could reach to touch his warm cheek or straighten already smoothed blankets.

Jeremy came in and stood near her. He placed his hand on her shoulder. "Dr. Ferris said it would be good if he would sleep for several hours—maybe sleep through the worst of the pain. It was a clean break, he said, and should heal nicely. Ned really was very brave the whole time—just gritted his teeth and endured. I've known grown men to be far less stoic in the face of pain."

Kate looked up at him through tears in her eyes. "Thank you for bringing my child back to me."

He pulled her to her feet and stood, just holding her close. "Mine too," he said softly, "but it's over now."

She nodded her head against his chest, then lifted her tear-filled gaze to his. "I—I don't know why I am such a watering pot. I did not cry all day! And now they are safe. . . . It doesn't make sense!"

"Relief?"

He lifted her chin to shower soft kisses on her forehead, her eyelids, her nose, and finally her lips. It was a tender whisper of a kiss—at first. Then she reached her arms around his neck, her hands in his hair, her body straining to blend with his, and kissed him back fiercely. She felt his body immediately respond, but he stepped back: reluctantly, it seemed to her.

"Come, Kate. Ned is safe now and he will probably sleep through the night."

She felt bereft at the separation, but assumed a normal tone. "What if Wynstan tries to snatch him again?"

"He won't. At least not for a while. The duke was injured in the accident."

"Badly?"

"I don't know. He was still unconscious when I left, but the doctor was with him. Now, come. Nell and Rosie will keep watch here and call us if we are needed. Aunt Elinor will be anxious to hear what happened."

Kate bent to kiss Ned's warm cheek again, overwhelmed by the fact that he was, indeed, safe. The fear and nearly unbearable tension of this day was over.

Back in the drawing room they found Lady Elinor exactly as Jeremy had described her: anxious to hear the news.

Jeremy poured sherry at an oak sideboard, and passed glasses to Kate and his aunt. "I think we've all earned this."

He settled himself into one of two wing-backed chairs flanking a small oak table, on which sat a porcelain lamp and an eight-inch-tall jade figurine. Kate occupied the matching chair and Lady Elinor sat across from them on a settee with worn upholstery but magnificently carved wooden arms and legs. Jeremy launched into an account of the rescue mission.

He had just finished by saying, "Thank God for Robert's military expertise. It helped tremendously."

"Did I just hear my name taken in vain?" Robert asked, entering the room with Lawrence and Phillips right behind him.

Jeremy laughed and rose to greet them. "Not at all. In fact, I was singing your praises. May I get you fine fellows something to drink?"

Robert eyed the sherry glasses and affected a Scots brogue. "Hmm. Perhaps a wee dram of the brew of the Scot?"

"Coming right up." Jeremy poured three generous glasses of whiskey and handed them to the newcomers. Robert sat next to his aunt and the other two sank into overstuffed chairs nearby.

"How's my favorite girl?" Robert asked his aunt flirtatiously.

"My dear boy," she said in a loud stage whisper, "you have that bit of blather down very pat now, so you can stop practicing on an old woman."

Robert grinned and shrugged and the others laughed.

"So, what is the latest?" Jeremy asked, reseating himself.

Robert's demeanor sobered. "The magistrate is holding an informal hearing later in the week. We have to be there. The Bow Street Runner had intended to return to London today, but when he heard what happened here this morning, he stayed on."

"I never cease to be amazed at the speed with which news travels in the country," Phillips said.

"What did the doctor say about Wynstan?" Jeremy asked.

Robert sipped his drink and said, "That news is not good at all. The man is paralyzed."

"Oh, dear," Lady Elinor said and Kate drew in a sharp breath.

"He regained consciousness while the doctor was examining him just after you left," Robert said to Jeremy. "He can move his arms, doc says, and has only slight difficulty breathing, but he has no feeling in his legs at all."

Kate drew in another sharp breath. She had no love for her father-in-law, but such a condition would be intolerable for a man of his temperament.

"Is it permanent?" Jeremy asked, and Kate thought he too had a shred of sympathy for the man who had been so ruthlessly indifferent to the feelings of others.

"Doc couldn't say for sure," Robert answered. "Too early, but he thought the prognosis was not good. He did not tell the duke—not yet, anyway. I suppose Wynstan will figure that out for himself soon enough." Robert's tone had become rather bleak—and Kate recognized it as the voice of a man who had seen too many battlefield wounds.

"How very, very sad," Lady Elinor said.

"I agree: it *is* sad," Lawrence said, "and mine may be an extreme view, but it does make one think of the hand of God, Providence, fate—or poetic justice."

Everyone was quiet for several moments after this comment; then Robert drained his glass and set it on a low table in front of the settee. "Am I the only one of us who is famished? We left before breakfast and did not have much in the way of lunch," he said apologetically to the ladies.

Kate jumped up. "I can remedy that problem."

"Kate, I did not mean—" Robert started.

"No. No." She assured him. "I am so immensely grateful to you—to all of you." Her gaze swept over the four men, but rested on Jeremy. She wrenched her eyes away. "I'll check with cook right away."

CHAPTER 21

The next day was relatively quiet at Kenrick Hall as everyone seemed to be adjusting to the near-tragedy of the previous day and the change in status of the Hall's housekeeper. *It's like the whole of Kenrick has put on a new cloak,* Kate thought, *and is trying to see how it fits.* She was glad to see Ned already on the mend and enjoying being the center of attention, but she was still worried about his future. Her worry extended also to Jeremy. She most assuredly did not want to be the cause of any setbacks in his plans for his own future. She invited Mr. Phillips and Major Lawrence to join her for a stroll in the garden.

"I need your advice," she said without preamble, "on what to do about Ned and since you are his guardians—"

"I just assumed he would be staying here with you," Lawrence said.

Phillips abruptly stopped walking and faced her and Lawrence. "Are you suggesting that Kenrick will not have your son here when you marry? That does not sound like the Jeremy I know."

"No, no," she said quickly. "Lord Kenrick has been very kind, but I—we—cannot stay here."

"But your betrothal—" Lawrence started.

"Is a sham. It was a plan Jer—Lord Kenrick concocted to divert gossip after Wynstan made—uh—certain comments. There seems no need for that diversion now."

"A sham?" Phillips repeated. "Are you sure Jeremy views it as such?"

"Oh, yes. We agreed that after a suitable time I could cry off."

"Sounds a little havey-cavey to me," Lawrence said, then walked on in thoughtful silence for a moment. Finally, he added, "I would invite you and Ned to stay with me, but, as you know, mine is also a bachelor household. And one without a Lady Elinor in residence."

"I had thought again of perhaps removing to the United States or to Canada," she said tentatively.

"Out of the question," Lawrence said flatly. "The boy must be educated as an Englishman."

"Well," Phillips said, "you *might* set up a household of your own, hire a companion, two or three servants, and a tutor for the boy . . ." His voice trailed off.

"I have funds enough for that?" She was surprised.

Phillips coughed. "You do now. I took the liberty of investing the funds Arthur left in the same cargo venture I talked Jeremy into. This is the first chance I have had to tell you."

"You did this without consulting me?"

She had steered them to the wicker furniture where she often sat to read with Lady Elinor. She sank into a chair at the glass-topped table and waited for a response from Phillips, who seemed embarrassed as he and Lawrence took matching chairs.

"I—uh—well, you see, if it hadn't worked out, I would have restored the funds myself."

"Thus making me a charity case," she said.

"But you would never have known. I—I thought of it as taking care of Arthur's business—of his family."

Kate reached to grasp his hand. "I appreciate that—truly, I do. And I know you had the legal authority to do it, but, all the same, I should like to have been consulted."

"My wife said you would feel that way."

"As Ned's guardians, would you be amenable to my living independently?" Kate asked.

"Where?" Lawrence sounded skeptical.

"London, perhaps—or on the outskirts of the city. Some place in Sussex?"

"Ned seems very content here," Phillips observed.

"Sussex is rather far away," Lawrence said. "I don't fancy a three-day journey every time I've a notion to visit my godson. And he *will* require the presence of some male in his life besides a tutor."

"London, then," she said.

They left it at that for the nonce, but Kate found herself as torn as ever. She was thrilled to know that she did have options. On the other hand, Phillips was right: Ned was very content. For the first time since leaving the army life behind, he seemed totally carefree and happy—as children should be, she told herself. He had access to horses and other animals that would be difficult to achieve in London. And he had playmates—in Cassie, of course, but also Porter's younger children and there were others. Of course he might make friends anywhere. Still, Lawrence was right: A boy needed a man to emulate—and always, when such a thought hit her, it was Jeremy's image that leapt to mind.

Accepting Jeremy's proposal was, of course, a perfect solution so far as Ned was concerned. A part of her wanted to grasp at that remedy. Another part resented always being subject to the whim and control of others. And there was another factor to consider: Yes, marriage would serve her material interests, but would it really serve Jeremy's interests? How damaging might a somewhat scandalous liaison be for him?

The day following what Kate thought of as their "down" day, the men had gone off on their own and were not expected back until evening. Kate and Lady Elinor were at home to visitors making morning calls in the afternoon. With her identity no longer a secret in the neighborhood, Kate was to be a fixture in the Kenrick drawing room whenever visitors were present, her position elevated to honored guest and affianced bride. Among the first of their callers was Mrs. Hartwick, accompanied by the elderly widow, Mrs. Clarkson, and her spinster daughter, Miss Clarkson.

"The Clarksons are two of the most dedicated gossips is our area—perhaps in all Yorkshire," Lady Elinor confided quietly to Kate after telling Wilkins she and Kate would receive the ladies in the formal drawing room. It was larger and more elaborately furnished than the comfortable room the family usually chose. A marvelous ceiling painted by a well-known artist of the previous century depicted the gods assembled for the wedding of Thetis and Peleus just before the spoilsport Eris tossed the golden apple in their midst. The dominant colors in the brocade furniture and embossed wallpaper were beige, gold, and a deep rose. An Aubusson carpet had obviously been commissioned especially for this room.

"Oh, my dear Lady Elinor," Mrs. Hartwick gushed on entering, "we simply had to call to see how you are getting on. So much excitement! A betrothal! An attempted abduction! One hardly knows how to begin to absorb it all."

"May I present my guest, Lady Arthur," Lady Elinor said, making the newcomers known to Kate.

Kate was amused at the intensity of the ever-so-polite inspection they accorded her. The Clarkson women turned matching dark, beady eyes on her. Mother and daughter, they certainly were, with the mother in her seventies and the daughter in her fifties. Both had long, sharp noses; each wore her black, graying hair in a no-nonsense bun; they were attired in nearly identical dark dresses trimmed with touches of white lace at the necks and wrists. Kate's initial impression of curious crows was intensified by their shared habit of bobbing their heads as they spoke.

"Lady Arthur," the three murmured acknowledgements in cultured tones even as they scrutinized her dress and posture.

Kate played the game for Lady Elinor's sake, responding to inane comments about unseasonably warm weather and answering with a straight face that yes, indeed, she was enjoying her "visit" at Kenrick Hall. Or, at least she had done so until her son's accident.

The visitors clucked sympathetically. "Such an unfortunate affair," Mrs. Hartwick said, clearly anticipating juicy details.

Kate and Lady Elinor fed them the story concocted at the breakfast table that morning: It was all a terrible misunderstanding. Somehow the duke had got it into his head that Lady Arthur was trying to deprive him of access to his grandson. The duke, well-known to be a man of firm opinions and decisive actions, had impetuously taken matters into his own hands. Yes, yes. It was, indeed, unfortunate, for it might have been resolved in a most civilized manner. And now a man had died, the duke was injured, and there was to be an inquiry— just when folks at Kenrick Hall had been anticipating the joyous occasion of a wedding in the family.

This shift in subject brought an additional gleam of curiosity in

Mrs. Hartwick's eyes. She turned to Kate. "I must say, Lady Arthur, you have quite stolen the march on our local damsels."

"Oh?" Kate murmured, all innocence.

"Quite," Mrs. Clarkson echoed with a laugh. "After all, handsome men with titles are, as they say in the colonies, scarce as hens' teeth. You have dashed maidenly hopes in many a heart."

Her daughter added with an arch look, "And in none more than in that of a certain knight's daughter who shall, of course, remain nameless."

Kate ignored this sally. She had no wish to discuss what she knew or had heard of Miss Charlotte Mortimer's designs on the Earl of Kenrick.

That first visit set the tone and pattern for the next two hours as it seemed every woman of any consequence in the entire parish had to see and judge for herself the figure at the center of a maelstrom of gossip. Kate endured and forbore making the caustic remarks that seemed to pop into her mind like a fisherman's bobbing cork.

When the last of the visitors had departed after spending their conventional fifteen minutes, Lady Elinor said, "Tomorrow we must go into town and procure proper clothing for you."

"What is wrong with this? Besides . . ." Kate swallowed the retort.

" 'Besides'—how do I know? My dear Kate, while my eyesight is certainly failing, it is by no means gone. I cannot read or do fine needlework anymore, but I still see colors and silhouettes. I'll not have you judged by these tabbies."

"I do not wish to expend my limited funds on buying new gowns."

Lady Elinor held up a quieting hand. "Since this charade is largely Jeremy's idea—if, indeed, it is a charade—he can stand the expense of a few gowns and dresses."

Not wanting to discuss with his aunt or anyone else the nature of her relationship with Jeremy, Kate said, "Well, if you think it absolutely necessary . . ."

"I absolutely do."

Jeremy and Robert had taken their guests out hunting in the morning, then ridden into town for lunch at the inn. As the four men entered the establishment, Mr. Finley came forward, wiping his hands on his apron. A boy was adding coal to a low fire on the hearth.

"My lord, gentlemen. Have you come to check on the duke?"

Jeremy responded. "Actually we came for lunch, but how is he faring?"

Sending the boy to inform Mrs. Finley of paying customers, the innkeeper answered, "The duke is not well. Not well at all. Doc told me he is sure the paralysis is permanent, but he's not yet told his grace that bit of distressing news. The patient does not seem to be in a great deal of pain, but he yells and complains something fierce—about simply everything."

"I am sorry you and Mrs. Finley have been saddled with his care," Jeremy said.

"Well, now, we haven't. Not really."

"Who . . . ?"

"That Cranstan woman and his grace's valet. They see to his personal care."

"Cranstan? Are you telling me the magistrate released her from custody?"

Finley chuckled. "No, my lord. He had the blacksmith attach a bracelet to her wrist; at night it is fastened by a chain to the oak post of her bed. She can get around quite a distance, but she ain't goin' nowhere. During the day she's allowed freedom of movement; she's watched all the time, you know."

"How does she take that?"

"As you might expect. Moaning and grumbling. But I think she's real scared about what might happen to her."

"As well she should be," Robert said.

"Has she had visitors?" Jeremy asked.

"Not a one. Squire Dennison informed Sir Eldridge Mortimer of her whereabouts that first evening too." Finley ushered his four guests to a table by the window.

"Interesting . . ." Jeremy murmured, but he let the subject drop as the four of them delved into Mrs. Finley's shepherd's pie and her husband's local brew.

"I missed English pub food in the Peninsula," Robert announced after a few bites.

"Amen," Lawrence echoed.

"Didn't find much of it on the American frontier, either," Jeremy said, "though I must say an Arapaho feast after a buffalo hunt is an experience not easily forgot." At the urging of his companions, he launched into a description of the hunt and the rituals before and after it.

"They actually smear paint on themselves? Everyone?" Lawrence asked.

"Everyone participating in the hunt."

"You too?" Robert asked, a teasing glint in his eyes.

"Yes. Of course. When in Rome . . ."

"I should like to have seen that," his brother said. "Perhaps one day you can show us—say, for a masquerade in London."

"Mr. Logan told us how he found you living among the savages," Phillips said, "but he was of the opinion that you had managed to preserve a measure of the civilized man."

Jeremy was dismayed at the direction the conversation was taking. "A masquerade? Never. That would be disrespectful of people I came to admire. And I rather take exception to the word *savages*. True, the style of life—nomadic, controlled by forces of nature—can be brutal, especially when judged by outsiders. But people are people. Things like honor and integrity matter."

Phillips cleared his throat. "I meant no offense, Jeremy."

"None taken, Wally. They are interesting people—the natives of America. But questions of brutality and savagery are wholly relative, it seems to me."

"I'm not sure I follow you," Phillips said, reaching for the pitcher to replenish his glass, then offer it to others.

"Well, think on it," Jeremy insisted. "In England we have men—and women too—working twelve hours and more a day in our mines and mills. In the winter, a miner never sees the light of day. Their pay is so miniscule that the men have to have their women working too, and they must put their children to work when they are still babes—barely out of their nappies."

"That's true," Phillips conceded.

"No Arapaho child would be forced to sort chunks of coal by size in some dank, dismal shed hour after hour after hour—walnut size in this bucket, apple size in that—the child himself rarely seeing a walnut, or an apple either—let alone something as exotic as an orange."

"Ye gods, Phillips! You had to get him started, didn't you?" Robert's tone belied his words. "And don't even think of asking his views on the penal system!"

Phillips grinned. "I must say debates in the House of Lords will be interesting once you take your seat there, Kenrick. You will let me know when you're pitted against the likes of Eldon and Sidmouth, won't you? The Whigs have a new champion! Those two Tories won't stand a chance!"

"Whigs. Tories. Who cares as long as they do the right thing?" Jeremy said, shoving his plate aside and swilling the last of his ale. "Drink up, lads. We need to enlist the aid of the magistrate before we visit the Thompson farm."

With the addition of the magistrate—Squire Dennison—five horsemen rode into the yard of the Thompson family home, a typical tenant farmer's cottage by outward appearance, though this one seemed to house folks who left outward appearance to chance. Chickens ran free in the front yard, which was mostly bare of grass. Window boxes boasted only dead stalks of what might once have been geraniums. Weeds had taken over a fenced kitchen garden off to the side. A rusty hoe leaned against the fence and a weathered wooden bench sat near the door.

Two dogs of uncertain pedigree started barking as the five men rode up. Two children that Jeremy guessed to be nine or ten emerged from the cottage, followed by a toddler. A girl dressed in a faded blue cotton print dress stood next to a boy in homespun trousers and a shirt of the same faded print as the girl's dress. They both seemed shy. The toddler wore a nappy and a short shirt. All were barefoot.

"Ma!" the boy called, holding one of the dogs by the scruff of its neck. "They's some men here."

A woman wearing a dress of the same faded blue print came to the door. Her eyes rounded in surprise at seeing five horsemen practically on her doorstep.

"My husband ain't here," she said nervously. "He's down at the barn there." She gestured to a building some fifty or sixty yards away.

"Perhaps you can help us, though, Mrs. Thompson," Jeremy said. "I'm Kenrick and this is my brother and our friends. I think you may know Squire Dennison."

She nodded and looked up at him with a tentative smile. She was missing a front tooth. "Yes. I remember you and your brother when you was just boys."

Jeremy looked at Robert, who dismounted, took something from his saddlebag, and extended it toward the woman. "Do you recognize this cloth?"

Immediately the older children crowded close to her to see the item.

"Eh!" the girl blurted. "That's a rag from Pa's old worn-out nightshirt!"

"It might could be," the woman said, her tone a blend of caution and suspicion. "It be pretty common goods, though."

"Have you any other bits of that—uh—garment?" Squire Dennison asked.

"I—I ain't sure." Fear tinged her words now.

"Would you mind checking, please?" the squire asked. Given Porter's report of how the Thompson men held a deal of animosity toward Kenrick people, Jeremy had agreed beforehand to allow the squire to take the lead in these initial questions.

Mrs. Thompson seemed to weigh her options, then shrugged. "Go get the rag bag, Tillie," she told her daughter.

The girl returned with a bag the size of a small pillowcase and dumped its contents on the bench. "Ain't much in here."

Squire Dennison stepped forward and pawed through assorted swatches of cloth. "This piece seems to be a match." He held a fragment of material from the bag next to the one in Robert's hand. Jeremy dismounted for a closer look.

"Hey! What's goin' on here?" The shout came from a man running up from the barn. He looked to be in his late forties or early fifties. He was followed by a younger man in his twenties. They appeared to be father and son, though the son had a full head of hair and the father's had been reduced to a fringe above his ears.

"Hello, Mr. Thompson," Jeremy said in an even voice.

"What do you want here?" Thompson demanded.

"We are examining two pieces of woven fabric that appear to be remarkably similar, though one is clean and the other soaked in lamp oil," Jeremy said, pointing at the rags in the squire-magistrate's hand and in Robert's.

Jeremy watched as the younger man's face turned a sickly white and he moved as though he might bolt. Lawrence casually edged his mount to ward off Billy Thompson's escape and the young man's shoulders slumped in defeat.

"Two pieces of rags don't prove nothin' to no one." Thompson spat at Jeremy's feet. "Half the kingdom probably has some just like 'em."

"That may well be true," Jeremy conceded, "but my solicitor, Mr. Walter Phillips here," Jeremy gestured at Phillips, who remained mounted, "and Squire Dennison assure me that this evidence, along with certain testimony from outside witnesses, would give us a very strong case if we were to go to court."

"Oh, Alfred, no. No." Mrs. Thompson had tears streaming down her face. Both children started to cry as well and the toddler, sensing the charged atmosphere, commenced to squalling until his mother picked him up and cuddled him with soft *shh*-ing sounds. When he quieted, she put him down again.

"You got no call to be accusin' me and mine of—of anything. An' what are you saying we done anyways?" Thompson seemed reluctant to give up his bluster, but there was a whine of fear in his voice as well.

"I think you know very well that we are investigating the fire that destroyed a portion of wool we had stored in the barns on the Kenrick home farm. My brother and I are convinced that you and your son are somehow involved."

"Oh, Alfred, is that true?" the woman wailed and grabbed her husband's hand.

"Gladys, be quiet," the elder Thompson growled. "They're just fishin'— ain't got proof of nothin'."

"We've enough to go to court, though," Robert said. "And it could go hard on all of you. You know that, don't you, Billy?"

Billy moved to stand closer to his parents and stared belligerently at the intruders. His tone blended defeat and hostility. "Don't say any more, Pa. The swells own the courts as well as everything else. What this country needs is a guillotine."

"You want I should arrest these men and hold them for the next assize court?" Squire Dennison asked Jeremy. "It meets about a month from now."

"Leave my Pa alone," Billy said. "He didn't have nothin' to do with that fire. I done it. Just me."

"But did he have knowledge of it before the event?" the lawyer Phillips wanted to know.

"No!" Billy said. Then he tempered this with, "I don't know. He might've guessed what I had planned."

Everyone looked at the father, who nodded glumly.

"Oh, no," Mrs. Thompson whispered.

"What I want to know now is *why*," Jeremy said.

"There may be mitigating circumstances," Phillips suggested.

"Ah, that's just lawyer talk," Billy said. "Do what you're gonna do, but leave my pa out of it."

"It may be 'lawyer talk,' as you say," the squire said sternly, "but it could make a difference—maybe even whether you live or die. Assize judges are trained in the law too."

To the three younger children, the father said, "Tillie, take your brother and the babe and go in the house and shut the door." Tillie clearly did not want to do this, but she did as she was told. Then Mr. Thompson said, "Tell 'em, son."

"Please, Billy," his mother whimpered.

"Just tell us why," Jeremy demanded.

Billy seemed near tears himself as he blurted out, "I done it for the money—and for Mina."

"Money? Mina? You'll need to explain that," Jeremy said.

"Go ahead, son. Tell 'em the whole of it." The elder Thompson's shoulders slumped and his wife clung to him, hiding her face against his upper arm.

The sky was blue and the sun shone brightly, but there was a distinct chill of foreboding in this scene.

Billy began hesitantly. "Things haven't been good for—for us Thompsons for—for a long time. I was away and didn't know all of it 'til I come home from the war."

"Please get to the point," Jeremy said.

Billy shifted from one foot to the other and looked unseeingly off into the distance. "The farm we had on Kenrick—it wasn't feeding us. So George and me—we took the king's shilling and joined up."

"George?"

"The next youngest brother," Robert supplied.

"Two less mouths to feed," Billy went on. "Also, George and me was excited to get away to see the world. Couple of kids—what did we know? George died in the battle at San Sebastian."

"I'm sorry," Jeremy said.

Billy shrugged. "Back home our not being there—here—made little difference. Kenrick and his steward ignored Pa's pleas for help. The barn needed repair, especially to the roof. Pa lost a whole season's hay and couldn't feed his animals. The earl's older sons were no help either—even when they were in residence, which wasn't often. Then they died in that boating accident and soon afterwards, the earl died too. There was no one to make decisions. Pa had already agreed to work for Mortimer when you arrived."

Jeremy was becoming impatient. "I am sure your family's hardships—painful as they must have been—were repeated in many a household, not just on Kenrick land, but all over England."

"Right," Billy said. " 'Twas no better here. Look at this place. See any livestock? Our milk cow died and the rest of the stock has been sold—or butchered—for food."

"So you took money to sabotage our wool sales?"

"Money—and he said he'd replenish our livestock, but he's real slow doin' that. Said when Kenrick is his . . ."

"Let us be perfectly clear about this," Jeremy said. "You are telling us that Sir Eldridge Mortimer paid you to set fire to my barns?"

"As God is my witness—and my Pa too. Sir Eldridge stood right where you're standin' now an' made the deal." Billy looked at his father for corroboration. The elder Thompson nodded.

Robert broke into the discussion at this point. "And you just—willy-nilly—agreed to do it? Fine sense of honor you Thompsons have, eh?"

Billy flushed a deep red. Dismay marked his mother's face and his father's hands were fisted in anger.

Billy sneered. "Honor? A Chilton is a fine one to talk of honor after what you did to my sister."

Robert stared at him in outrage. "You sister? Mina? I haven't even *seen* Mina in what—five? six? years!"

"Not you. Your brother Charles. That Chilton got her pregnant and refused to do right by her. Then he was dead and your father just laughed at her and Pa."

Mr. Thompson cleared his throat and said bitterly, "The earl just said, 'boys will be boys and who's to say the brat is a Chilton anyway?' "

Robert shared a look of understanding with Jeremy. Given the

character of their father and older siblings, this revelation came as little surprise to either of them.

"So Mina's in service in London now?" Robert asked. "What
about the babe?"

"The babe died. Mina couldn't feed herself properly to produce
milk for her babe, so it died." He emitted a harsh, mirthless laugh.
"Oh, yes. Mina's in 'service' in London. In Covent Garden!"

Robert stared at him. "Oh, my God! Mina is—"

"A whore," Billy said on a strangled sob. Jeremy thought perhaps
this was the first time the young man had admitted this aloud. "My
sister is a whore—and your brother, your father made her that way."

Tears streamed down the faces of all three Thompsons.

CHAPTER 22

Though not terribly surprising, the Thompsons' revelations were still appalling to Jeremy. He hastily conferred with Robert, then asked Phillips and the squire to join them, as Lawrence kept the Thompson men under surveillance.

"Obviously there *are* mitigating circumstances here to some extent," Jeremy said. "Robert and I agree that we cannot just ignore the roles our father and brother played in the hardships this family suffered."

Dennison's eyes widened. "You cannot mean to just let them get away with what they did. This is a hanging offense!"

"Not at all," Jeremy assured him. "But it does not appear that they have gained much from that act of perfidy—and we should not forget that there is a third party involved here."

"Proving *his* involvement in court will be difficult, perhaps impossible," Phillips cautioned.

"In a court of law," Jeremy said. "But there are other courts where one's actions might bring consequences."

"Hmm. You're right, but we have to act quickly."

Ever the lawyer, Walter Phillips, solicitor, never went anywhere without two important tools of his trade: blank paper and a writing instrument, in this case a graphite pencil. He sat on the bench and, using a saddlebag and its contents as a portable desk, quickly produced a record of what the Thompsons had said of the fire, including details of why and how it was started. When he finished, he read it aloud and the Thompson men signed it, then Jeremy and his companions signed it as witnesses. The Thompson men affixed their names to the document with a marked degree of reluctance and apprehension. Their doing so was the price Jeremy and Robert had exacted for not prosecuting them on what Dennison again pointed out was a hanging offense.

Mrs. Thompson, who had been standing on the sidelines through all this, burst into open sobs. "Alfred! What is to happen to us now? You? Billy? Me? The children? Sir Eldridge will find out about this—you know he will. We'll be evicted."

Her husband and son moved next to her and patted her shoulders awkwardly. "Don't take on so, Gladys. We'll figure somethin' out," the older man said, sounding none too confident.

Seeing and hearing this exchange, Jeremy looked at Robert in one of those silent communications family members or close friends often share. "What do you think?" Jeremy asked softly. Robert nodded and the two of them moved nearer the Thompsons.

"Mr. Thompson," Jeremy said, "the farm you had on Kenrick is still vacant. You can move your family back there. I have to tell you, though, it might be only a temporary situation. Still, it would give you a few weeks to find something else."

Thompson's head jerked up in wonder. "You'd do that? For us? After—"

"Yes," Jeremy said brusquely. He was slightly embarrassed at being caught out in what was, after all, an incredible act of magnanimity. He gestured at Robert. "My brother is the Kenrick steward now. He will see to it."

The Thompsons all spoke at once. "Thank you, my lord. Thank you. Thank you."

Robert said, "You were always a good farmer, Thompson. Surely you can be again."

"Oh, yes, sir." Years of defeat seemed to fade from Thompson's eyes and posture.

Jeremy turned away from the Thompsons' stark emotion. Mrs. Thompson's tears flowed freely and both the men had watery eyes. Well, Jeremy thought, was this not what people of his class were supposed to do—use their power, their wealth to help others?

"Careful there, Kenrick, you'll be signing on with that other Jeremy—Bentham—and his compatriot reformer, Robert Owen. Next thing, you'll be writing treatises on 'the greatest good for the greatest number' and building model communities."

And would that be so very bad?

He gave himself a mental shake and turned back to the Thompsons. "Uh . . . Mr. Thompson?"

"My lord?"

"I cannot do anything about the loss of your grandchild, but so long as I retain control of Kenrick, should you wish to bring your daughter home to this area, I can assure that her service in London will be whatever you say it was. Nothing said here today will be repeated." He glanced around to see his companions nod.

Now the tears spilled over and ran down the cheeks of the Thompson men.

Reasoning that the five of them might immediately overwhelm the knight, Jeremy thought an interview with Mortimer would go more smoothly if he were accompanied only by Phillips as a man of law. So, leaving Robert and Major Lawrence to sort out the logistics and timing of the Thompsons' return to Kenrick, Jeremy and Phillips bade good-bye to Dennison and rode the short distance to the main house on Mortimer's estate.

"You treated that family most generously, Jeremy," Phillips observed as they rode. "What's to keep them from bolting?"

Jeremy raised an eyebrow. "The fact that they gave their word? I refuse to believe that honor and integrity are limited to a single segment of English society. God knows that greed and chicanery aren't."

Arriving at Mortimer's ostentatious architectural wonder, they dismounted at the side of a wide expanse of steps, tied their horses to posts set there for that purpose, and climbed the steps to a set of double doors that could have graced a cathedral. A footman in purple and gold livery answered their knock, then left them in a huge, three-storied entrance hall as he took their cards to present them to his employer. Jeremy and Phillips sat on ornately carved chairs with seats covered in brocade. Ebony wood and pink marble abounded in the entrance. Lighting came from windows in a cupola in the ceiling.

"Good Lord!" Phillips said, craning his neck to look above. "One is reminded of St. Paul's Cathedral."

"I'm told that was the plan," Jeremy said. "New wealth cries out to be spent, you know."

A good fifteen minutes later, the footman still had not returned.

"This wait must be designed to impress upon us that we are intruding on a very important man," Phillips said.

"That or to give us time to admire this setting."

A very proper butler appeared and announced, "Sir Eldridge will see you now. This way, gentlemen."

He showed them into the library where Mortimer sat behind a large mahogany desk with some papers strewn about the blotter in front of him. He looked up as they entered, then rose and gestured to two chairs set in front of the desk, and resumed his seat. Jeremy glanced around. On previous visits, he had seen an ornate "Chinese" dining room, elegant drawing room, and, of course, the orangery, but never the library. The room was much larger than the library at Kenrick and lined with shelves of matching sets of books. The furniture, stiff and uninviting, boasted hand-carved wood and rich fabrics; it was arranged in several formal groupings. On the ceiling were carved geometric symbols covered in gold leaf, interspersed with medallions of paintings depicting stern Bible figures. It was not a room for a comfortable read. Jeremy wondered if any of the books had even had their pages cut yet.

"Good afternoon, gentlemen. To what do I owe this unexpected—and somewhat untimely—visit?"

Ah, Jeremy thought, *the great man is a headmaster grilling errant schoolboys.* Aloud he said, "I'm sure you remember Mr. Phillips."

"Of course. But let's get right at the business that brought you here," Mortimer said coldly. "Kenrick, you might have saved Phillips the journey up from London. Given your announcement of a couple of nights ago, I see no reason at all to renegotiate these loans." He tapped the papers on the desk. "I thought I had made my terms very clear to you . . . on more than one occasion."

"Yes, you did—"

"Well, then. I shall expect you to vacate the property so that I can take possession on the previously established date."

"That will not be happening," Jeremy said calmly. "And you may want to rethink your refusal to renegotiate certain aspects of the arrangement you originally forced upon a sick, grieving old man."

"A deal is a deal," Mortimer snapped. "I did not get where I am today by knuckling under to every hard-luck story thrown my way."

"No. I don't suppose you did," Jeremy replied. "I imagine your tactics run more to having paid informants in others' businesses and hiring out any work of a nefarious nature."

"Now see here." Mortimer half rose in his chair, his knuckles white as he gripped the edge of his desk. "I will not be insulted in my own home."

Phillips audibly cleared his throat. Jeremy took the hint and changed his approach. "As you know, Sir Eldridge, my brother and I have been investigating the circumstances surrounding that fire in the barn on the Kenrick home farm."

"Ah. I did tell you, did I not, that you would find that unfortunate incident to have been an accident?"

"But it was not."

Jeremy watched Mortimer's face closely and noted only a slight twitch in the jaw and mild curiosity in his "Oh?"

Jeremy went on: "We have just come from a rather interesting visit with Alfred Thompson and his son Billy."

This time Jeremy thought the man visibly blanched beneath his ruddy complexion, but Mortimer leaned back in his chair and said, "I cannot see that where you may ride of an afternoon has anything to do with me, though I should have thought it a matter of common courtesy to notify me—ask permission—before hunting on my property."

"Actually, we weren't hunting. Not for animals or birds, at least," Jeremy said. "We did find something of interest, however. Phillips, would you mind reading that document? I never could read your handwriting."

Phillips took carefully folded sheets from a flat leather case on his lap and began to the read the Thompsons' confession in a professionally neutral tone. Mortimer sat through the reading with no more outward show of emotion than a recurring twitch in his jaw.

When Phillips finished, Mortimer shrugged. "Lies. All lies regarding any part they say I had in this. And you'll have a very tough time proving that in any court of law." He rose. "Now, if you gentlemen will excuse me—"

"Hold on, sir," Phillips said. "It is true that hard evidence is somewhat weak as to your role, but circumstantial evidence is quite strong.

Your intentions regarding Kenrick holdings are a matter of public knowledge. My client is prepared to take the matter to open court and air the whole of it—including a supposed match you desired between him and your daughter."

"Well, let him do so. He won't win such a case and I still intend to foreclose on the mortgaged properties."

"Not if the money is repaid by the stipulated date," Phillips said.

Mortimer addressed Jeremy directly. "Are you telling me you are prepared to repay the entire amount—principal and interest?"

"Principal and reasonable interest," Jeremy said.

"Eh? What does that mean—'reasonable interest'? I negotiated these loans in good faith."

"No, sir, you did not," Phillips said calmly. "Since your rather surprising and generous agreement to extend the due date while we tried to locate the new earl, my staff has spent a good deal of time and effort investigating the exact circumstances under which the original loans were undertaken. The current Lord Kenrick's father was in extremely poor health at the time."

"His debauchery was killing him. So, was that my fault?" Mortimer asked.

"Not at all." Phillips sounded affable, but then more stern as he added, "However, you may be faulted for the usurious terms you squeezed out of a dying man."

"He got the funds he wanted. He knew what he was doing."

"He may have *thought* he knew what he was doing, but it is abundantly clear that it is highly unlikely he knew what he was actually signing."

"You cannot possibly prove such an allegation," Mortimer said with a dismissive wave of his hand.

"Perhaps not. But I have no doubt we can persuade a court of its probability. I have signed affidavits from Dr. Ferris locally, and from the previous earl's London physician as well, as to the likelihood of his being incapable of comprehending what he signed. Moreover, profligate and scapegrace though he was, the sixth earl of Kenrick was not one to assume serious legal obligations without seeking my father's advice. He had never done so before. There is no record of this having been done in this instance. I have also consulted the man who was his valet at the time, a certain Mr. David Bowers. Both he and Mr. Wilkins, the Kenrick butler of the last twenty years, will testify that when these papers were drawn up, the earl was heavily dosed with laudanum."

Mortimer leaned forward over his desk and gave Jeremy a sly smile. "So. Am I hearing this correctly? The oh-so-noble seventh earl is trying to wriggle out of lawful debts contracted by his predecessor?"

Jeremy leaned back, crossed his legs, and hooked an arm around the back of his chair. "Not at all. The basic, lawful debt? Not at all. But I do challenge the exorbitant rate of interest foisted on a man not in full possession of all his faculties."

Mortimer snorted. "And you just happen to do so mere weeks before I am to collect?"

"Initially, I accepted the situation at face value. But as I examined the papers more carefully, I became concerned and several months ago Mr. Phillips launched his investigation on my behalf."

Phillips added, "Let us not forget the timing of that barn fire, which seems to have been designed to cripple Kenrick's ability to pay."

Mortimer stood. "While I find your conjectures mildly interesting, you will, as I said before, find little that actually involves me. So sue me and be damned."

"Sir, I do not think you are seeing the entire picture here," Phillips said.

"I see enough. And don't patronize me! I can buy and sell a dozen fellows like you."

"Yes, sir, you probably can," Phillips replied. "But did I mention that Sally Jersey is my wife's cousin?"

Mortimer stared at Phillips as though the lawyer had lost his mind. "What? Why should I have the faintest inclination to care about a relative of some woman I have never met?"

"Sally Jersey is one of the patronesses of Almack's, London's most exclusive social club. I am sure you know with what high regard it is held by the ton, particularly the women. Sally is not known by the nickname 'Silence' because she is."

Mortimer became very still, apparently seeing where this was going. He slowly sat back down as Phillips spelled it out for him.

"It is well known that you are trying for a superior match for your daughter. What do you think her chances of snagging a peer as her husband will be when it gets around that her father has stooped to such underhanded means to buy her a husband? Even without the likes of Sally Jersey—and London is full of them—a public trial will spell an end to Miss Mortimer's being accepted in any but the very lowest social circles."

"This is blackmail—pure and simple," Mortimer sputtered, his face a furious red.

"I suppose one could view it as such," Phillips agreed blandly. "Rather akin to usury, wouldn't you say? I might suggest, also, that you try to distance yourself from the recent activities of the Duke of Wynstan."

"Hey! I had nothing whatsoever to do with that incident."

"Nevertheless, your name will be associated with it, if only tangentially."

Mortimer sat in stunned silence for several moments; the muscles of his jaw worked as though he were grinding his teeth. Then he slapped his hand against his desk. "All right. I did not get where I am today by not knowing when to cut my losses. What are your terms?"

"Rather more generous than you might expect—or deserve," Phillips said. "My client agrees to the basic principal of the debt and to the established going rate of interest for the entire life of the loan. He also agrees not to take the issue of the manner of the debt or the incident of the fire to court. Nor will he or members of his family discuss these things in any social context. The debt will remain a private matter and the fire an accident."

"I will not stipulate to any involvement in that blasted fire," Mortimer said.

"We are not asking you to do so," Phillips said. "However, we shall keep the Thompsons' statement on file."

Mortimer sighed. "All right. Draw up the revised loan papers and I'll sign them. The fewer people who know about this, the better."

"Actually, I have them already prepared right here." Phillips pulled them from the attaché case and laid them before Mortimer.

"Why do I not find this surprising?"

CHAPTER 23

The sun was beginning to set when the men returned to Kenrick Hall and Kate had already set the supper hour back. She and Lady Elinor chatted in the family drawing room as they waited none too patiently. She was thinking of putting supper back again when Robert and Major Lawrence arrived, bursting with news of having solved the mystery of the fire.

"Allow us to make ourselves presentable for the company of ladies," Robert said, "and we will tell you the whole story."

No sooner had those two disappeared above stairs than Jeremy and Mr. Phillips appeared. After greeting Kate and his aunt, Jeremy said, "Where are Robert and the major? We saw their horses in the stable."

"Ridding themselves of road dust," Kate said.

"Good idea," Jeremy said. "We'll do the same and be right back to fill you in on the adventures of the day."

"Men!" Lady Elinor said indulgently. "You can tell they are fairly bursting at the seams with their news."

"Yet they keep us in anxious wonder." Kate shared her tone.

Lady Elinor emitted an exaggerated sigh. "Ours is ever the plight of long-suffering women."

Kate rose. "I shall go and put our supper back again."

"Kate, dear."

"Yes?"

"Simply ring for someone." Lady Elinor pointed in the direction of the bellpull.

"Oh. I forgot."

In a very few minutes the men arrived in fresher clothing and obviously high spirits. Jeremy poured and handed around drinks of choice—sherry for the ladies, whiskey for the men—and they all seated themselves, eager for the reports.

"Phillips here was wonderful." Jeremy clapped his friend on the shoulder, then sat in a comfortable barrel chair near Kate's end of the settee she shared with Lady Elinor. The others occupied chairs nearby and Jeremy proceeded to summarize the scene in Sir Eldridge's library.

"So, we truly are free of that rather weighty anchor?" Robert asked.

"Just a matter of getting a bank draft to him."

"How did Sir Eldridge react to the news of your betrothal?" Lady Elinor asked.

Jeremy cast a questioning glance at Kate, who covered her slight confusion by sipping at her drink. "We did not speak of it directly, but his eagerness to foreclose bespoke volumes." Again he glanced at Kate, but she refused to meet his eyes. He grimaced slightly, then took a swallow from his own glass and leaned back in his chair. "Robert, how did it go with the Thompsons?"

"Very well," Robert said, but before explaining that cryptic reply, they had to inform the ladies of what had transpired in the Thompsons' front yard.

"You did the right thing, which in itself is not surprising, but I am proud of you—of both of you," Lady Elinor said to her nephews.

Robert shrugged and drained his glass. " 'Twas mostly Jeremy's doing. And I must tell you, big brother mine, you now have lifelong champions in the Thompson family. They could not sing your praises highly enough."

"I think it was your kindness regarding their daughter that made the real difference," Lawrence observed.

"Too bad you'll never be able to take public credit for that good deed," Robert quipped. "Just think—you might have been St. Jeremy or maybe St. Kenrick."

"Oh, cut line," Jeremy said. "And remember: I promised them discretion regarding the daughter."

The others nodded and Kate diverted the discussion by asking, "You said you stopped at the inn? Did you see Wynstan?"

"We did not *see* him," Jeremy said, "but Mr. Finley gave us a report."

Kate and Lady Elinor listened intently to this part of the men's day.

"So Cedric is indeed to be permanently paralyzed?" Lady Elinor asked. "How sad. He will hate—positively hate—losing his independence."

"According to Finley, he is not adjusting well. Not yet, anyway," Robert said.

"I cannot forgive his intentions toward my Ned," Kate said, "but one would not wish such a fate on anyone."

At this point, Wilkins announced that supper was being served in the dining room. The table conversation involved lighter topics and a good deal of laughter. Their late supper over, Lady Elinor announced her intention to retire early; Phillips said he had some paperwork he needed to catch up on; and Robert challenged Lawrence to a game of billiards. Jeremy and Kate reported to the nursery to bid the children good night. As they climbed the stairs, Kate was nervous, for she had not been alone with Jeremy since that kiss when he had returned after rescuing Ned and Cassie. The previous night Jeremy had bid the two children a perfunctory good night, then spent the rest of the evening closeted with Robert and their guests. She realized now that they had been planning how they would confront the Thompsons and Sir Eldridge. Kate had spent that evening reading, first to the children, then to Lady Elinor, and finally, when she'd gone to bed, to herself.

Now his hand occasionally brushed hers, sending tiny thrills through her at every touch. As he held doors to allow her to pass first, she caught a whiff of the familiar sandalwood and something else that was—well—just him, just Jeremy. This too sent a bolt of longing spiraling through her body. They passed the closed door to what had been her room in the nursery wing. She could not stop herself from glancing at him, and found him gazing at her, a warm twinkle in his eyes. She felt herself blushing and averted her gaze.

Kate had spent most of the previous day with Ned—and with Cassie, who hung around the schoolroom-playroom helping to keep him company; she had left him only for a riding lesson during which she had generously offered Lady Lobo as a companion in her stead.

Despite the welcome distraction of caring for and entertaining the injured Ned—along with frequent questions from the staff to ensure the smooth running of the household—Kate had not been able to escape incessant worry about what the future held for her and Ned. Even that constant stream of visitors had not deterred her from weighing the pros and cons of what she might do. Establishing a place of her own was now an option, but it was an option that had drawbacks. Wynstan could very well recover enough to try to make an issue of how "immoral" it would be for her to live independently, without an acceptable male protector. She was comfortable here at Kenrick Hall; more importantly, Ned was happy and thriving here. And Jeremy had not rescinded his offer of marriage; he had renewed it. And she loved him! By any objective analysis of her situation, she'd be a fool to reject him.

As Jeremy and Kate entered the main room of the nursery wing, the now fully recovered Rosie curtsied and left for her evening break. Cassie and Ned were putting a jigsaw puzzle together and eagerly welcomed the help of their parents.

"So, Ned, how is the arm today?" Jeremy asked, handing his daughter a piece of the puzzle that matched the blue sky of her section of the picture.

"It doesn't hurt so much today, but it really itches—right here." Ned tapped the middle of his cast.

"That must be really frustrating," Jeremy said, his serious tone treating Ned as an equal. Kate loved the fact that he never talked down to the children.

"Mm-hmm. It is." Ned was equally serious. "I went to the stable today, but I didn't ride. When will I get to ride again?"

Ned directed the question to Jeremy, who glanced at Kate for an answer.

"Perhaps in a day or two," she said. "But no jumping. We can't have you fall and injure the arm again."

"Ah, Mama—"

"No jumping."

The four of them continued to work on the puzzle together for a while, then Kate and Jeremy took turns reading to the children. Finally, when Rosie returned, they listened to bedtime prayers and kissed the children good night.

The utter domesticity of what had just happened hit Kate as she and Jeremy went down to the next floor to their own rooms. The scene had been incredibly ordinary, but beneath it was a thread of to-getherness and familial love that threatened to overwhelm her.

Jeremy must have sensed her emotion, for he said quietly, "Kate? Are you all right?"

"Yes, of course." Her tone sounded false, even to her own ears. They had reached her door. "Good night, Jeremy."

"Oh, no." He gripped her elbow and propelled her on down the hall and into his own room. "We need to talk."

"I—I—Jeremy! This is highly improper."

"And that night in the nursery wing, we were so very proper, weren't we?" he challenged with a grin, as he steered her to a couch set at an angle to face the fireplace in which a low fire glowed. A bedside lamp added more light to the room.

"That . . . that was a mistake," she said, feeling very nervous and unsure of herself. She hoped the light was dim enough to hide her blush.

He sat next to her and put his hand on her chin, forcing her to look at him. "Was it now? It surely did not feel like a mistake to me. In fact, it felt pretty damned right to me. I think you felt that way too."

He lowered his mouth to hers, his lips tender, searching. Without conscious volition, she responded, opening her lips to him. He lifted his mouth momentarily. "I knew it." On that note of triumph, he re-claimed her mouth in a deep, urgent, probing kiss that left them both breathless. Her arms found their way around his neck.

He drew back slightly to whisper against her cheek, "Kate. Kate, my love. Why are you being so stubborn? There's no need for you set up a house in London. Marry me. I can protect you and Ned."

She jerked away. "What? They *told* you? Mr. Phillips. Major Lawrence. They told you?"

"Yes. They thought I should know. We agreed that marriage to me is your best course of action. You will be safe here—both of you."

She stood and looked down at this face she had come to love and she wanted to cry. She willed her voice to be steady. "So you three men just decided how matters should proceed between you and me?"

"Four," he said. "Robert was there too."

"Oh!"

Exasperated, she turned toward the door, but he was too quick for her, leaping up and enfolding her in his arms.

"Let me go." She pushed against his chest.

"No." He held her firmly, but gently. "Not yet. Be reasonable, Kate. As a single woman in a separate household, you would be vulnerable to further plots and legal maneuvering from Wynstan."

She recognized this as one of her own arguments, but she was still stinging from those infernal men making major decisions about *her* life without bothering to find out what she might want or feel. "The man is likely to be a cripple," she said.

"In body, but not in mind. He will still have a great deal of money and enormous power to achieve his ends."

She went very still and lifted her head to hold his gaze, knowing he must feel the tremble of fear that coursed through her.

He hugged her closer. "Marry me, Kate. Together, we'll make Kenrick a veritable fortress."

"I—are you sure?" she whispered. "Won't the scandal ruin your plans to push for reforms in Parliament?"

"That is months, maybe a year, away. By then some duchess will have run away with her coachman and people will be saying 'Kenrick who?' and 'Lady Arthur who?' Yes, I'm sure. Please say you are too."

She held his gaze for a long moment, willing her eyes to ask the question uppermost in her mind. She read a sincere plea and a trace of uncertainty in his eyes.

"All right. Yes. I'll marry you."

"Oh, thank God," he said and drew her closer.

"But . . ." She pushed against his chest.

"*Now* what?" He sounded beleaguered.

"You said you wanted more than gratitude."

"Am I not getting more?"

"Oh, yes."

"Well, then . . ." He pulled her close again.

She turned her head so his lips brushed her cheek. She murmured, "I want more too."

"More than this?" Now he sounded puzzled.

"More than protection handed down from on high. More than having my life arranged *for* me. I want to be your partner, your friend—not just your lover."

He pulled back to hold her gaze. "*Just* my lover? Never. Kate, you are not *just* anything. You are everything to me." He grinned sheepishly. "But maybe we men were a bit high-handed."

Even as his lips claimed hers again, it occurred to her that he still had not said the magic *love* word. Nevertheless, she reveled in the fact that he cared for her and desired her. Perhaps she had love enough for both of them.

She stored this thought away and gave herself up to the sheer bliss of his touch as his hands caressed the length of her back, pulling her even closer. Despite their several layers of clothing, she felt a familiar hardness thrust against her belly. Brazenly, she slipped her hand between them and stroked that rigid flesh straining against his trousers.

He gasped in pleasure and whispered, "We are vastly overdressed for this, my love."

"I quite agree," she murmured as she eagerly allowed him to lead her toward the bed.

There was some confusion, soft laughter, and giggles of frustration as they hastily tried to divest themselves of their clothing.

"Do you need help?" he asked. Having already removed his own boots and his shirt, he watched as she carefully removed her dress, then sat on the edge of the bed to roll a stocking down one leg.

"Need? No. Housekeepers have to manage their own clothing. But would I welcome help? Oh, yes."

He knelt before her and slowly finished removing the stocking she had been working on, caressing her thigh, the calf, and then her foot.

She giggled. "I'm ticklish."

"That's good to know—for future reference."

He started on the other leg, his fingers caressing, teasing the soft flesh above the top of her stocking, then probing higher.

"Jeremy."

"Hmm?"

"You're taking too much time."

"I'm savoring," he said, bending closer.

"Well, maybe you'd like to savor these too." She slipped her chemise over her head to expose her breasts—and savor them, he did.

They made quick work of shedding what remained of their clothing and soon lay facing each other in the bed. He fondled her breasts, running his hand, then his lips and tongue over pebble-like nipples. Desire flared in her, centering in throbbing need in her nether regions. She drew his hand to the moist folds between her legs and then teasingly caressed his already hard flesh.

"Kate, you're driving me mad. I don't think I can wait."

She laughed softly. "Then don't."

He positioned himself on top of her and she raised her hips to accommodate him as he prolonged the pleasure of entering, until at last she felt full and complete. He moved slowly at first, testing their rhythm, teasing her, his eyes reflecting her own passion as he held her gaze. Then his strokes came faster and deeper and she matched him thrust for thrust. She felt a shuddering wave of ecstasy and heard herself cry out, "Oh, yes, Jeremy, yes!"

She felt him achieve his own release and collapse against her, though he carefully rested most of his weight on his elbows. "Oh, Kate. Kate." He kissed her, his lips tender and gentle. She felt her inner muscles still grasping, clinging to him as though to hold him forever as she fervently kissed him back. They both relaxed and he moved to her side, but continued to hold her close, spoon fashion, one arm under her head, his other hand idly caressing her body.

He nibbled at her earlobe. "I don't know what you did with my prim and proper housekeeper, but I *do* like her replacement."

"That's nice, for you seem to have seduced her out of existence and now you are stuck with what you get."

"I'll take it. I'll take it," he said quickly, then chuckled, "though I am not all sure who seduced whom this time."

"Does it matter?"

"Not at all, my love. Not at all." He stifled a yawn and added sleepily, "I was right about one thing."

"What?"

"This bed is much more conducive to this activity than the one in the nursery, isn't it?"

"Oh, yes. One could get quite used to this one."

"Count on it," he said, reaching across her to turn the gas lamp off. Then they both slept—for a while.

Long before the rest of the household stirred, Kate rose, slipped into her dress and shoes, and gathered up the rest of her clothing. Jeremy peeked out the door.

"It's clear," he said, giving her a quick kiss. "Soon enough, this won't be necessary."

"I know, but for now . . ." She returned the kiss and made her way down the hall to her own room. She crawled into her cold bed for another hour of two of sleep, already missing the warmth of Jeremy's body next to hers, the scent of him, the scent of him and her together.

"Well, the die is cast," she told herself. And if this was a taste of the rest of her life . . . well, it wasn't going to be so very bad—not bad at all.

Later, it was hard to pretend that nothing had changed. It was especially hard at the breakfast table, for when she happened to catch Jeremy's gaze, she knew very well they were each remembering some special nuance of the night before and she could not help smiling. Finally, she excused herself with a pretext of checking the day's menus with Mrs. Jenkins.

Just before noon, Cuthbertson drove Kate and Lady Elinor into town to visit the dressmaker. The town of Kenrick had almost all its businesses on one street. These included the Finleys' inn at one end of the town and a blacksmith at the other. In between were a mercantile shop that also held the post office, a bakery, a cobbler's shop, and the dressmaker's shop, which was run by a middle-aged woman named Madame Aubert.

"Violetta Aubert lost nearly her entire family in the Terror," Lady Elinor explained.

"But she escaped?" Kate asked.

"She was here in England at the time with her young husband and their baby daughter. He left her and their child here while he returned to try to rescue both their families, but they were all caught and served up to the rabble in Paris."

"How awful."

"She and her daughter, Jeanne, are both very talented with a needle. They can copy any of the latest fashions, and Jeanne also makes quite attractive bonnets."

"I take it you are assuring me I will be in good hands?"

"Very good hands."

The shop was bigger than Kate had judged from the exterior that faced the street. Besides examples on dress forms of the handiwork available here, there was a long counter for laying out fabrics and packaging purchases. In addition to the mother-daughter proprietors, two other young women worked on garments. Two large screens were arranged on opposite sides of the room to afford privacy for fittings. A cheval glass stood in front of each. Three tables with straight chairs and fashion magazines allowed clients some comfort in their decision-making. Three other customers, young women in fashionable dress, occupied one of the tables. Kate and Lady Elinor were already in the middle of the room before Kate recognized that one of those occupants was Charlotte Mortimer. Kate took a deep breath.

"Hello, Lady Elinor," Madame Aubert trilled. "How nice to see you. May I offer you a lemonade or tea?"

"Tea would be nice," Lady Elinor said, leaning on her cane. "I have brought my house guest, Lady Arthur Gardiner, to you for some new garments."

Madame curtsied to Kate, then clapped her hands and a young maid appeared from another room. "Tea, Mirabelle." Then she indicated an empty table. "Perhaps her ladyship would like to look at some of our fashion plates."

Kate guided Lady Elinor to the table and sat herself so she would not be facing Miss Mortimer directly. Lady Elinor looked around, squinting her eyes. Then she leaned toward Kate to whisper, "Is that—?"

"Yes," Kate whispered back.

"Oh, dear. Do you want to leave?"

Kate lifted her chin. "No. I will not be so intimidated."

Lady Elinor patted her hand. "That's our girl."

The maid brought the tea and Kate settled into perusing fashion plates, vaguely aware as she did so of the buzz of conversation at the other table. Finally, she chose three patterns she thought suitable. She signaled Madame, who hurried over.

"These will do nicely," Kate said. "Two day dresses and an evening gown."

"Those are nice choices," Madame cooed. "And perhaps you would like a bonnet or two to match the dresses?"

"My dear Kate!" Lady Elinor chided. "That will not do at all. Jeremy specifically charged me to see that you are properly outfitted." She turned to the French woman. "She must have at least five day dresses and two evening gowns to start with. And bonnets. Oh—and a cloak."

"And perhaps a wedding dress?" Madame said. "One hears rumors, you know."

"That too, of course."

Kate started to protest, but suddenly the discourse at the other table rose in volume and it was quite apparent that the three women there wanted to be overheard while pretending to a private conversation.

Charlotte Mortimer's voice was unmistakable. "—no better than she should be. I just think it really terrible that an honorable and noble man can be trapped into an unsavory marriage with a conniving female of a certain ilk just because she happened to convince him she had been compromised."

Knowing full well that she was the topic at the other table, Kate was profoundly embarrassed. She knew Charlotte Mortimer to be spiteful and pretentious, but she was also keenly aware that this young woman was a fixture in the Kenrick community while she, Kate, was a relative newcomer and unknown.

Miss Mortimer's companions tried to shush her, but she went on in the same loud tone. "No. I will not be silenced. I am not the sort to tolerate injustice when I encounter it and seeing a good man forced into a lifetime of unhappiness—well, it just fairly breaks my heart. It's just tragic. That's what it is: tragic."

"All right, that's it." Lady Elinor grabbed her cane and pushed herself out of her chair. She was halfway to the other table before Kate realized what she was about.

"Miss Mortimer," Lady Elinor said in a voice of authority Kate had never heard from her before. "I assume it is my nephew whom you are seeking to champion in an unseemly public manner and whom you would rescue from—how did you put it? Ah, yes, 'a tragic lifetime of unhappiness.' A tragic lifetime of misery is precisely what his lot would have been had your boorish father succeeded—with your full knowledge and complicity, by the way—in his ill-conceived plan to buy you a titled husband, thus putting you in the company of Covent Garden ware, in my opinion."

"Lady Elinor—" Miss Mortimer started to rise in an exaggerated show of shocked outrage.

"Sit back down there. I'm not finished," Lady Elinor snapped. Miss Mortimer sank back down and her companions cringed. Lady Elinor tapped her cane against the floor. "Marriage to some cit's daughter—a chit whose only interest is his title and elevating herself in society— that would be misery, indeed. Instead, though, Kenrick is getting a woman who loves him for himself. What's more, he happens to be very much in love with her—a condition he could not ever have known with you."

"Well, I never—" Charlotte Mortimer fairly sputtered. She stood and grabbed her reticule from the table. "Come, Fanny. Judith. I am leaving. I will not stay here to be abused so."

Her companions looked embarrassed and apologetic, but they rose and left with her.

Lady Elinor returned to her seat. "Oh, my. That felt good."

Kate gave a shaky laugh. "I must say, I had no idea you could be such a—a tigress! I do thank you for coming to my defense—even if you did rather overstate the case."

Lady Elinor lifted an eyebrow. "Hardly. I see better and more than you—or Jeremy—think I do." Her expression turned a bit sheepish. "However, my tirade is likely to become the talk of the parish. Ah, well . . . back to business. Really, Kate, five day dresses and two evening gowns to start. We shall discuss the wedding dress later."

CHAPTER 24

For Kate, time the next few days became a curious blend of routine and waiting during the day, and sheer bliss every night. On Sunday, the Reverend Mr. Packwood read the banns for the first of the requisite three readings to announce to all and sundry the forthcoming marriage of Katherine Emma Newton Gardiner and Jeremy Michael Chilton, Seventh Earl of Kenrick.

She felt a twinge of sadness as she sat in the church pew listening to the formal words. She remembered sharing the secret of her elopement years ago with her sister Beatrice and would have welcomed sharing her happiness with her again. After the service, she and Jeremy were besieged by well-wishers. On the way back to the Hall, they shared the carriage with Lady Elinor and Ned and Cassie. Then there was dinner to which the Packwoods and Dennisons had again been invited, so that, what with entertaining guests and seeing to the welfare of the children, she and Jeremy had scarcely any time together. The entire household had finally retired when she let herself into Jeremy's room. Both of them were already dressed for bed.

"Hello, stranger," he said softly and hugged her close.

"Hello, yourself." She lifted her face for his kiss.

"Come. I've poured us some port." He nudged her toward the couch. Two glasses of wine sat on a low table in front of it, the dancing light from the fireplace shining through the red liquid. He sat next to her, his arm loosely draped over her shoulder.

"What is it, Kate? Something has been bothering you all day."

"Oh, nothing, really."

"Yes, there's *something*. I sensed it in church this morning. I do hope you are not harboring doubts about—about us."

She smiled, aware that there was little gaiety in her expression.

"No. No doubts about us."

"But?"

"It—it's so foolish."

"Tell me anyway."

"It's just that this is the second time I will have married with none of my family in attendance. Arthur and I eloped, you know."

"You miss them, don't you?"

"Yes, I do. You'd think after all these years . . ."

"Some things do not change greatly just because time keeps ticking away."

"Thank you, Jeremy, for understanding."

"What are husbands for?"

"You are not my husband yet."

"Lovers, then. Speaking of which . . ." He stood, pulled her to her feet, and nudged her toward the bed, where they managed to banish the troubles of the day.

In addition to a wedding, the Earl of Kenrick, his family, and his guests were also waiting for the wheels of justice to grind inexorably on. Phillips and Lawrence were anxious to return to their respective homes, but they felt obligated to stay until the magistrate's hearing regarding the duke's attempt to abduct Ned and Cassie. Kate and Jeremy both wanted a sense of closure on this chapter of their lives. In the end, the hearing was both dramatic and anticlimactic.

Interest in the case ran high because it involved such a high-ranking member of the peerage, so it was moved from the magistrate's usual domain—a room on the first floor of the town hall—to the assembly room on the floor above. Getting the duke up two flights of stairs had posed a bit of a problem, but the blacksmith and the duke's valet managed to get his wheeled Bath chair into the temporary courtroom, with the chair's occupant complaining all the while.

The Kenrick party—Jeremy, Kate, Robert, Lady Elinor, Phillips, Lawrence, and Rosie—had followed Wynstan's slow progress up the stairs. Chairs had been arranged in rows on the dance floor. The magistrate's desk, along with a small table and chair for the court recorder, and a witness chair, were arranged on the musicians' dais.

Twenty minutes past the announced time for proceedings to begin, the magistrate finally rapped his gavel and said, "One man is dead, another and a child were seriously injured, and the lives of several have been profoundly disrupted as a result of actions taken by the principals in this matter. Therefore, this hearing is instituted as an investigative procedure to determine whether further legal action might be or should be undertaken and against whom such action should be directed."

The Kenrick party sat behind a table manned by Mr. Phillips and Sir Frederick Dunbar, a barrister with whom Phillips often worked in London. Dunbar had arrived two days before and stayed closeted with Phillips in the Kenrick library most of that time, though often conferring with members of the household. Wynstan too was represented by able legal counsel from the city, chiefly his barrister, Sir Algernon Stephenson.

"The barristers have both been knighted. That helps keep them on equal footing," Lawrence observed when Squire Dennison, in his capacity as magistrate, read out their names.

Dunbar quickly established the facts of the case to which Wynstan's counsel acceded, but insisted they were irrelevant as the duke was merely asserting his time-honored right to protect his heir. Dunbar overrode this argument by calling upon Lawrence, Phillips, and Kate to establish that the boy's father had clearly provided otherwise. Moreover, the duke's intentions regarding his grandson in no way made him less culpable in the abduction of Lord Kenrick's daughter. The legal questions then turned on who *was* culpable in terms of the overall picture—that is, who knew what, when? To this end, Sir Eldridge Mortimer was called to explain his involvement.

"My involvement?" he expostulated. "I had nothing whatsoever to do with this mess. I merely extended the hospitality of my home to the Duke of Wynstan when he was stranded in our neighborhood."

Dunbar took a different approach. "Wynstan's codefendant here, Miss Cranstan, has been with you for many years, has she not?"

"Yes."

"Practically a member of the family, would you say?"

"Why, no. She was a paid employee, that's all."

"She says otherwise."

Mortimer shifted in the witness chair. "Well, she is either lying or laboring under an insane misapprehension."

Miss Cranstan burst into loud sobs in her seat near Wynstan's wheeled chair. "Oh, Sir Eldridge, how can you be so cruel?"

The spectators murmured and the magistrate rapped his gavel for order.

Mortimer went on without looking at Miss Cranstan. "She abused my trust. Servants sometimes do, you know."

"But you encouraged me to help the duke. I was the only one who knew the plan of Kenrick Hall," she said, sending a gasp through the room.

The magistrate pounded his gavel again. "Miss Cranstan, it would be in your best interest to restrain yourself."

She subsided to whimpering sniffs, her head down, a handkerchief pressed to her face.

"See?" Mortimer said. "She is delusional. I have no vested interest one way or another in his grace's relations with his family."

"Miss Cranstan *is* employed by you, is she not?" Dunbar asked.

"Not anymore. I cannot have my name—my family—tainted by such sordid, not to say criminal, behavior."

Miss Cranstan jumped to her feet, raised her fist, and cried in obvious frustration, "Oh. Oh. You—you—"

"Miss Cranstan!" the magistrate said, "sit down and be quiet or I shall have you removed from these proceedings."

"You're not helping," the duke told her.

She sat back down and wiped her eyes and her nose, presenting a caricature of abused womanhood. When it came her turn to testify, she admitted her role in helping a respected member of society to secure what he had convinced her was rightfully his: custody of his grandson.

"That certainly provides a reason—of sorts—for your willingness to be a party to the abduction of Lord Spenland," Dunbar said, his tone deceptively mild. "However, we are left wondering what possible motivation you might have had for your crass indifference regarding Lady Cassandra."

"I meant the child no harm."

"No harm, eh? But the maid, Rose Davis, told us you suggested the child could be sold. Is that what you mean by 'no harm'—sell a little girl to God knows what kind of fate?"

A murmur of pure outrage sounded among the spectators. It was merely an echo of the horror and anger they had directed at the erstwhile nurse when Rosie had first testified to that stage of the events.

The duke's barrister jumped to his feet, protesting the "prejudicial language" of his adversary.

The magistrate pounded the gavel again. Kate wondered if his desk had dents in it.

Miss Cranstan swallowed a sob and made a show of shrinking away from her interrogator. "Rose Davis does not like me. She wanted my position—and she has it now. I never suggested— I would never— I have devoted my life to caring for children. Please, you must believe me."

Dunbar turned away in a show of disgust. "Methinks the lady doth protest too much."

Stephenson, the duke's barrister, rose to request a short recess. His client, he said, still suffered great pain as a result of an accident caused by reckless and irresponsible pursuit of his carriage on the day in question. Dunbar agreed to a recess so long as the phrase *reckless and irresponsible* was stricken from the official record of these proceedings. So far as Kate and Jeremy could tell, the request for a recess was a ruse to allow the legal experts to confer among themselves. Phillips rejoined the Kenrick party to confer with them.

"Stephenson, of course, just wants this to go away with the least possible damage to his client," Phillips said.

"Any damage is his own doing," Robert asserted.

"True enough," Phillips said, "but I am instructed to find out what your wishes are, Kenrick—you being the chief plaintiff in this matter, since neither the child, as a minor, nor his mother, because she is a female, is authorized to be such."

"A remarkably unfair aspect of English law," Jeremy said with a sympathetic look at Kate.

Phillips smiled briefly and said, "You can take up the issue of women's rights later, my friend. What do you want me to tell Dunbar and Stephenson?"

Jeremy took Kate's hand in his. He looked at her questioningly and she nodded. "We too just want to this behind us. Wynstan's punishment seems to have been taken out of mortal hands. The Cranstan woman deserves to be transported—or worse—for what she intended toward my daughter. But, frankly, I do not care at all what happens to her."

"She's been deserted by those she thought of as her family," Kate said. Jeremy squeezed her hand.

"Perhaps that truly is punishment enough for her," Lady Elinor said.

Robert snorted. "Hardly. But if she is to be free, can you not at least stipulate that she never show herself within, say, ten miles of either of the children she tried to harm?"

Phillips thought about this for a moment. "That seems reasonable—and most generous. I am sure the magistrate will agree."

So, by means of a good deal of obscure and legalistic language, the hearing ended with indeterminate findings: the carriage driver's death was an accident in which his own skill as driver was possibly a contributing factor; the children had been taken against the will of their parents, but said parents were not pursuing the matter further as a legal issue so long as the perpetrators of the deed maintained an established distance.

Two days later, Mrs. Packwood delivered the epilogue of the story during one of her regular visits to Kenrick Hall where, on this day, she had tea with Lady Elinor and Kate in the family drawing room. Rejected by the Mortimers, Miss Cranstan was to become Nurse Cranstan again. Instead of seeing to bathing, dressing, feeding, cleaning soiled linens, and generally seeing to the intimate needs of children, she would be performing these duties for the demanding, cantankerous Duke of Wynstan.

"She truly had no choice, you know," Mrs. Packwood confided. "The alternative would probably have been a workhouse. Her parents are long dead and she has never associated with any other relatives— if she has them. She has no one. At her age, few would see her as able to manage children."

"Luckily, Wynstan has a valet," Lady Elinor said.

"Not at the moment. He left the duke's service," Mrs. Packwood informed them. "He said he did not hire on to take care of an invalid—especially an ill-tempered one."

"Oh, dear. It just gets worse and worse for Cedric," Lady Elinor said, "but it is hard to feel truly sorry for one who was so much the agent of his own misfortune."

"I agree," Kate said, "and I think it applies to both the duke and his new caretaker. Still, it is hard not to regret what might have been.

My son does not know his grandparents on my side and now has only negative memories of his father's father."

Lady Elinor patted her hand. "Never mind, my dear. I shall happily fill that generational role for both Cassie and Ned. The Good Lord knows that Jeremy's stepmother, the current countess, is unsuited to such a role. So . . . you have me."

"To spoil them, you mean?"

"Is that not the proper role of grandparents?"

"I suppose it is."

CHAPTER 25

Plans for the wedding proceeded apace. Prior to the magistrate's hearing, Madame Aubert had delivered the first of the dresses Kate had ordered, along with suitable accessories. Now, having finished that order, she and her assistants set to work on a wedding gown for the woman who would be the wife of the most important man for miles around. What the new Countess of Kenrick wore at any time, but especially on her wedding day, would reflect mightily on her dressmaker. The gown, a pale green silk concoction trimmed with Belgian lace, brought out the flecks of green in Kate's hazel eyes.

"Think of it as supporting a local business," Jeremy said when Kate voiced a mild complaint about the expense and the time needed for fittings.

Kate sat through the second reading of her wedding banns alone, for Jeremy had accompanied Phillips and Lawrence back to London with a vague explanation about having items of business to take care of in the city. Kate thought that among these he might intend to screen possible candidates for two new positions in the hall—housekeeper and governess—though he had promised her a voice in the final selections.

When she made this observation in idle chatter with Lady Elinor, Jeremy's aunt offered another idea. "He may also be searching for the perfect wedding gift for you, my dear. As a boy, Jeremy delighted in surprising people."

Kate shrugged off wondering what Jeremy was up to. She was far too busy making preparations for the wedding itself. These included not only fittings for the wedding gown, but making other selections for a modest bridal wardrobe. In addition, she supervised plans and menus for the wedding breakfast and, together with Lady Elinor and Mr. Wilkins, arranged for an elaborate garden party to be held for servants, tenants, and locals having connections to the Kenrick holdings. She and Mr. Wilkins saw to the opening of the heretofore closed wing of the Hall, for Jeremy had sent word that extra rooms would be required. This meant hiring extra maids and footmen, but she left that largely up to Mr. Wilkins. She looked forward to seeing many of the guests. Mr. Phillips would be returning with his wife; Jeremy's sister Margaret would arrive along with her husband and children, and Kate looked forward to becoming acquainted with her. And there would be others, Robert warned; after all, the 46th Rifle Regiment would want to celebrate the nuptial of its angel.

"This is getting out of hand," Kate complained to Jeremy when he returned ten days after leaving.

He had arrived in mid-afternoon, disheveled and with a two-day growth of beard. Nevertheless, she threw herself into his arms, kissed him very soundly, and reveled in just having him close, road dust, scratchy whiskers, and all. After bathing and shaving, he pronounced himself fit for company again and grateful that he needn't sit in a saddle again for a day or two. Kate found herself feasting her eyes on him and manufacturing reasons to touch him throughout the evening.

Immediately on his arrival he had popped in to tell the children hello and give them little gifts he had for them—a gold locket on a chain for Cassie and handcrafted spurs for Ned's riding boots. He and Kate had joined them later for the nightly ritual of stories and prayers, but before that, they sat the children down on the couch in the schoolroom and themselves occupied cushioned chairs facing the two youngsters. Cassie and Ned looked curious, but not alarmed.

"My Lord Spenland," Jeremy said, sounding very serious and very formal, "I should like to ask your blessing and approval for me to marry your mother."

Ned smiled. "Really? Really and truly?" He looked at his mother. "That means we never have to leave here?"

She smiled back at him and nodded.

Ned then sat straighter and said very formally, "Then, yes; I give you my permission. But you must treat her nicely."

"Oh, I will. I promise," Jeremy said.

Cassie poked Ned in the arm. "See? I told you this would happen."

"No, you didn't. You just said you'd like it to happen. You never said it *would*."

"Same thing," she said.

"No, it isn't."

Kate interrupted this squabble. "Cassie, does that mean that you will be happy to have me as your mama?"

"Oh, yes." Cassie jumped from the couch to throw her arms around Kate. "Can I call you 'Mama' instead of 'Lady A'?"

Kate hugged her tightly and kissed her cheek. "Yes, of course. I shall have a lovely daughter and Ned will have a sister."

"I'd rather have a brother," Ned said, "but I guess this is all right."

"Whew!" Jeremy with a laugh. "I'm glad that worked out as it did."

"Now can we have the story?" Cassie asked.

Finally, Kate and Jeremy were alone in his bedchamber, enjoying a nightcap of port and each other. They sat on the couch laughing indulgently over that scene with the children.

Then their discussion turned to some of the details of wedding plans.

"This is getting out of hand," Kate said again.

"We cannot fault people for wanting to share our happiness," Jeremy said, pulling her close and kissing her yet again. "Besides, we have much to celebrate. Ned's future is secure. Our children are happy. The Chilton family once again has exclusive and unfettered control of all of Kenrick."

"And we have each other," she said softly, sliding her hands up his chest and around his neck.

"Yes." He paused for another long, deep kiss that threatened—promised—to reduce her to quivering desire. "Yes. The best part. We have each other. How lucky can two people get?"

For a long moment they simply sat quietly, savoring their closeness. Then Jeremy disentangled himself from her and stood to get a small box from the top of his dresser. "I brought you a present from London too." He opened the box to reveal a beautiful emerald ring flanked by two diamonds. He slipped it onto her finger.

"Oh, Jeremy," she whispered. "It's lovely." She felt tears well as she kissed him.

He laughed and kissed away her tears. "It's nothing to cry about."

"I've never owned anything so beautiful, so precious."

"Well, now you do." He hugged her again and whispered, "All the way home I imagined you wearing nothing but my ring."

"Mmm. I think we can arrange that, though the lady of the manor definitely needs more help with her clothing than the housekeeper did."

"Always happy to be of service," he quipped and fumbled only slightly with the tapes and pins on her dress.

Both were eager as they moved to the bed and wasted no time in engaging in the give-and-take of achieving mutual satisfaction. Afterwards, he continued to hold her close.

"I missed you," he said.

"I missed you too."

"By the way . . ." He still nibbled at her neck and ear and lazily stroked her body, but she sensed slight tension in him. "I stopped in at Finley's inn."

"And?"

"And I got a full helping of local gossip."

"I know you have a point here somewhere."

"I heard that Aunt Elinor gave Charlotte Mortimer a very proper set down."

Kate laughed. "Yes, it was. Classic."

"I heard the whole of it, I think." He sounded more serious now, but rushed on. "Aunt Elinor had it right on the mark, you know."

"About . . . ?"

"About me, at least. I *am* very much in love with you, Kate. I could never have been so happy with anyone else."

"Oh, Jeremy." She turned her head slightly to kiss him fiercely as she felt tears welling again.

"I gather that means she was right about you too," he said with a triumphant laugh.

"Of course she was."

"Then say it. I want to hear you say it."

"I love you, Jeremy. I love you, my Lord Kenrick. I think I have loved you since . . . since that interview in Grillon's Hotel. I love you. How many times should I say it?"

"At least once a day for the rest of our lives might suffice."

She held his gaze and said solemnly, "I promise to tell you I love you at least once a day for the rest of our lives."

"And show me too?"

"Oh, yes. We must show as well as tell, mustn't we?" She could feel that he was well on the way to being ready for another demonstration.

The next day was Sunday and marked the third reading of the banns. With the wedding set for the following Saturday, Kate was determined that nothing would spoil, or even taint her happiness. Truth to tell, there were so many visitors at the Hall now, she scarcely had time to dwell on the fact that she would marry again with none of her family present. Margaret Talbot breezed into the Hall with her husband William and their three children on Monday and immediately began to take her brothers to task, chastising Jeremy for not telling her sooner of this happy event and offering names of her female friends or their daughters or their sisters for Robert's consideration in achieving a similar degree of happiness.

The next day everyone had gathered in the larger, more formal drawing room for coffee or tea after the midday meal. Though Lady Elinor was clearly the hostess of this house party, Kate, as usual, assumed many of the actual duties of hostess. Margaret accepted her cup of tea and resumed teasing her younger brother.

"You're the only one of us left out now, Robert. We simply must do something about your single status."

He threw up his hands and cried, "Enough already. Stop. I'll marry the next female who enters this room just to make you quit nagging me."

Everyone laughed when the next female to enter the room was his own mother, who had just arrived at the Hall along with a male friend, whom she introduced as Baron Herbert Gordon-Smythe, a tall, handsome man with a large nose, white hair, and a courtly manner.

Margaret quickly said, "Oh, no, we'll have none of that Greek tragedy sort of thing. The next unattached woman who is *eligible*."

Everyone laughed again and the arriving countess said, "What? Don't tell me I am already missing out on the fun."

Kate thought Amelia, Countess of Kenrick and her prospective stepmother-in-law, seemed a bit hard around the edges, but gave her credit for fighting the good fight against the onslaught of time.

Introduced to Kate, Amelia said, "Ah, you are the one who is forcing me to take on the title *Dowager* Countess of Kenrick. I cannot like that, but, alas, what is one to do?"

The baron took her elbow and said, "Now, now, Amelia, my dear. I keep telling you that if you dislike the word *dowager* so very much, you may always take on the unadorned title of baroness."

"But, darling," she trilled, "then I would have to give up wearing the Kenrick diamond tiara."

"You will anyway, come Saturday," Lady Elinor said tartly.

Amelia affected a flirty moue at this and waltzed herself into the center of the room to choose a seat that Kate suspected was deliberately calculated to focus attention on her.

Jeremy, who had been standing next to Kate, bent down to whisper, "She's a bit overwhelming, but it's only for a few days."

Kate smiled up at him and happened to see a look of understanding pass between Robert and Margaret. Robert nodded, Margaret grinned, and Kate knew she had passed muster with her new sister, at least.

Phillips had returned with his wife, and Major Lawrence had come with them, along with another major, Templeton, and Templeton's wife Anne, who had also followed the drum in Peninsula. Kate was sure Jeremy had arranged with Robert for these old friends of hers to be here to make up for her own lack of family on this occasion—and she loved him even more for doing so.

Kate found Mrs. Phillips as unassuming and comfortable to be with here as she had found her in London. She was glad to see a blossoming friendship between Rosemary Phillips and Anne Templeton. She was also glad to find herself warming to the cheerful merriment that seemed at the core of Margaret's character.

"A penny for your thoughts, my lady," Robert said, plopping himself onto the chair next to hers.

"At the risk of turning your head with flattery, I was thinking I am going to enjoy very much becoming a part of your family."

Robert clasped her hand. "Margaret says we are lucky to have you—and she's right."

Jeremy approached and emitted a mock snarl. "Unhand my bride there, you—you—Don Juan."

Kate and Robert laughed, but before either of them could deliver a clever rejoinder, Mr. Wilkins approached with visitors' cards on a silver salver. Jeremy read the names, smiled, and extended his hand to Kate.

"Come, my dear, you will want to greet these guests with me."

Mystified, Kate accompanied him across the room toward the entrance hall.

"Who?" she murmured, but then she heard voices she thought lost to her forever.

"Are you quite sure this is the right place?"

"Yes, Mama, I'm sure."

Kate cast Jeremy a momentary look of surprise and wonder and dashed into the entrance hall to behold five members of her family: her mother and father, two sisters and a brother. A man and woman of the siblings' ages, both strangers to Kate, accompanied them.

"Mama! Papa! I cannot believe you are here." Kate could not restrain her tears. "Beatrice! Suzanne! Gerald! Oh, oh, my goodness! Oh, what a wonderful surprise." She hugged each of them briefly, then started over again, needing, rejoicing in their sheer physical presence. Her mother and sisters and brother kissed her and hugged her tightly.

Her father was rather stiff and, for the first time in Kate's memory, seemed unsure of himself. "Lord Kenrick assured us we would be welcome," he said rather gruffly.

"But of course you are," Kate said. She looked at Jeremy. "So *this* is why you insisted we prepare so many bedchambers!"

He merely grinned at her.

"And that business in London?" She raised an eyebrow.

"Was actually further south and west," he admitted.

She turned her attention to her family again. "Beatrice. Suzanne. Gerald. Oh, you are all so beautiful."

"Never quite thought of myself in those precise terms," her brother said. "Allow me to introduce my wife, Marianne. She truly is a beauty, as you can see."

The girl blushed and curtsied.

Beatrice brought the strange man forward. "And this is my husband, Hugh Parker."

"Suzanne?" Kate turned a questioning gaze on the sister who was her junior by six years.

Suzanne, with deep mahogany-colored hair and smoky gray eyes, was also a striking beauty. She flashed Kate a grin and said, "At twenty-three, I am the spinster in the family."

"Only because she turns down every offer that comes her way," Gerald scoffed.

"Kate," Jeremy said, "why don't you take your family into the library and get reacquainted? I'll make your excuses to the other guests and you can all join us in—say—an hour or so?"

"How kind of you, Lord Kenrick," Kate's mother said.

Kate spent the next hour hearing about her other siblings: a younger brother at university, another sister married and too close to her confinement to travel, and a younger brother and sister in their teens who were away at school. Gerald and Marianne were only recently married; Beatrice had left her two children at home. As Kate might have expected, the interview was most awkward with her parents. Her mother thawed rapidly, but her father remained somewhat aloof. Kate thought he was embarrassed and did her best to put him at ease.

"I am so very glad to see all of you—you have no idea!" she said, "but I am very curious as to precisely how it happened—your being here, that is."

Beatrice, who had been the chatty one in the group, answered. "Lord Kenrick simply appeared on Papa's doorstep and announced that he intended to marry his daughter. He was not asking permission, mind you, merely informing."

Suzanne giggled. "At first Papa thought Kenrick meant me—but of course I'd never met the man!"

Kate's father broke in. "He also pointed out to me the error of my ways and convinced me it was time to mend fences." There were tears in his eyes—another phenomenon Kate had never associated with her father—and he shook his head ruefully. "Your future husband is a very forceful and persuasive sort, my daughter." He wiped a tear away. "I've been a fool, Kate, and I am sorry. I know you can't forgive me—"

"But of course I can." She moved from her chair to sit next to him on the couch he and her mother occupied. She put her arms around him awkwardly, and for a moment they simply wept together. The others were tearful too.

When they had all managed to regain control and laugh at themselves, she took them to the formal drawing room and proudly introduced them to the other guests. Kate was amused to see Robert and

Major Lawrence immediately vying for Suzanne's attention and grinned when she heard Margaret's stage whisper to Robert.

"I did say the next *eligible* female."

Before the evening meal, Kate and her family trooped up to the nursery, where she introduced them to Ned and Cassie as the three Talbot children politely hung back. The family members greeted all the children formally. "Lord Spenland. Lady Cassandra. Masters Talbot. Miss Talbot." Kate was pleased to see that the children responded with correct, if not always smoothly executed, curtsies and bows.

"Your son is a handsome lad," Kate's father told her.

"Yes, he is," Kate agreed. "He looks very much like that portrait of you Grandmother Newton used to have in her parlor." Her father looked pleased at this comment.

"Lady Cassandra has interesting features—her complexion, that black glossy hair, and those startlingly blue eyes," Beatrice commented.

"Cassie is a beautiful child—in every way. She and Ned have become quite good friends—and that happened just when they both needed a friend," Kate said, then added, "My soon-to-be daughter's mother was part American Indian. I hope that won't be a problem for any of you." Her tone made it quite clear that if it were, it was *their* problem.

"No. Why should it?" Beatrice responded and the others nodded.

Kate breathed a sigh of relief, not aware until now that she had been apprehensive about their response. "Some people have been rather unkind."

"To a child?" Suzanne was aghast and the others murmured similar views. Kate was proud of her family.

Jeremy and Kate had agreed that, with a houseful of guests, they would not run the risk of having her caught leaving his room in the early hours of the morning. Nevertheless, after bidding the children good night, they snatched a moment alone in the schoolroom. He kissed her, then rested his head on hers and merely held her; both savored a quiet moment of togetherness.

"I've missed you," he said.

"And I you. Only three more days."

They kissed again.

"Jeremy?"

"Hmm?"

"Thank you for giving me back my family."

The wedding itself went off without a hitch. The bride—beautiful as brides always are—was attended by her sister and by her soon-to-be daughter; the groom, by his brother and by his soon-to-be son. After a wedding breakfast—at which champagne and toasts flowed freely—there was a festival in the garden for all the servants, tenants, and other locals who wanted to wish the couple well. Here too, beverages flowed freely.

To no one's surprise, the bride and groom retired early to the master bedchamber even as the party went on until the early hours of morning. They were both a little tipsy, but managed to do justice to their marriage bed—twice—and the next morning were seen to be in very good spirits, indeed.

www.ingramcontent.com/pod-product-compliance
Lightning Source LLC
Chambersburg PA
CBHW020740250626
47155CB00003B/846